'This original and high-concept coming-of-age adventure brilliantly evokes a claustrophobic future world, while its passionate young heroine fights her way to an unexpected and satisfying ending'
Laline Paull, author of *The Bees*

'A hugely gripping depiction of a future world, *The Ship* is all the more chilling for its sense of authenticity. Honeywell has written a story that will make you question the value we place on love and freedom and what we'd be willing to sacrifice for those precious commodities ourselves. I couldn't put it down'
Kerry Hudson, author of *Thirst*

'A disturbing story from a bright new talent'
Salley Vickers, author of *The Other Side of You*

'Honeywell's writing is clean and crisp, with a strong voice and great sense of emotion and atmosphere . . . This is a nugget of delight from an impressive first-time author'   *House of Blog*

'A wonderfully enchanting novel . . . thought-provoking'
Reviewed This Book

'*The Ship* is a wonderful first book – framing the utopian/dystopian genre in a coming of age story. It is both achingly sad and profoundly troubling'   *Cloudbanks & Shimbleshanks*

'*The Ship* has the language and ideas of a literary novel, combined with the pacing and twists of a thriller. It's an impressive debut'
The Writes of Women

Antonia Honeywell studied English at Manchester University and worked at the Natural History and Victoria and Albert Museums in London, running creative writing workshops and education programmes for children, before training as a teacher. During her ten years teaching English, drama and film studies, she wrote a musical, and a play which was performed at the Edinburgh Festival. She has four young children and lives in Buckinghamshire. *The Ship* is her first novel.

@antonia_writes
www.antoniahoneywell.com

THE
SHIP

ANTONIA HONEYWELL

WEIDENFELD & NICOLSON

A W&N PAPERBACK

First published in Great Britain in 2015
by Weidenfeld & Nicolson
This paperback edition published in 2016
by Weidenfeld & Nicolson,
an imprint of the Orion Publishing Group,
Carmelite House, 50 Victoria Embankment,
London EC4Y 0DZ

An Hachette UK company

3 5 7 9 10 8 6 4 2

A CIP catalogue record for this book
is available from the British Library.

ISBN 978-1-780-22734-4

Typeset by Input Data Services Ltd, Bridgwater, Somerset

Printed and bound by Clays Ltd, St Ives plc

The Orion Publishing Group's policy is to use papers that
are natural, renewable and recyclable products and made
from wood grown in sustainable forests. The logging and
manufacturing processes are expected to conform to the
environmental regulations of the country of origin.

www.orionbooks.co.uk

To James, who made it safe to open doors on dark places,
and to Oliver, Thea, Adam and Esme, who bring light.

ONE

Right up until the day we boarded, I wondered whether the ship was just a myth. There were so many myths in my life then. The display cases in the British Museum were full of them, and the street prophets crowding the pavements outside ranted new ones at my mother and me every time we walked past. From time to time, there was a government raid and, for a few days, the streets would be empty, except for the one prophet who always survived. He sat on the corner of Bedford Square and Gower Street, filthy in worn denim, holding up a board that said, 'God has forgotten us.' I don't know why the troops left him. Perhaps they agreed with him; in any case, he must have had a card. He was still there when we left, sailing past the car window as though he were the one on water. It was my sixteenth birthday.

I was born at the end of the world, although I did not know it at the time. While I fretted at my mother's breast, demanding more milk than she was able to give me, great cargo ships sailed out of countries far, far away, carrying people from lands that were sinking, or burning, or whose natural bounty had been exhausted. While I took my first stumbling steps, cities across the world that had once housed great industries crumbled into dust, and pleasure islands that had been raised from the oceans melted back into them as though they had never existed. And as I began to talk, the people in the surviving corners of civilisation fell silent, and plugged their ears and their hearts while the earth was plundered for its last scrapings of energy, of fertility. Of life.

I was seven when the collapse hit Britain. Banks crashed, the power failed, flood defences gave way, and my father paced the flat, strangely elated in the face of my mother's fear. I was right, he said, over and over again. Wasn't I right? Weren't we lucky that we owed nothing to anyone? That we relied on no one beyond our little trio? That we had stores, and bottled water? Oh, the government would regret not listening to him now. The government would be out on the streets with the rest of the population. Weren't we lucky, he wanted us to say, weren't we lucky that we had him? He ranted, and we bolted our doors; my mother tightened her arms around me, and for months we did not leave the flat.

Across the country, people lost their homes, the supermarkets emptied and the population stood, stunned and helpless, in the streets. My father watched the riots and the looting, the disasters and the forced evictions on every possible channel; he had the computer, his phone and his tablet and juggled them constantly, prowling about the flat and never seeming to sleep. The government resigned, and then came the tanks, and the troops with their terrible guns. My father vanished. Oxford Street burned for three weeks, and I watched the orange skies from the circle of my mother's arms, weeping for him. Hush, my mother whispered to me, hush. But I was only a child; I had not learned to be silent, and when he returned, tired and triumphant, I cried just as loudly and buried myself in him. But he was no longer the man who had walked away. The military government had listened; they had bought the Dove from him. He was a rich man now, and a powerful one, and he had more important things to do than cuddle me.

Within weeks of my father's return, the Nazareth Act came into force. I remember the queues, the identity checks, the biometric registrations, and surrounding it all, my father's jubilation at his success. Opponents called the Dove a violation of human rights, but as my father said, it worked. Your screen was registered, you were issued with an identity card, and from then on you were identified by your screen address, no matter where the social and financial earthquakes had left your land one. The satellites were still operational, so the authorities always knew where you were. What food there was could be distributed fairly. New laws could be communicated quickly and card-carrying citizens got the information they needed to survive. Food drops, medical assistance, re-registration requirements, work opportunities. New acts came in thick and fast: to the Exodus Act and the Optimum Resourcing Act were added the Land Allocation Act, the Prisoner Release Act, the Possession of Property Act – each heralded by a triumphant fanfare on the news bulletin, which was now the only source of information. The Dove was the ultimate firewall; anything it did not approve went onto the raven routes and over time, the raven routes became more and more dangerous. A screen open to raven routes burnt out in seconds; whether the virus that did so was a government initiative or a legacy from the days of unrestricted access, no one could say. And so, with cards and screens and the Dove, order was created from chaos. Regular biometric re-registration meant that stolen cards, and the cards of the dead, were only ever valid for a limited time. By the time I was ten, a valid card was the most valuable thing in the world, and my mother and I, duly registered, were able to go out for a walk.

'Where's your card?' my mother demanded the first time we went to unbolt the door. 'Show me.'

We'd practised so many times. I unzipped the inside of my pocket, felt through the hole, opened the card compartment of my belt and held it out to her. 'Seven seconds,' she said. 'It's not fast enough.'

'You do it then,' I said, but my mother was holding her card up before I'd even started the timer.

'The troops will shoot me if you don't show your card,' she said, 'and it'll be stolen if it can be seen.' And so I tried harder, but she wasn't satisfied, and took my card away to look after it herself. We went to Regent's Park, to look at the tents people had set up as temporary accommodation, although she wouldn't let me speak to anyone. We went to the new banks of the Thames, too, to see Big Ben and the London Eye peering mournfully out of the water, but even with the security of the troop patrols, London had become desolate and dangerous, and soon our outings became confined to the British Museum, just around the corner. We went there every day; it became my schoolroom, my playground, my almost home.

'Things will get better,' my mother said, holding my hand, and I believed her. The bulletins said the same.

And yet – and yet. Time went by, and still people starved. Still they slept in floating death-traps, or in the campsites that had been created in London's parks, now surrounded by razor wire. I saw these things through the bubble of safety and relative plenty in which I lived; I saw them so often that I became immune. My father saw them too. I think he was a little bewildered that his great triumph, the Dove, had not saved the world, and so he set about saving his own world – my mother and I – another way. He always did like to be in control.

The paper ran out, so my mother tore labels from tins and taught me to write on the back of them; when there were no pencils left, we burned splinters of wood and made our letters with scratches of black. And after a year or two, a new word began to creep through the wall that divided my parents' room from mine, whispered at night in hopeful voices. *A ship. What about a ship?* I scraped the word laboriously with my burned sticks. Ship. Ship. I grew quieter as I grew older, and listened as hard as I could to my mother and father's intense, whispered conversations. I was spelling out the titles on the spines of my mother's old books when I first heard the word spoken out loud.

'A ship,' he said to her. 'Shall we do it?'

And my mother said, 'But Lalage's future?' and my father said, 'There's no future here. We'll make one for her,' and from that time on he was barely ever home. It was years before I learned that Anna Karenina was the title of the novel and not the name of the author.

The ship. The word floated through my childhood, a thought with nothing to tether itself to. *There'll be paper on the ship*, my mother told me, when I complained about the labels. *There'll be rice on the ship*, my father said, when we ate the last of the rice in our stores. *The ship*, my father said when the public executions went from weekly to daily. When the marketeer riots spread from Oxford Street to Bloomsbury and the bodies stayed outside our flat for three days; when the screen crashed, or the rats got inside our building; when the water gave out, or a food drop failed, he always said, *Just you wait, Lalla. Wait until we sail.*

The only actual ships I'd ever seen were the stinking hulks that drifted up the bloated river every now and again, relics of the great evacuations, and I knew they weren't what my parents meant. Mostly they were empty; anyone left alive on them was shot as they swam to the bank, if they didn't drown first. The rusting carcasses lined the river from London to the sea, lowering into the water until they keeled over, complete with the homeless who'd taken refuge on them. My mother would go pale and clench her fists as we watched the bulletins on our screens. I hated seeing my mother so unhappy, but to me she seemed naive. After all, no one had forced those people to sleep on the Sinkers, any more than they were forced to live in

London's public buildings. My parents and I lived in a proper flat, with food and clothes and locks on the door, and because we had these things, it seemed to me that they were available, and anyone who lived without them was making a choice. My father was very big on choice.

'Turn it off,' my mother always said, but she never meant it. She would no more have missed a bulletin than she'd have let me go out into the streets alone.

Food became scarcer; on my twelfth birthday, for the first time since the Dove, there was no cake.

'There's no power spare for the oven,' she told us.

'Why can't you just melt chocolate over the fire and stir in biscuits, like last year?' I asked, but my father told me to hush, and my birthday was ruined.

My mother got thinner, and when my father came home the two of them pored over papers and screens while I read and played approved screen games and tried to remember the things my mother had taught me during the day. Daytime London gradually emptied, drained by the curfews and the Land Allocation Act, and the terrible penalties of being discovered by the troops without a card. My father's appearances were gala days; the rest were about survival. Food drops. Hiding the car, which my father claimed we'd need one day. The fingerprinting and flashing lights of the biometric re-registrations, which became ever more frequent. And the ship, the ship, the ship, held out like a promised land between them, hung on words like equality, kindness, safety and plenty. 'Wouldn't it be nice if the good people had a chance?' my mother would say, but in post-collapse London, my father and mother were the only people I knew, and in any case, she never seemed to expect an answer.

Who were the good people, anyway? The street people, or the prophets or petrolheads, who avoided me as instinctively as I did them? Were the strangers who came to the flat when my father was at home good people? I had no way of knowing; I didn't talk to them, and in any case they never came twice. You'll have friends on the ship, my parents told me. By the time I was fifteen, my parents were still all I knew, and their stories of the ship had become as fascinating and impossible as fairy tales. I didn't know that the people who came to the flat were being interviewed for berths, or that the hours my mother spent on the screen were spent exploring the forbidden raven routes, looking for stories of people who deserved to be saved. I didn't know that my father's frequent absences were spent tracking down supplies and vaccinations; I didn't know that he finally bought the ship itself from a Greek magnate who'd decided to tie himself to the land. I knew nothing. Except that I was lucky, and that was only because my parents kept telling me so. We walked to the British Museum almost every day, and the dwindling of the collections was the only marker of time I had.

The evening before my sixteenth birthday, I sat watching the news bulletin with my mother. At least, she watched the bulletin; I didn't bother. I couldn't understand how she could waste precious power when the bulletins were always the same. I never watched them; what I watched was my mother watching. She sat on the edge of the sofa, twitching and shifting as she sifted the presenter's words, her hand resting automatically over the pocket where she kept our identity cards, right up until the bulletin finished, as it always did, with the recording of the commander's original promise to the people. I could recite it word for word. 'Keep your card. It is your life. This Emergency Government has but one task – to ensure fair distribution of limited resources. I, Marius, Commander of the Emergency Government, promise that no card-carrying, screen-registered, law-abiding man or woman in this country will go hungry, or homeless, or watch their children walk without shoes. But with that promise comes a warning. Do not let your registration lapse. Carry your card and keep it safe. My citizens are my priority. I cannot feed those who are not mine. And without your card, I cannot know that you are mine.'

'Your card, Lalage,' she said suddenly. She had handed it over to me just before the bulletin.

I felt in my pocket. 'It's fine,' I said. Her face tensed. 'What?' I demanded. 'I've got my card. It's here, all right?'

'No. It's not all right.'

'Why not?'

'Because you'll be sixteen tomorrow. You'll be responsible for your own card. They will shoot you if you can't produce it. Not me. You. Your card, do you hear me, Lalage?'

'Happy birthday to me,' I muttered. But I listened. I always listened to her, although I rarely let her know it, and on the day of my sixteenth birthday, as we walked to the museum, I was so conscious of the little plastic rectangle nestled inside the pocket my mother had made for it that I forgot to complain that my father was away for my birthday. I was an adult; the card in my pocket said so, and I looked around at the museum dwellers with judgemental eyes, asking myself how they could have been so careless as to lose their cards and end up homeless. While my mother spoke with them in undertones, and handed over the food we always brought, I wandered the display cases.

So many objects had disappeared over the years. The Mildenhall Treasure. The Portland Font. My favourite exhibit, a little gold chariot pulled by golden horses, had vanished just after my fourteenth birthday. Instead, the cases were filled with little cards – *Object removed for cleaning, Object removed during display rearrangement.* Lindow Man was still there, though, huddled, leathern, against whatever had killed him two thousand years before. I stared at him, and through the glass at the sleeping bags beyond, inside which living bodies huddled against what London had become. My mother made sure we kept up our registrations, and she took me to the British Museum and talked at me, and we read her old books and waited for my father, and scratched letters with burnt sticks, and that was my life. A closed circle shot through with irritations, soothed by the promise of a ship that never seemed to come any closer.

'If the ship is real,' I asked my mother as we walked back to the flat, 'why don't we just get on it?'

'It's not that simple.' She tapped in our entry code and began to fit the separate keys into their various locks.

'Why not?' I asked. It was my job to keep watch while she did the door, but nothing ever happened. My mother liked things to be done properly, that was all. Even the milk, which came in cardboard bricks when it came at all, had to be poured into a jug before she'd let me or my father have any. When the outside door was safely bolted behind us, she began the long process of unlocking the front door of our flat. We went in, and the door clunked solidly behind us. As I began to fasten the bolts, she went to the pantry, took down one of the few tins on the shelf and stood staring at it. It didn't have a label. She held out the tin to me, smiling. 'It's your birthday,' she said. 'You decide. What do you think? Shall we risk it?' I refused to look and went into the drawing room. We had always eaten roast chicken on my birthday, and I'd never forgotten it, even though the last one had been five years ago.

There was a bang at the door, then a pattern of knocks. Before it was finished, my mother and I were both there, our almost-quarrel forgotten, racing to see who could get the bolts and locks undone first. 'It's my birthday,' I protested, but she still got to him first, and clung to him, and left me to close the door and start on the bolts again.

'I've got something for you, birthday girl,' my father said, leaning over my mother and kissing the top of my head. I wondered, wildly, whether he'd managed to find a chicken. But the box he produced as he grinned at my mother was smaller than the palm of his hand. 'We haven't seen one of these for a very long time,' he said, and I felt my mother trembling beside me, crowding in closely as he put the box into my shaking hands. I opened the box and her face fell. She began to cry and he moved away from me in consternation.

'I thought you had found a flower,' she said. And he held her, and while she sobbed against him and he said sorry, sorry, sorry into her hair, I shook a pool of white fire onto the palm of my hand. I remembered him bringing home diamonds years ago, when the banks were teetering and there was still roast chicken, but I'd never even been allowed to hold them, and before long the diamonds had given way to rifles and grenades, piled up throughout the flat. My mother's face had become pale and lined, and my father went away, and then the rifles gave way to stacks and stacks of screens, pristine in their boxes. Then the Art Trials began, and my father was gone again. And so it went on, but now I had a diamond of my own. I stared at it, gleaming in my hand, and could not imagine how any flower could be more beautiful.

It was good to have him back on diamonds. I think my mother thought so too, because she looked at the diamond in my hand and said, 'Another rivet in the ship,' just as she had done all those years ago, and once again I imagined a boat studded with sparkling rainbows, like something from a dream.

'How was the trip?' she asked, drying her eyes and settling onto the sofa with her sewing.

'Fine. And I visited the holding centre. Roger told me that the people don't believe in Lalla because I never take her with me.' He laughed, but my mother didn't even smile. He started to say more, then stopped and looked at me. 'Kitten, is there any water? Could you fetch me some?'

I went to the kitchen. The boiled water in the stone jug was mine; my mother knew I hated the taste of the water sterilising tablets we were given at every re-registration. But it was hard to boil water when power was so scarce; my father and mother always used the tablets. I looked about for them, but the tone of my father's voice stopped me. 'Anna, listen,' he said quietly as soon as I was out of sight. 'The troops are going to bomb St James's Park. They've put the razor wire round it, and moved out the people who've got cards. It's Regent's Park all over again. We need to leave.'

Regent's Park. It had been one of the first places opened up for people who had nowhere to go. I was thirteen when the government bombed it. Hundreds, thousands of people eliminated in a series of explosions that had made the windows of the flat vibrate. 'Be glad I didn't let you meet them,' my mother had said, taking away my screen so I couldn't see anything more. 'Then it would really hurt.' My parents had shut themselves away for hours after that; I heard them through their bedroom door, talking about the ship, then and for weeks afterwards. The ship, the ship, the ship, but nothing happened. There had been more food available at the food drops after the bombing, and my mother said it was because things were turning a corner, as she'd always said they would. But it hadn't lasted, and now my birthday dinner was coming out of a single tin. I stood in the kitchen doorway, holding my diamond in my hand, and watched as my father knelt in front of my mother and took the sewing from her limp hands.

'You brought home a diamond,' she said. 'You haven't done that for ages. Surely that means things are getting better?'

'No. It means people have given up. I got that diamond for a tin of peaches.'

'A tin of peaches?' she said. I opened my hand and noticed for the first time how hard the diamond was, how cold. My stomach rumbled, and I wondered what would be inside the tin my mother had lighted on.

'It was a kind of joke,' my father said. 'I was negotiating for the contents of a warehouse in Sussex. The guy said that diamonds were for those who believed in the future more than they cared about survival. I thought Lalla would like it, that's all.'

'What did he take, if he didn't want diamonds?'

'Munitions. He traded one warehouse for the means to protect the other, and pistols for his family. There is nothing left, Anna. Nothing. We have to leave. You won't dissuade me this time.'

My mother fastened her length of thread, shook out the material – it was a red velvet curtain that she was making into a skirt for me – and pointed the needle at my father.

'You created this situation,' she said. She unspooled a length of thread and bit it off, looking up at him sharply.

'Me?' He stared at her. 'Me? The Dove saved this country. Saved it.'

It hadn't. You only had to look outside our window to see that. But my father no longer looked outside our window. His mind was made up, and his eyes were on places far beyond our London square. My mother picked a black button from her sewing box and said, 'What about the people in the British Museum?'

'They're squatting,' my father said quietly, sitting on the back of the sofa and stroking her hair. 'It's all very cooperative, but how can they build an alternative society when there's nothing left to build it on? All the government can do – all it can do – is reduce the population in the hope of feeding what's left. Bit by bit. The museum dwellers are idiots, corralling themselves so they can be eliminated. It's time for us to leave.' He frowned and jabbed at his screen. 'It's been time for a long time.'

She bent her head over the button, and when she spoke her voice was so quiet I could barely hear her. 'I'm not ready, Michael. However dreadful the process is, soon the population will be manageable, and all this will improve. The ship will be the last thing we do.'

'The last thing?' My father laughed, putting his screen down, swinging his legs over the back of the sofa and landing beside my mother with a bounce. 'No, my darling, the ship is the start. Why do you cling to the end, when the beginning is waiting?'

'I want to grow things.'

He stopped bouncing and turned away. 'Still?' he said. 'The Land Allocation Act's a failure. People are coming back from the countryside as fast as they left. And if they don't come back, it's because they're dead. I've seen it.'

My mother put her sewing down. 'What about the Lakes?' she said. 'They didn't do industrial farming there. Or fracking. The soil might still be good.'

'And you'd take that risk, even though we've never heard anything from any of the families who left? Remember the Freemans? The Kings? The Holloways? Think of the security we'd need just to get there. And the loneliness.'

Freemans, Kings, Holloways – names from a time I could barely remember. A time of restaurants, a time when Regent's Park was a place to take a picnic, a time when people smiled at each other and sometimes stopped to talk. A time when there were still a few private cars in the street; when electricity was constant. Nothing but myths now, lost in time. But at sixteen, I knew about loneliness. I was lonely, so lonely that my stomach clenched with it at night.

'A life for Lalla,' my father said. 'Isn't that worth everything we have? A place to be a family, among friends, where we can learn and share without fear? A place for Lalla to grow in safety? Isn't that what we set out to create?'

'A place without money,' my mother said softly, putting her arms around him. 'No gold or guns. Just everyone working hard and sharing in the plenty we've provided.'

'No homelessness,' he replied, 'and no hunger.' He turned in the circle of her arms and stroked the hair back from her face. 'Tell me when, Anna. Please tell me when.'

'It was an insurance policy. Just that. Insurance. And now you're making it a life plan. I don't want to spend my life clinging to a lifeboat.'

'How much worse do you want things to get?'

'If you loved me, you'd stop pushing.'

'If you loved me, we'd have gone already.'

'I love you, Michael. I just don't think you're right.'

I stood in the doorway, forgetting I wasn't meant to be listening. I clenched my fist and felt the diamond cutting into my palm. 'I want to go,' I said. 'If the ship is real, I want to go on it.'

They looked at me in surprise. My father looked for his glass of water and realised that I wasn't holding one. My mother said, 'You don't know what you're talking about,' and took back her sewing, tucking her legs under her. 'We're going to Mughal India tomorrow.' But I had spoken out at last, and I couldn't stop now.

'I've seen Mughal India,' I said. 'I've seen Ancient Egypt and the Aztecs and Babylon and Abyssinia and Mesopotamia. I've seen them all day, every day, for years and years and years.'

'But you've learned nothing,' she said, standing up and marching past me into the tiny kitchen. I heard the drawer open and shut and the rattle of the utensils in it. I heard the tin opener puncturing the lid, and the ratcheting as she turned the handle. 'Seriously, Lalage,' she called over the rattle of the spoon as she scraped out the contents of the tin. 'What have you actually learned from the British Museum? From me? From your father?' I drew breath, ready to tell her about hieroglyphics and lunar calendars, about crucifixes and fertility symbols and currency, about kings being buried with gold and sandwiches to see them safely to the underworld, but my father spoke before I could begin.

14

'I don't care what she's still got to learn,' he called into the kitchen. 'I want her safe. I want both of you safe.'

'I want to go on the ship,' I said again, and it was as though someone else had taken over my body, someone who carried their own card and owned a diamond and said what they thought.

'Lalla wants to go on the ship,' my father said, and his eyes shone, and I felt the hairs on my arms prickle with electricity, because even though my mother had come back in the room, it was me he was looking at, my words that had brought that light to his eyes. I thought about the ship, and the promise of friends, and suddenly I needed to know, more than anything else in my limited, safe, grey world, that the ship was more than a theoretical hereafter for the hopeless, that it was not just one more of the many heavens I'd seen in the display cases at the British Museum.

My father stood up. 'Lalla is sixteen now,' he said. 'Maybe that will persuade you better than I can.' He held out a hand to me, and I stood beside him, his arm around my shoulder. My mother looked at us and, for a fraction of a second, her eyes widened. 'It's over, Anna. You know it. That's why we bought the ship in the first place.' He lifted his arm and I slipped out from under it, dismissed. He went to my mother, the two of them framed by the kitchen doorway, and stroked her cheek with the back of his hand. 'Darling,' he began.

I went to the window. It was quite dark now, and street people were gathering by the railings in the square opposite. One looked up at us, face stark white against his clothes. What did sixteen mean, when nothing ever changed? Behind me, my father and mother were kissing softly. Until recently, I'd just hidden behind the latest Dove-authorised game when they kissed, regardless of the power rationing. But now, I found myself staring, and wondering how it would feel to have my lips touched by someone else's like that, and whether it would ever happen to me.

'Come back into the room, kitten,' my father said, and I did as I was told. I knelt down to see whether my mother had laid the fire. The wood came from a man my father knew. Everything we'd ever had came from a man my father knew.

'Of course we'll leave. When we have to,' my mother said into the silence. 'But, Michael, we need to stay for a little longer.'

'What for? There's nothing left to see in the museums anyway. The stuff gets traded on all the time. What do you think the museum dwellers are living on?'

My mother's voice began to rise. 'They need people like us. If we don't keep visiting the museum, then those people will be next on the government list.'

'There are no more people like us.' He gestured around the room, at the fire, the working screen, the spaghetti hoops in tomato sauce that my mother had emptied into three small bowls and put on the table in the corner. There were sausages hiding under the hoops, and I realised that my mother had known the contents of the tin all along and had saved it for my birthday. We went to the table. My mother didn't like sausages; I ate them for her, and for a few moments nothing was said at all. I waited for the miracle that sometimes happened on my birthday – not a cake, but chocolate or sweets; even a tin of peaches. But when my mother finally spoke, it was as though my birthday wasn't happening at all.

'You wouldn't want to leave the museum people if you'd actually talked to them,' she said. 'They're organising themselves, working together. If we desert them, it's over. We might as well kill them with our own hands.'

'I talk to the people who matter. You, and Lalla, and our people in the holding centre.'

'And people who give diamonds for tinned peaches.'

'Yes,' my father said flatly. 'Face it, Anna. If we don't walk past the people who need us, we'll never save ourselves.'

'I won't walk past them,' my mother whispered. I took the armchair, and thought about the people who had once lived in tents in Regent's Park, their bodies blown apart and scattered across the ruins of their makeshift homes. Who had gathered them up? And my own death. What would that look like? In a tent, by a bomb? *Lucky Lalla, lucky, lucky Lalla.* In the warmth of the fire, I lost myself in thoughts about people so valued that their dead bodies were buried with gold and jade, and of others so hungry that they would steal stories to feed themselves. Where did the difference lie? Which was I?

I sat up when my father said, 'Tomorrow.'

'Tomorrow?'

'We're ready. We've been planning this for years. What's it all been for if we don't go? It's time. I've warned you, Anna. For Lalla, if not for you.'

My mother put another piece of wood on the fire. It was prettily shaped; it must have been part of a chair once. Or a table.

'Lalage,' she said. 'We named her Lalage.' I waited for them to look at me, to bring me into focus, but they didn't. My mother sat staring into the flames; my father sat watching her.

'We had to find the right people,' she said.

'We've found them. The manifest is full. Five hundred pages. Five hundred people. They're in the holding centre, waiting.'

'But what if things get better?' she asked, turning to him. The light of the fire shone in her hair. 'How can they get better if we leave?'

I could feel the press of people outside. Dark had long since fallen. There were firedrums lit on the street corners; I saw their burning orange on the white walls of the drawing room. I could feel the longing of the street people for what we had, pulling them towards us like gravity. I could feel the air, pressing change upon me, and a sensation in my belly that was new, gnawing at me like hunger, although we had only just eaten.

'I can't keep paying for the guards. For the holding centre. For all the food you and Lalla take to the museum dwellers. There's enough petrol to get us to the quay, but no more. Do you understand, Anna? I can't get any more.'

'A little longer. Until the museum dwellers have a proper plan.'

'What plan can they possibly have?' my father asked, but the words were barely out of his mouth when there was a scream from the street.

'Don't,' my father said as my mother started up from the sofa.

My mother stood up. 'Someone's hurt.'

'Stay away from the window.' He took her arm and pulled her back.

'I want to know what's going on out there.'

'You know,' my father said, tightening his grip. 'You just won't see it. What do I have to do? What?'

'What?' I cried, suddenly panicked. 'What is going on?' But they weren't looking at me. They were staring at each other, locked into a battle that was nothing to do with me.

'Didn't I see you and Lalla safely through the collapse? The establishment of military government? When have you ever been hungry, or in danger?'

'You're hurting me,' she said through clenched teeth.

'Tell me we'll leave tomorrow. Tell me.' He gripped her upper arms and held her against the wall. The screaming continued; more voices joined in, piercing and demented. 'Tomorrow,' he said. There were tears in his eyes; he was shaking. 'I mean it. We've waited too long already. Say it. Say it.'

She shook him off and ran to the window. I went to follow her, but he grabbed me and held me back, and I was too taken aback to protest.

The silence lasted for three heartbeats. Then the air was split by a sudden crack and the window fell away. The fire guttered in the wind and a sudden chill wrapped itself around me. My mother stood tall and beautiful, frozen in time, her eyes unnaturally wide and her lips parted in surprise. She folded in two and slumped backwards, and as she did so, the cord connecting me to the land snapped, fibre by fibre. There was blood, and as I ran to her, I knew that my sixteen years counted for nothing, and that nothing of this old life was relevant anymore.

'Close the curtains,' my father said, and as I did so I saw a small black-clothed figure move away through the crowd and vanish into the dark.

'Look,' I said, but my father was kneeling beside her body, kissing her cheeks, her hair, her lips, holding her hand in both of his as though he would never let her go, sobbing, 'Anna, Anna,' over and over again. I fetched a towel and pressed it to her abdomen, where blood seeped wet and dark, and he looked at me through his tears.

'I saw someone,' I began, but he held a warning finger to his lips, and I stopped.

'Lalla,' he said. 'Help me to take her to the ship.'

'The ship?'

He nodded, and even as I held on to my mother's hand, I felt my heart beating faster.

'Everything I have promised you is true, Lalla. Remember that.'

Together, we laid my mother gently on the back seat of the last car in London. I remembered everything I had ever heard about the ship and sat with her head on my lap, whispering tales of doctors, of medicines, of healing. Every now and then, she tried to talk, but my father told her to save her strength. I watched her blood soaking the towel, but what I felt more than anything was the irrepressible beating of my own heart. It drowned out the engine starting, the protests of the street people as they moved out of the road, the cries of the children as we passed. It filled the silence of the empty streets beyond the city; it banished the fear of an ambush or a breakdown. On a smooth wide road in the middle of nowhere, two jeeps were waiting for us. 'Our escort,' my father said, and we drove on through the night flanked by guards and guns. It's beginning, I thought. My life is about to start.

TWO

The ship. The whispered word had done nothing to prepare me for the dizzying reality. It towered over us as we drove onto the concrete at the water's edge, solid and magnificent, a palace. A temple. It was as though my father had taken the British Museum, made it shine and put it on water. Ropes as thick as my father's arms tethered it to the quay.

'Doesn't it make you feel small, Lalla?' my father asked. But it didn't make me feel small. It made me feel that I could fly. I craned my head to marvel at the ship's whiteness, its grandeur, the rising sun reflecting on the windows and filling them with gold. I almost forgot my mother until she groaned in my father's arms.

'It's here,' I breathed. 'It's all true.'

'Yes, little one,' he said. 'It's all true.'

The escorting jeeps had disappeared. For a moment, the three of us were alone, the ship rising from the water before us. Then I saw the guards leading a procession of people towards us. As the people came closer, I realised that many of their faces were familiar. The man with the dark grey beard that had one white strand running through it; the woman whose eyes were like my mother's; another woman, old, old, with black eyes bright in her dark face. They had all come to the flat; I had watched them through windows, from behind doors, and now they were here. I remembered a boy with green eyes, who had smiled at me once. I looked for him, but when I saw him I pretended I hadn't, afraid he wouldn't smile at me again.

'Lalla,' my father said as I stared, 'run up ahead to the ballroom and open the doors.' And it was their turn to stare at me as I ran across the quay. I was the first to touch the ship, and it was unyielding and real. My heart lifted as I unfastened the gangway gate. My red shoes set the gangway jangling as I ran up.

At the top, I stopped and turned around, breathing hard. I wanted to shout out to the sky up above and to my parents below. We were getting away. For years I had waited, dancing on the periphery of my parents' vision as they worked and prepared. Now my dress blazed orange against the white of the ship; I was a torch, a flame, I was forging the way. The gangway was held to the ship with a bolt on either side, each longer than my forearm. I put my hand on one, and imagined the moment when the bolts would be drawn back.

On the quay, the people parted to let my father through. Where he walked, they followed, like water swirling in the wake of a trailing hand. In my father's arms, my mother in her silk dress seemed to float like a flower. The ship. The beginning of every tomorrow there would ever be. The guards formed a corridor to the gangway; the people filled it. There would be a doctor among them, I was sure, and medicines and bandages. The deck rail was cold under my outstretched hand.

My father looked up and I remembered that he had told me to go straight to the ballroom. I had no idea where or what the ballroom was, but ahead of me I saw a pair of doors with golden handles and panels of decorated glass. I pushed them open and entered a vast hall, with blue velvet benches running the length

22

of the walls and three chandeliers, sparkling with crystals, hanging from the ceiling. At the top of the room was a raised podium; on the podium stood a polished wooden desk; on the desk, fat and leather-bound, sat the manifest. This, then, was the ballroom, unreal in luxury and cleanliness. I stood and stared at the manifest. Those thick, dark covers held the details of every one of the people my parents had invited on board. If I read it through, there would be no such thing as a stranger, for as long as the ship sailed.

I saw my father through the window and ran to hold the door. He laid my mother on blue velvet and knelt beside her. Her palms were sticky, and her forehead shone with perspiration. Her skin was marble white. Only the movement of her eyes behind her closed lids and the blood seeping through the front of her dress said that she was still alive. I looked to my father for instructions, but he would not look at me, however hard I stared at him. He held my mother's hand to his forehead, his eyes tightly shut, while I watched the people coming in. 'For Lalage,' I heard him say under his breath, as though there was no one else in the room. He looked at the manifest, and then at me, and I was glad I had not touched it. He rose and I took his place beside her.

The people began to enter. First was a man with a grey face, lined and tired. As he came closer to my father, his shoulders straightened and he held his head higher, and I saw his blue eyes, eyes that belonged in a younger face. The rest of the people oozed behind him. They filed in and sat on the blue velvet benches, shuffling up, making room for each other, eyes meeting then looking away. Now, those people are Finn, Helen, Patience, Gabriel, Jamila. They are Luke, Emily, Tom. They have names, and stories that I know. But on that first day, they were images of hunger and sadness and loss, each as desperate as each other, and all I cared about was that one of them was surely a doctor.

From where I knelt, I could see the quay. The embarkation

exposed its grey concrete in patches that grew bigger and bigger, until all that was left were the last few people stepping onto the gangway, the abandoned car and the two lines of guards. When we'd gone they'd tear the car apart for shelter, for food, for the dregs of petrol left in the tank. Beyond the car, the obsolete road unwound, hemmed in on either side by broken warehouses. Then my mother coughed and I forgot the guards. I forgot the ship and the people. I went and pulled at my father's jacket, as I had been doing ever since I was tiny. The six people he had been talking to left the ballroom at a run, and he turned to face me.

'Father,' I said, 'which one is the doctor?'

'Wait,' he said.

'But Father . . .'

He looked at me then. 'Lalla,' he said, and his voice was low and urgent. 'We've got to sail. The government troops will be coming. There is no doubt of that. And they will be armed.'

'Then why aren't we sailing?'

'We have to start the engines. Register the people.'

Register the people? My father's time and my mother's time were running at different speeds, and if I could not bring them together, my mother would die. This, then, was fear, and even as my heart pounded and my fingernails carved half moons on the palm of my hands, I thought how strange it was that I learned to feel fear the moment I was brought to safety.

'Roger!' My father beckoned to a man who had entered in a rush, looking anxiously about him, his floppy hair swinging lank across his face. In the flood of light from the huge windows, his skin looked translucent and crumpled. I wondered when he had last eaten, or slept. He thrust the parcel he was holding into the hands of a woman with red hair and ran to us.

'How is Anna?' he said at once. Then he saw her, and he closed his eyes as though he was in pain. My mother sighed, and then coughed again, rearing up as the bloodstains on the towel darkened and shone. The doctor grabbed a cushion from the bench – deep blue velvet, soft, new, untouched – and gave it to me. 'Press this over the bleeding,' he said. I started to try and remove the towel but he stopped me. 'No,' he said sharply, as though he'd expected better of me, 'just hold it over what's already there.' He put his hand to her forehead and snatched it away almost immediately. 'She's burning up,' the doctor said. 'The wound must be infected.'

'So quickly?' my father said, and I let go of the cushion; it fell to the floor just as the doctor was turning to my father, and his foot sent it spinning away.

The cushion came to rest in front of my father's desk, blood-stain uppermost. The manifest sat on the desk, fat and solid, and the three of us stared at it.

'Lalage,' my mother whispered softly. 'Michael?'

'I'm here,' I said, squeezing her hand.

'Anna,' my father said, kneeling. 'Anna, I've sent the engineers straight down. The doctor's here. We'll be sailing soon. Try, Anna. Please try.'

'Register them first,' she breathed. Then her eyes opened wide, and no matter how many times I said, I'm here, I'm here, no matter how close to her I held my face, her eyes kept darting from side to side, seeing nothing. I kissed her forehead and was startled by its heat.

'The infirmary's ready, isn't it?' my father asked the man Roger. 'It's all done?'

'It's been ready for a long time,' the doctor said, and my father strode to the desk. The red-headed woman was standing next to it; she stepped aside, and my father opened the manifest. The cover thudded heavily; the pen sat fatly in his hand.

'Sign,' he said, trembling. The doctor took the pen from my father's hand. He could not help lifting the pen to look at it first, and I thought the delay might kill her. Then he signed, and as he did so, my father leaned into him and whispered fiercely, 'You save her, do you hear me? You save her.'

The doctor paled, then lifted my mother in his arms. 'I'll try, Michael. I'll do everything I can.' A dark-haired woman opened the door for them, and I followed them.

'No,' my father said. The word was a bullet. 'Not you, Lalla. Let Roger do his job.'

I stopped and turned, incredulous. Whenever our unit of three had been separated, it had been my father striding off alone, sometimes for weeks at a time, and my mother and I left together, counting the days until he came back. I did not know how to leave her to be with him. And whatever the doctor's job was, I was a part of it. The room had filled while I had been bent over my mother; wherever I looked, there was a face fixed on me. I had never been so close to so many people; I stepped backwards and tripped over someone's feet.

'We're going to register,' my father said. I protested, but a voice above me spoke softly; I looked from the feet into the black eyes of an old woman.

'What would your mother do if she were with us?' she asked.

'But she's still with us,' I said, looking around. Hundreds of eyes stared back at me, wide with sympathy, and I began to panic. 'She's still with us,' I repeated, as though repetition could somehow make it true.

'Come here, Lalla,' my father said. I walked to the podium and sat down beside him; he placed his hand on my head with tears in his eyes, and I knew I had no choice.

No one picked up the cushion.

My father spoke into a small black stick. 'Hello,' he said, and his voice cracked a little and then suddenly came from everywhere, as though a thousand of him had surrounded the ballroom and spoken together. He pulled back a little, startled, then leaned in again. 'Can everyone hear me?' The people called

26

back, and my father continued, 'That's good. That works, then. So, welcome. We – we all – I mean, here we are, come to the ship at last. It's been a long wait but you've made it. You're free to breathe now. As you know, Anna's been hurt, but she's in good hands. In a few moments, we'll be off. But while the engineers are doing their work, shall we greet each other? I know you've been together in the holding centre for a long time, but let's meet each other once more, as the people of the ship.'

All around the room, people smiled and held their hands out to each other. The people drew together before him, all rags and grime and hungry eyes, until I was utterly alone in the room.

I could not bear to look at them. The bloodstained cushion sat like a reproach; my mother was somewhere, bleeding, needing me. And I needed her. In this great crowd, I was still alone. I skulked behind my father, looking over their heads, desperate to avoid eye contact. Through the big picture windows I could see the guards on the quay gathered in dark blotches, waiting for us to unbolt the gangway so that they could wheel it away, release the ropes and send us on our way. They were hunched over; one of them, at least, was crying. Were they so sorry to see us go? Beyond the guards sat the little car. I went to the window and gazed at the car until I almost saw my mother's blood on its back seat. Along the road, the broken windows made dark gaps in the warehouse facades. And at the end of that road I saw a grey shape that had not been there before.

'Father,' I said, moving closer to him, but the ballroom doors opened and six people walked in, nervous and proud.

'Our engineers,' my father called through the microphone, and my plea was lost in cheers, and then in a wave of movement as people began to move towards the desk. My father called their names. The first – Diana Aabri, dark-eyed and serious – picked up the cushion and laid it gently on the podium where no one would step on it, and I felt a burst of gratitude that made me want to run to her. But there were other names, and Diana had moved away long before I had found the courage to approach her. One by one, they stepped onto the podium and signed the pages of the manifest, fascinated by the pen, the smooth ivory paper, the kindness of my father smiling upon them. One by one, they stepped off and gathered excitedly together, looking curiously and yet kindly at me as they did so, exchanging names, exchanging looks. Exchanging stories. And as they did so, I saw the anonymous mass resolve into dozens, hundreds of individuals, and wondered whether any one of them would help me.

'Father,' I called again, my breath catching, but the buzz of the people drowned not only my voice, but another, fainter buzz that might have come from my father's microphone.

And then the new darkness at the end of the road spat out a globule of black. The globule moved with strength and purpose down the centre of the road, and as it grew bigger I realised it was a group, running in formation. In a few short seconds, they reached my father's guards and separated, and, for the second time since we boarded, fear rose in me. Those were uniforms. Not the makeshift clothes of the street in which everyone looked the same, or the worn fatigues my father had found for his guards, but clean, sharp, deliberate clothes, in unfaded black. I had seen them in the bulletins, batons lifted against marketeers. I had seen them at registrations and at food drops, patrolling the queues, removing those whose cards had become invalid, invalidating the cards of those who resisted. My card was always valid and I did not have to use the markets, but the black uniforms frightened me now. Government troops.

'Father,' I said, more loudly this time, but the rhythmic jangling of heavy boots on the gangway silenced me. Beside me someone screamed; the whole room seemed to harden; people who had been smiling gently at each other stiffened and drew apart. The ballroom doors burst open and my father's chief guard strode in. The registration stopped.

'The troops are here, Mr Paul,' the guard said, breathing hard. 'Shall we shoot them?'

My father shook his head. 'No, Greenlaw. Not as a first resort. And you should have left your gun with the others. You know the rules. No guns on the ship.' But before Greenlaw could leave, the ballroom door was flung open by a man in true black. He had a craggy face, one which we had all seen on the bulletins. He, too, carried a gun. So did the two soldiers who stood behind him.

'Michael Paul,' he said, and his voice needed no microphone.

'Commander Marius,' my father said. His voice was pinched and light. 'In person. We are honoured. And your armed guards. Delighted, I'm sure.'

'We're here to arrest you.'

'On what charge?'

'Stealing state property.'

My father smiled with relief, and the room settled with him. Greenlaw went back to the quay, gripping his rifle. 'The ship is mine,' my father said. 'It's registered to me, and it's been re-registered every time the regulations have changed. I've kept a hard trail.' He took a sheaf of printouts from his case and offered it to the commander with a look of pity. 'I'm sorry you've had a wasted journey. Did you run all the way?' My mother's voice floated over us. *Above board, Michael. Legal. Nothing that might shame us.*

I will be with you, I promised her silently.

'I'm not talking about the ship,' Commander Marius said contemptuously.

My father leaned forward, his face alive with interest. 'What, then? The provisions?'

'No. We can't trace those to government supplies.'

My father raised his eyebrows as though he was acknowledging a compliment. 'I didn't know that the state had any property left,' he said. 'Everything on board is mine, I assure you.'

There was a gentle ripple of sound; I looked around me and realised that I had just heard strangers laughing. It felt light inside me; it was a feeling I liked, one I wanted to have again. My fear bubbled away; I thought this must be a game, something my father had arranged for everyone before we sailed away, and I laughed too, confident that I'd be with my mother shortly, and that she would be all right.

'Look,' my father said, irritation shading his voice. 'My wife and I have kept up with every single new law. There is no obscure amendment, no loophole, no adjustment you can surprise me with.'

'The Exodus Act,' the commander said triumphantly. My father's expression of amused tolerance did not change, but it set hard and the palms of my hands began to feel damp. 'You've forgotten the Exodus Act.'

'The Exodus Act?' my father repeated. Astonished eyes travelled from my father to the uniformed men and back again. My father spoke slowly. 'The Exodus Act was twenty years ago. More. Under the previous government. The elected one,' he added pointedly. The amusement had gone; now my father looked wary, alert, ready to produce whatever snippet of knowledge was required.

'But the principle still holds. No state assets can be exported from the state.'

My father nodded. 'Of course,' he said. 'But the ship is not a state asset. And how can I export when there's nowhere to export to?' He gave an exasperated sigh. 'We're not your problem. We're just five hundred fewer people for you to feed. Please, Marius.' He swallowed. 'My wife is injured. I need to get to her.'

The commander turned away from my father and indicated the ballroom. 'Have these people all got valid identity cards?'

'Of course they have. They wouldn't have lasted long without them.'

'Then they're state assets.'

'State assets?'

'The Nazareth Act promised provision for all registered citizens. But it works both ways. You're stealing. From the state. And that's a death penalty.' I heard a man whisper, 'What isn't, these days?' but nobody replied. So many laws had just slipped in quietly, without fuss, like a stone held to the surface of the water before you let it fall in.

The commander stepped onto the podium and hefted a black armoured case onto my father's desk; the brass handles on the desk drawer rattled as it thudded down, and the red-headed woman flinched. He took out a screen; his bodyguards trained their guns on the crowd. A man in dirty checked trousers felt for his card, and he set off a ripple of similar movements along the benches. It was a market raid, except that no one was trying to escape. The very act of producing the cards seemed to galvanise my father.

'Look,' he said. 'Check our identities by all means. But you can't stop us from sailing.'

'I can,' the man said. 'If nothing else, we're armed. You're not.'

'They are,' my father said, pointing at his guards on the quay.

'Fine,' the commander said. 'My men shoot your men, your men shoot mine, and then we'll carry on. Have you got a gun on you now?'

My father hesitated, then shook his head. *No guns on the ship*, I remember my mother saying to my father. *Let the guards keep them. God knows they'll have earned them.*

But . . .

Not on the ship, Michael. Do you know how many times I would have killed you if I'd had the chance? I don't want to have that chance. They smiled, the way they did when a serious point was wrapped in a joke and offered as a present, and the conversation ended in laughter and tinned peaches. But the truth is that my father did not want guns on the ship, either. When he went on his trips, he told me, he carried only his toothbrush and his wit. The episode in the flat, before my mother was shot, was as violent as I had ever seen him. He armed the guards because he had to, but words were what he liked. Words, arguments, debates. He liked to win. But for as long as I can remember, winning meant convincing you, drawing you into his vision so completely that you would defend it with your last breath.

Not your last breath, Mother, I whispered. *Not your last.*

'You should have a gun,' the commander said. 'Look.' He gestured at the horizon. I looked in the direction he was pointing, past the quay and the car, down the road. The darkness I had noticed earlier had become a rolling cloud of smoke. My father left the desk and walked towards us. The commander lifted his gun, but my father pushed its barrel to the floor as he passed and the two men walked to the window together. In the silence I heard a noise that I thought was the whisper of conversation, but no one in the ballroom was talking. Then I realised that the noise was coming from outside the ship and that it was getting louder. The sound rose, at first like the rhythmic swish of the waves, then more insistent, harsher, like the noise the mighty ropes would make when they were let loose and sent crashing into the water. The black smoke in the distance was solidifying into a mass, like water made thick with detritus, oozing down the road we had travelled. The commander looked towards the approaching darkness. I saw fear in the way his hands would not stay still, in the way his head kept twitching as though he could not decide where his priorities lay. The people began to nudge each other, to exchange worried glances and to look, again and again, towards my father.

The commander turned to his bodyguards and said, 'You'd better go down. Don't let them storm the ship. Yet.' The bodyguards hesitated and the commander snapped, 'He's not going to shoot me. He hasn't even got a gun,' and the two men tramped down the gangway, guns raised, leaving my father and the commander facing each other.

'Are you going to shoot us?' my father asked.

'You're committing a crime.'

'I'm saving the human race.'

'No, Mr Paul. I am saving the human race.'

'By killing off the surplus population?'

The commander shrugged, the crags in his face deepened and for the first time I saw a person behind the uniform. Here was a man; maybe he had a wife, a daughter. 'This is not a democracy,' he said. 'This is government for survival. What else do you suggest?'

'It's over, you know,' my father said gently. They leant on the sill; in another time, another place, they could have been friends contemplating a stroll on deck.

'I can't let you go,' the commander said. 'You've got food and medicine on board. Tools, equipment . . .'

'No more than we need,' my father said hastily. 'There's no law against holding the food you require for survival.'

'Even so. Essential rations for five hundred – that's significant. We could create a few more citizens, get some people off the Sinkers . . . You've got all five hundred on board, I take it?'

'All except one.'

'Your wife?'

'She's in the infirmary. She's going to be fine. No, a young man. He died last night.'

'Then you're over-stocked. That's a criminal offence.'

33

'I'll surrender his share. Just let us go.'

The approaching mass became distinct; these were men and women, with voices raised in anger. Individual voices jutted from the cacophony – stop them, get them, take them, bring them down. Inside, the people of the ship, afraid and silent. On the quay, my father's guards and the government troops, armed and awaiting orders.

'You knew they'd come,' the commander said.

'Of course.' My father shrugged. 'I had hoped to leave before they arrived, but they don't change anything.'

The mob were surrounding the car now, and for a moment they were distracted, jumping on it, pulling at the door handles, kicking the doors, tearing at the seats. My father's guards and the government troops stood together, defending the gangway.

The commander looked directly at my father. 'I have seen what hungry men will do for food,' he said. 'And if I were you, I would be afraid. I would be on my knees, begging me to let you raise the gangway and sail before they notice you standing here.'

'Why?' my father said. 'Why would I beg? You can shoot us all, one by one, and throw our bodies into the sea. You can de-register us and put us in tents and bomb us later. You can hold us up here until those desperate men and women swarm on board and destroy us all. Or you can let us go.'

The commander looked from the mob on the quay to my father, from his black-clothed colleagues to the stricken faces in the ballroom. My heart was racing. We had to release the gangway and cast off the ropes. Part of me was waiting for my father to produce a weapon from some hidden store, for an army of his own to leap fully formed from the ballroom panelling and blast the commander and the mob and the quay into oblivion. But it didn't happen. Instead, the commander levelled his gun at my father and the horizon contracted so that the descending crowd and the road and the car and the quayside became one. *Fear makes men blind*, my mother said, and at that moment I understood what she meant. There was life, and there was death, and the fragile divide between them, held in the hands of a stranger. Metallic clangs echoed around the room, vying with the deeper, distant pulsing of engines ready for the off. I wondered how long it would take the crowd to break through the barrier of armed guards and storm the ship.

I needed my mother. My father's eyes kept straying to the internal door; he needed her too. He was restless, biting his lips and rubbing his thumb in the palm of his hand.

'I offered you a government post when you sold us the Dove,' Commander Marius said. 'You should have taken it. You'd have had food, security, privilege. But no. You wanted freedom. Look where your freedom's got you. I am arresting you, Michael Paul. If you resist, I shall have no alternative but to shoot you.'

My father looked around at the people, his lips pale. 'I . . .' he began, but his voice cracked and he said no more.

'We'll take you all off the ship and empty the hold. And if you're lucky, we'll shoot you quietly.'

'Please . . .'

'And if you're not lucky,' the commander continued, 'then I'll tell my troops to stand aside and let the mob deal with you.'

My father had failed. I saw the people being marched off the ship at gunpoint and sent away from the quay. I saw a chain of people in black uniforms passing boxes from one to another. I saw everything my father had worked to amass evaporating over the starving city. And in that one short moment, as my father crumpled on the window sill, his head in his hands, dwarfed by the commander's black case and the weapon at his side, I found myself growing angry. My mother would die. We would never sail; my father's vision would become dust, the ship would go back to being a myth and we too would starve, just to bring the commander a moment of glory on the bulletin.

And where I had felt fear and guilt, I now felt anger. I was angry with the commander, the troops, the government they worked for that my father had been too principled to join. I was angry at the stupidity of the generations before mine that had brought us to this place. And I was angry with the people – my father's chosen people – quietly shuffling into a queue before the commander's screen, cards in hand, as though this was just another registration. My father was shrunken and motionless. My anger spread through me, like a virus eating away the information on a screen. It destroyed all the questions, the doubt, the distance. It brought me on board. To untie the massive ropes that held the ship to the shore, to let the grinding engines leap into life – above all, to be gone and be with my mother, became my overriding mission.

'If he takes me, you execute him for stealing from the state?' I asked the commander. The crags in his face shifted as he raised his eyebrows and nodded. 'What will happen to me? To all of us?'

'Nothing,' he said. 'You don't prosecute the bread for being stolen.' He smiled sadly, and I remember thinking that, however sharp his uniform, his teeth would not last much longer. He addressed the people as a whole. 'Leave now, and you will all retain your registration. My men will protect you, and you will be given food from the stocks we reclaim from the ship. For as long as you have your cards, you are citizens still.'

A whisper of relief escaped the people. They were going to give in, I thought. They were going to walk down the gangway as quietly as they had walked up it. For a moment, I hated them all. For years, my parents had talked about them, planned for them, argued about them. Ignored me for them. And they were here, in this room. Not a bland mass, but individuals, each unique, all gathered in my father's name. The people. Men. Women. Even a scattering of children. My parents had chosen these people to be my world. If I did nothing, I would never know them. Already I knew that I couldn't go back. I had breathed salt air and spoken to a stranger. I couldn't go back.

I undid the zip in my pocket and took my identity card from its belt. I pulled open the door to the deck. The noise of the mob on the quay hit me like a blow to the face. The commander followed me; the people followed him. Why aren't they more afraid? I asked myself, looking at their empty faces. If they had been marched back down the gangway and left to find a life, their expressions would not have changed. *It was always too good to be true*, they would say, just as my mother did every time a food drop turned out to be no more than a rumour. But the ship was not a rumour or a false promise. It was here, solid and white, the giant engines throbbing under our feet, ready to take us away. I climbed up onto the deck rail and braced myself against a vertical bar. I held my card aloft. I didn't know what the ship was, but I knew I wanted it. My blood coursed wildly through my veins; I was alive; I was going to act. The latest biometric re-registration had only been a couple of days ago; my card would be valid for a week or two yet.

'Look,' I shouted. My father joined the people on deck, staring at me until I met his eyes. His eyes grew bright, his shoulders squared, and I loved him. On the quay, a woman in a pink dress saw me and stopped still, pointing; the stillness rippled from her until the mob and the troops and the guards were all staring up at me, as silent as the people of the ship crowded onto the deck.

'This is my card,' I called. 'Without it, I am no one. Without it, I have no state, no rights, no claims. Without it, I have no screen access. I'll be a non-person, and no one will know when I die.'

'Don't,' came a voice from the deck. 'He'll shoot.' I looked towards the sound, and the eyes that met mine were green.

The commander raised his gun to his eye. Like mother, like

daughter, I thought, except that she had not known the shot was coming. I heard the click as he prepared to fire.

'Shoot me,' I said, and as I let go of my card, he lowered his gun with incredulous eyes. My card turned over and over as it fell to the quay. It hit ropes that held the ship and rebounded into the water. I saw it floating, a speck of white on a grey-brown strip of sea.

The mob began to jostle at the water's edge. The woman in the pink dress lay down, stretching her hands to the water, but the water level was too low. A man held her ankles and she grabbed, but my card floated out of reach. Others joined in; a soldier bent down and used his gun to try and sweep the card towards him; yet others shouted advice.

'We must release the gangway,' my father said quietly to the woman with red curly hair, who was standing beside him. 'Now, while the people on the quay are distracted.'

'What about the commander?' the woman said, moving to the bolts that held the gangway to the ship. She tried to draw them back, but they were heavy, and she looked about for help.

My father hesitated. 'We've got a space, haven't we?'

I was too scared to ask what he meant. Now, I urged him silently. Now. The bodies on the streets had been ghastly; the government bombings had been horrific; the battles at the food points had been violent and bloody, but none of them had had anything to do with me. Now my card had gone, and with it any chance I had of survival in the old world. Like my mother, I had given myself wholly and completely to my father, or to death. We had to sail.

Then, as my father drew breath, the woman looked up from the gangway bolts.

'I've waited five years for this,' she called out over the deck rail. 'You can have mine, too.' The crowd looked up, and she threw her card onto the quay. A group of people hurled themselves at it. My father watched, intent.

'And mine,' shouted the man who had led the people on board. His card caught the sunlight as it fell into a mass of out-stretched hands.

'And mine,' called the green-eyed boy, climbing up onto the deck rail to join me. He swayed dangerously and I caught his arm, and for a moment we stood clasped together, high above everyone else, and I felt something glorious in the air around me, as though the ship really was studded with rainbows from the diamonds that had paid for it. And suddenly the air below us became full of white plastic rectangles with gold chips glinting, spinning and turning as they flew. The snarling mass sepa-rated into pairs of dancing arms. And the green-eyed boy and I climbed down and looked at each other, laughing, and for a moment we did not let each other go.

'I'm Tom. Tom Mandel,' he said, but before I could answer, someone called out behind me.

'Be me,' they said, and we separated to let others reach the deck rail, and my arms felt cold where he had let me go.

The commander looked down as the laughing crowd caught at the confetti of cards. My father, who had come to stand next to me, was laughing too, his body brimful of energy, his eyes alight. 'Will you?' he asked the commander, pulling out his own identity card and holding it aloft. 'We lost one of our number last night. You can have his place.'

'It's suicide,' the commander said quietly. 'You'll never be able to come back.'

'We don't want to. We know where we're going.'

Commander Marius looked thoughtful. He looked from my father's card to his face, from the cards still raining onto the quay to his colleagues, as eager as the homeless to catch them. My mother's voice in my head said, *Michael, you can never know*

what depths people may have until the waters have a chance to settle.
What lay behind the commander's lined face, his yellowing eyes?
He took his card from a pocket and studied it, turning it over
and over in his hands.

'Where are you going?' he asked at last.

'Join my people,' my father said. 'Find out.'

'People?' the commander said wearily, putting his card away.
'You know the Nazareth Act. No card, no presence. There aren't
any people on this ship now.' He put his gun into its holster.
'The people are all down on the quay. I'll take my screen down
to them while those cards are still valid. Then at least they'll be
able to get to the next food drop.'

My father held out his hand. 'Why stay?' he asked.

'I have to do what I can. I don't have a choice.'

'I'm giving you a choice, right now. Throw down your card.'

'I don't think so,' the commander said quietly. 'I had a daughter once.' He looked at me and took my father's hand without
taking his eyes from my face. *I'm sorry*, I thought, although I
did not know why, and before I could say anything he turned
and walked along the deck and down the gangway. His ringing
footsteps grew fainter. The gangway gate groaned, and as the
commander stepped onto the quay, my father threw his own
card. It paused in the air, a flash of gold, before the commander
caught it. The people on the ship cheered. My father's guards ran
to the ropes; others crowded around to help, making so much
noise that no one heard my father's panicked shout. 'Not yet,' he
screamed, running to the gangway bolts, but the ropes fell into
the sea before the cheers had subsided. The engines kicked in
with a deep roar, and the ship began to drift.

There was a screech of tortured metal. The gangway was still
bolted to the ship.

'It'll slam into us,' my father said desperately, struggling to
slide the mechanism free. Others joined him. But the movement

of the ship had tightened the bolts against their casings, and they would not give. As the ship moved slowly, inexorably out to sea, it dragged the gangplank across the quay. I shouted, but I was too late. Three women lay on the quay, still trying to reach the cards that had fallen into the water. They had no time to stand. The gangway swept them away with industrial efficiency; they barely had time to scream. The resistance of their bodies momentarily slackened the bolts; the bolts gave and the gangway fell into the sea with an incredible splash.

I watched the water crash white over the falling metal, and I watched as the waves subsided and the sea became smooth. The strip of brown water between the ship and the land became a river, a lake, a sea. But the three women did not come to the surface. Tiny figures lined the quay; I heard far-off cries. But we were gone. The gangway was in the sea, the ship was safe, and soon the land was nothing more than a panoramic postcard pinned to the sky.

My father returned to the desk and opened the manifest.

'Lalla,' he said, inclining his head. He handed me the pen and I felt its unfamiliar weight between my fingers.

'But those women . . .' I said.

'Sign your name, then go to your mother,' he answered, and I formed my name as quickly as I could, struggling with the strange sensation of the paper against the nib, my hands trembling with gratitude and relief. But at last there it was, Lalla Paul, thick, black, indelible. A pen with ink, a paper page. Irrevocable paper, that could not be reprogrammed, hacked, crashed, deleted. No matter what happened to the power supply, my name would stand there, for ever. I wondered whether this was why my mother had been so insistent on teaching me to write without using the screen. 'Go, quickly,' he said. 'Up the first staircase, third door.'

'Aren't you coming?' I asked.

He waved the pen at the queue of people before him, alight with hope and adoration. He shook his head. 'I've got to register the people,' he said. 'Tell her . . .' he began, but his voice gave way and he stopped, breathing hard. 'It's a metal door,' he said at last.

Behind me, I heard my father calling out names, the shuffle of feet, the ordered method of things being done properly. Hope insinuated itself into the controlled space. I glanced over my shoulder as, one by one, the people signed the manifest. Three lives had been lost, but one hung in the balance, and that was the one I cared about most. I ran. I ran as fast as I could. To the infirmary. To my mother.

It never occurred to me to wonder how we would disembark, now that the gangway was gone.

THREE

A steel door ❀ *a doctor's joy* ❀ *and now who is
Lalla Paul?*

I found the steel door and pushed it open, feeling the metal grow warm under my hands. When I took them away, there were two perfect hand shapes outlined in mist on the silver. They vanished before I had walked through. My mother lay still, her eyes closed. The doctor was there too, adjusting the valve on a bag of fluid hanging over my mother's bed.

'Miss Paul,' he said, standing in the way of the bed. His eyes did not meet mine. His hair was coarse and pale and fell over his ears. He stepped aside as I approached the bed.

'Mother?' I said. 'Mother?'

I reached out to stroke her face but the doctor caught my hand. 'Wash your hands before you touch her,' he said gently, 'then rub them with the gel in the blue bottle. And put on a gown.'

I turned on the tap. 'There's water,' I said, surprised, watching it cascading into the silver bowl. I turned off the tap, then turned it on again. 'It's still there.'

'There's electricity too,' the doctor said. 'All the time, apparently, although I don't quite see . . .' His voice trailed away. I unfolded the gown slowly, and I began to feel that the change in my life was not contained in the exchange of water for land, but in the fact that the doctor could not meet my eyes, that his hands pulled restlessly at the elasticated cuffs of his own gown, that he had no words for me. He pushed his hair back and I saw that there were hairs growing from his ears, too. I didn't like it. The gel sat cold on my skin.

'We should wait for your father,' he said, and his ear hair moved when he talked.

'He's registering the people,' I said. 'We've sailed now.' The sound of the engines had grown fainter since the first great roar. 'They're signing the manifest. My father sent me here. He said . . .'

'Yes?'

'He said the infirmary had a metal door,' I faltered, watching the doctor take down a crisp sheet of startling whiteness from a stack on a shelf. 'Can I . . . ?' I nodded at my mother and he stepped aside. I kissed her and squeezed her cold hand and then I stared and stared, looking for the rise and fall of her chest until my eyes watered. Footsteps moved past the infirmary door in little groups. I heard voices and laughter. I heard doors opening and closing and the bubbling rush of taps being turned on and off. 'Water!' I heard a distant voice shout, and a chorus of babbling voices took up the cry.

Water. How could there be water all the time, when time itself had stopped?

Then my mother heaved a sudden breath and an ooze of blood spread through the white cotton over her stomach.

'Mother?' I whispered. But she did not answer, and the doctor just watched, the white sheet folded over his arm.

In the cabins around us, the water continued to flow. Baths she had given me when I was a very little girl, when we still took water for granted, soap refusing to be caught as we chased it with slippery hands. Water cascading over her head as she washed her hair, turning it dark and shining. I forgot about the times I felt I had let her down, about never being quite clever enough, about

44

feeling unimportant. I thought about rain making puddles on the pavement and the sudden anger with which she pulled me away when I asked why we couldn't drink from them as the street people did. I'd never thanked her for boiling my water. I'd just complained about having to drink it when it was hot. And so she had found a stone jug to cool the water in, and filled it, and poured cool water from it, just for me. She had to live, so that I could thank her.

I thought about the stone jug.

The blood spread but the very fact that it was there made me dizzy with hope.

The steel door opened and my father walked in.

'I'm sorry,' the doctor said, hanging beside my father like a trailing thread, and my knees felt weak; I clung to her hand, although there was no answering pressure. My father approached the bed and the doctor did not stand in his way.

'Can she hear me?' my father asked.

I stepped back and leaned against the wall; I found myself sliding down it, the green gown rustling around me. I folded my arms over my knees and hid my face. I waited for my mother's voice to ask, *Lalage, what's wrong?* then felt the floor lurch as I realised that she was not going to ask.

'The bullet ripped through her bowel,' the doctor said. 'There isn't anything to be done except make her comfortable.'

I looked up and saw that my father's face was grey.

'I'm sorry, Mr Paul,' the doctor said again. 'I'm so sorry. The blood loss, the infection. It was too much for her. It would have been too much for anyone.'

My father closed his eyes. He clenched his hands into tight fists.

'It'll be peaceful,' the doctor continued. 'I'm making sure of that, at least.' He gestured towards the bag of clear fluid dripping into my mother's arm.

I looked at my father, willing him to produce another miraculous ship, one in which my mother had not been shot. But he kept his eyes closed and took a long time to draw breath. 'Is there anything you don't have?' he said at last. 'Is there anything you need that might make a difference? That might . . . save her?'

'No,' the doctor said quickly. 'I've got everything I want, more of everything than I could possibly need. It's all here for me. The morphine, the saline, the sterile needles and the drip . . .'

My father opened his eyes and colour returned slowly to his face.

'I cleaned the wound with swabs and dressed it with surgical muslin. Mr Paul, I had fresh water and antibiotics. If it had been possible to save your wife, I could have done it with what was here.' The doctor finished, and my father stepped forwards and held out his hand.

'Thank you,' he said as the doctor took it.

'No,' said the doctor, 'it is you I thank. If I had had all this . . .' He stopped, and my father put his free hand on the doctor's shoulder.

The sound of footsteps still surrounded us – pattering ones underscoring chatter and effervescent giggles, heavier ones accompanied by deeper voices – but this time they were going the other way, back to the ballroom.

'What?' I demanded from the floor, pulling my hair away from my face. 'If you'd had all this, then what?'

Neither man replied. They stepped apart and silence flooded between them.

'I told the people to gather in the ballroom after they'd found their cabins,' my father said. 'I have to talk to them. If I'm not there, they'll be uncertain. They'll look to each other, they'll look back to what we've left behind. It could all . . . I need to be there. She'd understand that. She told me to do it properly.'

'But she's not dead,' I said. They looked down at me. I

scrambled up with my back to the wall and faced the doctor. 'You said she's not dead. She took a breath. And there's blood. The blood's still coming. Dead people don't bleed.'

'It's only a matter of time,' the doctor said quietly. My father stood bowed, his eyes on my mother, his senses alert to the sounds outside and the constant dark rumbling of the engines taking us onwards, onwards, we knew not where.

'Does she know we're here?' my father asked.

'The pain relief is very strong. It needs to be.' The doctor paused. 'I could go to the ballroom for you,' he said. 'They'll understand.'

The footsteps on the walkway became quicker, skittering over the background bass of the engines and fading towards the ballroom. I took my mother's hand again. I felt the shallow quick fluttering of her pulse and watched the deep rise and fall of my father's breathing as he thought. I held my breath.

'No,' he said. 'It has to be me. They need to see me, to hear me. The ship was my plan. They put their trust in me. With all due respect, Roger . . .'

The doctor inclined his head in acknowledgement.

'Perhaps,' my father said, moving towards the door and then coming back to the bed, 'perhaps you could go to the ballroom and tell the people to wait.' I breathed again and lifted my head. 'Tell them that I . . . that Lalla and I . . . that we will be with them shortly. They'll wait. Of course they'll wait. They've waited so long already.'

The doctor nodded. 'Mr Paul,' he said. 'Michael. I want you to know – you need to know – that at no time in history could more have been done for her. And I thank you.'

'You're happy,' I said to the doctor as my father began to open the door for him. The doctor took a breath as if to deny it, then sighed. He leaned his forehead against the steel door and spoke to the floor.

'I've watched so many people die without being able to help. And to be able to help someone, to be able to do everything I can and then let what will be, be – that's life, Miss Paul. What's happiness, more than that?'

'And will you?' I said.

'Will I what?'

'Let what will be, be. You've stuffed her with drugs so she can't even hear me. She doesn't even know I'm here. She wouldn't want that. She wants to talk to me, even if it hurts her. She'd rather be in pain than be like this.'

The doctor straightened up and turned to me. My father took a step backwards, as though he wanted a better view. 'You think?' the doctor said. He pointed a finger at me. The slightest tremor at its tip betrayed the effort he was putting into controlling himself. 'What do you know about pain, Miss Paul? What do you know?'

My father took my hand and held it tight. I felt the strong pulse in his thumb, the warmth and resilience of his flesh, and I stared into the doctor's face, which was as white as my mother's. 'Life is pain, Miss Paul, and a pain-free death is a gift. You should thank your father. You should thank him on your knees for what he's given your mother. That's what you should be doing.' He took a breath. 'I'm sorry,' he said, but this time he was talking to my father, not to me.

I pinched my lips together with my teeth and felt the blood being driven away. I hated him. I called down thunderbolts to strike him dead on the spot; I decided to find out where his cabin was and poison the water; I would track down the person he loved best in the world and shoot them through the bowels and see how strongly he held to his precious philosophy then. The door clanged shut behind him and the misty outline of his forehead faded with the noise. My father put his arm around me and we looked down at my mother.

'Don't be angry with Roger,' he said. 'He did all he could.'

'But she's not dead.'

'She's leaving us peacefully.'

'I threw away my card,' I said. 'I stood on the deck rail and I threw it down to the people on the quay.'

'I know.'

'I did it for her,' I said. 'I did it so that we could sail quickly and I could come and be with her.'

'No,' my father said, tightening his arm around me. 'You did it for me. For the ship. I knew you would make me proud, but I did not know how soon it would come. I owe you my life, Lalla. And so does everyone on board this ship. They are your people too, now. And so soon.' He was excited; I could see his eyes dancing a little, even through the misery in his face.

'But I don't want them,' I said, the image of my mother before me beginning to swim. 'I want her.' I blinked and she was back, pale on the infirmary bed. I took her hand and knelt down beside her. Her hand was cold; I rubbed it between my own, trying to communicate my warmth to her as I had done to the steel door. But her skin resisted me as wholly as the steel had absorbed me. I looked at my father, but his eyes were far away, seeing things I had never been a part of. He bent over my mother and kissed her forehead, but it was I who felt the warmth of his lips. 'I want her too,' he whispered.

We stayed like that for a moment, until he said, 'Lalla. I have to go and talk to the people. Not for long. It won't be for long. I know exactly what I'm going to say.' He patted his pocket and I heard the rustle of paper. 'And then I'll be back. Right back.'

I rested my head on the pillow beside hers and stared at him.

'It would be easier for me if you came with me,' he said. 'Will you, Lalla? Please.'

'She's not dead,' I said again, because that was the only thing I was sure of. I turned away from him and buried my face in my mother's pillow. I heard him sigh, then I heard the steel door open. I lifted my head and had to shield my eyes against the copper gold of the sun. My father hovered, silhouetted against the bright outside. He held out his hand to me; I shook my head and he was gone.

My father was always walking out of the room after an argument, leaving an important statement hanging in the air behind him. As soon as he'd gone, my mother's anger would melt and she would turn to me, eyes bright, ready to play or to walk or to teach. I thought she might sit up now, smile, ask me what I would like to do next. But this time there was no private wink, no secret smile to let me in on the joke. And my father was gone.

I settled my head on the pillow next to hers. The voices and running water had stopped; everyone was in the ballroom with my father. Through the silence, I felt the vibration deep in the heart of the ship. My heart learned to beat in time with the engine, and I was back in London, walking to the British Museum, my mother's steady steps undeterred by the emaciated faces, the blackened teeth, the smell of the end of the world. *What right do we have,* I heard her asking my father on our return, *what right do we have to a place to call home?*

It's for Lalla, he always said. *All of it. For Lalla.*

Yes, she said, *but has she ever eaten an apple?*

'Mother,' I cried, and a cold gust of wind blew on me. My father had left the infirmary door standing open and I could see that the sun had set. I tried to stand and found that my legs had gone numb. My neck was stiff and I realised that I was cold and light-headed with hunger. We had not eaten since we left the flat. I shut the door. Where was my father? How long had he been gone?

'Mother,' I said, and then again more loudly, 'Mother.' There was no response. I could not help myself; I pressed her stomach gently, and a fresh patch of blood glinted. Her blood was

50

flowing, therefore she lived; only the doctor's magic bag of fluid was keeping her from me. 'Mother,' I said, 'it's Lalla,' as though that information alone would be enough to provoke a response.

I looked up at the plastic bag and the drip, drip, drip of the drugs that were keeping her still and quiet, keeping her away. The doctor was sedating her. Therefore, by stopping his drugs, I could wake her up. I could ask her what she wanted me to do. I reached up and turned the valve, and the dripping stopped.

I sat by the bed. For a few moments, nothing happened. Then her breathing became deeper and stronger. Her cheeks turned red. My heart outstripped the engines. I gripped her hand; I lined up my thousand questions.

Her eyes started open, pupils vast and unseeing.

'Mother,' I began, but she did not answer me. Her face was turning purple. Her hands began to flail uselessly, reaching for help I could not give. Blood flowed faster, gathering in a pool and dripping from the bed to the floor. I stood over her, trying to give her wild eyes a glimpse of my face, to bring her back to me, but her mouth opened and she began to scream, an animal cry that carved out new lines in her face. She reared off the bed and curled into a ball, her head against her knees, as though pain was the only thing in the world. Then she fell back again, hard, her face drained grey and old. The bloody sheet fell to the floor, taking the sodden dressing with it. The wound beneath was swollen red and purple and black with white dots like dead maggots. I recoiled; I could not bring myself to go near enough to cover her again. Instead I screamed with her, and we filled the small room in ghastly unison, drowning the sounds of the ship. I stopped to draw breath, but she did not, and her scream became a thin wail that faded to nothing.

'Mother?' I was too scared to put my hands on her shoulders and shake her. My whole body was trembling as I waited for her chest to rise so that she could speak. 'Mother?'

I heard pounding footsteps outside and the door burst open. My father grabbed my shoulders and pulled me away from the bed; the doctor reached for the valve on the bag of fluid.

'What have you done, Lalla?' my father shouted. 'What have you done?' The doctor stepped back, and the echoes of the screams and of my father's shouting rang from the walls as we stared at the thin, grey body on the bed and its terrible wound.

'She's gone,' the doctor said.

'Gone?' my father repeated. They stared at each other. I tried to take a step towards the bed but my legs were not working. I fell, and neither man helped me up. The doctor took a clean white sheet and wafted it over my mother's body. It settled over the wound; he drew it gently over her face and I was glad, because the pain inscribed there made me feel so guilty I couldn't move. The light of the infirmary streamed out into the night; my father's shadow became a black path. The doctor looked at me, and his face was thin and sour. He did not like me, and I did not care. He passed before my father, through the open door and into the night, and if they exchanged words I did not hear what they were. But I saw my father's hand on the doctor's shoulder, and the way the doctor shook his head as he walked away.

My father turned towards me. I looked around; I saw the bed, the outline of the body beneath the sheet, the sink, the fluid in the plastic bag, dripping its contents once more. I did not dare turn it off again. My father and I stood alone.

'I just wanted to talk to her,' I said.

He was silent. He stood staring at my mother. The bloody sheet lay on the floor between us. I wondered if the world without my mother was so different that he would raise a hand and hit me. I wondered whether I would feel anything if he did. But he did not hit me. He did not even look at me. Slowly, he slumped to the floor, folded on the threshold of the infirmary. Here, too, was pain, except that my father was not dying. Through the open door, the sky was black.

I listened for his breathing and saw that he was shivering. I looked at my own arms and realised they were covered in goose-bumps. Slowly, I crept towards him and sat beside him, so that our arms were touching. I thought he might push me away, but he lifted his arm and put it around me, and we stayed like that for a long time, staring at the shape on the bed that was my mother's body.

What would my mother do? I asked myself, over and over again, but my anchor was gone. My father shivered, and I remembered seeing blankets on the infirmary shelf; I think I had an idea of shielding ourselves against the inevitable dawn, when the sun would rise without her. The shelf was behind the door, and as I was standing there, reaching for the blankets, feeling the blood fighting its way back into my legs, the doctor came back. He did not see me, hidden as I was, and I said nothing. There was someone with him – the woman with red curly hair. The electric lights of the infirmary shone through it and made it look like fire. Together they knelt down beside my father; one on either side of him, they lifted him gently. He gave a start and looked around as though he could not remember where he was. Then he saw the bed and the sheet, and he rushed over and pulled back the sheet, and kissed the stricken face again and again. She was his wife, I thought, shrinking behind the door. She was his wife before she was my mother. And for the first time, I caught a glimpse of a world beyond myself. The woman and the doctor stood quietly by, and when he fell back, they caught him and led him away, supporting him on either side. I longed to call out, to go with them. But my mother was dead; I had made her death a painful one. And so I hid, unable to move, unable to cry out to the doctor who thought I'd killed her, or to the father who had, however briefly, forgotten me.

I sat on a chair beside my mother's body and felt under the sheet for her hand. I was so chilled that her hand did not feel cold in comparison. *I'm sorry*, I said, again and again. *I thought you'd want to know I was here.* Through the pain, I saw the face time would have given my mother, had she been allowed to grow old. I lay down beside her, undeterred by the blood, and stared through the door to the night sea beyond.

The doctor was right; I had never felt pain. I had never felt loss, or hunger, or genuine fear either. My parents protected me so well from what the world had become that I had no means to navigate it. They had surrounded me, made their plans to keep me safe, made sure that my only compass through life was my own experience of it. And it wasn't enough. How could it have been? A lifetime ago, the sun had set in front of the infirmary door. Soon, it would rise on the other side of the ship. Already the sky was imperceptibly lighter, like a screen that has just been turned off. And as the light grew clearer and brighter, I realised that my parents had been wrong. That, far from being the pivot around which the world turned, I was smaller than a mote of dust, less significant than a gnat.

FOUR

A new world ❀ *I choose to live* ❀ *the boy with the green eyes*

I woke up in my father's arms, being borne into a new, colder world.

'Hush, Lalla,' my father said, 'you're safe now.'

I looked around. The sun hung high in the sky, bathing the white painted metal walls and the lines of rivets in light. The textured surface of the steel walkway was set ringing by his London shoes.

'Where is she?' I asked.

'She's in good hands,' he said. We reached a door and he used his elbow to open it, keeping his arms tightly round me. He set me down on a bunk and stroked my hair. I ducked away from his hand and looked around, sniffing for damp, expecting to see the crumbling bricks and decaying plaster of our London walls. But here was only polished wood and the smell of soap, and smooth cotton pillowing under my hands. He kissed me and I missed the scratching of the stubble on his chin.

'Darling,' he said softly. 'It's all right. Everything is all right. My darling.' He had never called me darling. Always kitten, sweetheart, little one. *Darling* had been my mother.

My hands began to shake and I could not keep my voice steady. 'Did I kill her?' I asked.

'No, Lalla. Oh, no.'

'I wanted her to know I was there. I just wanted to say good-bye. And she screamed.' I began to sob. 'I thought I could save her, and instead I—'

'Hush, darling, hush. All that pain – there are people here who will just smooth it away. When you see her again, she'll be beautiful, like she was before.' *Before I killed her*, I thought, but I couldn't find the courage to say the words. 'I've talked to the doctor, and to Emily. We're going to give her body to the sea, and as we sail, she'll be part of the seas that support us.'

Except that she'll be dead.

I heard people walking the decks, learning the way around their new home, pulling their new-found safety about themselves. I overheard scraps of their conversations as they felt their way towards friendships, friendships that, only a few hours before, I had longed for. *I lost my home in the floods. My parents died in the first pandemic. My child was killed for the bread in her hands.* If there was any competition in their words, it was cancelled out by the undertow to every exchange: *What right do I have to be here? Why was I chosen? What did I do to deserve this haven? What did you?* And with every sentence that floated into my cabin, my father smiled slightly, and I saw my mother's death slipping away from him. The lines that appeared on his forehead when he cried for her were still there, but his mind was drawn to the people and the gratitude and awe they were pouring into the air outside.

'Where's the stone jug?' I asked suddenly.

'What?'

'The stone jug. Where is it?'

'What stone jug?'

'We had a stone jug. In London. Mother used to put the boiled water in it, so it could cool down.'

He looked confused. 'You don't have to boil the water on the ship. There's cool water flowing from the taps. We didn't bring a stone jug.'

'But I want it.'

'Why?'

Why? Why did I want something so redundant, so heavy, so futile? Because she had touched it. Because she had seen the need for it, and got hold of it, and used it to make my life happier, even as she scolded me. I closed my eyes and tried to hear her voice, to hear what she wanted me to do, what she wanted me to learn from the emptiness inside me, from the terrible thing I had done to her, but she was silent. I set my mind running through the galleries of the British Museum, searching for a stone jug, but although I ran from the jade axe to the Portland Font to the Mildenhall Treasure, all I could see were empty cases, and cards that marked where the treasures had once stood. *Object removed for rearrangement. Object removed for cleaning. Object removed for research purposes.* I could not find a stone jug, and from the far galleries, the sounds of hunger and loss hunted me until I was too afraid to stay silent.

'Come and have some breakfast,' he said. But when I got to the door, I could not follow him. I could not step from my little cabin out into that bright white golden world of metal and rivets and endless sea. It seemed to me that if I were to take that step, I would become someone new, and I did not want to change. I wanted my mother, and my mother was dead.

'I can't,' I said, and he put his arms around me.

'I have to,' he said. 'Please come, Lalla. I want us to be together. That's what all this was for.'

I tried. I went to the door, and the air was so fresh it frightened me. I clutched at the doorframe, dizzy and heartsick. My mother would have led me out, holding my hand, or she'd have sat beside me and stroked my hair, and whatever she did would have been right, because she was doing it. Without her, I had nothing to lean on, and I flopped, empty and useless, back onto my bunk. I couldn't bring her back. Nothing I could do would bring her back, and so there was no point in doing anything. He held out his hands to pull me up, but I curled into a tighter ball. He put his hand on my head and I was grateful, although I didn't say so, because my head felt floaty; I thought I might fall if I stood up. I noticed red-headed Emily hovering in the doorway; my father saw her too.

'When did you last eat?' he asked me. 'Emily, was Lalla given anything to eat yesterday?'

'I'm sorry,' Emily said in consternation. 'I didn't know – I didn't think – Oh, Michael, I'm so, so sorry. Our departure – the cards, and poor Anna, and . . . shall I fetch something?' Her voice went quiet and soft. 'Michael, I'm sorry. I'll understand if you appoint someone else. Diana, perhaps. She seems very capable.' Emily's voice shook; I lifted my head and dropped it again, bewildered by the abject misery on her face.

'It's all right,' my father said. 'We're learning. We're all learning.'

Emily darted off, and my father said, 'I have to go. They're waiting for me. But I'll be back, and Emily will bring you something to eat, and . . .' He put his hand on my arm and said, 'Lalla. You're cold.'

I wasn't cold. I was afraid. He was going to pull me out of the cabin, I knew, and force me into the terrible, unknowable world outside, without my mother to help me through it. How would I know where to go? What to do? How could I even put one foot in front of the other without her? She had walked alongside me for my entire life.

'It's going to be all right, Lalla.' He was holding out a biscuit and a glass of water.

My hands felt too heavy to move; still, I picked up the biscuit, rested it on my bottom teeth and began to gnaw. But the crumbs were too dry inside my dry mouth. 'Haven't we got anything else?' he asked the woman Emily, who was dancing about in the doorway holding a plate. 'Something that might be easier for Lalla to eat? Some soup, maybe, or . . . ?' His mind gave out. He had never planned our meals; that had been my mother's job. 'Just something better,' he snapped, and Emily flinched at the anger in his voice. I was glad, and then hated myself.

I put the biscuit down; I felt that to eat any more would be like Persephone eating pomegranate seeds, fixing me for ever in this world without my mother. And the thought of Persephone brought my mother's voice to life, and she was standing holding my hand in front of a little Greek bowl. 'Which one is Persephone?' she'd asked, and I remember the way that I had looked and looked, searching for the big important figure at the centre of the story. But the Persephone moulded into the bowl was small, so small, holding her hands out to her mother as Hades drove away with her to the underworld. *Look*, my mother had said, *look*, but I couldn't see what she was trying to show me. I was overcome by the sudden conviction that all I had ever done was let my mother down, over and over again. I remembered the pain on her face, the terrible screams with which she had died. I hadn't told her I loved her. I couldn't even cry; instead I shrank, until I seemed to consist solely of a space in my chest made of compressed air that pushed outwards, against my ribs, squeezing my heart upwards to the base of my throat, where it beat painfully. I pulled my covers over my head. Everything was over. Everything.

'Go away,' I wailed, my voice made dead by the blankets. 'Go away.'

'Lalla,' he said, putting his hand where he thought my head was. 'Lalla. Come on, darling. You can't stay in here for ever.'

I heard Emily's soft, light voice suggesting I needed time, and my father asking her to go and tell the people he'd be there in a minute. Then something heavy landed just next to my feet, and for a wild, joyful moment it seemed that my mother had come to sit on my bed and tell me how stupid I was being, how selfish.

'Here,' my father said, 'look,' and something in the tenderness of his voice made me reach out a hand, and he slipped something into it, something heavy and flat and smooth.

'It's a screen,' I said, astonished.

'A screen,' he said, 'yes, but not the kind of screen you're used to. This is a screen for the ship. See? It's more like a portal. Let's call it a portal. We've had enough of screens.' He opened it, and I wondered how he would access it without a card. But there were no demands for registration numbers, no requirement to scan a card and wait for the dove's wing to sweep the screen. There was not even a calendar or a clock. Just my father's smiling face. He tapped it.

'You see,' he said, 'there's the library, and there's the art collection – and here, Lalla, look.' There, among the myriad of icons, was the British Museum. He tapped again. Every single gallery my mother and I had ever visited was listed. There was the Portland Font, its detail as clear on the display as it was in my memory. Lindow Man, just as I had left him behind the glass of his case. Even the little gold chariot with its gold horses was there. I called up object after object. 'This was Anna's idea,' he said, but I hardly heard him. 'She said that the only thing to be said for technology was that we'd be able to bring every museum and art gallery in the world with us.'

I took the screen – the portal – to my desk, and my father left, closing my door behind him very gently. I tapped and tapped, and in the darkness I felt that my mother had come, and that I had the chance to set things right. There, for example, was the Aztec mask. She had shown it to me so many times, but I always glowered and told her that human sacrifice was disgusting. Now, too late, the words I'd always known she wanted from me tumbled forth. *It's not bloodthirsty, Mother. They believed in human sacrifice, the honour of offering your own life for the continuation of the life force itself.* I found the jade axe. *It's ceremonial,* I said confidently, bathing in her smile. *It's to show people in the afterlife how respected the dead warrior was.* In the darkness of my cabin, we wandered the museum, together again. But this time, I made up for my sulking and silence, my resentment of the museum dwellers who took her away from me for hours at a time.

Someone knocked; I jammed a chair under the door handle. 'Lalla,' came my father's voice. 'Lalla, let me in.' But I didn't want him. I didn't want anyone except my mother, and she was in my cabin with me, and if I opened the door she would escape and fly into the golden sky and I would never find her again. I scrolled through the vases and statues and friezes until they began to swim; I could still see them when I closed my eyes, still hear my mother's voice. The banging at the door started again, but the door, and the person knocking on it, were both a long way away. I was looking at the Mildenhall Treasure – all the Roman silver had disappeared from the display cases long before we sailed, but I remembered the decoration, the size, the sheer beauty of it all, and I lost myself in wondering where it was now. I held the screen to my chest, put my head on the desk and tried to sleep, but I couldn't stay rooted. I floated, and when the voice outside the door came back and shouted that I would kill myself if I went on like this, it made perfect sense. To die would be to be with her always, to feel her hands, to walk with her, to drink cool water from the stone jug. I dragged my desk to the door, pushed it against the chair and took the screen under the covers of my bed, where I breathed and rebreathed the same warm air, resolved to stay shut up until I had used up all the oxygen and suffocated, or starved. I held my mother's hand, and together we carried tins of apple to the museum dwellers, only to drop them in the Great Court and see them bouncing

61

up the staircase in defiance of the law of gravity, thumping and banging while people shouted. Bright spots danced across my vision regardless of whether my eyes were open or closed, and as the door moved and the desk scraped across the floor, the chair slipped and wedged against my bunk. Outside, my father swore and shouted, and I realised with delight that he would never get in unless I let him in.

I sank back on my pillow and my mother's hands weighed dry and warm against my cheek and sweetness spread over my tongue and I nestled under my quilt and searched for a word to describe the feeling, and then came to with a jerk and realised that I had been happy.

Before we sailed, we lived in England.

In England, my mother and father had lived and laughed and sheltered me.

Had my father loved her so little, that he could embrace this new life without her?

Fresh air came in through the partly opened door. My father was calling my name. I fought, but he was stronger, calling me on, on, into the ship and the world he had made.

'I'm fetching the engineers,' he shouted. 'We'll break this door down if we have to.'

'Go away,' I cried. 'Go away,' but the very act of speaking brought me back to myself, to my cabin, to the reality of my situation. 'Go away,' I said again, and as I heard his footsteps running away, I found myself reluctantly reborn, hungry and miserable, into the white order of his future.

I left my willingness to think behind, in the warm chaos where my mother had been killed. I moved towards the door like one already dead. I dislodged the desk and the chair and opened the door. The exhilaration was terrifying. I recoiled and stepped back, slamming the door shut, grateful to return to the warmth of spent, stale air that smelled of sweat and grief and the salt of tears. Of me and only of me. I regretted the familiar air I had allowed to escape and would never breathe again. But even as I sat on my bed, panting and shivering, I felt a tightly wound spring in my stomach suddenly come loose. I was desperately hungry. And my lungs, having snatched a breath of clean air, started complaining. I had stopped thinking, but I had not died, and my body started asserting itself. *Air*, said my lungs. *Food*, said my stomach, and I stood up, feeling dizzy. I opened the door once more, not out of disloyalty to my mother, but because I was not yet dead.

I almost tripped over a tray. Sandwiches. More biscuits, this time with raisins in them. A glass of clear water. As the fresh air brought warm blood to my cheeks, I realised that I had lived through a kind of death. I was alive. I would continue to live. But time and my mother were gone, and my life now would be defined, not by their absence, but by their absolute and irrevocable loss.

'Are you all right?' said a voice, a voice I recognised, a voice that belonged to a tall boy with green eyes who, once upon a time in London, had knocked upon my door. We had stood together on the deck rail, and he had taken my hand and we had smiled together. Tom, he had called himself, back in that different life, where my mother was still alive. He held a soft cloth; he was wiping the walls, but I had no energy to ask him why. My limbs were weak and I leaned on the deck rail for support. All around, the sea was grey and green and flat to the edges of the world.

'Where's my father?' I asked.

He looked at me. I remember thinking, *He is seeing me now for the first time*, and wishing that I had brushed my hair. We stood there, facing each other, and I felt a tiny shard of light cut through the dark emptiness inside me, as though I had lifted a corner of the blind in my cabin.

'I'm sorry about your mother,' he said.

The air liquefied; the sun caught the green of his irises. I felt my heart beating again, and I stepped towards him. But he was not looking at me anymore, but past me, and I remembered that my mother was dead. I followed his gaze and saw my father approaching, with people running behind him.

'Lalla,' he called. He waved the others away and said, 'Tom. Go and tell everyone to wait in the ballroom.' Then he put his arms around me and crushed me against the crisp cotton of his shirt, which smelled of soap. His body beneath the shirt was warm. I looked down and saw he had exchanged his London shoes for dark blue canvas ones with white rubber soles. 'My darling,' he said. Then faintness and nausea took over and I slumped against him. My father reached for the tray and gave me tiny sips of water, and although I strained for more, he would not let me control the glass. 'Little by little,' he said gently, 'too much at once and you'll be sick.'

Tom came back and between them, he and my father supported me to the ballroom, where the people swam in and out of my vision as my father settled me onto a bench. He's still called Tom, I thought, and my heart beat less reluctantly, for here was something that had not changed with my mother's death. As I grew accustomed to the light and the space, and the little sips of water spread through my exhausted body and brought the room into focus, I saw that the people were sitting upright, alert, excited. I looked on the floor for the bloodstained cushion, but it wasn't there anymore. This was a new, clean version of the ballroom and, I realised as he walked to the podium, a new, clean version of my father. His skin was glowing with certainty. He wore a white shirt, its collars and cuffs unmarked by any signs of wear or use. The people, too, were clean, their clothes bright. They've been updated, I thought, and for the first time in my life, I felt left behind and lost.

Then my father held out his arms to me from the podium. 'My daughter,' he called.

There was a heartbeat of silence. I looked down at my dress, saturated with the filth of the London air. My hair felt heavy, loaded with a build up of grease and grime. I wondered whether my father would tell me how I could wash it, and how it would feel to stand in the sparkling air of the sea and let it dry. And then the people began to cheer. They called my name, they shouted, they smiled and held out their arms to me as my father had done. They were cheering for me, and they would not stop.

'People,' he said, and his voice was deeper than I remembered it, and more resonant. 'Lalla has come. Lalla has chosen.' Chosen? What choice had I made? I just hadn't been ready to die. But there was no chance for me to speak. 'With Lalla beside me,' he continued, 'I can finally welcome you all. Here, together, we will create, not an existence, but a life. A life of like-minded people, joined together in love. A life, my friends, that may truly be called life. Remember work? Remember art, and music, and laughing over food in the company of friends? Remember conversation? Words exchanged, not in barter or pleas, but for nothing but the joy of sharing them with another human being?

'We have brought words, but left arguments behind. We have brought tools, but left weapons behind. We have brought love, but left betrayal behind.

'Together, Lalla and I give you safety. Not a temporary loan from a government that will take back as soon as it gives. An unconditional gift, given for nothing other than your happiness. We are a family now. People of the ship, we give you freedom.'

The noise of the people was such that I thought the sea had crashed its way into the ballroom. I saw the man with the grey beard murmuring with his eyes closed. Michael, he said, as his tears flowed. He was not the only one crying. Michael, my captain. My father's name was taken up and whispered around the room. I read it on their lips, I heard the words *Michael* and *Captain* floating, bobbing up again and again above the soft wash of blended voices. They took my father from me and turned him into something new. Or something he had always been, that I had never seen before. He had grown and moved on, but I was simply me. Lalage. The babbling waters of a small stream, lost in an ocean of salt.

FIVE

The first meal ❀ *pineapples* ❀ *I wash and change my clothes*

From the ballroom we all moved to the dining room. There were no clocks on the walls or on our portals, but at the sound of the gong the people stood up and filed out. I was the only one unsure of where to go, and I simply followed my father. He led me to the seat beside him, at the head of the top table, and I thought, I am in my mother's place, and that is why he is not broken. He told me that lunch and dinner were served every day, and breakfast was set out on the buffet tables for everyone to help themselves. Emily, the woman with red curly hair, was in charge of the dining room; I would meet Gerhard the chef later. Freedom and plenty. I was lightheaded with hunger and dizzy with the sensations of colour and sound.

Plates were brought to us, filled with something that smelled savoury and maddening; I could smell garlic and salt and my mouth filled with saliva. It looked like chicken. I swallowed, and swallowed again, and I put my hand out for my fork. A quick hand prevented me from picking it up. A man with skin like a pickled walnut nodded towards my father. 'Respect,' the man said softly, his dark eyes shining. The chicken and garlic smell hung tantalisingly in the air. My father picked up his knife and fork; everyone in the dining hall did the same, and the moment was gone. I ate, and the sensation of taste drove every other thought from my mind. I remember roast chicken, I thought, and I was eleven again, and my mother was holding out a plate of drumsticks and warning me that they were too hot to hold, and it was my birthday, and she was running to shut the window so that the smell of the chicken would not attract the street people to our home.

'Father,' I said, because I wanted to see if he remembered it too, but the main course was over, and the kitchen team were bringing out rings of gold, set in squares of pliant cake and covered in sticky sweetness. A ripple of excitement spread across the room as the plates were placed on the tables.

'Pineapple,' my father said, smiling at my amazement. 'A tropical fruit, with sharp leaves and prickly skin. A symbol of hospitality.'

'Which part of this is the pineapple?' I asked, prodding the cake with my fork.

'The round, yellow part on the top.'

'You said it had leaves and prickly skin.'

'Yes, but they weren't necessary. They were the parts we didn't need. The parts that prevented the pineapple from being truly itself, the best that it could be. They've been done away with already. The work has been done by those who came before us, and we are reaping the benefits now. This is a pineapple,' he concluded, pointing at my plate.

'So a pineapple was not the same as an apple?' I said as he sat back down.

'No.' He finished his cake and pushed his plate away.

'Was a pineapple an apple that grew on a pine tree?' I asked.

That's good thinking, Lalla, I heard my mother say, but my father was talking to someone else, and just said, 'If you like.'

The people began to get up and move around. I saw Tom

hover at the doors and scan the room; my face burned and I stared at the table until he had gone.

'Where are the people going?' I asked.

'Some are going to the gallery or the cinema,' my father said, coming back to me as the room emptied. 'Some will be going for a walk on the deck, or to listen to music, or simply gathering together to talk. But most of them—' He paused, and I waited. He turned dark and stern, as he used to do when my mother disagreed with him. He sighed. 'They're going to watch the bulletin in the ballroom. We usually have it before dinner, but today there was you.' He smiled at me, as though he had just remembered how.

'The news bulletin? Like at home?'

He stroked my cheek. 'The ship is our home now, darling,' he said. 'But yes, we have the news bulletin here as we did in London. We have everything we had in London, and a great deal more that we could never have had in London.'

And suddenly, I had had enough. The food sat heavily in my stomach; the effort of digesting after not eating for so long made me sleepy. The noise of conversations and the constant movement of so many people had left me bewildered. I wanted our flat, and the little fire, and the dancing flames of the oil-drum fires in the street, and cooled water from the stone jug. I wanted my mother. *Have an apple,* she used to say when I asked for the impossible. Because there were no apples anymore where we had come from. I wondered whether the same would be true of where we were going. A pineapple was not the same thing as an apple.

He looked at me sadly. 'Stop looking back, Lalla. She's gone. We'll have the funeral tomorrow, and then we move on. You've got everything here, darling. Everything she ever wanted for you. But you won't benefit from it until you let her go. Let her go, Lalla. Let her go.' He wrapped his arms around me and pressed his new smooth face to mine; I felt damp on my cheeks, although I was not crying. 'You have had the time to grieve,' he said, wrapping himself around my shoulders far too tightly. 'Be grateful for that.' But I could not let her go. She was with me now; I had heard her voice. In life, her mind had always been on the next task, the next duty, the next thing that had to be done. In death, there was nothing to distract her. She was beside me, and I clung to her. My father let me go. I stumbled, and my dress caught on a corner of the table.

He stared at the dress as I unhooked it. 'Do I remember that dress?' he asked.

'It was hers,' I said. It had once been long and full with red and orange flowers all over it, so big that they were lost when my mother cut the dress down for me. Now, the dress was stiff with London dirt, with sweat and tears and loss and misery, flowers and flame puddled alike with grey. I held out the skirt to him, searching his face for a clue that he, too, was remembering her looking through her dresses for something to alter for me, the way she muttered *Impractical, impractical*, to the red silk, the golden gauze, the velvets she threw aside.

'She was making it the day you asked her to make the bags,' I said. 'Five hundred bags, for the five hundred people you were going to bring with us.'

'I remember she didn't want to make the bags,' he said. 'I don't remember you being there.'

That's because I stood so still, I thought. That's because I worried that if I moved, you'd remember I was there, and change the subject. 'You said it would be symbolic,' I told him. 'A new start, the same opportunities for everyone.'

'So it would have been. I could have got the material. I knew a man who had sailcloth. But it doesn't matter anymore.'

He kept staring, and I wondered whether he, too, was remembering my mother draping the fabric round me, whether her voice was sounding in his head as clearly as it was in mine.

'We've got bags,' she'd said through a mouthful of pins. 'We don't need more bags.'

'This is different.'

'It always is. It always was. I thought we were trying to make sure that it won't always be.'

'It would be nice if the bags matched. That's all I'm saying.'

'Nice? Nice? Oh, for crying out loud. Have an apple, Michael.' She looked up, and I saw dark circles under her eyes. She's tired, I remember thinking in surprise. She's really tired. 'Shall we print them?' my mother had asked suddenly, falsely bright. 'If we're going to use our precious resources to make bags we don't need for a plan that may never come off, we might as well have them printed. *I owe my life to Michael Paul.* That would be good. That's your vision, really, isn't it, Michael? A symmetrical line of grateful clean people, with matching bags.'

'They will owe their lives to me.'

'You've got to forget that, Michael. Life can only be given as a free gift. If our people come on board carrying bags that say, Michael Paul Saved My Life, we're sunk. They're sunk.'

I had no way of knowing whether my father was thinking of that now. He only said, 'You should go and change,' and I watched him walk out of the dining room through an avenue of smiles.

I went to my clean and shining cabin and took off the dress. It had always seemed so easy – take a full, ornate dress and make it smaller and simpler. But now, as I buried my face in the fabric and tried to find her there, I saw the complexity of the task she had undertaken, the thousands of stitches all put in by her hands, the little darts and gathers that made the dress mine rather than hers. I realised then that I could never do what she had done. I could never ask the questions she asked, or tell the truth like she told it. She had resisted him, and through that resistance, she had disciplined his vision and given him strength. And that same resistance had given me my life. I had been born from it, nourished by it, educated by it. She had given me her life like she had once given me her clothes – carefully chosen, contrived from the best that was available, cut to fit. To fit me. Who was my father without her? Who was I? He was without boundaries now, and I half expected that the next time I saw the people, they would be sitting making five hundred matching bags from sailcloth, ready to be printed. *I owe my life to Michael Paul.*

I realised that the dress smelled foul and I was embarrassed that I'd worn it to dinner. I opened the cupboards. Clothes hung there, fresh and smooth. A pile of white squares sat on a shelf; I shook one out and saw that it was a nightdress. I could not hang my London dress amidst all that crisp purity. I showered, watching the grey water dancing lightly to the drain; I washed my hair, letting the soap run into my eyes and revelling in the pain of it.

Mother, I whispered quietly. *If this is what you wanted for me, I will do my best.* I scratched a mark on the wall beside me, slipped into my bunk and slept. When I woke up, the orange dress was gone.

SIX

The wind farms ❀ the broken button
❀ I find my place of work

On the morning of the funeral, as the sky in my porthole lightened, my father came and knocked at my cabin door. I let him in and climbed back into my bunk.

'Lalla,' he said, perching on the corner of my desk. 'How are you?'

'Fine.'

'There are other clothes, you know.' I looked down my cotton nightdress and felt exposed. I had never given a thought to what I was wearing in front of him before. This was a strange new world, in which I did not feel comfortable sitting with my father in my nightdress. 'If you wanted to wear something new for the funeral,' he said, 'I can show you where the clothes are.'

'Do you want me to wear black?' I asked.

'This isn't about what I want,' he said. 'Think about what would be fitting. Think of what would be the right thing by Anna.'

'I don't think she would have wanted to die in the first place.'

He frowned and his eyes darkened. 'She chose what happened to her, Lalla. We all do.'

I opened my mouth to speak, and my cabin went dark. A vast trunk of grey and rust was blocking my porthole. I got down

73

from my bunk and looked out, so surprised that I forgot what I was going to say.

'What's that?' I asked.

'It's a wind turbine,' my father said. 'We're going through the wind farms.' He got off the desk and stood beside me. 'We were going to save the world with offshore wind farms.' I stared at the peeling flakes of metal, the coastlines of rust, spread before my eyes as though my porthole were a magnifying glass.

'Look to the horizon,' my father said, and as the ship sailed past the trunk, it moved aside to reveal a leafless forest stretching as far as I could see. On the horizon, I saw the motionless blades reaching uselessly to the sky, to the sea. I had only ever seen the wind farms on my screen before – now here they were, larger in life than I had ever imagined. It seemed a beautiful thing to me, to take the movement of the winds and turn it into power for humanity.

'Why don't they work?' I asked.

'They're disconnected,' he said.

'But why? Why can't we connect them again, get the power going?'

'Look at them, Lalla. They're rusting away. Useless great hulks. Nothing lasts if it's not cared for. If no one could pay for the power, where was the money to come from to maintain the turbines? Or the oil derricks, for that matter? Who would create power only to give it away?'

I thought of the ship, of what it must have cost. 'You could have done it,' I said. 'Instead of this.'

'For Marius and his politicians to get fat on?' Anger flared in his eyes; I saw him control himself, and I did not dare to say more. Then he said, 'Labour, and the fruits of labour. When those things were connected, the world turned. When the disconnect became absolute, it stopped. Politicians looking out for themselves. And all those street people in London, sitting

74

around waiting for food drops. What were they doing, Lalla? Why weren't they working?'

'There wasn't any work.'

'There's always work. Easier to sit around and complain than find it, though.'

We passed another turbine and in the dark, I appealed to my mother, *Tell me what to think. Tell me what to ask.* It didn't seem to me that the street people had had an awful lot of choice.

'When we've passed the wind farms, we'll be on our way,' my father said at last. 'That's all the wind farms are now, a staging post on our journey.'

'What's a staging post?'

'Somewhere they used to change horses. Before cars and trains and aeroplanes. So they could get where they were going more quickly.' Horses. Aeroplanes. Words so impossibly exotic that they made little sense to me.

'Where are we going?' I asked.

My father smiled and went to the door. 'You'll know when we get there,' he said. 'We all will.' He looked at me and inclined his head. 'We might not all arrive at the same time, that's all.'

'But we're all on the same ship.'

'Yes,' he said. 'Yes, we are. We are all on the same ship.' He repeated my words as though they pleased him.

There was a gentle knock on my cabin door. My father called, 'Come in,' and the woman with red curly hair opened the door and looked in, smiling at me with pity in her eyes before turning to my father. Emily.

'We're ready for you,' she said. He nodded and she withdrew, keeping her eyes fixed on him until the moment the door closed behind her.

He went to the door. 'Shall we?' he said, holding out his hand.

'Why are you so angry with her?' I asked suddenly.

'With Emily?'

'No. With my mother.'

'Angry?' He looked warily at me, and I remembered the way he had looked at Commander Marius when he mentioned the Exodus Act. As though he might have been found out.

'You said she chose what happened to her.'

'She did.'

The nightdress smelled of soap, not of London. 'She didn't,' I said. 'She didn't, and neither did I.'

I expected him to come over and put his arms around me as he had done before. I expected him to say that, although I had lost my mother, I would never, ever lose my father, and that he loved me, and that everything he had done in setting up the ship and this life was for me. That, at least, would be familiar, and by burying my face in his shoulder, I could maybe find a link back to her.

But he didn't. He just said, 'Grow up, Lalla,' and I felt as though a blanket had been ripped from me. 'We could have left long before we did. Before the gangs began to gather. Before the Land Allocation Act, even. We didn't have to wait to see blood being spilt on the streets. We could have gathered you up years ago, Lalla, and brought you here.'

'You could have forced her,' I muttered sullenly.

'Anna would have kept finding excuses until London rotted and the people in the holding centre were all dead. I was terrified that something terrible would have to happen before she would agree to come away. That one of you would be hurt. I am only grateful that it was not you.'

'Why did we have to come away at all?'

'Because of you.' He smiled, and a terrible thought that had come into my mind popped like a bubble of soap. I was back at the centre of the universe, where I was comfortable because it was where I had always been.

'Me?' I asked. I felt warm again.

'You. I wanted you to have a chance to live with higher thoughts than where to find food. I wanted you to experience all the wonders of being human, without worrying that some starving, terrified soul was going to kill you. I wanted to give my daughter herself, so that she could find out who she is. When you were born, you gave me the strength and inspiration to reach for something higher, for everyone. And this is that place. Your mother will always be a part of you, so what need have I to weep when you are with me?'

At first I clung to him as I wept. I saw my mother walking down Great Russell Street, holding the hand of a little girl who looked a bit like me. Except that little girl was smiling, and I knew that I would never smile again. I wept for the water she had cooled for me in the stone jug, and for the dress she had died in, that would never be cut down for me. I wept because my days had been so empty, and because I had wasted so much time thinking that I was letting her down, when all she had wanted to do was to love me. My chest hurt; I could not bear that, if I stopped crying, it might stop hurting. And I wept in gratitude for my father's words, which had given me permission to cry.

'I've got something for you,' my father said, putting a velvet jewellery box on the desk.

I stopped crying. Was I to be given another diamond? But I didn't want one. In death, I had drawn my mother closer. She had yearned for flowers, not for diamonds.

'Open it,' he said.

I did so, and the world around me shifted.

One day, on the way back from the British Museum, I saw a couple standing on the corner of the street. I must have been ten or eleven, I suppose – after restaurants and shops, but before the museum dwellers became entrenched. I let my mother walk ahead and I watched, and I saw the man place his hands around her face and kiss the woman. It was a bitterly cold day, and he pulled his coat around the two of them so that they looked like only one person, and as he did so, a button fell from his coat and rolled to my feet. I wasn't allowed to talk to anyone, so I picked up the button, and when we got home, I put it into an empty jewellery box and gave it to my mother.

'That's a story, little one,' she said. 'We'll put it in our museum, shall we? With a label saying, *This button shows us that there was still love amongst twenty-first century man.*'

'It's just a broken button, Anna,' my father said. 'It's not worth anything. It's hardly a diamond.'

'Diamonds are just diamonds,' she said quietly, her skin shining soft in the pale daylight. 'They're too hard. Nothing marks them. This button – look, those are the scratches where it rolled along the road. The pattern's worn away on one side. That must have been where the man used to push the button through the buttonhole. Think how long he must have been doing that for, to mark the button in this way. And think what it meant to him, to share his coat, maybe his only shelter, with someone else.' She turned it over in her hand. 'See?' she said, holding it out to both of us, although I was the only one who leaned forward. 'The shank's worn so thin that it snapped.' She turned to my father. 'Don't you see, Michael? Don't you see that this button is more valuable than your diamonds?'

'What good's that button going to be when you get hungry?'

'So we're to eat diamonds, King Midas?' She pushed me towards him. 'Go on, Michael, touch her and see if she turns to gold.'

He held me, but I never did turn to gold. And yet, my father had taken the trouble to bring the button in its little box on board the ship. What could it mean, except that, in his own way, he loved me, just as my mother had in hers? Would he have to die, too, before I began to understand him? It was time to make of this life what I could.

The grey sea swelled around the ship. 'It's you and me now, Lalla,' my father said quietly. 'Shall we go?' He gave me his arm, as though we were wearing the long, old-fashioned clothes I had seen on my screen and were about to dance.

And so the first funeral took place. My father hopped around, alternately exultant and subdued, disappearing after breakfast and coming back with artificial flowers, which he dumped in the ballroom before disappearing again and bringing a black dress from somewhere and giving it to me. Food was put out in the dining room and people snatched their lunch when they could, in between the dusting and the polishing and the dress-ing of tables. And at last, as the sun began to give up its gold to the sky and the wind farms disappeared behind us, we all came onto the lower deck. I wore the black dress, full-skirted and held at the waist by a thin belt with a gold buckle. All around me, people held handkerchiefs and looked sad. The children stood in a small group holding the flowers, and theirs were the only feet and hands that moved.

My father spoke over my mother's body. She wore the blue and green silk dress, cleaned and mended. She looked younger, as though at any moment she might open her eyes and jump off the board she was resting on and offer to play a game. My father was right; there was no trace of her suffering or her violent death upon her face, and I realised that this would make it easier for me to say goodbye. Someone had put her hair up. She looked as though she was going to a party in the time before the time before the ship.

'So lovely,' someone whispered, and someone else said, 'Such a terrible shame,' and soft shimmery whispers moved around the gathering. Beside me, a woman wiped her eyes with a handker-chief. I saw her stare in wonder at the handkerchief, so clean and so new, and was not surprised that she found it more fascinating than death, which even I had seen every day until we sailed.

Then my father stood beside the body and faced us, and there was silence.

'We have come to let Anna go,' he said. 'We are here to say goodbye. We will commit her to the sea, which is our support now, and she will become part of it, bearing us up in death as she always did in life.' I thought of the piece of paper he had patted in his pocket the night my mother died, upon which he had written his welcoming speech. He held no paper now. Where had he learned to speak like this? How much further from me was he going to travel?

'Love Lalla,' he said to the people. A wind blew from the sea and I shivered. 'Enfold her. Teach her the universality of goodness; show her your love for mankind, the love for which you were brought on board. Anna is dead. You lost her before you came to know her. But the very fact that you are here is testimony to Anna's vision, her love, her faith in you. You will find Anna in each other. Her death will draw you closer together, because during her life, she created this life for you. But Lalla – Lalla is just a child who has lost her mother. Can you bear that for her? Can you enfold Lalla in yourselves, as surely as the sea will enfold Anna and take her to itself?'

A child? Was I still a child? I felt that I had aged a hundred years since we boarded the ship. I imagined all the people coming towards me, holding out their arms, and I panicked and had to fight for my breath. A hand touched my arm but I pulled away. I did not need pity. I needed to be held. I needed to be held as my parents had held each other, as though each was only complete when the other was there. The people were alive, and my mother was dead, and I hoped they felt as guilty as I did. I stood and glared, my arm cold where the touch had been withdrawn, and the people shrank from me.

My father tilted the board on which my mother's body lay and she slipped into the sea with a small splash.

But the waters did not cover my mother's body. It floated without direction, without control, the blue green dress tracing its ebb and flow. As her dress took up the water, it clung across her body, outlining the wound on her stomach. The hair that had been arranged so carefully pulled loose with the water's weight and washed across her face in dark shadows. Each wave sloughed a layer of paint from her face, so that the peace and loveliness that had been created there melted away. She was no longer sleeping until we met again, the honoured guest of the sea; she was white and damaged and soiled and dead, and the pain I had forced on her was written all over her face.

I felt my father stiffen beside me. His fists were clenched. He did not move, but all around us, people began to look at each other. He continued to watch, his eyes fixed on the body as though he could draw the waters over it by the force of his gaze. I felt unease seeping into the atmosphere. People began to shift their weight from foot to foot; the children looked up ready to ask questions and were shushed; my father's lips thinned and his eyes became fixed and shone blue. He was Michael, their captain; food appeared on tables; stories were told, people gathered together, fresh water flowed, all at his command. And yet he could not push my mother's body beneath the waves.

And I understood that the next death would be different. At the next death, he would weight the body down with something, and the sea would rise to welcome the dead at my father's bidding. The next death would be perfect. But this time, my father stood white and unmoving, deaf to the rustle and shifting of the people around him. Slowly, they left the deck. Those with children went first, shoulders hunched apologetically over their fidgeting offspring still clutching their flowers. Others followed, throwing glances of concern at my father's granite back as they left.

He remained, staring at the body.

'He's grieving,' I heard one departing mourner say to another, as the last of the people left the deck and the sun dipped slowly into the sea in front of us, glinting in the cabin portholes.

But my mother still refused to sink. Night came on, and her body became a stain on dark water. I grew cold, then colder. My arms and legs began to hurt; my fingers burned as I chafed them out of numbness. My father had not moved. I strained my eyes but the black water was unrelieved now. There was no moon, and I knew from the ancient calendars in the British Museum that this was because the earth was standing in the way of the light of the sun. The moon is still there, I told myself, even though I cannot see it.

Night time was new to me. In London, going out in the dark would have been akin to plunging a hand into boiling water or eating from the pavement. Although I had seen the night from our flat, there had always been some light out there – from the oil drums, from street fires, from screens. Here there was nothing. I could not even see whether my father was still there. I stepped carefully towards the sound of his breathing, feeling for the deck rail and gasping with the cold of it. Then I felt my father's hand, and I placed mine over it. He opened his coat and wrapped me inside it.

'Shall we jump?' he said quietly. 'Now, before the sun rises. Before they come to start breakfast. Do you want to jump, Lalla? I'll come with you if you do.'

To jump and to be with her. To jump, and join her in the sea.

'What about the ship?'

'It doesn't matter,' he said, his arms tightly around me. 'This was all for you. Only for you. Anna is gone. I can't change that. But if her death means there's nothing left for you, then I will jump, whether you do or not.'

I burrowed into his chest. I imagined jumping, my body flying weightless through the air, my misery and loneliness left on the ship. Yes. Yes, I would jump, for the sake of that brief moment before the water hit. And when it did, the coldness of it, and the struggle for breath, and the fighting that would come before the peace would be worth it, because I would be with my mother.

The sun began to rise. I searched the horizon, but my mother was gone at last, taken by the receding darkness.

'What do you want me to do?' I said.

'Eat. Smile at me. Be happy.'

I felt the deck beneath my feet. I saw how far it was down to the water; I saw the layers of cabins and rooms above us. I smelled the breakfast being prepared in the dining room; I felt my hunger and realised that my father was the reason it would be sated before I'd really realised it was there. And there was Tom, too. If I were to jump, I would never know him. What if I were to change my mind mid-air? My father stared out at the empty sea, waiting for my response.

'I don't want to jump,' I said.

'But will you live? Really live?'

'I'll try.'

'Promise me. Promise!'

I promised. In the half light, I slipped out of his coat and found my way to my cabin. No one took him from me this time; it was I who left. I took off the black dress and the belt with the gold buckle and pushed them into the laundry chute. I scratched another line upon my tally of the days. I put on clean clothes and made my way to breakfast. And I wondered whether these mechanical things could, actually, make a life. Whether, if I stopped thinking so much, I might find that my father was right, and that life without my mother was possible. After all, he was managing it. The rising sun warmed the air. People arrived in the dining room and smiled through me at each other, looking for the one person that was missing.

And then my father entered, red-eyed but touching every

hand that reached out to him as he made his way to his seat. The woodwork glowed, the white paint on the deck outside gleamed through the windows, the plates and cutlery shone. My father stood at his place and raised his hand, and into the ensuing silence he called, 'The sun has risen on a new day.'

And so it had. From that day on, the new days just kept coming. The ship became a busy place, a bright place, a place where people smiled and talked and revelled in their safety and fullness. I watched the people as they went to meals, their cabins, the galleries. I explored my screen and found the library – hundreds, thousands of books. Books I had read with my mother, books I'd read on my own, but for the most part, books I'd never heard of. And for the first time since my mother's death, I felt a flicker of excitement. I was given work in the laundry; I had a role. I saw Tom talking with other people and vowed to find the courage to speak to him again. And I saw a life begin to take shape. What had seemed impossible only days before became normal, and any questions I'd had became less and less important, until they no longer mattered and vanished, like frost at sunrise.

The scratched markings by my bunk increased in number and the people began to coalesce in groups. New activities started – for example, a net was cast out from the lower deck and some people began to swim inside it. There was a little white boat on the lower deck too, a relic from the ship's former existence that my father had kept for its entertainment value. 'A life boat, it was called,' he said, faintly amused, as he watched the people lower it into the sea. It had a solar-powered motor and a small chamber below its tiny deck, where the children liked to hide. You could go all around the ship in it, although the novelty seemed to fade after the first couple of trips. Others got together and watched films, or went to Gerhard in the kitchen and learned to make cake. I couldn't walk from my cabin to the ballroom, or the kitchen, or anywhere without passing two or three people deep in conversation. Another group of people put the same book on their screens and then met in the dining room to talk about it. Emily with the red hair took them biscuits while they were talking, then she and her team set up for the next meal and collected the empty plate. I still spent hours in the British Museum on my screen, but my mother had fallen silent, as though she was waiting, watching to see what would happen next.

'You should join a group,' Patience said when we were folding the ironed sheets. 'Make friends.' Patience was from Africa, and she was in charge of the laundry. When she smiled, her new white teeth flashed against the black skin of her face. My teeth had been passed by the dentist with an appreciative glance at my father, but many of the adults were in the process of having theirs repaired or, like Patience, replaced altogether.

'Aren't we friends?' I asked.

'I'm old. You are young. You cannot spend all your time working.'

'I like working.' And so I did – not so much for the lengths of fresh clean cotton sheeting, or the piles of laundered clothes ready to be delivered back to people's cabins, or even for the feeling of having something to contribute, but for my conversations with Patience. My father had always been hurried, determined, his every action dictated by a horizon that held something bigger and greater than whatever was happening in front of his eyes. Once he'd established that I wasn't going to jump into the sea, he was off again. My mother, too, had given everything to her part of the plan; I had simply been there, the reason for everything and the focus of nothing. But with Patience, on the ship, the horizon was a far off thing, a hazy line that meant and demanded nothing, and there was time.

'How did my parents find you?' I asked. 'Were you still in Africa then?'

We had moved from sheets to clothes, and Patience's iron moved like a thing alive through the creases. 'I was. In Mombasa, when the boats were leaving the burning lands with the last of the people.'

'Why didn't you get on one?'

'If you thought your mother would return, would you have left your cabin? You chose to live. And to live, you must leave behind.' She paused. 'I was waiting for my daughter.'

'Did she come?'

'Tola? No.' Patience threw me the finished trousers, and began to work the iron's point into the gathers of a flowered skirt. 'She took a different way. The way of the young. The young never believe there is an end. For them, there is always a tomorrow, and another, and another. But I remembered Africa before the earth baked dry for good, and I knew it was the end.'

I checked the laundry mark on the trousers and began to fold them. 'But you still waited for her?'

Patience added the finished skirt to the pile. I handed her a shirt and waited for her to speak.

She ironed the collar, the cuffs and the sleeves, then arranged the left front over her board. 'Tola was angry,' she said. 'Her father put razor wire around our farm. He said it was for her, to keep safe the goats and chickens that fed us. She said he was a murderer, for the wire would kill anyone who tried to enter.' I thought of the fences round Regent's Park, and their twisted barbs, that my father said could cut to the bone.

Patience rested the iron upright and lifted the shirt from the board. Her eyes rested on the wall beyond and above me, and her voice dropped so I had to lean forwards to hear her.

'One night,' she said, 'I looked out of the window. And in the moonlight, I saw the body of a young man, draped bleeding over the razor wire fence. I went out, but he was dead. So little blood, and so thin, I could lift him alone. I buried the body, glad to save

86

my Tola this terrible sight. But Tola in the morning, she saw my cut arms. She said more people would come, and more, and were we to kill them all? Yes, said her father, if we must. And Tola left us. She was gone, and without her, her father moved around the farm like a forgotten spirit.'

Patience's forearm caught on the iron. She flinched, and I ran to the sink and soaked a handkerchief in cold water. But when I took it to her, she waved it away, laughing quickly. 'Michael warned us about looking back,' she said, her voice suddenly light. 'I look back, and see what happens? You are bad for me, Lalla. You and your questions. Join a group and bother some other person.'

She rearranged the shirt and began smoothing the right front, then the back.

'But what happened?'

'It doesn't matter.'

'Please, Patience. Tell me what happened in the end. Did Tola come back? Is that when my father found you?'

Patience's smile fell away and she worked on that shirt as though it was the only thing that existed in the world.

'Tola returned with fifty young people, all hungry, all wild. She told us we must feed them, with our goats, our cheese, our little bread. Her father fought them. But they were hungry, and they knew only to survive. They had clubs, and broken glass, and strength. Oh such strength.'

'Did they kill him?'

'Tola killed him. She would not let her father be killed by a stranger.'

'And then?'

Patience took the shirt and folded it carefully. 'I gave Tola the keys to the farm. I walked three hundred miles to Mombasa, to the ships, and there I cared for the departing people. For their children, their elderly. I soothed their fears and promised good things in their new lives.'

'But you chose not to go?'

'I had left all I had with Tola. And always, always, I hoped she might come.'

'So you could punish her for killing her father?'

'So I could tell her she was forgiven. What else was she to do?'

'And my father? What about my father?'

'The people on the ships spoke of me. They wrote of me on their screens. Michael heard my story, and he sent a message to the authorities.' She smiled. 'In the office of the harbour master, I talked with Michael on the screen and I knew then that I would come if he asked me. And I wanted him to ask me. More than anything, I wanted that.'

'But you said you were waiting for Tola.'

'And so I am. She will come to me here, on the ship. In Mombasa, I had only a dream of Tola, and only a burning death to meet when the evacuation was done. On the ship, I know I will see her.'

'But I don't understand. I don't understand why Tola ran away.'

'You cannot understand what you yourself did not choose to do.'

'Should I have run away?' I asked, perplexed. I saw Great Russell Street, unrolling diseased and dangerous before me, and the troops with their batons and their guns. 'How could I have run away? Where would I have gone?'

'Forgive me, Lalla. You are a child still. Tola was a woman.'

'How old was she?'

'Then? Thirteen. Now? Twenty-six. Maybe she is a mother herself, and her children will come with her.'

'I'm sixteen.'

Patience held up the iron with warning in her eyes. 'Tola's was a different life. You had nothing to run from. But now – now, Lalla, you must become a woman too, and then maybe your mother will be holding Tola's hand when they come, and we will be women of the ship together.'

The clothes were ironed, the piles made up. All there was now was the deliveries, and those were up to me.

'All right,' I said. 'I'll join a group.'

SEVEN

A busy life ❧ *the last bulletin from land*
❧ *we destroy the mast*

I was busy. For the first time in my life, I was busy. There were my conversations with Patience, my trips to the cinema, the meals. I learned to swim and swam in the net most days. A little boy called Gabriel was often there at the same time; I played with him in the water while his mother, Helen, who taught the small children, looked on. I could call lots of people by their names. Above all, there was my work, and I walked with pride as I carried clean clothes and bedding to the cabins.

My busy life was plentiful, too. I cleaned my teeth, and when the bristles around the edges of the toothbrush began to bend outwards, a new toothbrush appeared in my bathroom. If the soap dispenser began to spit when I pressed the pump, the next day it would be back to laying a fat slug of scented gel in the palm of my hand whenever I wanted one. Meals were regular and varied, and the people of the ship gathered around tables to talk and to compare and to laugh. My sheets were smooth and soft, my mind occupied, my body nourished and exercised. Everything had its place, its allotted portion of the sun's journey over the ship and down the other side. There were even times when I looked up from the damp washing, or my screen, or Gabriel's little face, and realised that I had not been thinking about my mother. The sun shone, and although there were storms from time to time, they were nothing more than a reason to gather together in the ballroom and marvel at the sheer quantity of water that could fall from the sky.

My father watched me and I watched him watching. If he was there when I was in the net, I laughed just a little more loudly; if he came upon me talking to someone, I would nod more vigorously, agree more heartily, then pretend I had only just noticed him. And when he passed me carrying the clean laundry, I would hold myself just a little taller. *Are you happy?* he would ask me at dinner, and I would grin and say, *Yes, yes of course, of course,* and carry on talking with even more energy. He smiled, and I saw that he was pleased.

And Tom sat next to me at breakfast one day, and I found out that he liked toast with chocolate spread, but never drank coffee. He told me that coffee was for old guys, and I pulled my long hair over my chin so it looked like a beard, and he laughed, and the next day I saw him looking for me across the dining hall, and my breath came quicker and I sat next to him again. After the rain, the sun dried out the water on the deck and Tom and the deck team cleaned the tide marks away. Life can be like this, I remember thinking. Happiness is possible. Is this what my parents meant when they bought the ship? Is this what they wanted?

And I felt that it was, but for one thing.

The news bulletins.

My father made the bulletins available in the ballroom every other evening, just before dinner. And every other evening, the people came into dinner diminished and grey, walking as though time had turned backwards. On bulletin nights there were leftovers on people's plates and the goodnight meetings were subdued. I could see my father's frustration in the deep breaths he took before he spoke, in the emphasis he placed on the words 'here' and 'now' in his goodnight speeches. The bulletins brought heaviness into the air, and made people less ready to enjoy the films, the book group, even work. And yet they went, bulletin after bulletin, pulled there by a longing that was never satisfied.

I went to the bulletins because Tom went, but I spent more time looking at him and blushing wildly when he looked at me than I did watching the news. I sighed when the others sighed, but I quickly realised that the news never changed, any more than it had when we were still living in London. Riots, short-ages, market raids, more Sinkers going down, the same stories over and over again, recited over film footage that never seemed to vary. As far as I could see, the bulletins depressed everyone and told us nothing, and I knew my father thought so too from the way he met my eyes across the ballroom.

And then, one night, when the scratches by my bunk num-bered twenty-two and I had learned to fold a sheet without any help, the news was different.

'That's the British Museum!' I called out when the bulletin started. 'We used to . . .' My father caught my eye and put his finger to his lips. The British Museum meant my mother, and as I stared at the screen, searching for her, my loss burst afresh through the sheet-folding and the Tom-following and the swim-ming and everything I had carefully built around myself since her funeral. I knew, sharply and absolutely, that the reason – the only reason – the people kept coming was to scour the footage for those they had left behind. My heart battered against my ribcage and I watched in silence. My mother was dead. I knew it, and yet I had trouble remembering to breathe.

'Today saw the commencement of the Heritage Restoration Act,' the voiceover on the screen announced.

I don't have answers, Lalla. Only questions. That's how you learn. Mother.

'The Heritage Restoration Act restores citizens to the

enjoyment of public buildings. When government cleansing is completed, citizens will once more enjoy unencumbered access.'

'What's happening?' a voice beside me asked, and I turned to see that Tom had come in late and was sitting beside me. But I was inside the museum with my mother, my head spinning. I could not speak for remembering, and I forgot to blush.

For a moment, it seemed that nothing was going to happen. *They wanted to show how valuable the man's life had been . . .*

Then troops appeared on the roof of the museum. They stood for a moment, outlined against the sky, and then they abseiled down, like locusts swarming over the screen, slicing the building with dark ribbons. They stopped at the windows and produced great rolls of tape from nowhere. They ripped lengths of tape – the tearing sound was clear on the screen – and pressed them to the window frames.

'What are they doing?' I heard myself asking. *Watch, Lalla. Look at what you can see, then think about what you can't.* Yet more troops arrived in trucks bearing huge reels of yellow hose. They unrolled reel after reel into the Great Court, forming a yellow carpet through the main doors. Then they exited the museum and closed the doors. More abseiling troops sealed the doors, then released their cables and joined the others, positioned around the museum with their guns and rifles.

All around me, I saw hands stealing into hands, bodies moving closer together, faces illuminated by the screen, open-mouthed. Tom's hand lay next to mine; our little fingers were touching, and his skin was dry and hot. 'I don't know,' I heard myself saying. 'I don't know what's happening.'

For a few moments the only sound from the screen was the mechanical rhythm of the pumps starting up. The yellow hoses swelled, the carpet of hoses plumped into a mattress. The windows were dark and I briefly hoped that the faces I had seen there had existed only in my imagination.

Mother, what is the most valuable thing in the museum? I asked her once.

Life, she said loudly. *Life,* and a woman looked out from under a layer of cardboard, longing for ours.

Those staring faces appeared again now, marked not by hatred but by despair. They pressed up against the windows, mouths stretched into dark caverns. A woman held up a baby; another dragged her away, then beat at the window with weakened hands. Hundreds of them, thousands, hammering at the windows, kicking at the doors. Lifting their children to the glass, hoping that someone, somewhere, might see them and care. Desperate hands clawing at the inside of their giant sarcophagi. There were no numbers. There were no names. The museum, the announcer told us, was empty, and yet when she drew breath, we heard distant screaming. The scrawled notice at the window – *Mums 4 Community* – fell away.

I thought of everyone I had ever met. The men and women who staffed the re-registration points. The people hiding in the museum. The waitress who, back when there were still restaurants, had brought me a plate of food, unable to hide the jealousy and hunger in her eyes. A man whose coat was now missing a button, and the woman who had sheltered with him. Commander Marius, who did not believe in suicide. I knew people now; I knew what it meant to look forward to seeing someone, to plan, to be glad that, when the sun rose, they would be there still. And I knew that, although the museum would have been dirty and crowded and full of fear, there would have been friendship there too, and care. And that through the empty display cases, a girl might have met a pair of eyes that made her heart beat faster, and that even in the squalor and deprivation, a mother would have lived and breathed for her child. Tom put his hand on mine, and I took it, shaking.

They would all have died one day. But not like that.

Life, my mother said. *Life.*

The museum windows emptied, the last reaching hands sinking below the sills. The troops donned gas masks. They ripped away the sealing tape and stood with their guns as the main doors were opened. *Run,* I pleaded as seven hollow figures staggered through the doors, fragile and dazed. *Run.* But they collapsed before the troops had had time to aim their weapons. No one else came out, and soon, the troops entered in groups. They wrapped the first bodies in sheets and carried them out on stretchers. But after the first half an hour, the bodies were just slung into handcarts and wheeled into the backs of the waiting vans. Body after body. The British Museum emptied of its treasure. Reclaimed for the nation, the announcer said triumphantly. No identity cards, no casualties.

A woman with long dark hair began to cry first. 'It could have been me,' she said between sobs. I knew that my own dreams would be haunted by the thought of those people, whose eyes I had once felt burning into me as my mother explained what I was looking at.

Look carefully, darling. We can tell what these people thought about life by looking at how they treated their dead.

And what they think about death by the way that they treat their living.

The gong rang for dinner, but nobody moved.

'They've gassed the British Museum,' Tom said, his voice a stunned monotone. Our hands were still woven together; bones and heat. 'They ran pipes into it, and they've carried out hundreds of bodies.'

'Thousands.'

'There were faces at the windows . . .'

'They were trying to break out . . .'

'We have to go back,' I said, and I felt my mother's arms around my shoulders, squeezing me tight as she did when I had given the right answer. I looked for my father, expecting to see his face stunned and overwhelmed, like those around him, but his face was fixed and stern. I spoke again, more loudly this time. 'We have to go back,' I said. Tom let go of my hand and I stood up. I waited for everyone else to jump up and join their voices to mine. It was our departure all over again, when throwing my card to the crowd on the quay had been the only thing to do.

'Turn the ship around,' I told my father. 'We need to be in London. We need to help. We've got to stop them before they gas the National Gallery too, and St Paul's, and . . .' Beside me, a pair of green eyes moved gently left to right as their owner shook his head and I shrank from him in disbelief. My hand was still warm where he had held it.

My father stood, and the people were silent. He looked around the ballroom. Savoury smells floated in from the dining room. The gong rang again. Still no one moved. Only the occasional lowering of a head here, eyes closed in pain there, said that these people were alive. I hated myself for thinking about food amidst such horror. But I could not stop the growling of my stomach, and wondered how long the horror was going to keep us all in the ballroom. We had witnessed a terrible thing. We knew what we had to do. We would eat, and we would go back.

My father looked at me.

'What good has it done you, to watch this?' he asked me.

'It's shown us what to do next,' I said eagerly, watching for his approval and pride, certain that, somewhere, my mother was listening. 'We must go, now. There are people sheltering in all the public buildings. Dr Spencer can treat them, and we can open our stores and give them food. And clothes.' I thought of my orange dress and of the piles of clean clothes in my cabin. I did not need so many. 'If they were stronger, they'd be able to do something. Resist the troops. I don't know.' I searched the room for help. But no one would meet my eyes. My father remained unmoved.

'What good has it done you, to watch this?' he asked the ballroom as a whole.

The only sound was the clinking of plates in the dining room, and concerned voices wondering whether the gong had been heard.

'Are you surprised?' he asked, and his voice was deeper, his tone more certain than I had ever heard it. 'Have we not seen it before, again and again? The consequences of criminal decisions squeezed downwards until the ones at the bottom pay the price?'

He looked around the ballroom. 'I ask you again, what good has this bulletin done you?'

Helen stood up, her dark hair blending into the shadows. 'Michael,' she said, and I winced, because she was looking at him as though he was the only person in the world, and I still wanted him for myself.

'Yes, Helen?'

'While the bulletins are there, I must watch them. I might see Simon.'

Across the ballroom, heads nodded in agreement and names were muttered. Tola. Paul. Grace. Nisha. Salvator. Mark. A gentle litany, murmured for the lost.

'Where's Gabriel?' my father asked Helen.

'I didn't bring him, Michael. He's still so young. He's helping Emily in the dining room, with the other children.'

'In the dining room? Where your dinner is, even now, getting cold, while you weep here for something you cannot change?'

Helen looked at her feet.

'I did not bring you on board the ship for a ringside seat at the end of the world. I brought you that you might have life, and have it in abundance. We've left all that behind – the state

97

murders, the mourning, the misery.' Frustration broke through his voice. 'I brought you here to be happy.' He swallowed, and pulled himself up tall. 'The past is over,' he declared. 'There is nothing now except what is here, on the ship, with us. We are the world. We are the entire universe. The old world is turning in on itself. We are no longer a part of it. In a few short weeks, they will have fallen apart. Will we fall with them?'

'I'm not watching another bulletin,' someone said, and agreement spread through the room like a tide.

'No more bulletins!' came the cry. 'No more news.'

'No,' I shouted over the cries of agreement. 'We need to know what's happening.' I thought of all the bulletins I'd ignored in London, back when I had been free to watch as many as I liked. Could I have changed things then? Is that what my mother had been waiting for?

'I don't want the bulletins,' Helen said, turning on me. 'While they're there, I'll watch them. Michael's right. We can't help those people.'

'But we have to try,' I cried, looking around the room, but it was too late. They had made up their minds.

'Lalla,' my father said softly. 'If we go back, we'll never reach our destination. Everything on this ship is necessary to get us there, and to support us when we arrive. Trust me.' There was silence now.

'But people in London are going to be gassed. Or drowned. Or shot.'

'So you want to return so that you can be gassed, or drowned, or shot? How is that going to help them? Or anyone?'

One of the engineers shouted out, 'We're helping them by not being there.' There was a murmur of agreement.

Then Tom stood up. He looked around and turned red, and then he coughed. For a moment I thought he was going to tell them all that I was right, and insist we should go back. I remembered standing on the deck rail with him as we threw our cards, and I clasped my hands together.

He said, 'I think we should take the mast down.'

'What?' I stood up too and looked around, waiting for the people to react. My father looked from Tom to me, from me to Tom, and said nothing.

'The thing is,' Tom said, 'if we don't want to see the bulletins, what's the point in having the mast?'

'So soon?' my father said. To anyone who didn't know him, his expression would have looked uncertain. But I knew that look. It was the look he used to give my mother and me when he had made up his mind about something and was waiting for us to catch up. And I knew, as surely as if it had already happened, that he would stand still and say nothing, and that the people would fall over themselves to do what he had wanted them to do all along.

'The bulletins rule my life,' Patience said. 'I wait all day for the next one, and when it comes, it is the same as the last, and the last, and the last. Tola will not come to me on a bulletin.'

Tom turned to me. 'If we could help those people, it would be different.'

'But we can.'

'No, we can't.'

'They're already dead.'

I couldn't keep track of who was speaking. Voices tripped over one another, and they were all saying the same thing. *Get rid of it. What good is it to us now? We don't want the mast where we're going.*

'Destroy the mast,' they cried. 'Destroy the connection.'

And they did. My father sent the engineers off, and their dinners went cold as they untangled the wires that connected the mast to the ship. After our meat pie and vegetable bake we left our places to watch them drag it down to the small deck. Tom had not come to sit beside me, but I saw him cheering with the rest, standing with a group, clapping each other on the back. The engineers heaved the mast into the sea after my mother. It sank immediately, the water closing over it as though it had never existed.

I watched my father's face as the mast went down. His hand was on Tom's shoulder, and for the first time, I wondered how he had known to stock the ship with my mother's funeral flowers.

EIGHT

We remember our missing ✦ *the stores*
✦ *an apple*

When we came back from sinking the mast, everyone helped each other to pudding, hot from the kitchen. I put the first forkful into my mouth mechanically, but I was no longer hungry. I could see Tom, far away on the other side of the dining room, accepting the praise of his neighbours. He used his arms to mime the falling of the mast, and they laughed. The whole room pulsed with energy as though a great weight had been lifted from it. The woman to my right was talking energetically about what she was going to do with the extra time she would have spent watching the bulletin. The air was bright. But to me it felt brittle, as though the laughter was coming from people's throats rather than their hearts. Tom was talking away as though he had never held my hand, and I pushed my plate away.

'Is your meal not to your liking?' the man with the pickled walnut skin asked politely, but I didn't know how to answer him. He glanced at my father and back at my plate, then quickly swapped my full plate for his empty one and dispatched the crumble and custard efficiently into his own system.

'Are you hungry?' I asked, taken aback more by the appropriation of my plate than by his appetite.

'No,' he said quickly, 'no, my dear. Not hungry. How could I be?' My father was standing now, waiting for everyone to notice and fall silent so that he could speak. 'But Michael will not like to look out and see that his provision is not being enjoyed. Not tonight. Tonight of all nights. Tonight we have done a great thing.'

'A great thing?' I queried, but at that moment my father drew breath, leaving my words ringing round the dining room like lost children.

'I am proud of you,' my father said without preamble. 'Your actions tonight have proved your worth. Had you not taken the decision you did, you would not be the people I thought you were. You would not be the people I brought onto the ship. To-night, we say goodbye to the dead and the dying, and then we live. Live!'

I looked around the ballroom, expecting a cheer, but saw only thoughtful faces gazing at my father. He lifted his water glass.

'I offer myself as a father to your children, as a brother where a brother is needed, and a companion to anyone who has been left alone. I drink to the people we would have given our lives to find and I thank them for the love they bore you. And I bid them farewell.'

Across the dining room, Helen stood up. She, too, held up her glass, and in a voice that was quiet yet firm, said, 'I drink to Simon, my husband, who left to claim a plot in the Land Allo-cation Act and never came back. Gabriel will find a new father in you, Michael.'

Then Patience. 'I drink to Tola, my daughter, lost in the burn-ing lands. May she find me here.'

One by one, the people stood.

'To my child Sanjeev, gone without trace in the drowning of Bangladesh. May he, too, find a new father.'

'To my grandparents, who ran to escape the second pandemic.'

'Tripp, my friend, arrested under the Nazareth Act.'

And the list continued. The faces the people had searched for in the bulletins were all given names. The sun set; Emily and her team quietly cleared the plates and the tables. Sounds of crockery being cleaned underscored the recitation.

'Mia, who missed her re-registration.'

'Sam, my brother, made homeless by the Possession of Property Act.'

'My twin Gill, who went to trade our books.'

The moon rose clear and full through the windows; the earth had moved out of her way. The children's eyes became heavy; the grown-ups held them, or settled them in on the carpet with pillows of cardigans and jumpers as the names rolled on.

'Lynde, who lost her card.'

'Victor, who went to school.'

'Rebecca, arrested in a market raid.'

The people had already said goodbye to their dead; in the course of that long night, they let go of their missing. Some, like me, had nothing to say, but like everyone else, I stayed awake all night and listened to the story of the collapse of the world told through a listing of names. Only when the sun had risen again, and the children began to stir, rubbing their eyes and asking what was for breakfast, was the last name committed to the air and set free.

'Let this be the end of longing for what is gone,' my father said. 'Let our children grow up in safety, knowing that the people who are with them now will always be with them. Think about any mementoes you have brought on board. Do you need them? Or are they holding you back from becoming part of the free, loving family of the ship? Think about why you were invited on board. Think of why you chose to accept. Be worthy. And let us eat!'

Breakfast was curved bits of melting pastry and sweet dark jam. The baskets emptied as fast as they were put onto the table.

'It's a croissant,' I heard Helen tell Gabriel. 'They used to eat these in France.'

'So what?' the little boy said, sticky with pastry flakes and jam, and my father smiled. 'Are there any more?'

'Are there any more?' I echoed, wondering how long this bounty could continue. One day, surely, someone would ask the same question and the answer would be no. Where were we going? Would there be croissants there? My father stretched out a hand and stopped Emily in her path.

'Emily,' he said, 'Lalla wants to know whether there are any more.'

'Any more?' Emily laughed. 'Any more? Lalla, you could eat croissants every day for a year and there'd still be more. And more.' My father's hand was still on her arm and she looked at it, her cheeks going slightly pink. 'Would you like to come, Lalla, and see for yourself? Michael, would that be all right?'

'Of course. Unless she'd rather go and help Tom with the football?'

'Football?'

My father smiled. 'I've moved Tom to new work. He's going to teach the children to play football. Up in the sports hall.'

No wonder Tom had looked so happy. I shook my head, and Emily looked pleased. 'I'll tidy away here, then we can go.'

'You two go,' my father said. 'I'll manage here.'

'But Father,' Emily protested. 'I can't let you do my work. I'll take Lalla later on.'

'I have to be in the laundry later,' I said, with an obscure feeling that I was losing a competition I did not know I had entered.

'There,' said my father with amusement in his eyes. 'Lalla

needs to be in the laundry later. You'd better go now.' He turned Emily around slowly and pulled the ties of her canvas apron loose. As he lifted it over her head, I heard him speak softly into the back of her neck. 'Emily. Take Lalla, and help her lose the last of her doubts and fears.' I saw Emily's hands trembling as she folded the apron and surrendered it to him.

And so, as the people finished their croissants, and stood up from the tables and made their way out of the dining room, Emily and I went through the wooden doors into the white and steel realm of the kitchen. I looked back through the round window and saw my father holding Emily's apron, gesturing to the tables to be cleared. Emily stood beside me, her hands clasped under her chin.

'It must have been wonderful,' she said.

'What?'

'To have lived with him all your life. Just think. There's never been a time when you didn't know him.' I stared at her, but she was staring at him. Had I ever known him? He had brought home diamonds and guns and strangers, but he had found tinned peaches, too, and shoes, and had never, ever forgotten to tell my mother to keep me safe. Now he belonged to five hundred people I had never met, and their children were to call him Father.

Somebody tried to take Emily's apron; my father held it out of reach with mock warning in his eyes. The woman – Alice, her name was, an old lady with grey hair and bright eyes – looked disappointed. From nowhere, my father produced a second apron and bestowed it on her, and she took it, beaming, and began to clear the plates.

'Look, Lalla. Michael won't let anyone else touch my apron,' Emily breathed.

All I'd seen was that he didn't touch a single dirty plate himself.

'He's *my* father,' I burst out. 'Mine. What does he want a load more children for? What did I do wrong?'

'I think it's more a question of what you did right,' Emily said softly. 'Why would he want more, unless he loved the one he had?' And with that she turned, and I followed her, through the kitchens and down, down, down to the stores.

When Emily said she would show me the stores, I'd expected to see something like my mother's larder in London, with its modest piles of tins and packets neatly arranged. But when Emily pushed open the storeroom doors, the comparison melted away. This was no larder, but a warehouse, as big and bigger than the atrium of the British Museum. The tins in my mother's larder could be comfortably lifted between a thumb and a finger. Here, the tins were bigger than my head. They were piled upon great pallets, their black lettering repeated over and over again, to the sides, up, down and back to the distant walls like an optical illusion or a game of mirrors. We walked and walked; the black lettering gave way to pictures of red tomatoes; we walked some more. I stepped backwards and craned my head to see to the top but, like the wind turbines, they were constructed on a scale that one person standing alone could not comprehend. My mother had had bags of dried rice the size of my hand; now we were passing sacks the size of a small child, stacked twenty high and twenty across in layered towers. Like tiny dolls in a giant's larder, Emily and I walked the stores.

She opened another door. Drums. Bigger than the oil drums the street people had used for their fires. 'Cooking oil and fat pellets,' she said. 'Hermetically sealed, fresh until we need to use it.' I started to calculate how many there were and gave up. Further on, I recognised the squat white buckets of dried egg, the taller ones that held milk powder, the blue paper sacks of sugar.

'But why is there so much?' I said, feeling more and more

like the king who tried to turn back the tides. My feet were aching.

'We've not even finished one of these drums of oil yet, Lalla,' Emily said. 'Not one.'

Another door, more sacks. My legs were tired and I wanted to sit down. More tins, more pallets, more drums, more sealed buckets. I felt dazed. We went down another steel staircase and I sat on the bottom step and rubbed my feet. I had asked a simple question; this heavy artillery of reply was bewildering and exhausting. But one thing I learned – that whatever else happened on the ship, we were unlikely to starve.

'This level is the same again,' Emily said, and my mouth fell open. 'Want to walk it?'

I shook my head but she had already set off. 'Biscuits,' she said, gesturing to the left and pointing forwards. 'And on this side, cooking chocolate. Milk chocolate. White chocolate. Dark chocolate. Syrup. Crackers. And I can't remember what this is; I forgot to bring the catalogue. I think it's marshmallows. We haven't opened any yet. Do you remember marshmallows?'

I shook my head. 'What's the catalogue?'

'It's like the manifest, but for the stores. There's a map in the front and it shows us where everything is. I'm beginning to find my way around now. Sometimes I feel like I'm going down into the depths of the mountains and bringing up gold. At the moment, Gerhard and I manage alone, but one day we'll need a whole team. Do you want to walk to the end? Or shall we go down now?

'Down?'

'Yes, down. All this is just the dry stuff. There's more.'

At the foot of the stairs, beside a heavy white door, hung two padded bodysuits, with gloves and hats and face masks. There was a shining silver handle on either side, each one the length of my forearm. Emily felt in the pocket of her dress and produced two keys.

'Here,' Emily said, holding one of the keys out to me. 'We put on the suits, then unlock and turn the handles at the same time. That's to make sure no one goes into the freezers alone. Ready?' she asked, her eyes dancing. 'The freezers are bigger than the storerooms upstairs.'

I had had enough. My stomach was rumbling. I thought of the day we had sailed, of Commander Marius threatening to take the ship's stores and distribute them over the city. My father had said that there was no more food than we needed. And I had felt that our stored food wouldn't have made any difference to the city. But Emily said it took one sack of rice to make a meal for the ship. So just the sacks I had seen would have fed the museum dwellers for weeks, let alone the layers of sacks behind those, and the layers behind those, and the layers behind those. We had missed lunch and I had no idea where my father was. But to walk away from the chance to see what the freezers contained seemed to me to be insulting to the people who were still in London, de-registered and dying.

I pulled on one of the suits, and Emily pulled on the other, and as I turned my key and wrenched at the handle, I felt like the Antarctic explorers in my mother's old picture books, back in the days when there was an Antarctic. Lights blinked into shuddering life as Emily and I entered, and my breath rose in a mist. We were in a narrow corridor of wire crates. The ceiling was lower than in the warehouses, but still high enough to need ladders and pulley systems.

'It's smaller than I thought,' I said when I realised I could see the back wall from where I was standing.

'Really?' said Emily. She opened another door, which led into another frozen room, and another, and another. I counted seven before I realised I could no longer feel my nose. 'Michael partitioned the freezer stores,' she explained. 'It'll be more efficient when the fuel's completely gone and we start relying on the solar panels.'

'So what's all this?'

'Concentrated orange juice, I think. And the next chamber is my favourite.'

'Why? What's in it?'

'Look.'

I looked, but the racks of wire crates didn't look any different to me.

'It's dough,' Emily said. 'Cookie dough. You get a great long sausage of dough, and you slice it and put the discs in the oven, and fifteen minutes later there are fresh cookies for everyone.' The word sounded out of place, light and frivolous in a serious world. No one was going to die if they didn't get cookies. I couldn't imagine turning up in London and offering cookies to the homeless.

'I've never had a cookie,' I said.

'Poor Lalla. They're lovely. Warm and sweet, and when you bite into them the melted chocolate chips ooze into your mouth.'

'When did you have cookies?'

'Oh, decades ago. When I was much younger than you are now. And then the other night Father came down and got some dough and we tried it out in the kitchen with Gerhard and Tom and some of the others.'

'Tom?' Why hadn't I been there? Why hadn't someone come to get me?

She nodded. 'Oh, they were good. I'd forgotten how good. Oh, Lalla, you have so many treats in store for you. Cookies are just the start.'

'What about apples?' I asked.

'Oh yes. Dried, tinned, even some frozen – and there are some biscuits upstairs with apple pieces in them.'

'No,' I said, 'apples. Real apples. Like in books.'

Emily looked at me as though I was speaking a foreign language, and for the first time I noticed that she had lines around her eyes. 'Lalla, sweetheart,' she said gently, 'apples grew on trees, didn't they?' And for a moment we stared at each other, and the soil sickness seemed to creep right inside me. I thought of the stores I had already seen, their landscape of provision waiting to be mined, and of the ship sailing away from the barren country. And I remembered the film of the last polar bear, swimming and swimming in the empty ocean, in search of a mass of ice that had finally melted away. The freezer chamber felt smaller and smaller and I found myself looking around anxiously for the door.

'What about seeds?' I asked.

'Seeds?'

'Has my father brought seeds? Things we can plant?' I was walking around the chamber but the door seemed to have gone.

'Where would we plant seeds?' Emily asked, bewildered. 'Not that way, Lalla, if you want to go back. That door goes to bagels and crumpets.' She put her silver padded arm around my shoulders and led me back the way we had come. I didn't protest. I had seen enough, and could barely find the energy to toil after her, back through the freezer chambers and up, up, up through the vertiginous mountains of our future meals.

Emily gave me some biscuits, and I took them to my cabin. I lay on my bunk to eat them and ran my fingers over the scratches I was making to mark the days. Twenty-three days had passed – almost a month, not counting the time I had lost in mourning – and yet five hundred people had not even made a dent in the food stores. I closed my eyes, replaying the sleepless night of goodbyes. How many of those missing people might have been saved if this food had gone to the city instead of into the ship?

Tins and sacks and drums rising in great walls, solid and substantial, nourishment for thousands upon thousands for weeks, days, even years.

We have left hunger behind, my father said, and I knew now that he was right. But even as I admired the extent of his preparations, I felt that they had altered the world's balance – that the ship was not so much an escape from hunger as the cause of it. I thought about the women who had been swept into the sea by the flailing gangplank of the departing ship. My father had killed those women, and nothing had been said. Had he also killed others by his actions? His concern for our safety? His longing to get away? I remembered something about a man who'd died the night before we sailed and wondered what had happened. Why had my mother been so reluctant to board? I fell into an uneasy sleep. Then I heard a voice and I froze in earnest.

'Have you ever eaten an apple?'

I could not see. I had slept for longer than I thought, and my cabin was dark. The voice was familiar, but I could not place it. It was musical and confident; it put the question urgently, as though much depended upon my answer. It was not my mother, who would not have needed to ask. It was not my father, who now only asked questions that contained their own answers – *Do we want to return to a life of terror? Who is there among us who does not care, above all, for his fellow man? What are we here for, if not to take humanity to its natural, unfettered destiny?* He would not have wasted a word on an apple, especially now that there was no such thing.

'Have you ever eaten an apple?' the voice asked again, and this time there were breaths snatched between some of the words, as though its owner had been running fast.

'Mother?' I called, but the dark night was silent.

I felt a sudden pain under my ribs, as though my lungs were being forced upwards, and I could not get my breath. I tried to raise myself from my bunk but could not move. I had never eaten an apple, never even seen or held one. *She's here,* I thought, and the words carried such conviction that I knew they were true. I lay clutching my sheet, not daring to move, telling myself that if I stayed completely still, time would not be able to move forwards, and I would not have to live without her anymore.

Mother, I shouted silently, *how could you leave me? What did you want? If the ship was what you wanted, why didn't you come on board when you were well, so that you could have looked after me still? At least in London, I had you. Now I have lost everything, everything. I don't even believe in the ship.*

Child, she said, *child. Good things are happening.* But I could not listen. I lay trapped by my numb and motionless body, and inside I screamed and yelled and stamped my feet until the walkways and the staircases and the metal hull were ringing with my grief and anger. *I do not want to be here. I did not ask for this. Who are you, that you forced me to come here? How dare you leave, when you have not told me who I am? Who am I, Mother? Who am I, and what am I here to do?*

I smelled the fresh, tingling scent of an apple I must have dreamed of in my childhood. Cool, sweet flesh burst over my tongue; my teeth ached at the pleasure of piercing its skin. It was pain, yes, but it was also wanting more, more, and overlying that was the feeling that I would never, never taste that sweetness outside of my dreams. I wanted my mother, and that was impossible, because she was dead flesh tucked around with silk, still floating somewhere beyond the horizon. I wondered if every sensation I would ever have now would be a yearning for something that did not and could not exist.

Have an apple, Lalla.

I ran to my cabin door and pulled it open. The walkway rang, a distant echo of a disappearing footstep. A door closed. I went to follow but there, at my feet, was an orb of bright, vivid green with shining skin. A small stick of a stalk. A springy brown leaf still attached.

An apple.

NINE

The beginnings of my museum ❧ goodnight
meeting ❧ dinosaurs

I brought the apple into my cabin and turned on the light. It sat in my palm, lighter than I had imagined, its green skin smooth, unblemished and cold to the touch. The little leaf bounced slightly when I touched it. I didn't want it to break off and so I put the apple down on my table. I went to my cupboard and took out the velvet jewellery box containing the button my father had given me when my mother died. How many objects make a museum? Eight million? Two? There, on my desk, were the beginnings of a new British Museum, a museum for the ship.

Safe on the ship, I looked at the button, nestled in its velvet box, and I saw how my parents' words to each other were translated in the air, as a beam of light bends when shone through clear water. My mother dismissed diamonds; my father heard ingratitude. My father refused to wait until the people of the museum had formed a plan, and my mother heard him condemn his fellow human beings to death. They were both right, and both wrong. When things fall apart, you cannot save everything. That was the button's story. The man wanted to save his companion from the cold. He wanted to love her, to keep her safe. And the little worn button couldn't cope with the pressure of his expectations. It cracked and fell away. It could have been ground to dust. Instead, it was caught on a tide that brought it to me.

An apple and a button.

Our museum, my mother had said. *Our museum.*

There it sat on the shelf of my cabin. A worn relic of the life before; a shining miracle of life on the ship. I put them together and the sight pleased me. I'd keep these things for someone. And when we got to wherever we were going, I'd build a home for them, and people would come and see them and ask questions and I'd say, *I don't have any answers. Only questions. That's how you learn.*

I was learning now, and the night of the last news bulletin taught me two things. It taught me that, if we were to turn around and go back to London, I would have to find people on the ship who agreed with me, and get them to help me persuade the rest. And it taught me that holding someone's hand can turn them into a stranger. I had not spoken to Tom since the night of the last bulletin. But I watched him move around the ship. I learned him until his face was as fixed in my mind as my mother's. I knew his voice, his eyes, the lines that ran from the edges of his nostrils to the corners of his mouth and deepened when he smiled. The children ran after him all the time, laughing as he demonstrated kicks and turns and bounced the football from knee to knee while they counted and cheered. I began to eat toast and chocolate spread, and to say no to coffee.

But just as real in my mind were the suffocated museum dwellers. Someone, I knew, would say, *Yes, Lalla, you are right. We must go back to London and do what we can to help.* It would be like the moment I threw my card away – just one person speaking the truth would bring everyone else along with them. We could set the ship up as a clinic, a rescue centre. We could all stay on it, living our happy lives, and no one would have to leave. It was too late for the British Museum. But there were other public buildings. Maybe a community had been formed in one of them. Maybe another mother and another daughter took food from their own stocks and shared it when they visited. We could not have been the only ones in the whole of London. And there were other cities too; who knew what was happening in those? We could save those people.

It was so simple that it was bound to happen. I waited for a while, watching for the resolve I'd expressed at the last bulletin to take hold and spread. But the ship had been invaded by a blissful content. Patience was walking taller, laughing more, even singing as we folded the clean clothes. Doctor Spencer's walk had developed a bounce and the very lines on his face seemed to have smoothed. Helen played with Gabriel, and adults began to join the children in the sports hall as Tom's green eyes flashed among them, chasing his football. There was a small group who met each other in corners, looking over their shoulders, but whenever I approached them they separated and melted away until I convinced myself I had imagined their connection.

In desperation, I defied my father's request that we should not look back. At a goodnight meeting, I talked openly about the sealing of the museum, the pumping in of poisonous gas, the thousands of deaths that resulted. But my words simply energised the community on the ship. Far from depressing them, the horror of the museum gave them a common currency for conversation. It would start with two or more people trying to find a name by which to refer to the deaths. It couldn't be called genocide, because it was not a concerted attempt to eliminate a particular race or religion. Nor execution, which implied that the victims had done something wrong. Elimination gave the impression that something undesirable had been wiped out.

Murder was too small, too domestic a word for the sheer scale of what had happened, although it found favour because it was unequivocal in its statement of crime. And as I waited for some-one, anyone, to make the connection between the museum dwellers and ourselves, and to declare with me that we should return to land, I realised that they were enjoying themselves. That the people in the museum had become ciphers to the ship dwellers as much as they had ever been to the government on land, and that any doubts anyone may have had about leav-ing the land for the ship had vanished in the dying breaths of the dispossessed.

Once communication with the land was impossible, people began to live on the ship. Not just to eat and to sleep and to smile at each other, but to live. I was watching and listening, and I noticed the difference. Experiences stopped being calibrated in losses – homes, friends, a parent, a child – and began to be measured in gains: a book discovered, a painting understood, a film watched for the first time. I noticed, too, that my father's way of speaking, his turns of phrases, the words he used most often, became a kind of currency. There was nothing so obvi-ous as a manual of approved words and phrases, or instructions on the screen. Nevertheless, when I woke one morning hoping that breakfast would be croissants and jam again, I didn't say a word. Meals meant wide-eyed gratitude for whatever my father had chosen to provide, and personal preferences were better left unspoken.

Similarly, the conversations in which life on the ship was overtly compared with life on land ceased. For example, I re-membered the feeling I had when we came home from the museum having learned something new. There was something about having avoided danger, about having escaped the atten-tions of the wild people gathered on the streets, about having survived the journey and brought home our precious nugget of knowledge, that had made my heart race and my eyes shine. Now that the knowledge was there, a short deck stroll away, behind an unlocked door, it did not carry the same thrill. But I never said so out loud.

I could not help wondering how many of the books I was reading, how many of the works of art I looked at, would have been created in a life of such pleasant and easy luxury. Here on the ship, the button I had given my mother truly was nothing more than a button. On the ship, Jane Eyre would not have had to escape her evil aunt and cruel cousins by going to a terrible school, or have gone to work in a strange country house, because there would have been no cruelty and no need to escape. The Fossil sisters would never have had to learn to dance, because they would never have needed to earn a living. Macbeth would never have murdered Duncan, because on the ship, Macbeth would have had everything he wanted.

I did not want anyone to be cruel, but I wanted a reason to get up every morning.

I found myself saying less and thinking more, and the girl who had once stood on a deck rail and addressed a mob shrank away, leaving only a person unsure of what and who she was in a world she had not asked to join. And although I never lost my conviction that we should turn around, I stopped saying so, and once I had stopped saying so, I began to understand that it would never happen, and to think more closely about where we were, and where we might be going. My father and Patience had both told me to grow up. I wasn't sure what they meant, but I felt older.

'Why do we need the net?' Gabriel asked me, when he wanted to swim but the net had not been lowered. 'There aren't any sea creatures left.'

'Maybe not,' I answered, 'but if there are, you can bet they'll be hungry.'

'But I'm bored,' he said, and so I took him to the research room and we looked up sea creatures. We found out about sharks that could eat you with a single bite and jellyfish that could wrap you in their tentacles and poison you through your skin and fish that shot darts into your feet that could paralyse you in an instant. But the carbon the generations before us had burned had turned the water into acid, and the coral reefs were gone.

'Isn't it awful?' I said to Gabriel. 'Isn't it awful that so many kinds of animals and things have died out?' And when he looked at me puzzled and I said, 'Gone. Extinct. Like the dinosaurs,' he looked at me anxiously.

'Dinosaurs aren't gone,' he said.

'They are.'

'No, they're not. I held a dinosaur bone once.'

'You didn't.'

'I did. I found this big bone in the road, and I took it to mum, and she said that it came from a dinosaur and I was never, ever to leave the holding centre in case the tyrannosaurus rex got me.' His eyes took up his whole face.

'But that wasn't real,' I said, 'it was just a story to keep you safe,' and I started to explain about fossilisation the way my mother had explained it to me, about rainwater seeping through the ground and dissolved minerals precipitating in the honeycomb of buried bones, but Gabriel ran off to play football with Tom. I sat alone and thought, and the more I thought, the more I felt that everything was balanced against everything else, and that no one had the right to sail over a dead sea and say, I am not responsible for this.

I began to listen in the goodnight meetings. I knew my mother would have done so, and as I emerged from my grief older, I found that people's stories were a way of connecting with her. Each evening, the people took it in turns to tell their stories, and when they'd finished, my father would tell them to consign their sadness to the past and never look back. It was a kind of ritual. Testimonies, my father called them. I heard my mother say, *Testimonies, or, How Michael Paul Saved My Life,* and could not help smiling, even when the tales were of loss and death and despair.

'I was sentenced to thirty years in prison,' Finn said softly, the night he was asked. 'Because of the Thursday Project.'

'You were the Thursday Project?' someone said, incredulous. 'The Thursday Project saved my life.'

'It made so much sense,' Finn said, the people drawing around him as the moon shone through the ballroom window. 'This was decades ago, remember. Before the crash. Before the Dove. The big supermarket near where I lived threw away food every single night. There were people starving in doorways right outside, but the supermarket threw what hadn't sold into these big bins in the car park.' I saw Emily nodding her head. 'So every Thursday, I took that food from the bins to the people who needed it. And I organised other people to do the same in other places. When they started locking the bins, I started using bolt cutters.'

'They gave you thirty years for that?'

'We started raiding farms as well,' Finn said. 'The industrial ones that supplied the supermarkets in the first place. They threw out all the vegetables that weren't right – crooked carrots, rusty potatoes, all that, they just threw them out. And Thursday Project volunteers used to break in and take all that stuff, and give it away. Because people were starving, weren't they, even then?'

My father said, 'But it was already too late, wasn't it?'

Finn nodded. 'The soil was already dead. All those chemicals, they were all that was making that stuff grow. Ironic, really. Making stuff grow and killing off all the insects.' He paused, then carried on. 'Anyway. After a bit, the big supermarkets stopped using the bins. Army trucks came to take the food straight to landfill, and three of us got shot when we tried to break into one of the trucks. I was arrested.'

'For theft?'

'No. For threatening national security and undermining the economy. That's why my sentence was so long.'

'No,' my father said. 'Your sentence was long because you started something with power and passion and momentum. Because you were right, and there was no way the government could argue otherwise. But mostly, they gave you thirty years because you brought others with you. Your goodness made you a threat.'

'Are you bitter?' Emily asked.

'I'd only done twenty years before the Prisoner Release Act,' Finn grinned. 'Prison was full of social criminals by then anyway. The real murderers were all on the outside, running gangs and joining the government troops and that. There wasn't any food left anyway. That's why they set us free, so they wouldn't have to feed us.' He turned serious, and as his smile faded the lines on his face smoothed slightly. He looked a little younger, a little less certain. 'It didn't feel like much at the time,' he said, rubbing at his grey beard, now neatly trimmed. 'It was only what anyone could have done.'

'But they didn't, and you did,' my father said. 'And that is why you are here. Now, Finn, consign your story to the past. Move forwards with the ship. Don't look back.'

'Don't look back,' the people murmured in response. Finn opened his mouth as though he wanted to say something more, but my father held up his hand and Finn bowed his head.

'I won't look back,' he said, and the goodnight meeting was over. As I stood up, I looked at Tom, and he looked at me, and

I remembered how he had held my hand as we watched the last bulletin, and I thought of the way the first star appeared over the horizon when the sun set, and that maybe, just maybe, happiness was something I would have to go out and find.

TEN

The people settle ❧ *I spend time in the cinema*
❧ *the boy with the green eyes again*

We could hear nothing of the land, and the land could know nothing of us. I began to wonder what was real and what I had made up, and whether, if the gassing of the museum existed only in my head, that meant it did not exist at all. People sat with their screens reading, or looking at the instructions for some forgotten activity. Alice, the old lady with grey hair and gentle eyes who helped out in the dining room, went to my father, and he disappeared and came back with a bag, which she opened with a kind of surprised and fascinated delight. Whenever I saw her after that she was sitting holding a wooden circle with fabric stretched over it, making patterns in coloured threads with a tiny silver needle, an admiring audience around her.

Tom ran his football games on the second deck and, when I wasn't in the laundry, I wandered up to the sports hall. If the door was ajar, I watched him with the children, teaching, playing, comforting them when they fell over and then giving them water that they gulped down, red from exercise and laughter. I saw him with my father, too, the two of them talking earnestly as they walked along the deck. *You'll make friends on the ship*, my mother had said. And I had – but Tom had thrown the mast into the sea and turned his back on London. My mother had taught me all about fossilisation, but she had never taught me how to disagree with someone who was wrong, and now I was here, and she was not, and when I tried to think of something to say to Tom, I felt myself crumble with missing her.

I spent a lot of time in the cinema. I could hide there; it was dark and you didn't have to talk to anyone. And I loved the films. In them, monsters terrorised ordinary people, eating them, attacking them, driving them to live in underground caves or remote mountains. I found the noises satisfying; I liked the violence, which seemed to answer something in me I had not known was there. I liked the way my heart and lungs seemed to suspend themselves as a head was torn off here, a body torn apart there. In the cinema, and on my screen, I worked my way through the listings for Horror, for Disaster, for Apocalypse, film by film, and counted the forms the monster came in. There were Gabriel's dinosaurs, and men who had been turned evil by power, and aliens from other planets set to take over the world. There were diseases, and people coming back from the dead. There were walking plants and creatures that could change to look exactly like things that were not evil, so that they could win the trust of the innocent masses. There were asteroids about to crash into the earth. But always, always, there were many, many people who died, and a handful who survived. And one day I realised why I was watching these films.

The museum dead were the masses and we were the survivors on whom the future of the world depended.

Perhaps it was because I had so little else happening in my life, or because I had so little control, or because I didn't fully understand what was going on, but I began to love them, watching my favourites over and over again alone on the screen – the portal – my father had given me. They made sense; they gave me a context in which to understand what was going on and permission to stop worrying. The more I watched, the more I felt that the films were what was real, and that the day-to-day ship life of meals and smiles and clean water was nothing more than a story. After all the trials and the threats and the deaths, someone wise and elderly, one who had been sagely watching events unfold, would eventually sacrifice himself to save the young hero, who himself would have already tried to sacrifice himself for the young heroine, and they alone would survive, ready to replenish the world. And the earlier in the film you met the character, the more certain they were to survive.

I began to look at the people of the ship differently. When Godzilla rose from the sea, or the evil ruler of the Galactic Empire attacked, I thought of the black-clothed troops, the screens, the re-registrations. We were the good people who had escaped from the bad people. It was a comforting way of looking at things. *Don't look back,* my father told us at every goodnight meeting, and with the films to think about, I did not have to. I could think quietly and place myself in the framework of the story. I had been part of the ship from the very beginning. And I was young. So whatever threat came to us on the ship, I would survive. Finn would be eaten, because he was old. Emily would be eaten, because she was happy. Gabriel would either be eaten to show the ruthlessness of the beast, or left behind for me to adopt and bring up as my own, but either way, Helen would be eaten, because otherwise no one would cry and Gabriel would never have to grow up. I had a context for my mother's death, too. She was the prologue victim, the one in the opening scenes who died mysteriously in order to show that there was a threat, before anyone had understood that there was a threat at all.

And my father. Strong, valiant, truly good, my father would rush in during the final moments, when the young man was about to throw himself into the beast's jaws in order to save me, and use his knowledge and power to defeat the beast, rescue the young man and die nobly in the process. And the young man and I would always remember him, perhaps with a giant photograph on our wedding day, or his wedding ring, pressed at the last moment into the young man's hand as he whispered, *Look after her.*

And if I was the young woman, I knew that Tom was the young man. The films, the swimming, Alice and her embroidery, came further and further forward in my mind, and the question of our responsibilities receded. I ate my dried eggs scrambled and my tinned apples baked in pies without thinking where they had come from, never doubting that they would be replaced. I trusted that we'd get where we were going and stopped asking where that was. I stopped dreaming about the gassed thousands in the museum; my lovely apple was more real, still shining greenly on the shelf in my cabin. And as I made more and more sense of the ship, and of my place in it, so my courage grew, and it made less and less sense to avoid Tom.

And so, one day, when the cinema had filled me with pink mist and kissing and brave rescues and a sense that the ship was, after all, a right and proper place in which I had a home, I went up to the sports hall while the football was going on, and I waited, my heart pounding. The outer doors stood wide open but the inner ones were shut. I heard people running and laughing; I heard Tom's voice raised above the others, shouting instructions, and I heard a long whistle blast that meant the game was over. Then the inner door slid open and out they came – adults, which surprised me. I hadn't realised that the grownups were learning too. Finn and Luke and Gabriel, Helen, Jamila who had lost her home in the Indian floods, Ingrid who had lost hers in the Dutch ones. They all looked at me and smiled as they passed, and I felt that they knew something I did not, and that they had known it for a long time, and that they would be glad to see me learn it too. My father passed at that moment, flushed with victory.

126

'Come for the football?' he said, raising his eyebrows. He kissed me, and although I smiled for him, I waited until he'd gone before I went to the door. It wasn't his kisses I wanted anymore. I stood and watched Tom stacking coloured cones and carrying them to a cupboard. *Hello*, I said in my head, and the very thought of speaking made me blush. What could I say? *You shouldn't have thrown away the mast, but I wanted to be your friend.* And yet I wanted to talk to him. *What's the worst-case scenario?* my mother used to say when I wanted to go out on my own, or walk through the park. In those days, the worst-case scenario was being attacked, killed, catching a fatal disease, and ending up dead. It was her way of saying no. Now, the worst that could happen would be that he laughed at me, or ran away, or never spoke to me again, and suddenly these possibilities seemed like a death in themselves. I turned to leave, but my hard-soled red shoes clicked on the walkway and he looked up. And there it was: hope and apprehension and joy, all shining through those green eyes as he saw me, and I knew that I was welcome.

'Lalla,' he said, dropping the cones and running towards me. 'I knew you'd come. I knew you would.'

And something about his certainty made me almost wish I hadn't. Almost, but not quite.

'You could have come to find me,' I said.

'You kept running away,' he replied, and his face was so close to mine that I felt his breath on my nose, and I saw that when he smiled, his left eye creased up more than his right eye. And suddenly, I stopped wanting to turn the ship around. The tips of his ears went red and little fires started under my skin all over me. 'And I did try,' he said. The fabric of his shirt brushed the hairs on my arms, and they stood up as I shivered. 'I brought you the apple.'

'You gave me the apple?' I asked. 'That was you? Why?'

'I wanted to give you something.'

'So why did you just leave it by the door? Why didn't you give it to me yourself?'

'I didn't know what to say. I only knew what I felt.'

We stood staring at each other and my heart started to beat more loudly. 'Would you like to come to the cinema with me?' I asked at last, and my voice was far too loud in the echoing space. He would laugh at me now, I knew it, and I wished I hadn't come.

But he didn't laugh. 'I've just got to tidy up here,' he said.

'I'll help.'

'You don't have to.'

But it didn't take much to tidy up. A few black and white balls put into a cupboard, the stacked-up coloured cones put with them and it was done. I couldn't help contrasting it with the work of the laundry; I had ironed seventy-five sheets that day and my arms were still aching. I told myself that this was why I was trembling when he went to the doors; I imagined him shutting them and leaving the ship outside so he could kiss me, here, in the hall where he played his games. But he went out. He doesn't want to kiss me, I thought, blood rushing to my face in shame.

He beckoned me out onto the deck, then slid the inner door shut behind us, and pressed a button in the wall. The main doors began to close. I had not expected them to be so thick, or to move so slowly. 'They're hermetically sealed,' Tom explained, watching my face. 'They have to be left open when we're playing.'

'Why?'

'So that we get enough air. You use more oxygen when you're exercising. If these doors were shut we'd all suffocate inside.'

We walked together down the stairs to the main deck. Where had he found an apple? Were there more?

It had been my father's suggestion that the people of the ship should watch films together at the cinema instead of alone on our screens, and so Tom and I were not alone when we settled down on the velvet seats. But I didn't see who the others were. Everything I had learned at the cinema seemed to be concentrated on Tom's hand, his fingers curled softly around the armrest between us. Would he take mine? Was I going mad, to think that he might like me? That he went to sleep thinking of our fingers touching at the bulletin? There were thirty-seven marks on my cabin wall. Thirty-seven wasted days.

He drew breath, then leaned close to me and said quietly, 'Lalla, I remember the first day I saw you, hiding behind the door of your father's house when I came for interview. When Michael was talking to me, all I could think of was you and the fact that, if he chose me, I would get to see you every day for the rest of my life.'

I looked at my hand, now held between both of his, and tried to remember to breathe. His words were hot against my ear. I turned and pressed my lips to his, and felt myself get smaller and smaller at the centre of the picture, as the camera pulled away and our kiss became the centre of the cinema, the ship, the sea itself. And then, with our hands locked tightly together, I think we watched a film. I don't remember. All I remember is my hand in his, the warmth of his skin, the feeling of flesh against flesh and the thought that here, surely, I had found whatever it was I'd been looking for.

'Sit with me at dinner?' he said. I nodded, disappointed. Not because he'd asked me to sit with him – where else would I want to sit, now? But I had sat at dinner a thousand times. My heart was out of control, my body and my blood crying out for more – I did not know what of, but I knew I would not find it in Gerhard's cooking, in the neat place settings of Emily's dining room, in my father's after-dinner speeches.

'What's the matter?' Tom asked.

'I don't know,' I said, on the verge of tears. The cinema had emptied. He lifted his hand to my face and stroked his finger-tips along my cheekbone, and although I felt his touch there, it was my palms that burned, my diaphragm that suddenly melted away so that my insides seemed to shift. It was impossible that anyone else had ever felt this way – it was so new, so unexpected. So absolute. It felt like my assertion of my self in this world of my father's creation.

'Do you know?' I managed to whisper, although my breath was coming short, 'do you know where we're going?'

He bent his head to hear me; he touched his lips to where his fingers had been, then breathed, 'I think we've arrived.'

ELEVEN

I want to go back ❧ *the fourth deck and what I
found there* ❧ *Tom and the skylight*

We had not arrived at any geographical place – there was no
quay, no harbour to receive us. But I had certainly arrived somewhere new. I sat with Tom at breakfast; I met him at lunch,
and we always sat together for dinner. I moved away from my
father's table, and people arrived earlier and earlier every day in
an effort to be the one who took my old seat next to him. We
both had our work, but I could usually plan my route through
the ship with the clean laundry so that I saw him in the sports
hall at least once during the day. He was patient with the children and the grown-ups who were only just learning. But with
those who had played before, he was challenging, tough, setting
them ever harder goals until they all stopped, panting, with their
hands on their knees and their sweat dripping onto the sports
hall floor. They looked up at each other, grinning, and I was
envious of their connection. After dinner, and before the goodnight meetings, we went to the cinema, or walked on the deck,
and although I hadn't exactly forgotten about the people we had
left behind, they became less and less important. When Tom
held my hand, I didn't want to say anything or do anything that
might make him let go.

I could have learned football with him, but the sports hall was his territory, just as the laundry was mine. If he had come to help me fold sheets, the sheets would never have been folded. And if we'd been together in the sports hall, the football would have been left rolling around like tumbleweed. We needed to be in the same space, because when we weren't, there was a cold gap. But when we were, everything was complete, and the laundry and the football weren't important. There were thirty-eight, thirty-nine, forty marks on the wall in my cabin. Time was stretching in our minds, whole lifetimes passing in single moments. An age. A few weeks. Forty days. What did it matter anymore? We sat quietly in the goodnight meetings, and he stroked the back of my hand with his thumb. I was no longer alone; I had a friend, a friend who would listen. A friend the world felt cold without.

'Don't you think,' I would say sometimes, 'don't you think we should go back?'

And he would say, 'I'll come with you, wherever you want to go.'

And the thought that I had an ally made it harder and harder to remember why I wanted to go. I knew I was right, and yet when I tried to explain, the reason bobbed away, like the old days with my mother, when we tried to catch the soap in the bath. And instead of trying to catch it, I would ask again, 'Would you really come with me?' and he would say, 'Of course. If it's honestly what you want.'

But my thoughts about London were changing. Whereas before, I saw the homeless gratefully receiving the food we gave out, now I remembered the mob on the quay and thought of what would have happened to us if we had not given them our cards. I had been so sure; now I had an uneasy feeling I could not explain, like trying to sleep on my bunk when the sea was rough. I had a friend. Was London what I really wanted now?

'You're kind,' Tom said. 'But don't forget to be kind to the people here, too. What would little Gabriel do back in London?'

'I don't know,' I said, and it was a relief to let go of something so heavy, that I had been carrying all alone. 'It's not so much that I want to go. But I think we should.'

'Why don't you talk to Michael?'

'I barely see him. He keeps saying that the ship was created for me, but if that's true, why won't he turn it around when I want to?' I was starting to cry. 'He's all I've got left and I don't even see him anymore.'

Tom took my hand and said, 'He loves you, Lalla, more than anything in the world. Just look around you, and you'll see how much. And don't forget that you've got me.' Tom hesitated, then added, 'Your mother, too.'

I pulled my sleeve over my hand and wiped my eyes. 'I know she's gone,' I said. 'But I can't feel her anymore. I don't know what she would say. What she would want me to do. It's like I walk the ship, and she's nowhere. I had one single thing of hers – a dress – and it's gone. Sometimes I close my eyes and I can't even remember what she looked like.'

He held my hand in silence for a moment, then said, 'Can I show you something? Something that might help?'

'Where?'

'Follow me.'

I had not been up the infirmary staircase since my mother died. It was near my cabin and I'd never been aware of anyone using it. It was a silent place, half-forgotten, the way we do forget things we no longer need. But when Tom and I got there, we saw Helen with Gabriel, tucked behind the staircase as though they were trying to hide. Tom squeezed my hand and we stepped as silently as we could.

They were busy with something; at least, Helen was. She was holding Gabriel on her lap and he was fidgeting. In front of them, they had a thick book. Not a screen, but a book, like the manifest, only smaller. When they turned the pages, I could see that they were stiff and thick. There were photographs taped to them, photographs of a man.

'Can you see his eyes?' Helen was saying. 'They're just like yours. Look.' She held up a little mirror, and Gabriel squinted into it. Helen held him more tightly. 'He loved us. He helped me to make you, and he was there when you were born.'

'I've seen them before,' Gabriel said, wriggling away. 'Can't we go swimming? You said Michael was my father now. You said Daniel could be my brother. I want Daniel to be my brother.'

My shoe caught the walkway. Helen jumped to her feet and put the book behind her back. As I got closer, I saw that she was trembling. She did not say hello.

'What are you doing?' I asked.

'We're looking at my father.'

Helen bit her lip and closed her eyes, and Gabriel looked at her with a concerned expression. 'Have I been naughty?' he asked. 'Am I in trouble?'

'Oh, no, darling,' Helen said, trying to kiss him. 'No. Not you. Never you.' But Gabriel shrank from her, and Tom knelt down and put his hands on Gabriel's shoulders.

'Want to play football later?' he asked. Gabriel nodded, his furrowed little face smooth again. 'Remember,' Tom continued, 'remember that Michael gave you the football? Hey? And the sports hall. And the food that gives us the energy to play. All right?' Gabriel nodded, and Tom ruffled his hair. Helen tucked the book into the gap between the staircase and the wall. I wondered how long she had been keeping it there.

'Why don't you keep it in your cabin?' I asked. But even as I asked the question, I realised what the answer was. I was in and out of the cabins all the time, delivering the laundry. She didn't trust me.

'What was that all about?' I said as they left.

Tom stared after Helen. 'She shouldn't be showing Gabriel

photographs. It's not on, and she knows it. Michael told us to let our missing go.' I shrugged. I couldn't see the harm in a few old photographs, but if there wasn't any harm, why had Helen been hiding? And if Helen was hiding one thing, maybe she was hiding more. If I could get her to trust me, maybe she would tell me where we were going. If she knew. Then Tom said, 'Race you, Lalla,' and started running up the stairs.

'Where to?' I called after him.

'Fourth deck,' he shouted. He ran, and I ran and Gabriel and Helen and photographs and London, even the dead in the museum, fluttered away in my wake and the staircase rang like bells. Like wedding bells, from the time before.

He got there first; I was panting by the time I caught up.

'Look,' he said, pushing open the door onto a dark corridor, lined with doors on either side. The corridor was illuminated with frosted glass circles shining white in the ceiling, shedding regular pools of soft light on the floor. I slipped my hand into his and he squeezed it, and together we stepped from pool of light to pool of light, looking at one another with wide eyes in the dark places in between. Then he put his hands on my shoulders, and I turned to him, and he bent down and kissed me.

My mother told me that all life was contained in the display cases of the British Museum. But now I realised that she had been wrong. What was happening to me now was not about cold stone and history. This was warm and glorious and alive. So alive. Every vital sign – blood flow, beating heart, breathing, sensation – was here, doubled because there were two of us, then trebled, quadrupled, because it felt so good. His breath was so hot, and came so fast. I pressed myself against him and lay my hands flat against his back, pulling him in closer. His body was firm beneath his shirt; I wanted to take the shirt from him and feel his skin, touch it all at once. This wasn't about tomorrow or yesterday. It was about now, this moment, this glorious moment of knowing that Tom liked me as much as I liked him, of my flesh against his.

And then he pulled away. 'I'm sorry,' he said. 'I didn't mean – this isn't why I brought you here.'

'But . . .' I began, then stopped. If he wanted to stop, I wasn't going to tell him that I didn't. I turned back to the staircase and smoothed my dress. My hair was pulled back into an elastic band; I took it out, wishing I had a hairbrush. I gathered it all back up and secured the band tightly, to prove I didn't care, and walked back the way we had come.

'Don't go,' he said.

I didn't want to go, but I didn't want him to think I wanted to stay. I turned aside and pushed open one of the doors, and what I saw made me forget I was annoyed. The room was full of great rolls of carpet, propped against each other like the columns of the Parthenon just before the last pieces fell. Behind the next door was a room of tins of paint and varnish. Brushes. Sandpaper. Tools in boxes. Another room, larger this time, full of crockery – endless duplicates of the plates and dishes we used at every meal. I picked up a plate and held it up, white and whole, like a full moon. 'What's all this for?' I asked.

Tom was following me. 'It's amazing, isn't it?' he said. 'This is what I wanted to show you. And there's more.'

'More?'

He tugged at my elbow, but I was still holding the plate. 'It's all white,' I said.

'What?'

'The plates and everything. They're all white.'

'What's the matter with that?' he asked. He had found a new supply of energy from somewhere and was striding towards the next door.

I stayed where I was. I was still staring at the white plate when he came back. 'What are you doing?' he asked. 'Come on.'

I looked up at him. 'Do any of the plates have pictures on them?'

'I don't think so. They're all the same. Isn't that the point? Does it matter?'

But it did matter. Here on the fourth deck, away from the activity of the galleries and the ballroom and the dining room and the laundry and the cinema, there was silence, and in the silence, my childhood came back to me. I looked at Tom, and he stopped fidgeting and looked back at me. 'When I was little,' I said into the stillness, 'I had a small plate with a picture of lots of little rabbits picking red and yellow apples on it. I loved that plate. And then one day it broke. It must have had a crack we'd never noticed or something, because it just fell apart in my mother's hands. I was really upset. I wouldn't eat from any other plate. My parents were really worried.' I remembered my mother and father arguing about it over my head. *I'll find another one, just the same,* my father declared. And my mother. *Don't be ridiculous, Michael. We've got plates. She's got to learn.*

'What happened?'

'I got hungry, I suppose. I don't remember. I just wish . . .'

'What?'

'I wish I'd known I was eating from that plate for the last time.'

I looked at the storeroom, at the plates the same as all the other plates, the cups, the saucers, the bowls, all the same as each other. Gabriel would never stare at the details of a favourite plate, fascinated by tiny paws closed round an apple. Gabriel would never look at the coloured ribbons on the dresses, the many shades of green on the trees, and wonder whether rabbits really did wear clothes and how they cooked the pies with which the checked cloth in the foreground was spread. Our apple pies came ready-made. I wondered whether Helen had thought of this, and whether it would matter to her if I pointed it out.

Tom took my hand and led me into the next room. It was full of deck shoes, the entire population of the world reduced to twenty-three sizes. Fabric uppers, man-made soles, it said inside every single shoe. Most people were wearing them now. But I still clung to the shoes I had worn on land – dark red, hard leather, very scratched, with a bar across and a little silver buckle. I slipped sometimes on the walkways, and everyone could hear me coming, but I didn't want to let them go. Part of me felt that if I were to surrender my red leather shoes and start wearing the blue canvas deck shoes with the white soles and the blue stripe and fabric uppers and man-made soles, I would forget about my life on land entirely. I would forget my mother anxiously buckling the bar across my foot, making me stand straight and walk to and fro across the drawing room while she tried to tell whether they were rubbing my heels. And my father laughing and saying, *Anna, she's got shoes, and that puts her ahead of most of the population these days.*

Where did you get them from, Michael?

It doesn't matter. The point is that she's got them.

(To me) *Do they fit?* (To my father) *Where, Michael? Who wore them last?* (To me) *Do you like them?* (To my father) *Because if they used to belong to someone else, I want to know who, and exactly how you came to have them.*

I would wear them until they fell apart.

But Tom had dropped my hand and was already in the next room.

I followed him. My reverie was giving way to panic; there was too much here I did not understand. I pushed past him, into a room the size of the ballroom, with rails suspended from the ceiling, rows and rows of them, hung with clear plastic envelopes the length of a man, swollen with colours. Each one bore a name, marked on the plastic in heavy black letters. The first six were marked for Diana Aabri. She had dark eyes; I had never yet seen her smile. Then two for Solomon Asprey, the man who'd eaten my dinner when I could not. I wondered whether he had missed me at the dinner table once I'd started sitting with Tom. Five for Garth Britten, who sat on the bench to the left of the stairs down to the galley staring out to sea for so many hours of every day that other people simply never sat there, even when Garth himself was somewhere else. I pushed through to more distant rails. Here were eight for Roger Spencer, the doctor. People I saw every day, lined up in vacuum packs of clothes, arranged in alphabetical order.

Suddenly it struck me. My mother would be here. Was this why Tom had brought me here? I walked through the stiff, heavy packages, pushing them aside as I forced a path between the rows searching for her.

'Lalla,' Tom called behind me. 'Lalla?'

Here was Hiro Oka. Here was Harry Oz. Here was Lalage Paul, then Michael Paul, then Mercy Perkin. Frantically I went back on myself. There was no Anna Paul. Nothing stood between Harry and me, and for the first time since my mother's death, I felt the chill wind of complete exposure. Buffered on both sides by my parents, I had grown up immune from the cruelties of the alphabet. When we were required to present ourselves for bio-metric re-registration, to get new food purchase authorisations, or renew our permit to remain in the flat we owned, I would be sheltered between my mother before me and my father behind me. My mother would entrust my card to me for the few moments it took to present it to the officials, but she and my father were there all the while, anchoring me on either side, so my little foray to the tiny opening in the glassed-off window was nothing more than the slight stretching of an elastic band.

And now she was gone. Hiro Oka, Harry Oz, Lalage Paul, Michael Paul, Mercy Perkin. And that was all.

I sat on the hard floor and closed my eyes. The place smelled of new plastic, chemical and unyielding. Once, there must have been a package in my mother's name. At some point since her death, someone had taken it and put it . . . where? The ship was finite. There were only so many places it could be. But if it was finite, it was also vast, so vast that I could well spend my life searching for it. For them – for if there were eleven in my name and five in my father's, how many would there have been for my mother? *There are clothes, you know,* my father had said before the funeral. *If you wanted to wear something else.* And here they were. Clothes. Clothes for everyone, for a lifetime.

'Lalla.' Tom was coming closer, pushing the packages aside.

What if my mother had not died? Would I have come to the fourth deck with Tom? Would I have kissed him? What if I had stayed downstairs? Would I feel so restless, so dissatisfied? I had never asked *what if?* before. My father had asked the *what ifs* for everyone, so that no one else would have to.

What if I am attacked when I go outside?

What if I become ill?

What if I have nothing to feed my child?

I had just taken, taken, taken. My questions had not been *what ifs* but simply *whats.*

What am I doing here?

What is my father?

What is going to happen to us all in the end?

I became methodical. I started at the beginning and I walked the rows. I looked at every name on every package. I thought she might have been filed out of order, that her clothes might have been moved rather than taken away. When the names ran out, the packages carried on; the remaining labels bore the names, not of people, but of ceremonies. Birth. Naming. Coming of age. Funeral. And at every turn, Tom pursued me, calling my name.

I reached the last rail, and when I found the wall behind the plastic packages, I saw twelve flat boxes, all identical, each bearing a small label printed with a black and white picture of a baby's cot.

And that was where Tom found me.

'You see?' he said, coming up behind me.

'See what?'

'All this. Everything on the fourth deck. This is just the start. This is what I wanted to show you.'

'Why? Because you thought my mother would be here?'

Tom looked startled. 'Your mother's dead, Lalla. Anna's dead. We gave her to the sea, remember?'

'But is that all? She's dead, and she vanishes without trace? Gone? Look,' I said, pushing back through the clothes, 'she should be here. It's all alphabetical. She should be just here.'

'It's all right, Lalla,' he said, putting his hands on my shoulders. He began to stroke my collarbones with his thumbs. 'Everything we'll ever need is here. And we've got each other. Haven't we?'

Everything, he said. This was it. I thought of London, of the cracks in the walls, the yellowing paint in our flat, cement wearing away between the bricks, so that the bricks themselves could be prised out and taken away. Of rust, and buildings falling. Everywhere bearing the marks and scars of the passing of time. *That house had a balcony once, with plants in pots.* Or, *That was when we had the blue plates with white flowers, remember?* Or things so obvious that there was no point in speaking, such as the fact that the house on the corner would fall if people kept chiselling out the bricks and stealing them. Tom's hands were on my neck, his fingers tracing the contours of my chin, my lips, my cheekbones.

Here on the ship, yellowing paint would be covered with new paint. Rust would be sandpapered into oblivion. A plate broken? Here was the means to replace it – not only to replace it, but to create the impression that the breakage had never happened. I thought of Tom wiping the walls the day we'd met, and realised how blind I had been.

'Get me out of here,' I said to Tom, my skin flaming trails where he'd touched me. I ran away from him, pushing past the fifteen million plastic bags to the corridor, looking for a way out. But there was only the corridor, with its round skylights and the storerooms leading from it. I walked its length, searching for ladders or hatches. I remembered how the ship had appeared to me on that first day, the day we came on board, looming over the quay like an old-fashioned wedding cake. Was I walking the top tier now? The small one. The one that people once put away in a box until their first child was born. And even as I was struck at the strangeness of the whole idea of baking an enormous cake and keeping bits of it, and of covering it in sugar and stuff that looked like embroidery, and wondering what that had to do with marrying someone, and what indeed marriage was and why, I suddenly knew that one of these rooms held a white dress and a plastic figurine of a man and a woman. I knew that, if I searched through all the boxes, I would find garlands of artificial flowers and bolts and bolts of white fabric; I'd find green silk leaves wired into long wreaths; I'd find dresses in the same colours as the little cakes we ate after dinner. Pink. Lemon yellow. Sky blue. Lilac.

I didn't bother to look. I didn't need to. I saw my father, his hands tight upon the ropes by which he drove his people. And at the ends of those ropes, I saw, not Emily and Patience and Gerhard and Helen and Daniel and Gabriel, but the things we had left in the broken world. Weddings and funerals and childbirth and books and music. Birthdays and dancing and football and graduations and qualifications. Because all these were milestones that belonged in the place behind us. Not only behind us in space, but behind us in time. My father had reached back, back, past the squatters in the British Museum, past the thefts from the display cases, past the oil drums on the streets and the rats and the wild dogs and children and market raids, and pulled things onto the ship from the life that had been his before the crash. We were not creating, we were simply existing, building lives upon the flotsam and jetsam of something that had gone. We were not finding new ways to live. We were living in accordance with some ideal of a former age, which we saw in films, read of on our screens, but no longer knew or understood.

I pushed open door after door, door after door, and in every room, there was nothing but boxes and smooth ceilings. No trap doors, no ladders, no way up. The ship was a tin can, hermetically sealed to preserve us all. The corridor went on and on, unravelling before me until I had indeed lost all sense of time. Tom followed me, looking worried. His lips were moving but I paid no attention to what he said. I needed to get out, not onto the deck but out, right out, to where there was air and sky and nothing surrounding me. My body was crying out against this sterile safety. I was hungry for danger and dizziness. I wanted mess and sensation; I bit my lip so hard I tasted blood.

I looked again at the fourth deck, so featureless that I felt utterly lost. I knew that, if we did not go to dinner when the gong rang, my father would come looking, and that, were we to hide, he would find us. He would find us without effort, just as Gerhard's practised hands automatically fell upon the very thing he needed in the kitchen. My father had created this place. He had conceived it, filled it, ordered it. He knew where everything lay; he knew what everything was, and if I were to disappear myself within his provisioning for the future, he would see what had been disturbed, and where lay the irregularity of me in hiding. He would see it as surely as I would know if anyone had interfered with the marks in my cabin, or with the things I had collected for my museum.

'Let's go back downstairs now,' Tom said nervously. 'I just

wanted to show you, that's all. To stop you from worrying.' I flapped a hand at him to stop him talking and looked up at the skylights. The glass circles had shone white when we had arrived; now they were a yellow gold. This meant that the circles, which I had assumed were electric lights, were actually frosted windows. Where there were windows, there was access to the outside. I thought, if I can get up there, I could prise away a pane, crawl out, even climb up the outside of the ship to the top if I had to. The golden light meant that the sun was setting, and soon it would be dark.

I looked into Tom's anxious green eyes. 'Pile up some boxes and take off one of those skylights,' I said.

'But why?' I was already hauling boxes. 'Lalla, there's no need for this. Michael wouldn't like it. Anyway, there's no time. Look, the light is almost gone. We'll miss dinner.'

'I have to get out, now and now and now. I can't breathe.'

'If you couldn't breathe, you would be dead.'

'I am dead,' I said. 'We're all dead.'

My breath came in short, shallow sobs and my head was spinning. I wondered how the wall had fallen, then realised I was lying on the floor. My lungs contracted; hot metal bars snapped around them and gripped so tightly that I gave up trying to draw in air. And then I felt a sting on my cheek, as sharp and painful as if someone had slapped me. My physical body registered its living presence in pain, and I heard my mother's voice. *Stop this at once, Lalage. If I had wanted drama, I would have gone to the theatre. You are perfectly alive. You are also about to faint. Do think things through.*

I shuffled to the wall and pressed my back against it, hard, so that the metal bars gave slightly and I could force air into my lungs. *And again, Lalage. And again.* The voice grew fainter, and was replaced by Tom's anxious fussing. 'Are you all right, Lalla? Lalla?'

'I am not dead,' I said, and the echoing of my voice down the corridor told me I had spoken out loud.

'No,' said Tom, nodding eagerly. 'No, you're not. Let's go down. I'll help you. We could walk on deck if you want air.'

I stumbled to my feet; my lungs were released, and my mind began to clear. I went over to him and stood squarely in front of him. All the hand-holding and the heart-pounding and the watching him in the sports hall came together in the now. I reached for his hand, and he pulled me up, and I stood so close to him I could feel his breath on my cheek. And then I kissed him, and as I kissed him, he put his arms around me, and he ran his hands down my arms and over my back and I felt my blood rising to meet his hands wherever they touched me. 'No,' I said as he began to tug at my dress.

'But I thought . . .'

'Not here. Up there.' I pointed up at the skylight. I could see screws holding it up. 'Find a screwdriver.'

'But Lalla . . .'

I started to climb onto the boxes I'd piled up. 'Find a screwdriver or go to dinner, Tom.' I looked down and saw concern mixed with the desire in his green eyes.

'What if you fall?' he said. But I was determined and excited and the danger was all part of it; if I fell off the boxes and hurt myself, I'd know I was alive. And if I got into the open and fell into the sea, maybe I'd find my mother there. I wanted to pull Tom through with me into the open air, and then I wanted to kiss him so hard that I could feel his teeth; I wanted him to crush the breath from my body. I wanted us to cast off all the provision my father had made and set each other alight under the unconstricting sky. I watched Tom, my father pulling him one way, me pulling him the other. The golden light made a circle around me. It would be the difference between learning something at the museum and learning it in the research room.

'You look like an angel,' he said.

'I'm not an angel,' I said grimly. And then, suddenly, he made up his mind. He pulled boxes together. He fetched two screwdrivers. He climbed up beside me. And together, balanced precariously on our future lives, we took the twelve screws from the skylight and worked on its grey metal rim, pulling on it, using the screwdrivers as levers, until it surrendered with a screech and a crunch, showering us in plaster dust and debris.

'I can get through there,' I said, coughing. 'I'm sure I can.' I reached through with my hands; he pushed me, grunting with effort, his hands on my bottom while I scrabbled for his shoulders with my feet. I pushed against him, hard, and as I pulled myself up to my waist and hung on my forearms, I heard a crash below me and Tom's voice crying out in surprise and then, with a final effort that tore my dress and scraped the skin from my knees, I was standing on the top of the world.

'Are you all right?' I called, but I didn't really care. I could not tear my eyes away from the last sliver of the setting sun, laying out a pathway of fire across the sea. And above and behind and all around me stretched the sky. I closed my eyes and reached my arms up as high as I could, standing on my toes and feeling my muscles cry out in celebration of their freedom. And then Tom's head appeared at my feet, covered in dust, a piece of ceiling stuck in his hair, and I laughed.

'The gong will have gone,' he complained, and as he wriggled his awkward way through the skylight, fighting off debris and muttering about madness, he became mine. Not a boy with green eyes, but a friend, an intimate. Someone I could talk to, for whom I could be Lalla. Not my father's daughter, but a young woman all her own.

'Come here,' I told him. I beat the dust from his thick blue shirt. I ran my fingers through his hair and threw the piece of ceiling towards the sunset. I pulled him towards me and pressed my lips against his, and then I pressed my body against him, feeling the buttons of his shirt marking circles on my chest and my stomach, and the flap of his shirt pocket pressing a line against my breast. And there was fire, spreading from my nipples to the palms of my hands, and when he stood back to take off his shirt, a cold wind spread goosebumps across my arms and my chest. 'Lalla,' he said, the gong and the ship forgotten, 'Lalla.' And he tried to put his hands under my dress, but the skirt was too long and he ended up tangled in crumpled cotton. I laughed, but he seemed annoyed, and so before he could change his mind, I pulled my dress over my head. When he undid his jeans, I could see that his hands were shaking. I unbuttoned his shirt, and he took it off and spread it out so that I could lie on it.

He lay on top of me, and all the breath was squeezed from my body, and he was pushing against me and whispering, 'Does that hurt?' And it did, but it was pain I wanted, the pain of something opening and expanding and reaching up to the stars that were appearing overhead, and suddenly he cried out, his back arched, his body tensed. And then he simply lay, his body limp against mine, his head on my shoulder, and I thought, whatever it is, we have just done it, and wondered whether it would always hurt like that. Under his shirt, the top deck was cold metal, and it began to bite through the fabric as night fell. The hairs on my arms and legs stood up and I shivered, trying to make sense of what had just happened. Was this rebellion or just a way of catching pneumonia? I wondered if I was bleeding; certainly I was sore. What was I now? A girl? A woman? Tom was staring out, out over the dark sea; I put my hand on his arm and he came back from wherever his thoughts had taken him.

'I'm cold,' I said, and he jumped up and pulled on his jeans, and then he wriggled through the skylight and came back with blankets. I put my dress back on, and he tucked one blanket around my shoulders and another around his, and we sat a little way apart from each other. All the diamonds the world had left had been ground like flour and spilt across the sky; if I reached up, I could write my name in them. I remembered searching for a blanket to cover my father once, and a button that had fallen from a coat.

'What do you think would happen if we stayed up here all night?' I asked.

I waited for him to say, *I don't think Michael would like it*, and braced myself to send him away. But he didn't. 'We'd get hungry,' he said.

'There'll be breakfast.'

'I can wait till breakfast.'

I moved closer to him, and we wrapped both the blankets around both of us. It was warmer that way. He stroked my hair, and I rested my head on his shoulder, and we fell asleep. As I drifted off, I heard Helen saying, 'It's hardly subversion, is it?' But this was subversion. I had found a place of my own, a way to get to it, a way of being with someone way beyond my father's control. *There's a conversation we'll need to have when the time comes*, my mother had said the first time I bled, but the time had never come. Now I had grabbed it and dragged it to me. It was mine now. My time. I had found my freedom with a pair of green eyes. Perhaps it wouldn't always hurt – and oh, the wanting. The wanting had been sweet.

When we woke up, the sun was rising. It was rising in front of us, exactly where the path of fire had been the night before. We put the blankets back into their plastic wrapping, then squeezed through the skylight. We didn't replace all the screws, just six of them, enough to hold the skylight in place, and we put all the boxes back. I put the spare screws in the pocket of my dress, where once I had kept my card. There were only five; I could not find the last one.

'We'll find a ladder next time,' Tom said. Only the dust on the floor and a little tiny crack in the glass of the skylight showed that we'd been there. I liked looking at that dust. The ship was so clean. But dirt told stories, too. I liked that I could smell Tom on my skin as we climbed back down to the main deck, and that the smell was not of soap, but of sour milk and the warmth of the iron.

We said goodbye by the infirmary stairs. And as I walked to my cabin, I held the precious secret of my freedom inside myself. Where there had been only me, now there was me and Tom. And the sunrise showed that, wherever we were going, we were on our way. We had provisions enough to last until we arrived, and to give us a good start when we got there. Tom was happy. I could be happy, too.

The spare screws were for my museum. I put them in the jewellery box with the button. The apple was there too, still shining as brightly as the day Tom had left it for me. It showed no signs of withering, and I was glad. We were on our way. My mother was dead, but I was no longer travelling alone.

TWELVE

My secret ❀ *shell eggs* ❀ *the mystery of the
missing sunset*

There is nothing like having a secret to make you see secrets in others. As I walked to the dining room – I was extremely hungry by this time – I saw people talking in corners, walking to breakfast tables together, or slipping away from them, or catching other people's eyes and then smiling and looking away, in a way I had never noticed before. I remembered Tom pushing himself inside me and caught my breath. A trickle of warm fluid oozed from me and dripped down the inside of my thigh. I could feel a new story traced all over my body; surely these people could see it? Did everyone have a secret? What other thoughts were going on in all these people around me? For a moment I felt almost sorry for my father, with all this subversion going on under his nose. But there he was, eating an omelette and smiling, and my pity was drowned out by elation when I met Tom's eyes across the dining room. I wondered what my father would say if he knew, and whether he was going to tell me off for missing dinner last night. But he just waved at me across the dining room. It was Emily who frowned, Emily who raised her eyebrows and pursed her lips.

But Emily I could ignore.

I took my omelette. Patience had told me that you could hold a shell egg comfortably in your hand, and I held my hand out, trying to imagine what an egg might have felt like sitting in my palm. Crack, you broke them and they flooded out. Crack. Had I broken Tom last night, or had he broken me? *You can't make an omelette without breaking eggs*, my father had said to my mother too many times for me to count. But the omelette in front of me had been made without breaking any eggs. How could it be otherwise, when there were no eggs left to break? The only eggs I'd ever known were dried. What was this place, and where were we going?

'Meet me on deck for sunset,' Tom whispered as we left the dining room, and my cheeks flamed again.

I was due in the laundry after breakfast. Patience was already there, pulling sheets out of the big machine and tumbling them into the dryer. I stuffed the machine with more sheets and set it going.

'When did you last see a real egg?' I asked.

'In my omelette this morning,' she said shortly. She was busy over a pile of sheets and didn't look at me. I fetched the basket from the chute – it was a plastic crate really, but we called it a basket – and started sorting the clothes. There was a long silence, but we often worked that way. I drifted away, thinking about Tom, the weight of his body on mine. Why had it taken me so long to go to him? Why had my parents kept me so enclosed, so safe? What else had they been keeping from me? They had kept me a child for so long. I smiled.

'So, you are enjoying yourself now?' Patience pulled out a dry sheet and flapped it straight, ready to fold for ironing. The smell of washing powder wafted over, so strong that it masked the human smells of the used clothes I was sorting. Her voice came from behind the sheet, as though she was playing ghosts.

'You found a good thing, yes, and you are your own woman now?'

I felt my face go scarlet. I took the basket of dark clothes and pushed them into another machine, hiding my face behind the door.

'You be sure you keep right. There's a right way and a wrong way. You stay right and you'll be right.'

'What do you mean?' I asked from behind the door.

'I mean it's time to stop asking about eggs, Lalla. If you going to grow up now, you need to ask better questions.'

Lalla? Patience had always called me *child* until now.

She finished folding her sheet, and I couldn't keep the machine door open for ever. I shut it and stood up, and realised that I was taller than she was. I had never noticed it before.

'Like what?' I asked.

'Like how to knit.'

'How to *knit*?'

'Or sew. How to sew would be a good question.'

'But I don't want to know how to knit. Or how to sew.'

'Then you got no right to call yourself your mamma's girl. You and me, we used to talk, Lalla, and I worried about you then, losing your mamma like that. But we here now.'

'Where are we?'

'Here. Like Michael says. Right here, exactly where we are. And this right here's where you got to start living. Your mamma didn't keep you in dresses by fretting over eggs.'

I sat on an upturned laundry basket and stared. She looked at me and I felt that she could see everything, from the redness between my breasts where Tom's stubble had scratched me, to the wet patch on my thigh, to the sweet-tasting swelling on the inside of my lip where we'd kissed too hard.

'Do you know where the ship's going, Patience?'

'What're you asking me for? I've arrived where I'm going. If you listened more to Michael and less to what voices are in your head, you'd know that. I'm not clever. I never went to a museum with my mamma. But I know that we in a good place, and that you asking the wrong questions. You want to be a woman, you got to grow up. Now. Not in a while, but now.' She paused, considering, then added, 'And go see the doctor.'

Grow up? I grew up last night, I wanted to say, and there's a pile of dust and a cracked skylight to prove it. As for the doctor, I hadn't spoken to him since the night my mother died and had no intention of doing so now. Patience turned back to her sheets and I looked at her stiff and frightened back, and I imagined myself in a film, running towards Tom as molten lava exploded around us and bits of falling building rained down, and saying, *We have to get out of here! Now!* But I was still sore and the dust in my hair was making my scalp itch. The wetness between my legs was cold now, sticky and uncomfortable. Already the monster films seemed a world away, the preoccupation of a child with nothing more important to worry about. But the thought stayed with me. We have to get out of here, now.

'I only asked about eggs,' I said at last.

Out of here to where? There were no windows in the laundry, so it was easy to imagine worlds beyond its closed walls. I imagined a house surrounded by grass, flowers growing out of the ground, a chicken laying an egg. But even before the collapse, these things had belonged to picture books, not to London, and as Patience would not talk, my imaginings were colourless. I found my mind drifting to Tom and his hands and the top of the world, a dream of freedom I had touched for myself. We worked the rest of the day in silence. I didn't bother with lunch and by the time I had taken the clean sheets to Leyton, who coordinated the making of the beds, I was exhausted.

The light was goldening through the windows. It was sunset time; I wanted to stand with Tom and see the fire on the water and pretend we were on top of the ship. Knitting, I thought. Sewing. Alice and her embroidery hoop. Rows upon rows of clothes in plastic bags, so many for each person, but none for my mother, who was dead. Twelve flat boxes with babies' cots printed on them. A sprinkling of plaster dust. A crack. I pushed open the doors and stepped onto the deck, mindful that the golden light was already fading. There was a strange heaviness in the outside air, and it was hot; I found that I was sweating just walking along the deck.

Under the darkening sky, a group of people walked past me towards the dining room. The gong rang out and I moved with them. I had come to watch the sunset, but where was the sun?

'Coming to dinner, Lalla? Hasn't it turned hot?' It was Mercy, a woman I'd noticed because she looked about the same age as my mother, although Mercy's hair was fair rather than dark and I'd never seen her pink, round face frown. Mercy never disagreed with anyone. She was smiling now. 'Or is there somewhere you would rather be?'

'I missed the sunset,' I said, too distracted to notice that I was being teased.

'Too busy in the laundry?'

'No. I was here, but . . .' *But the sun wasn't.*

Mercy patted my shoulder kindly, as though I'd turned up for breakfast at the wrong end of the day and was asking for a croissant. I could feel her hand damp through my dress and dodged away. 'You need to go to where the sun is if you want to watch it set.'

'But it should have set here. On this side.'

She looked at me strangely. 'It'll be this deck again,' she said comfortingly. 'Soon. Maybe even tomorrow.'

'How do you know?'

She gazed at me with radiant confidence, tempered with just a little pity, and shook her head. Mercy, I wanted to say, Mercy, there are five packages hanging in a storeroom on the fourth deck with your name on them.

'You do a lovely job in the laundry, Lalla. My clothes always feel like new.' She looked almost shy as she offered her compliment, and whereas before I was sure she was approaching fifty, now she could have been forty, or thirty, or even younger. Too young to be my mother. I wondered how I could ever have seen anything in common between them.

'What if they wear out before we arrive?' I said suddenly. She looked startled, but I didn't stop. I was hot and troubled, and the heavy air was hard to breathe.

'What do you mean?' she said. 'I've got more clothes in my cabin, more than I've ever had before.'

'But they'll wear out too.'

'I'm going to learn to sew,' she said eagerly. I rolled my eyes in exasperation, but before I could speak she went on. 'And if the knees of my trousers tear, I'll ask Alice to embroider a square for me and she'll sew it over the hole and the trousers will be even better than they are now.'

She looked at me. 'Lalla,' she said more gently as she pushed open the dining room doors, letting out a blessed draught of cooled air, 'there's no need to be angry. Michael has thought of these things. Just trust, and everything will work out.'

'But,' I began, but Mercy had already left me then and gone to her table. Finn pulled her chair out for her and I looked around me, my damp blouse cooling against my back. Five bags for Mercy. Eleven for me. Three for Finn. Ten for Tom. And I knew that Mercy was right. Of course my father had thought of these things. There were packages of clothes for everyone, the more packages the younger you were.

But why so many? Were there no clothes where we were going?

'Where were you at sunset?' Tom asked, bringing me a plate of quiche and peas. 'I waited.'

'How did you know where to go?'

'Michael told me.'

Think, Lalla, think. Look around you. What can you see? What does it tell you?

We finished our quiche and peas and now I saw four hundred and ninety-eight people eating chocolate tart and cream. I knew their names, I knew most of their stories, but I could not see one single person of whom I could say, *You. I trust you to tell me the truth.* Even Tom didn't seem to have any questions.

I pushed my chocolate tart away, and one of the children grabbed it. I wasn't hungry anymore. I wanted to run up to the fourth deck and look again, to tear open one of the packages and check inside. I was sixteen. Maybe I would live to be sixty, or seventy. That meant one package every four or five years. And the sun. I had watched the sun rise that morning in the same place as it had set the night before. And I had been on the wrong deck to see the sunset; this had amused Mercy and annoyed Tom. We were clearly heading somewhere. But where? Where was this place to which we were travelling, that was so far away, yet made everyone so happy? Why would no one tell me? The behaviour of the sun was as real as the little golden chariot drawn by the little golden horse in the British Museum, even if it had been stolen.

Then I saw Helen. Gabriel sat next to her. Helen alone had not accepted my father's offer to be a father to all the children; she had hidden away with Gabriel to show him all she had to show of his real father. I could not articulate why, but I felt that her determination had something in common with the questions I was framing so badly. *Look, Lalla. Look carefully, because that's how you learn.*

'I need to talk to Helen,' I said.

'Be careful, then,' Tom replied, making little ravines in his chocolate tart and filling them with cream. As I waited for everyone on our table to finish, I saw Roger beckoning to Abigail, and Abigail exchanging words with Vikram. Perhaps it was just that I had a secret myself, but I was sure that they were looking over their shoulders. Tom was the last to finish; he begged the others to carry on to the meeting without waiting for him, and we were left at our table alone.

'Why should I be careful of Helen?' I asked.

'Because Helen's still got a lot to learn,' Tom said. 'She shouldn't have been showing Gabriel those pictures of her husband.'

I couldn't help laughing. 'They were photographs of Gabriel's father,' I said. 'Why shouldn't she?'

'You've got a lot to learn too.'

We heard my father's voice coming from the ballroom. The goodnight meeting had started, and we were together in the empty dining room. He grinned and kissed me so quickly that only the taste of chocolate on my lips showed it had happened. There it was again – that wanting – and the soreness became an ache. We crept silently to my cabin, and this time he kissed me very, very slowly. I forgot about Helen, and the goodnight meeting happened without us.

'My Tom,' I whispered to him, and he was. My rebellion, my growth, my discovery. My proof that I was alive.

THIRTEEN

'Time no longer' ❧ *Tom's story* ❧ *Tom asks a question and ends the film*

Tom and I proved that we were alive all over the ship. We found each other in our cabins, the sports hall, the laundry. Wherever I was, whatever I was doing, I found myself thinking of him, and all the energy I had once put into wondering and remembering went into him. I was confident that we were going somewhere, even if no one would tell me where; when we got there, there would be other work to do, and so the time I spent helping Patience to make sure that everyone had clean clothes and clean bed linen seemed important, because it was limited. Some days I was so busy I didn't see Tom at all, which was why we went to the goodnight meetings. Even without clocks or watches, we could be sure of seeing each other there. When my father announced at a goodnight meeting that we had heard the last testimony and that we could now set ourselves free from the past altogether, we were looking at each other, and later we could not even remember whose the last testimony had been. When my father called triumphantly, 'There shall be time no longer,' I cheered along although I had no idea what he meant. We read the same books; we laughed at poor Garth, sitting staring out to sea, and at Emily, for whom a clean white plate was the most important thing in the world, and at Finn, who seemed to say,

Yes, Michael, Yes Michael, more than he said anything else. We tried to find a way of spending the nights together, but my father watched everyone return to their cabins after the goodnight meetings and then turned out the lights. Tom's cabin lay in one direction and mine in the other, and the nights were far too dark for roaming.

More than anything, I wanted to go back to the fourth deck. But the ship kept us too busy. Tom was wiping the walls again now as well as teaching football, and a girl on another laundry shift sprained her wrist so the piles of washing were bigger. I stayed until they were done. I didn't exactly mind. Not being with Tom was almost as seductive as being with Tom, because the fact that I loved him created a secret place that had nothing to do with my father, nothing to do with the ship. I didn't bother with the research room or the galleries, or even the cinema, anymore. I lost interest in food. The menu card would say confit of duck, creamed potatoes, petits pois, raspberries and ice-cream. Or casseroled chicken, sweetcorn, peach melba. Or beef and dumplings, green beans, sticky toffee pudding and custard. But whatever the card said, it all tasted the same and left a dull, metallic aftertaste. I played with the food on my plate, imagining myself with Tom. When I wasn't working or making snatched love or forming patterns with tinned sweetcorn and rehydrated potato, I lay in my cabin, staring at the scratches on the button or the shine on the apple, and listening to the sounds of busy people busy about the business of keeping the ship clean and comfortable. I knew it all so well by then that I could see what was going on with my ears. The heavy, regular stride was Gerhard Goltz, the cook, trekking to the stores. The lighter step that clipped alongside was Emily, come to help with her soft skin and bouncing curls. The doctor's footsteps always slowed as he reached the infirmary stairs, then clanged as he took them two at a time. When I was mourning for my mother, footsteps had come in single sets. Now they came in rattling collections, as though the feet themselves were chattering along with their owners. There were fewer slow, contemplative strides and more quick ones, as though people had places they wanted to be, as though there were things to be anticipated, looked forward to, raced towards. Tom raced too, and sometimes, the footsteps I heard would be his, and his face would shine with delight when I opened the door to him.

I watched the sun, too, and sometimes it rose over the prow and sometimes it rose over the stern. Sometimes it rose in the place where it had set. People asked my father where the sunset would be and gathered where he said, and he was always right. Sometimes I asked, 'Where are we? Where are we going?' But no matter who I spoke to or when I spoke, the answer was always, 'Right here, Lalla. We're right here, right now.' Once, Tom asked me at breakfast whether I would watch the sunset with him that day, but I hated the thought of having to check with my father first so much that I said no and went to bed early. I sat on my bunk with the apple in my hands, its surface smooth and cold, and stroked it against my cheek pretending it was Tom's hand.

The marks on my cabin wall became more and more important to me as time began to count for less and less. In the beginning, I had known time in other ways – hunger, tiredness, the rising and setting of the sun. Time just was, like death and the sun. And of course, in the beginning, I'd known time through the tenderness of my breasts, the aches in my belly, the dull passing of unnecessary blood. I don't suppose my father had even thought of that.

But things were different now, and the marks were all I had. Even the bleeding had stopped. I knew this meant I needed to eat more – it had happened once before, in London, when my father was still refusing to use ship stocks at home. My mother had told him that I had to eat; more food came into the flat and the blood came back. But I had no mother to make me eat now. I worked hard, I went to my cabin, and from time to time I walked aimlessly, staring around at the people running about, living their cheerful lives with their white teeth set in their delighted smiles. I looked at my museum, and I waited for Tom, and the fact that I felt light-headed for much of the time felt right.

What I wanted from Tom changed too. I loved his body, but I wanted more. I wanted him to take my hand and lead me to some rust, or dust, or a worn-out cushion he had saved from the ballroom. He wanted me to stop making the marks on my cabin wall, but I wanted him to watch them mounting up. I wanted him to show me something – anything – and say, yes, Lalla, of course there is time, and however much of it passes, I will stay with you and love you as I do now.

Oh, the ship was a busy place! So much joy and hope and anticipation that there really wasn't any space for the grumbling cloud I carried around. Gerhard had small teams going into the kitchen, learning how to bake. My father produced tins in different shapes, and for a while we ate crescent moons and ellipses decorated with tiny stars in pink and blue and green and yellow, and hats and shoes and coats of shaved chocolate and swirled cream. Something different, people said delightedly, while my father smiled on. But they weren't different. They were the same things in different shapes. The same flour, egg powder, fat pellets, sugar, mixed to make the same cake. Whether it was shaped like a hat or a shoe, or a cone or a chair or a dinosaur, it tasted the same. It was the same. There was nothing new, and while everyone in the ballroom exclaimed delightedly and laughed as though something extraordinary had happened, I wondered what was missing in their minds that they thought these cakes were anything to be pleased about. What is being alive if it is not to grow? And what is it to grow, if not to make something new?

But they ate the cakes and left nothing to show for the time that had gone into their making.

Patience began to knit. My father gave her needles and wool, and soon she had a circle around her, learning to follow patterns. No one except me ever seemed to wonder why, when Gabriel was the youngest child on board, they made toys and baby clothes. They knitted and knitted and knitted, and as I watched the booties and sleepsuits growing on their knitting needles, I wondered whether Patience might be my ally after all. Because if there were four pairs of booties where once there had been none, there was proof of the passing of time. But before I could speak to her, they all unravelled the little clothes and wound the balls of wool up again to be knitted into something else. Whenever anyone wanted to join in, my father gave them knitting needles, and the unravelling meant that there was always wool. 'The point is the process, not the product,' he said, offering me knitting needles as I walked away.

The weather grew warmer and the winds grew less. My father gave us clay. We all made little models, then left them to go hard. I looked at them – a cat, a fish, a pot that looked like something from the British Museum, and the shapeless lump that I had intended to be a copy of my button – and thought, now there is a time before we made these models and a time after. But after a while, they were all put into a bucket of water, soaked into shapelessness and made back into clay for others to use.

I heard a plate break in the kitchen when I went in to dinner, but there were no fewer plates at the table when we sat down.

I called up the library list on my screen. There was more material there than I could read in my lifetime. Was this the answer? Could time be measured in the books you had read and the books you had not read? I took my screen and scrolled through every single book title available in the library, the titles passing down the screen so quickly I could not read a single one.

But after three hours, during which Tom knocked twice and went away without an answer, the titles came to an end. The library was a vast, stagnant pond. I might as well just sit and re-read *Ballet Shoes* until the day I died. The only fresh and un-expected thing was Tom, and even so, I was beginning to know exactly where he would put his hands, and when, and to feel less desperate for him to do so.

'Where are we going?' I asked, again and again.

'Why does it matter so much?' Tom answered, every time. 'We're here, now. Isn't that enough?'

But it wasn't enough, and for three days I punished Tom by avoiding him, angry that he would not share my anger. But I missed him. When I lay in my bunk at night, I thought of him. My fingers were not his hands, and without the weight of his body against me, I could not lose myself as I longed to be lost. I kept my tally of the days, hating him for wanting me to stop, yet hating the marks too, which could not love me as he did. Patience looked at me with pity, but I did not talk to her. I did not talk to anyone, and I tried not to notice them staring at me as I went about my work.

'It's a process,' I overheard my father saying to Emily on the way to dinner, and I shrank into a doorway. 'Tom will explain it better to her than I can. She'll catch us all up, and then she'll overtake us. You'll see.' I didn't see, and I didn't follow them into the dining room. I lay on my bed and listened to my stom-ach growling, and imagined the house I would build for myself when we arrived, and how far it would be away from everyone else's. It was hot – I found myself thinking of a book called *Robinson Crusoe*, of a picture of a beach and a tree that only had leaves at the very top. I would collect branches and build a hut.

On the third day – the seventy-fourth mark – I went out onto the deck in the hope of a breeze, and as I stood staring into the warm sky, Tom came to me. His hair was floppy over his eyes; he brushed it back and his forehead was damp. 'Lalla,' he said, and his face was so serious and his hands so still that I knew something was about to change. He's going to tell me where we're going, I thought, and my heart began to beat faster. *The fear is part of the love*, my mother had said. Looking at Tom, and looking through him to the rest of my life, I felt that I was touching the edge of what she meant. Would we be going back to London and hunger and pain and chaos and yes, maybe death? Would it be Robinson Crusoe's island, and this heat? Whatever it was, it would be us, together – and that would be life. I burst into tears and clung to him as though he was the one who'd been running away.

'Lalla,' he said simply. 'Why are you so angry?'

'Are we going back to London? Are we looking for an island somewhere? Has my father sent you to tell me?'

He shook his head. 'We're never going back to London.' He took a deep breath. 'Listen to me, Lalla. Michael says that we shouldn't think about time anymore. That if we let time go, then everything happens together. Like the knitting wool and the baby suits. They're the same. The wool is the sleepsuit, and the sleepsuit is the wool. And I didn't really understand. But when we went up, when you pulled me through that skylight and we did – what we did – I did understand. I understand every time we're together.' He took my hands in his and we stood facing each other on the deck. 'I'm everything, Lalla. My parents, my grandfather, the Land Allocation Act. Michael saving my life and coming here and meeting you and being with you. It's all concentrated here, in me, whether I'm wiping the walls on the deck or teaching football or wanting to be with you.'

'And tomorrow? And the day after that? And the day after that?'

'Tomorrow's already happened. That's the point. Nobody's

frightened anymore, because everything is here. Why won't you see? It doesn't matter how long the journey is, if we've already arrived.'

I tried to pull my hands away, but he held them tighter and pulled me close. 'What do you want, Lalla?' he said, and his breath was urgent against my ear. 'I want you. I want to stop hiding, and be with you, openly and for always. I want us to tell Michael, and to get his blessing.'

'I want . . .' I began, but I did not know what I wanted, and before I could find any words his arms wound around me, more confident than before. He kissed my lips, my cheeks; he swept my damp escaping hair from my face and kissed my ears. He pressed the length of his body against me and I could feel him growing hard. I felt my face burning. The cracked skylight and the pile of dust beneath it appeared in my mind like the answer to everything, all surrounded by light. The dust. I wanted the dust.

'Come upstairs with me,' I said.

'Now?' He smiled. 'Your cabin's closer.'

'Upstairs. Now,' I said, and took his hand.

We ran to the infirmary stairs. The thought of the skylight drove me on; I barely noticed that the photograph album had gone. Tom ran behind me, setting staircase after staircase clanging. My work had made me fit, for this time I took the stairs with ease. There would be a pile of dust, and a cracked skylight, and we would fetch a ladder and go out onto the top of the ship, and wherever the sun set, we would see it without having to ask.

That would be freedom. And if we were free, we could choose each other, and that would be love. And then Tom would be right; it wouldn't matter how long it took us to find our island and start again.

I burst onto the corridor of the fourth deck and stopped. Tom followed so eagerly that he ran into me. We fell onto the floor and he lay on top of me, kissing my face, stroking my hair so hard it felt like he was trying to wipe it off. I pushed him away and went to the skylight.

'It can't be this one,' I said, 'there's no crack.'

'Does it matter?' He stood firmer now, his feet planted solidly on the floor. He was undoing the buttons on his shirt.

'Where's the dust?' I demanded. He walked towards me. 'Where's the skylight with the crack in it?' I walked along the corridor, looking up, walking in and out of the pools of light.

'Stop it, Lalla,' he said, and his voice sounded older, less hesitant. But all I could see was the clean floor.

'The dust,' I said, starting to run, 'the dust. I want the dust.'

'Dust?' he said, catching up with me. 'Life, Lalla. That's what we want. And it's what we've got. All of us. Life. Come on.' He grabbed my hands and pulled me around, breathing hard. Where was his softness, his hesitancy, his uncertainty? 'What's dust got to do with us? Have I got to fetch a ladder, Lalla?'

I jerked my hands free and faced him squarely. Everything about him that had made him a boy had gone. Here was a man, a man like my father. Telling me what to do. So certain of himself that there was no room for anyone else to breathe.

He looked at me. 'What's wrong with you, Lalla?'

'What's wrong with you? With all of you?'

He laughed then, and it wasn't a kind sound. 'We're happy,' he said. 'We all enjoy our food and our work, and we play games and care for each other. You're the one who skulks around, avoiding the people who love you.'

'But you're all mad. Nobody cares about where we're going, or how long it'll take us to get there.'

'Because it doesn't matter! Don't you listen to anything Michael says? Or me? We're here, together, you and me. Why are you forcing us to hide? You act as though we're doing something wrong.'

He was pleading now, and reaching for me, and the trouble with love is that it shuts off the part of your brain that wants to understand, because there is nothing to understand about the burning under skin that longs to be touched, and your lips and your stomach going soft and the centre of the universe gathering to be exploded under his hand.

I pulled away. 'Tell me something you miss,' I demanded.

'I miss you when we're not together.'

'No. That doesn't count. Something you miss from before. From before we sailed. That's not on the ship. That can't be hidden behind one of these doors.'

He looked over his shoulder. I heard the humming of the solar panels, sending the sun to the desalination unit, the ovens, the engine room. I thought I felt the throb of the engines through my feet, but they were in the bowels of the ship and we were on the fourth deck. It must be my blood, then, I thought. It must be my blood.

'Nothing,' he said. 'There's nothing.'

My blood pounded harder. 'Not your father?' I was goading him now, willing those blazing green eyes to burst into flame. 'Not your mother? Your home? Come on, Tom. There's something you miss. Something you'd go back for. Something you'll never, ever have again. Like Helen and her husband.'

For a moment I thought he was going to hit me, and I almost wished he would. But as I pushed harder, the tension went from his body and he leaned against the wall.

'You don't get it, do you?' he said, and his eyes were soft again. 'We all miss things. People. But it doesn't matter anymore, because all those things, everyone we've ever loved, are part of where we are now. We don't need to go on about them. Or show our children photographs of them.'

I didn't say a word. I sat in silence, wishing I had a photograph of my mother. It wasn't that I couldn't remember what she looked like; when I closed my eyes and concentrated I could see her eyes, her skin, the pale blue veins that pulsed over her collarbones, the thousands of different smiles that betrayed her true feelings, whatever her actual words. But a photograph would have let me show her to other people. I suddenly wanted to go to my father. Not to talk, not to ask where we were going, but simply to breathe the same air as someone else who had loved her. Who could see her face as clearly as I could. I stood up, but Tom grabbed my hand.

'My mum had relatives in Shanghai, in China,' he said. 'She used to message them all the time before the borders closed. And then one day, right out of the blue, they sent her all these pictures. Bodies lying in the street. Bodies piled in factories. Hundreds, thousands of them, like they'd just fallen where they stood.'

'I never saw that on the bulletins.'

'No. Almost as soon as she'd opened the pictures, all communications from Chinese servers were deleted. Gone. And there was a Dove warning that anyone retaining messages from China would be in contravention of closed borders. That was a death penalty, Lalla. We deleted everything. Even the message her parents sent when I was born. My dad said that all the Chinese people must have lain in the streets to make everyone think they were dead, so that China could just get on. But my mum cried. Oh, Lalla. She cried and cried. I couldn't get anything on the bulletins. It was like China never existed. But I'd saved one of the pictures onto my own screen.'

'Wasn't that illegal?'

He nodded. 'I thought it would be all right. They weren't de-registering minors then. I waited. And after a couple of days, when nothing had happened, I put the picture on my blog.

And the stats went wild. Hundreds of thousands of hits. After a couple of hours, I got scared, and I took it down. But it was too late. The troops came on the same day.'

'The troops? Did they de-register you?'

He shook his head. 'They de-registered my parents. Said they should have controlled me.' I stared at the floor, as though I could make the dust reappear if I looked for it hard enough. De-registered. I remembered the way my parents looked at each other when they said the word, the fervour with which the people on the quay had scrambled for our cards.

'My grandfather said it was time to use the Land Allocation Act. He remembered growing things in the ground. He talked about apple trees and carrots, and planting clover in the first year to make the soil safe again and bring back the insects.'

'What's clover?'

'Something you plant, I suppose. I don't know.'

'Did you go?'

'My grandfather got his allocation code. We left my parents with the last of our provisions and promised we'd go back for them. My grandfather and I walked out of the city, and what we saw . . . oh, Lalla, what we saw. It was frightening. You don't know who anyone is. We hid more than we walked. And no matter how far we walked, there was nothing green. Nothing growing at all. And we were so hungry. My grandfather got slower and slower. He just kept saying, tomorrow we will find a garden. I was so scared. We got to a shelter, and when we signed in, Michael was there, waiting for me. He'd been tracking me through my screen, ever since the blog. I've never been so glad to see anyone in my life, never.'

I leant on the wall next to him and we slumped down side by side, our backs against the wall, our legs making four mountains, our toes pointing at a storeroom door.

Tom spoke to the floor. 'Michael told me that my parents had been executed. They'd tried to use their cards at a food drop. He said he wanted me for the ship.'

'And your grandfather?'

'Michael told me I had to decide. He said that a man in love with the soil would always long for the soil. He said that my grandfather could never be happy on the ship. We were still citizens then, so we were allowed to sleep one night in the shelter, and in the morning . . .' He looked at me as though he was trying to make up his mind about something, and then took a small piece of paper from the pocket of his shirt. 'In the morning Michael gave me this.' I unfolded the paper. The writing on it was small, faint and shaky, and by the end, the words were so close together it was hard to read them at all.

Dear Tom, it said, *I give you to Michael Paul, who will be your father now. I am going to find a garden for I am sure one is there. I will tend my garden knowing you are safe and happy and that one child on this broken planet we called earth may live to see his family's prayers for him answered for this is no place now and you are so young this is no time in your young life to die or see such deaths. I hold you in my heart and let you go. Your loving Granpa.*

Tom took the note back and held it between his fingers, turning it around and around, a soft, regular rustle of a beat, counting seconds, minutes, time itself until we spoke again. Such a simple thought, to place a seed in the soil and watch it grow.

'I shouldn't have kept it,' Tom said. 'Michael said to get rid of our mementoes. I can hardly blame Helen for keeping hold of those photographs when I'm just as bad.' He looked down at his hands. Strong hands. I could see his tendons moving beneath his skin as he turned the note.

'You're not bad,' I said. 'Or if you are, I am too. If I had a letter from my mother, I'd never let it go.'

'But that's the trouble, isn't it? Not letting go. That's why you make those marks in your cabin.'

'I'm scared of stopping.'

'If you stop making the marks, I'll give up my grandfather's letter. We ought to be raising each other up, Lalla, not holding each other back. I love you. I love you so much.'

I took the letter from him and read it again. *I hold you in my heart and let you go.* How could Tom honour his grandfather's wish for him unless he did the same? How could I live the life my mother wished for me, unless I forgot her?

'Maybe we're on our way to China,' I said at last. 'We could be. We could have a life there. Start the factories again, make things. Grow rice.'

'The photos looked like a pandemic,' he said. 'Like they'd all just dropped dead where they stood.'

'Maybe we're going to go and see.'

He rested his elbows on his knees. 'A country full of dead people behind closed borders? I don't think so.'

I shut my eyes, and leaned my head back against the wall, and thought about the survivors in my monster films. I thought about how people lived and died and made love in films, and how different it was in real life.

'Did you ever see anyone smoking?' I asked eventually.

'I saw a pile of bodies being burned. Just outside a village on the way to Oxford.'

'No, I meant cigarettes. Like in the films. If we were in a film right now, we'd be smoking cigarettes. You'd light the cigarette, and then you'd pass it to me, and we'd be sitting here talking just like this.'

He laughed. 'You're funny, Lalla.' I moved closer to him and rested my head on his shoulder. He kissed the top of my head and we stayed like that for a while. I don't know what he was thinking about, but I was thinking about my mother.

'The worst thing is . . .'

'What?'

'Michael thought I was so brave, putting that picture on my blog. He thought I was telling the truth to the world at my own risk.'

'And weren't you?'

He shook his head. 'I just wanted to see if anyone knew what had happened. So that I could have something to tell my mother. Instead I killed her.'

'You didn't kill your mother.' But maybe he had. Maybe that was what drew us so closely together, whether we knew it or not.

'I'm an imposter,' he said. 'Everyone else here has done incredible things. I'm scared too, Lalla. I'm scared Michael'll find me out. He's told everyone I'm some great truth-telling hero. But I was just an idiot.'

I loved him more at that moment than at any other since I'd first set eyes on him.

'Let's go down,' he said at last. 'You should eat something. You're so thin, Lalla.'

'I can't help it.'

'It's just not . . . It's like there's not enough food or something. Like you're rejecting everything Michael's given us.'

I said nothing, just sat and looked for non-existent cracks in the wall opposite.

'Let me talk to Michael,' he said. 'Let's stop being a secret.'

'I need a secret.'

'No, you don't. Not now.' He stood up and gave me his hands, then pulled me to my feet. He kept his arm around me as we made our way down the stairs, and although it was a bit awkward at the turns, it was nice. By the time we reached the bottom, I had made up my mind. I stopped and turned to face him.

'We're not the only ones with secrets,' I said. Tom raised his eyebrows and I went on. 'There's a group of people – a small group – I see them meeting and whispering. But I don't know what they're saying. And there were clothes upstairs once, clothes for my mother. There must have been, but they're gone. And the sun never rises and sets in the same place. Ever. There are never any lights on at night. The ship's full of secrets. It's not just us.'

Tom laughed, and then his face softened and he put his hand to my cheek. 'Your mother's gone,' he said softly. 'Like my grandfather. You miss her. And I wish I'd known her. She loved you so much.'

'How do you know?' I asked, my voice shaking.

'Because she was part of the ship. Part of what made it happen. Because she was part of what made you. But she's here, Lalla. Like my mum and dad, and my grandfather, and Patience's daughter, and Roger's baby. All that has been and all that is, all that will be. Right here, right now. If you need to ask where we're going, then you haven't learned to trust. Secrets just hold us back. And looking for secrets in others – that's worse.'

I shook my head; a tear splashed onto his hand and he kissed my wet eyes, very softly. 'That's for you,' he said as he kissed the right one. 'And that's for the people we lost, who are here with us now,' he said as he kissed the left. 'Do you really love me, Lalla? I love you. We could get married.'

Married? The shock of the word brought on a wave of nausea, and I took deep breath after deep breath, trying to quell it. And yet why was the suggestion such a surprise? What was marriage, except two people who loved each other and wanted to be together? What more did I want than what I already had?

Marriage. It meant that things had worked out. That the film was over. I felt as though I was back in the museum, staring at a shapeless lump of stone while my mother told me how exciting and interesting it was. What was wrong with me, that I saw only a shapeless lump of stone? The world should have been tinged pink and gone misty, and I should have been happy.

I made Tom go into the dining room ahead of me. I wasn't ready to give up my secrets. I hadn't answered his question and I certainly didn't feel like eating.

FOURTEEN

Helen's trial ❀ *Tom's confession* ❀ *what I want*

I ate what I could of my dinner, and Solomon Asprey ate the rest. I wondered what would happen to the packages of clothes if I grew too thin for mine and he grew too fat for his.

Tom kept catching my eye and smiling. I smiled back, but my attention was focused on the doctor's small group. They came together at the table where the water jugs stood; they passed each other in their quests for cutlery, for napkins, for second servings. Why don't they just sit together? I asked myself, but when they saw me looking, they separated as though they'd burned each other. I sat over a glass of water until everyone else had left, including Tom, borne away by a chattering group I didn't care about.

I left the air-conditioned dining room and went out into the heated air to walk to my cabin. Most people walked through the ship to get from place to place; it was more comfortable, especially in the heat, and usually quicker. But I liked to watch the sea, to feel a connection with where we were. I hadn't intended to go to the goodnight meeting, but as I passed the ballroom I heard a noise, soft whispering overlaid with something harsher and more urgent, like a high wind. Curious, I pushed open the doors, and the first person I saw was Helen herself, white-faced and slumped at the desk on the raised podium where once my father had checked the manifest. The people, instead of being sat on the blue velvet benches, stood surrounding the podium talking at her. Helen's eyes were red, and although I was half a room away from her, I could see her lips forming the single word, 'But,' over and over again. But . . . but . . . but. No one gave her the chance to finish, and no one met her eyes. They fell silent when they saw me, and shifted uncomfortably.

And then I stopped dead. There, on the desk, sat the photograph album. All around the room, people were looking at the album, then at Helen. She looked at Finn, at Greg, at Alice, at Mercy, but they all turned away from her. Then the doors opened and my father came in. Everyone turned towards him, and I slipped quietly onto an empty bench.

My father looked at where Helen sat, sobbing and shaking her head.

'Sit, friends, sit,' my father said, and as he walked to the podium, they moved to the benches, as though the sea itself was making way for him. I bit my lip and wiped my palms on my dress.

Look carefully, Lalla. That's how you learn.

My father stepped onto the podium. Helen concentrated on him, her eyes wide and adoring. He surveyed the room slowly then asked, 'We have no laws on the ship. Why do we need a courtroom?' He stood next to Helen and put his hand on her shoulder.

'Where is Gabriel?' he asked.

Finn stepped forwards. 'It was better that he didn't come tonight,' he said. Several of the people nodded. But Emily did not nod. The doctor's head was still. Was there a division among the people of the ship? The exhilaration of thinking I was not alone brought my mother before me with startling clarity. I felt a hand on mine and saw that Tom had slipped onto the bench beside

176

me. His hands were hot and damp; he must have been walking outside too.

My father frowned. 'You think Gabriel is better without his mother? Did his mother agree?'

Finn stood up. The air he displaced pressed heavily on my shoulders. 'Michael, you said we must not look back. You said there should be time no longer. And we threw away the mast and we said goodbye to the people we left behind.'

My father nodded, gesturing at Finn to continue, but he did not take his hand from Helen's shoulder. Finn's voice rose in pitch, filling the ballroom with unease. 'You became the children's father. So Gabriel is your child. Our child. But Helen's keeping him from you. From us. How can we be family to him, when she keeps showing him photographs of a man who's dead?'

'He's mine.' The voice that broke across Finn's rising pitch was so thunderous that I thought it was my father who had spoken. It was not until I saw Helen standing, shaking, her hands clutching at the desk for support, that I realised that the words had been hers. Finn stepped away, staggering on the edge of the podium as he did so. The ballroom pulsed with the collective instinct to steady him, but he saved himself and kept his feet, staring at Helen. Helen stood still and white, the blood completely drained from her lips. I willed Finn to say nothing. We had all seen fights in the time before, people so driven by one need that they forgot everything else. And it was that single-mindedness – the single-mindedness that forgets humanity and community and all thoughts of tomorrow in the pursuit of bread, or blankets, or shelter – that we saw suddenly flash before us in the challenge the mother threw down before the old man. The sky beyond the ballroom was black and oppressive, pushing at the windows.

Finn and Helen were looking at each other, breathing hard.

'Helen?' my father said.

'Simon was my husband, Michael. I loved him, and we had

177

Gabriel together. I brought the photographs to the holding centre, and I brought them onto the ship. And I show them to Gabriel. But I've never spoken against you, Michael, or the ship. Never.' My father's expression did not change and Helen's voice tailed off. 'Michael, have I done wrong?' she asked him, her eyes damp and wide.

My father shook his head. 'You've caused a storm, that's all.' He pulled the photograph album to him and turned the pages slowly. 'So this is Simon?' he said. 'He looks like he was a good man.'

'He was. He left just after Gabriel was born, to claim land under the Land Allocation Act.'

'And he never came back. What did you do when he didn't return? Did you give up and wallow in your misery?'

'Everyone's already heard my testimony.'

'Everyone except you.' He was speaking as he spoke to the children, with soft encouragement. 'I wonder whether you've ever really listened to your own story.'

'I didn't do anything,' she faltered. 'Everyone else did incredible things. But I . . . I didn't do anything. I don't deserve to be here. I'm not like all the others.'

'Is that why you cling to what is gone, because you don't believe in your own worth? I didn't choose you because you loved Simon. I never knew Simon. Neither did Gabriel. I chose you because I saw the stories of the children you saved. People wrote about you, Helen. Do you know how far some of them travelled to find you? The hope you gave to parents who thought everything was lost? I read about you, and I saw at once that you embodied not motherhood, but ship-motherhood.'

'All I did was feed the babies,' Helen whispered. 'That was all. I was lucky. I made so much milk for Gabriel, and so many of the babies were starving. And Gabriel loved it. They held him while I fed their babies, and – oh, he was so loved.'

'Can't you see that it was a heroic thing to do, Helen? That the ability to let others love your child was what marked you out for the ship? Have all the testimonies, all the time we've spent together, taught you no more than that? It's not just Helen.' He turned to the room, frustration verging on anger etched across his forehead. 'Every single one of you – every single one – was chosen. No one slipped onto this ship by mistake. If you doubt yourself, then you doubt me.'

Tom sat beside me, his gaze fixed on my father, his eyes wide.

'All this *I'm not worthy* rubbish. It has to stop. It's dangerous. If everyone had acted as you did – each one of you – then the ship would never have been necessary. Think about it. If every nursing mother fed a starving child alongside her own. If every able human took the food they did not need and gave it to one who did. If every witness of injustice, or cruelty, or exploitation, or murder, stood up and said, *Here is something happening that is wrong.* If everyone put another's ease ahead of their own pain. I'm not talking about other people.' He looked around the room at the upturned faces, the clasped hands, the tears. 'I am talking about you. All of you.'

'But what about love?' Helen cried out, and I saw my father flinch. He turned to her slowly, and I saw a dangerous light in his eyes that made me wish she had not spoken. 'Simon loved Gabriel. Why is it wrong to keep that love alive?'

'I had photographs of Debbie,' Luke called out, speaking very fast. 'I threw them overboard. After that night we all said goodbye.' Other people spoke in agreement; Michael had said to get rid of mementoes, and they had done so, and they felt better. Relieved. Lighter. Helen could feel better too. Misery was unnecessary.

My father crumpled slightly, as though something had tugged painfully at the very centre of his being, and all of a sudden I felt that, little as we seemed to speak these days, there was nothing I would not do to save him that pain. Emily, braver than I, walked over and laid her hand upon his arm, and he put his hand over hers and pressed it for a moment. Helen looked at Emily, and two red patches flamed on her pale, pale face.

Patience stood up, but before she could speak, there was a movement at my side and Tom was marching to the podium. He stepped up on to it and raised his hand, and for a moment I thought he was going to strike Helen. 'Because love is where we're going!' Tom cried, bringing his hand down onto the desk so hard that the drawer handle rattled. 'The ship is the important thing now. If we all sit around loving what's gone, we might as well have died in London.' He looked across the ballroom, straight at me, and I was overwhelmed with piercing green and longing. 'If you don't let go of the past, you'll never find the love that's here for you. On the ship.'

My father fell on Tom, hugging him so hard I could barely see him. The entire room burst into applause, and my father let Tom go and joined in. I looked at Finn, expecting to see him triumphant, but he seemed younger, uncertain, and he looked at Helen as though he was hungry. I saw a *but* rise from Helen's heart to her throat; I saw her swallow it; her face cleared, and I knew that I had lost her.

The meeting broke up. The people made themselves into smaller groups. Helen and Finn ran to each other as though they'd been joined by elastic, and my father stayed with them, and although I could not hear what they were saying, a golden glow seemed to come from them. Tom was there too, looking over and beckoning to me. He did not come and fetch me. He wanted to stay with the laughing, touching, happy people, inside their magic circle. Eating cookies. People who were a shining example to the world. I was no shining example. What would the world have been if everyone had done as I had done? Exactly what it had become.

My father's shadow fell over me.

'Lalla,' he said. 'It's so good to see you at a meeting. I'm glad Tom brought you.'

'Tom didn't bring me,' I said. 'I heard the noise and wondered what was going on. That's all.'

My father nodded. 'And what do you think?'

'I think you're all wrong.' I spoke louder than I meant to, and the people near us fell silent. 'You can't stop Helen showing Gabriel photographs of his father. I think Helen should be allowed to teach Gabriel anything she wants.'

'But she can.' My father called to Helen, who came hurrying over to us. 'Helen,' he said. 'Lalla's worried about you. How are you now?'

Helen held out her hand so we could all see it trembling, and she laughed. 'It's like being found all over again,' she said. 'I was so worried I couldn't think straight. And there was no need to worry. No need. Simon will always be a part of Gabriel, but Gabriel needs a mother who's with him now. And a father who's able to give him what he needs.' She turned to Finn. 'And new friends,' she said quietly, and he took her shaking hand and squeezed it.

'Michael,' Tom said. 'Michael, I have a confession.'

My father inclined his head.

'Shall I leave?' Helen asked.

Tom shook his head. He spoke very fast. 'You know my story,' he said. 'But what you don't know is that I've been worse than Helen. I've been clinging onto something that I should have let go.' He felt in his shirt pocket and took out his grandfather's letter. I leaned forwards to stop him, but he held it out to my father. My father stood aside and gestured Tom towards the podium.

'Michael,' Tom said, 'everyone.' The room fell silent. 'This is the last letter my grandfather wrote to me. I have kept it until now. Please forgive me. I'm giving this letter up, in the hope that might help anyone who's still struggling. I didn't think I was worthy either. But Michael thought I was, and I'm glad. And I'm going to do what my grandfather told me, and look to Michael as my father, because he believed in me enough to bring me here.' He looked straight at me. 'And by being happy on the ship, as my grandfather wanted, I'll be keeping him with me.' My father strode over to the podium. He put his arms around Tom and held him as close as he had ever held me. The applause broke out again, stronger this time, and I thought that if the applause went on for long enough, I would be able to tell who else was still keeping mementoes of the life before simply by studying the force with which they clapped.

'Let it all go!' my father cried over the noise. 'If it happened before the ship, then it didn't happen at all. Life starts here!' I joined in, hoping to keep the applause going for longer, and I saw Roger and Abigail exchanging looks, and glancing across to Vikram and Luke, and I knew then that this small group, who met secretly, were like me. They saw no threat in the last words of a grandfather to the child he had loved, or a photograph of a father who was dead. I would find them, and I would join them.

My father and Tom left the meeting together, and I looked the other way as they passed me. I stayed in the sticky air of the ballroom until everyone had gone. When the ballroom was empty, I rescued the abandoned photograph album. I took the letter, too, and I put them on my desk and lay staring at them through the long humid night, sweating where the sheets touched me. I did not sleep, and went to breakfast simply for the air-conditioning in the dining room.

The British Museum had been full of objects, and every single one of them had a story. I had five now. The button, the apple, the photograph album, the letter and the screws. When I looked at them, I was filled with a sense of what we had lost. Not just my mother, but our connection to things. To people. Without connections, there was no learning. Without learning, there was no journey of discovery. And without discovery, there was nothing but a full plate at dinner and a soft bed at night.

It wasn't that I cared much about Helen's Simon. I'd never known him. But he was part of a past that was part of our present. Helen's trial and Tom's confession had crystallised my thinking, although not in the way Tom had hoped.

I loved Tom and he wanted to marry me.

But I did not want to marry Tom. Not now. I wanted to be with him for ever, to love and fight for him, to give my body up to his and to take him into me. I wanted to fear for him, and need him, and ache when he was gone. I wanted him to stand with me on the deck rail and declare with me that the sun rises in the east and sets in the west, and that its journey across the sky is called a day, and that many days together make a lifetime. I wanted the people to hear us, and cheer, and take the ship as quickly as possible to our tropical island, or China, or even back to London, and start again.

FIFTEEN

The storm breaks ❧ *the temptation of Tom*
Mandel ❧ *the message of Alice's tapestry*

The weather broke; it rained for an entire night, fat drops
slamming against the portholes like stones, and in the
morning, the world was new. I stepped through the puddles
on my way to the laundry, and in the clean, vibrant air, I
realised that since I was the only one for whom it existed,
time was on my side. Someone knew where we were going,
even if I didn't, and when we finally got there, Tom would
begin to understand me, and the stores would give us a
good start. He might even be glad, then, to have his grandfather's letter back. And so I relaxed a little and began to enjoy
myself once more. It was no challenge to get Tom to take
his clothes off; the real excitement began to come from getting
him to break my father's unwritten rules by talking about the
time before.

'Do you remember the Nazareth Act, Tom?' I would ask,
pulling him into my cabin and pressing him against the wall
with the full length of my body.

'No.'

I untucked his shirt. 'What about the Dove?'

'Nope.'

'Money,' I'd say, undoing the buttons on his trousers one by

184

one. 'Do you remember money? Actual notes and coins you held in your hand?'

'Nope.'

'Did you ever go to a restaurant?'

'A what?'

In my cabin he was on his guard, and I rarely won. The conversation usually ended with him grumbling, 'Why do you keep all that useless junk?'

But in the safety of the fourth deck, just sometimes, I triumphed, and we would talk, and that was when I loved him most.

'My mum would have loved all this,' he said once. 'The cookery and the crafts. The book group. You.'

'Your mum would have liked me?'

'Well. She'd have worried about your obsession with dust.'

I hit him then, and he grabbed my wrist and stared at me until I thought I'd melt. 'Why won't you marry me, Lalla?' he asked.

'Because I'm alive.'

'What do you mean?' He loosened his grip, but I didn't take my wrist away.

'I mean that nothing's allowed to happen.'

'Then make something happen,' he said, and his green eyes sparkled through his fringe. 'Marry me.' I moved away from him and stood looking up at the whole, perfect skylight with its new full complement of shiny screws. Then he laughed. 'Anyway, there's so much happening. Take a look around. There's the cooking, and the swimming. And all the books in the library to read. You could learn how to play football. Come on, I'll show you.'

'I don't want to play football.'

'Tennis, then. On deck, even, while the weather's like this.' The storm had given way to clear blue skies that felt as though they'd last for ever. 'Michael's got all the things.'

'What's tennis?'

'We'll find out. Or knit.'

'I don't want to knit. It all gets undone anyway.'

'Learn Latin.'

'What?'

'There's a Latin class starting. Charles is going to teach it and then he's going to show us round the Roman Galleries of the British Museum on the screens and we're going to recreate Pompeii in one of the empty rooms next to the sports hall. It's all right,' he said hurriedly as I felt my mouth fall open, 'Michael says it's all right. It's not looking back because it was so long ago and none of us have ever been there. It's honouring our heritage.'

'The Heritage Restoration Act,' I muttered, but he didn't hear me, or chose to ignore me. One or the other.

He stood up and joined me under the skylight. 'Shall I fetch the ladder?' he said hopefully. But I didn't feel like it. His enthusiasm had driven mine out of me.

'What will it take?' he asked me softly, one finger stroking the nape of my neck. 'What will it take to bring you with me? With the rest of us?'

I looked up at him. 'What will it take to bring you with me?'

'You've got me, Lalla. Look, I'm here with you, aren't I? I'll get the ladder, we'll make more dust if that's what you want. Tell me what it is you need and I'll find it. We've been happy, these last few days, haven't we?'

'I want to be somewhere. Do something.'

'The ship is somewhere. And there's loads to do.'

'I know that. I know. But none of it's important. Helen fed all those babies. Finn had the Thursday project. Patience helped loads of people.'

'But you're the reason any of us are here at all. You should be proud.'

I tried to think of another way to explain. 'Look at the library here,' I said. 'If you did nothing but read, and lived for long enough, you could read it all.'

'Of course. But who does nothing but read?'

'That's not the point. There's nothing infinite here. There's nothing that doesn't have an end.' I paused, then realised that, for once, I had said what I meant. 'Everything on the ship,' I said carefully, for Tom deserved that I should try, 'everything, every single thing, contains its own ending. The cooking, the knitting, the clothes, the library. Pompeii. Whatever you look at, you're also looking at its final point. Its end.'

I looked at him, waiting to see a flash of illumination on his face. But the only light there was, was pouring over him through the skylight. And I understood that, even if we went through that skylight and joined our bodies together and brought the stars down all around us and became one with each other again, I would still be alone.

'Why can't you be happy, Lalla? Why must you worry? Is it because of your mother?'

I shook my head. I missed her. I missed her every minute of every day. But that wasn't a worry. It was a sadness, a misery, a visceral longing for a world in which she had not died. But not a worry. Why, then, was I worried? Food? I had seen the towering stores in the holds. Health? We had a doctor and dentist and more medicines than we'd ever need. Occupation? We hadn't yet scratched the surface of the playthings my father had provided for us.

And then I realised. I was worried precisely because everyone was so happy. Everyone was so content. No one seemed to care when we were going to arrive, or be worried about what we would find there. No one was making plans. We were learning to play tennis, not learning to build houses. They didn't even mind that they were no longer counting the days and the weeks and the months. It was a relief to them not to have to. And more and more, it became borne upon me that we simply could not go on. We needed to arrive. Who would listen to me? Not Helen; I had lost her in the ballroom. Not Tom, who was looking at me with adoring incomprehension. He had given me an apple, but even now I was not sure what that meant.

What were the secret group doing while I was trying to explain myself? Maybe they had a map, a compass, and were charting our location. Maybe they were creeping into the engine rooms and speeding up our progress. Once, I thought I heard a dog barking, and became convinced that they had a pet somewhere. But whatever they were doing, they were my allies.

'Lalla,' Tom said suddenly, his eyes alight, 'if I could show you something that was growing and developing on the ship – if I could show you something that will be different tomorrow from what it is today, and different the day after that and after that – then do you think you might be happy?'

I expected him to fetch a ladder and a screwdriver. I could tell he wanted to by the way he kept touching me as he was talking – my hair, my face, my arms – as though he needed to be sure I was really there. But he stayed beside me, drowning in sunlight.

'Something that hasn't come from my father?'

He raised his eyebrows at me and I gave up.

'Follow me,' he said.

He went back down the stairs, and I followed him, dreaming of subversion and dissension and somebody other than me standing on a blue velvet bench and saying, 'The sun rises in the east and sets in the west, and this is called a day,' and everybody cheering. They'd cheered me once before, when I'd made it possible for us to leave. If I could only make them see what was so clear to me, they'd cheer me again, for making it possible for us to get to land.

But I had to give Tom his chance. I loved him. Maybe there was a garden on board, a secret space of grass with an apple tree in the centre laden with fruit. A farm, a pig, a rolling field, a horse to ride, a house made of red bricks with a garden and a child's swing moving to and fro in a gentle breeze.

A place where he and I could live and be together until we died.

We clattered down the stairs together. He pulled me through the ballroom and up to the gallery and the research room. I was all ready to tell him that these places didn't count, that there was nothing new in them, only thousands of things we hadn't looked at yet, but he didn't stop. I was wondering how much further he was going to take me when he pushed open a door and said, 'There, Lalla. What do you say to that?'

And, sitting on a chair in the middle of an otherwise empty room, with the sunlight streaming through the windows behind her, was an elderly lady surrounded by a sea of silk. I had not seen Alice's embroidery since the early days, when she worked with her hoop on a single length of silk in the ballroom. Now the silk filled a room that was three times the size of my cabin. Here and there were patches of colour, but for the most part the silk was bare, except for a grey outline of the ship itself. The patches of colour were people. I was there, a little figure standing on the prow of the ship, reaching up my arms to the sky. I knew it was me because I was wearing the orange dress I'd been wearing the day we boarded, but I looked like a little girl still, with two plaits sticking out of my head. Helen was there, watching Gabriel swimming in the net. I would rather have been in the net with Gabriel, but this was Alice's work, and I had no choice but to stand where Alice had stitched me. There was Roger, resting his hand on the forehead of a prone figure in the infirmary. The figure was wearing green and blue, and I realised it must be my mother. I looked up at Alice.

'Do you mind seeing her there, Lalla?' she said, and I shook my head. Finn was there with his grey beard, screen in hand before a group of listening people, and the engineers, clustered together, tools in hand. And there, in the centre, was my father. He was ten times the size of anyone else and he stood on the deck of the ship, his arms outstretched, outlined in gold, waiting to be filled in with millions of tiny stitches. More gold stitches outlined a rope coming from his right hand, and at the end of the rope was a circle. I wondered how long all this had taken, and how long there was left until the tapestry would be complete. But there was no doubt that there was time, time, time, stitched into it as securely as the lengths of coloured thread that made the picture. I looked at Tom; he met my eyes in challenge and I was the one who looked away.

'Why is my father bigger than anyone else?' I asked.

'Because he is,' Alice said, putting blue stitch after blue stitch into a section of the sea.

'What's he holding in his hand?'

'If you can't tell,' she said, 'you'll have to watch and wait.' She fastened off the blue and took a reel of silver. She held the end of the thread and drew it away from her body, setting the reel spinning between her fingers, then cut the thread and held the cut end in front of the eye of her needle. She made a few attempts to thread the needle, screwing up her eyes and holding it up to the light, before the thread finally went through and then she began to stitch again. With the blue thread she had made a solid block of colour; we watched as she made a silver upside-down V-shape on top of the blue.

'Is that a wave?' Tom asked.

'No,' I said, 'it's the ghost of a shark.'

'Oh, there are still sharks,' Alice said, looping the silver around her needle and pulling it taut. 'There were sharks before there was almost anything else and there'll be sharks long after we've gone.'

'How do you know?' I asked.

'I just know.'

'Why don't they come after us when we're in the net, then?'

Tom cut in. 'Why do you think Michael thought of providing the net?'

I looked at him and this time I did not look away. 'Do you think that there are still sharks?'

Tom shrugged. 'I don't think there aren't. I don't know if there are. All I'm saying is, whatever is the case, Michael thought of it.'

'But if a shark came, the net wouldn't stop it. They're really fierce. They've got never-ending rows of teeth that never stop growing and they can detect one drop of human blood in a million parts of water.'

Alice and Tom laughed. 'You've spent too long in the cinema,' Tom said.

'It can be the ghost of a shark if you like,' Alice said, her eyes kind. 'That's the thing about work like this. You make of it what you will.'

'But I don't want to make of it what I will. I want to know what it really is.'

'Then you will never be happy,' she said quietly.

No one spoke after that. Alice stitched at her silver shapes. Tom stared out of the window at the original of the sea. I watched Alice's fingers as she made one stitch, two stitches, three stitches, just as once upon a time I might have watched the second hand on a clock. Time passed here and could be measured. Eight, nine, ten. Twenty-one, twenty-two, twenty-three, and another ghost shark was complete and she went on to the next.

'Better than dust, isn't it, Lalla?' Tom said. I nodded. Maybe by the time Alice finished the sea, we would find a better way out onto the roof of the ship. Maybe by the time she finished the sky, Tom would understand me. Maybe, by the time she'd finished the ship, we'd have arrived and started building our home. There was a measuring stick here, and that was something I wanted. I felt content flood through me, and I moved closer to Tom.

Then I realised.

'It's the sun,' I said. 'That circle at the end of the rope in my father's hand. It's the sun.'

'Indeed.'

'Is that really what you think? That my father holds the sun on a rope?'

'It's what I see,' said Alice. 'I embroider what I see.'

I felt my content seeping away.

'It's not true, though.' I looked from her old face to his young one, her pale to his golden. 'You know it's not true.'

Tom smiled. 'Shall we meet up and watch the sunrise in the morning?'

'But we never know where the sun is going to rise.'

Tom and Alice laughed. 'Michael knows,' they said, and I felt sick. I went to the porthole and tried to open it, but there was no fastening, no handle. I stood still and tried to breathe, long slow breaths. I wanted rest and tranquillity; for a brief second I had found it, and now here was something else. I seemed destined to a constant struggle.

'What will you do when you've finished, Alice?' Tom asked.

'Oh, I'll never finish this. Look at how long it's taken me to get this far. If I've done before I die, I'll be lucky. I'll spend the rest of my days looking at it. And if I don't, well, my days will have been filled with something good. And someone else will have to take it on. There'll always be unfinished work, and there'll always be someone left to finish it. That's the way.'

But it wasn't the way. It was the way for tomorrow, maybe, and for the day after, and the day after, and the day after that. But not for ever. Everything anyone said seemed to point to some kind of collective blindness, as though the whole community had taken sleeping pills from the infirmary and swallowed them together with our evening coffee.

Tom turned to me. He never could sit still for long. 'Come on, Lalla. Alice wants to get on. We've disturbed her enough. And I bet people are waiting for football.'

'Michael has taught us to wait, Tom,' Alice said. 'I am enjoying your company, and Lalla is enjoying mine. Michael would tell you to leave if you want to, but don't put the responsibility for your actions on the shoulders of others.'

Tom bowed his head and said, 'Thank you, Alice. Please excuse me.' Alice nodded a benediction, and I stared at them, amazed.

'Are you coming, Lalla?'

I shook my head.

'See you at the gong, then.' He went to the door, grinning as though he had done something clever.

'Alice hasn't answered your question,' I said, but Tom left the room and closed the door behind him.

Alice picked up her needle again. 'We are too quiet here to contain such energy,' she said. 'Let us be thankful for Michael's provision, that Tom and I may both be happily occupied.'

'What will happen when you've finished?' I asked.

'I told you, Lalla. I'll be dead before that happens.'

'But I won't be. And neither will Tom. What will happen to us?'

Alice smiled at me, a warm smile right from her eyes. 'Tom, is it?' she said. 'I did wonder. Well, Lalla, mankind has been asking that question for millennia. The first moment that there was man, there were questions. Who am I? Where am I going? What happens when I'm gone?'

She was working on a figure now. It wore blue deck shoes, so it could have been anybody. She selected some deep red and rethreaded her needle.

'Well?'

'They told stories that explained what was going on around them. They said that the dark was a dragon that ate the sun every night, that the sun itself was a flower that grew when his back was turned.'

'Is that true?'

'As true as that the world was created when a god sneezed, or that winter came when the king of the underworld took the goddess of the harvest's daughter away with him. Or that thunder was because of a god who worked as a blacksmith.'

'A blacksmith? Like from the olden days?' My mother had told me about men who, once upon a time, had heated metal until it glowed red hot, so that they could bend and shape it. She had said they made gates, fences, tools. She'd also said they made shoes for horses, an idea so unlikely I'd never bothered to ask for details.

I asked now. 'Did horses really have shoes?'

'Yes. Horses had quite soft feet, so they used to make curved pieces of iron and nail them to the feet so that the horses would be comfortable walking for long distances.'

'Is that true? Or is it like the god sneezing thing?'

'It's true.'

'How do you know?'

'I went to school, remember. I read books.'

'You didn't have a screen?'

'There were two. In the corner of the classroom. Fixed to the wall. We used to take it in turns to use them. But it was better to read a book.'

'There aren't any books here.'

'No.' She took her scissors and snipped off the red thread, and I thought, well, no one will ever use that thread again. Then she chose a new colour, a lighter, golden orange, like a tinned peach. She cut a length, then unravelled it, so that instead of one thick thread, there were six thin ones. Her needle threaded with one bright strand; she made tiny knots with the point of her needle against the silk, each knot so close to the next that the stitches became a living, shimmering mass of curls, catching the sunlight as they moved. Emily. Emily with red hair, who was never still.

'Alice?'

'Yes, Lalla?'

'The way you've done my father, with the sun on the rope like that. Do you really think that's true, like the horse shoes, or is it like the dragon eating the sun?'

Alice put down her needle and looked at me. 'What is it that you see, Lalla? Where does the sun rise in the morning? Where does it set at night? Who made that happen? Look, Lalla, and decide for yourself.' She bent her head over the embroidery threads and I knew that I had been dismissed.

I could not resist. I went close to her and whispered, 'You know it's not true, Alice. Help me tell the others. Help me to get us to our destination.'

She spoke softly, moving her hands through the colours.

'My hands have work. My body is nourished. I sleep, and I am not afraid.'

'But Alice . . .'

'I will be dead before I have finished, Lalla. Before your father found me, I was finished, but I was not dead, and it was hell. Now, I look out of my porthole in the morning and I see the sun. I look again in the evening, and I see it again. It is a better world, Lalla. Let it be. What harm?'

So, I thought, here it is. My father stands on the deck of the ship, holding the sun by a golden rope. He swings the rope over his head, and the sun arcs over the ship. He transfers the rope to his left hand and rests. Once we have all slept and restored ourselves, he swings the rope back. And the sun passes over us all once more, and his right hand resumes control, and we rest, and he brings forth the sun once more. Our world was not sneezed out, or created in six days to end an eternity of loneliness. Ours was salvaged from decay and destruction by one who was part of it, and saw where it was leading. And he chose those who were worthy and carried them with him, and thus birthed life from death, hope from despair, love from fear.

And the sun shifted to illuminate the new centre of the universe and submitted itself to my father.

And the evidence was there, every single day. Twice a day. As long as people like Alice could look out of their portholes and say, *This is what I see*, I would be unable to say, *Yes, but it is not what you think*. Because they knew. They already knew.

At dinner that night, I watched Alice cut her food with the same grace as she made her stitches. What harm, she had said. What harm. But to me, the harm was clear. If there were eighteen thousand tins of pineapple in the stores, then they would one day be gone, the same as if there were a hundred thousand, or a hundred, or only one. Alice would reach out her hand for a skein of coloured thread and it would not be there. First the blue, then the grey, then the gold would run out, and there would be nothing left but the outlines of a child's colouring book, made of the shadows of thoughts and ideas that could never be brought to life. The longer we took to get to land, the fewer resources we would have to start our new lives.

Tom's green eyes danced in front of me, and I knew that if I were Alice, and the tapestry she was stitching was the story of my life and thoughts, it would be the green thread that would run out first, because everywhere I looked, all I could see was the green of his eyes. It was for him I had to act. For him, so that we could know time, know ourselves, and be truly together. We could not lose ourselves in each other until we knew where we were. After all, if you do not know where you are, you are lost already, and how can you ever hope to find anyone else?

For Tom, because I loved him.

I went over to her table. 'Thank you, Alice,' I said, and I kissed her soft, wrinkled cheek. She put down her knife and fork and squeezed my hand.

'Try to be happy, dear,' she said. 'It's much the best thing.'

I would go to the goodnight meeting and I would listen with all my heart. And then I would go back to my cabin and wait for the dark.

It was time to talk to my father.

SIXTEEN

My plan to save the ship ❧ *I go to find my father,*
but my father finds me ❧ *I fall*

I sat in the goodnight meeting and looked from face to face. At
last I had a plan, a way to prove to the people that things were
not as they thought. My father did not control the sun. It rose
in the east and set in the west. That was the truth, and whether
they admitted it or not, they knew it. I would force them to
admit what they knew to be true. Helen, I thought, when I bring
my evidence, you will be free to teach Gabriel as many truths as
you please. Patience, you will knit for a purpose. I will find out
where we are going, and when we are going to get there, and that
knowledge will set you all free.

And Tom. Tom. When we know where we are going, we can
marry. Make plans. I had come to the goodnight meeting in-
tending to listen, but I had been so lost in my own thoughts that
the discussion was underway before I realised it had started.

'Of course we should write,' my father was saying. 'But let
us consider why. In the time before the time before, any words
that were to be heard by more than a few people had to be
written down and published in a book, printed on paper. And
because this was a process that cost money, the mere existence
of a book meant that someone, somewhere, thought that what
was in it was worth reading. That is why only pre-published

works were authorised by the Dove. A reminder of a nobler time.'

'But, Michael,' Finn said, 'without the raven routes, you would never have known of me.'

'Or me,' Tom agreed.

'For every one Finn Johnson,' my father said, 'for every one Tom Mandel, there were hundreds of thousands of people pouring words into the ether, words that meant nothing. An hour with a book expanded understanding; an hour with the screen contracted it. Since you had the strength and the wisdom to cast away the mast, the danger of suffocating yourselves with irrelevances is significantly diminished. The portals I gave you are tools. Just tools. A way to access important things that have stood the test of time. Cast aside ephemera. And before you dare to write, make sure your words are worthy of standing alongside those that have gone before you. Read. Before you write, read.'

'Read everything? All the books on the screen?' Finn asked, his face reflecting his struggle to understand. He owed his life to the very thing my father was dismissing – an unrestricted flow of words, pouring from him to anyone reckless enough to access them, unfettered by paper and ink and someone else's controlling mind. Unreliable, uncensored and illegal as the raven routes were, they were the only way of circumventing the Dove. People like Finn had hacked, decoded and tampered to pass on what they had to say. Now there was no Dove, there was no risk, or danger either.

But I was going to find my evidence, and then talk to my father. In the morning, we would be on our way; the risk and danger would be back and Finn would be free to write again.

My father smiled and he held out his hands, just as he did in Alice's tapestry. I had never seen him stand like that before; now, he drew himself up and held his hands out with his palms towards us. It was as though he had seen an idealised version of himself in Alice's work, and decided to become it.

'You are my books,' my father said, and I knew that this would be all I would hear from anyone for the next few marks on my cabin wall. *We are Michael's books. I am a precious book, belonging to Michael. I am a glorious book that Michael has written.* He continued, 'You are my library of the best of twenty-first-century man – of all man, across all time, all ages. What need have we of more books, when we have each other?'

Your mother will always be a part of you, Lalla, so what need I weep when you are with me?

That night, I did not change into my cotton nightdress. I stayed in my clothes, and when the night noises of running water and creaking bunks had subsided, I slipped out of my cabin door. The dark was more than dark; it was black in a way London nights had never been. It made no difference whether my eyes were open or shut. I could see nothing. I felt my way forwards, along the corridor of cabin doors, until I reached the bigger doors that led out onto the deck. When I pushed them open, the thick air took me by surprise. The days had been cooler since the rain. But the dark seemed to have brought back the heat, and in any case, the night was a strange place to me. There was a wind too, a hot stifling breath that brought no relief. I blinked as air blew into my eyes. I felt tears forming, swelling, spilling onto my face and I celebrated them as a purely physical reaction to a purely physical thing. My body had a reflex with which to protect my eyes from wind. Self-preservation, not preservation by the father.

And the night had a different smell, too. In the day, the smells were of food, washing powder, the warmth of an iron on rumpled cotton. Soup. Soap. Now, those smells were gone, and there was only salt and emptiness, with a warm dank undertone of neglect. After all, when had any of us really acknowledged the presence of the sea? If there was anything still living there, it would not come in the daytime, when everyone was busy, but in the night, when we slept. I felt for the metal wall and stood with my back to it. In the dark, there was no horizon. The ship, the sea and the sky were one expanse of black, less than an arm's stretch away, or miles and miles beyond me. It was impossible to tell. And because I could not see its edge, the sea ceased to be a vast barrier, a cage without bars, and became one with the ship and the sky and the land.

I could leave just by putting my foot over the side.

I thought of going back to my cabin and trying again when there was a moon, or at least replacing my clothes with my cool cotton nightdress. But I had no way of knowing whether there would ever be a moon, and it had taken me long enough to inch my blind self this far. It had to be now. A fat drop of water fell on my hand and I heard thunder, far away. I felt like yelling, *You didn't see this coming, did you, Father?* I left the security of the wall and took a step towards the deck railings opposite. I could not see my feet upon the deck or my hands stretched out in front of me; I was blind, and the sense of possibility made me dizzy. I took another step, and another, following the smell of the sea, expecting at any moment for my fingertips to meet the deck rail. Warm, heavy drops splashed onto my reaching arms and the thunder rolled closer. But the further I travelled, the more remote the deck's edge seemed to become, until I was surrounded by nothingness, turning this way and that, groping above the unsteady deck for a fixed point from which I could navigate. Then the rain came in earnest, great sheets that were draped over me by the winds. It felt as though the sea itself was pouring onto the deck; I was soaked in an instant, as thoroughly as though I had fallen in. The infinite union of the ship, the sky and the water enfolded me, and in that infinite and terrifying blackness, I heard my name.

'Lalla.'

The walls and bars sprang back into being. I turned towards

the voice, but I had no idea where it was coming from, or whether to seek it or hide from it. The thunder was all but drowned out by the noise of the downpour, hammering on the deck, the walls, the window. Through the chaos the voice came again. *Lalla*, it said, *Lalla*, and I panicked. I ran towards the dissolved edges of my world. My hard soles slipped on the water-coated deck; I fell, and cried out as my face hit something cold and hard. White lights exploded inside my head; my mouth flooded with warmth. I put my hands to my face then got to my knees, struggling for breath. A flash of lightning ripped through the sky. I saw my hands red and shining, with bits of them dripping onto my shoes. I saw a figure in the doorway, silhouetted by the light, its shadow falling so close to me that only a shard of light separated us

'Lalla.'

My father had called me; now he had come for me. I scrabbled along the wall, my bloody hands slipping, trying to find a hook or a handle I could use to pull myself up. The metal was smooth, and the rivets had been beaten into perfect hemispheres. My legs refused to act. I crawled away from his shadow as though it would burn me if it touched me, but my strength was gone. I was wet and shaking, and when hands closed around my ribcage and pulled me up, I could not break away.

'What do you want?' I demanded, but the words were slurred and indistinct in my damaged mouth.

'You came looking for something, Lalla, and you have found me. So the question is not what do I want, but what do you want?'

What did I want? I remembered my mother, lying in the infirmary with her green and blue dress tucked over her.

'I want to know,' I shouted over the rain, while the wind whipped my sodden hair around my face.

'Then you had better come with me.' I could not move without his help. I pulsed and throbbed where my skin had broken, and I wondered how I could possibly have done myself so much damage. It was as though the ship itself had slammed into me, the full force of its tonnage crashing against my fragile human frame. *I am bigger than you are*, it said. *I have been created by a brilliant mind, a mind that saw the future; I am knit together, not of metal and rivets, but of dreams and ideas. Mine is the power; you are a mayfly, a gnat, a minor irritation. You are rusting; I am eternal.*

I limped beside my father, dependent on his arm. The next flash of lightning showed me the deck rail, strong and silver, the sea and the sky beyond still as black as each other. I tried to remember that, for a fleeting moment, the sea had been, not an insuperable eternity of dead water, but simply so much space, at one with the land. For a moment, the darkness had been my friend; now I could only feel pain and trembling.

'It's all right, Lalla. I'm here. Feel me. Everything is all right now. You know it is.'

Did I? Did the fact that I was stumbling alongside the man who had brought me into the world mean that everything was all right? His arm was strong, his flesh beneath the soaked shirt warm; as I surrendered to its support, tiredness stole over me. My aching body was no longer my own. The pain receded as I leant upon him, glad to feel that he had strength enough for both of us. What was thought, after all? Only a means for self-torment, self-doubt.

'Lalla,' he said into my hair. 'My Lalla, at last.'

I heard the sound of a key in a lock, and my father passed before me into a room full of screens, lights, control panels. I saw books. I saw maps. I saw something that looked like a clock, but it had only one hand and just four numbers. I looked more closely and realised that they were not numbers, but letters. N, E, S, W. North, East, South, West. A compass. I had last seen this one in a museum, inside a glass case, and won-dered how it had come to be here. I saw two chairs, padded in dark blue, on wheels. My father led me gently to one, then sat on the other, his right arm leaning on the arm rest, his shirt stained with my blood. I wondered how long it would take me to get the stain out. He disappeared briefly and came back with towels, soft white warm towels, and wrapped one around me. He closed the door behind him and the noise of the storm ceased completely.

'You wanted to know,' he said. He leaned over and kissed me on my temple, where there was no blood and no bruising. 'Are you ready, Lalla? Are you ready to learn?'

I was tired. I wanted my mother. I wanted Tom. My face hurt. My eyes burned with the pain in my nose and I could feel the cuts in my mouth with my tongue. I sniffed, then coughed as the warm metal taste of blood oozed into the back of my mouth. The blood dripped onto my clothes, onto the carpet, and I dabbed stupidly at it with the towel, which clung to me damply. My father produced a handkerchief and I sat holding it to my nose.

Then he reached for a switch and the overhead light went out, and with the blackness came clarity.

In the darkness, leaving seemed possible, because everything was one. If infinite is truly infinite, then it is as close as it is dis-tant, and as far away as it may be, you can reach out and touch it with nothing more than an outstretched hand.

A green light flashed on a screen as a green line swept over it. Bleep. Bleep. Bleep. 'There we are, Lalla. That's us, that dot. You're always asking, and now you know.'

'Where are we going?'

'Didn't Tom tell you? I told him to tell you. We've arrived. This is the ship, my darling. When you get to where you are going, you stop.'

'What's that?' A solid green patch appeared in one corner,

with an uneven edge, like torn paper. 'That's land, isn't it? Is that where we're going?'

'Keep watching.'

I watched, leaning forward and using the handkerchief to stop the blood dripping on the instruments. The green dot went bleep, bleep, bleep. And as I watched, the solid green corner receded until the little dot was once more bleeping in a circle of nothingness.

'Why are we sailing away?' I asked. 'That was land. What are you doing?'

'Look at the charts, the radar, the patterns of the sunrise and sunset. Look at the compass. You know what I'm doing. You only have to look.' He paused. 'Your mother would have worked it out weeks ago.'

'You're turning the ship,' I said at last. 'You take us so far, and then at night you turn the ship around and go back the other way. That's why the sun never rises and sets where it should. We're going round in circles.' I paused for a moment. 'The people will kill you when they find out.'

'Why would they do that?'

'Because they think we're going to a place where we can make a new start, where we can leave the misery behind . . .'

'Which is exactly where we are.'

And I thought, and my thoughts all ran into each other like toppling dominos. The gangway, released to the sea, never to be used again. My mother, so reluctant to leave the land. Alice's tapestry. And Tom. *I know where I am, Lalla. I'm right here, right now.* The stores. The readiness with which the people knitted and used clay, all the while knowing that their work would be undone. Photograph albums.

'The ship is where we're going?'

'The ship is where we're going.'

'The people knew?'

'The people knew.'

'We're not heading to an island somewhere, or a place that still works?'

'There are no such places. There is nothing left.'

'It's madness,' I said, the enormity of the truth breaking at last. 'You'll kill us all.'

I expected him to be angry, but he simply cocked his head as though he found me interesting. 'How so?' he said.

'The engine parts will give out. They'll wear away and stop working, and then you'll have no control at all over where we're going. The solar panels will break off and fall into the sea. The bolts under the water will rust through, and they'll fall away, and the sea will pour in and the ship will sink. Like the Sinkers back in London, remember? Or that village Jamila lived in, that ended up under water. Or else someone will get ill and it'll spread. We'll run out of food.' I stopped, astounded at having to explain. 'It's just not sustainable,' I concluded lamely, and even in the darkness I could hear my father smile.

'The Sinkers were deliberately scuppered by troops. And Jamila's village was at the mercy of a world that didn't care about it, that could barely be bothered to acknowledge it existed. Her village was under water once a year for decades and nothing was done. The warnings were all there. But they weren't acted upon, and that was it. One year, the waters didn't recede. That was the end of her village and everyone in it.' He paused for a moment, then added, 'It was the end of most of Bangladesh, actually.'

'I know.'

'But the ship isn't Bangladesh. The ship is cared about. Maintained. If something is wrong, it is sorted out. If there is a problem, it is solved. What do you think the engineers do all day? The world was destroyed by blind eyes. We of the ship will never be blind to her needs.'

'It's a machine. A machine. It's not a person, it's not a country. It's not organic.'

'Listen to yourself,' said my father. 'Sustainable. Organic. You should have been born fifty years ago.' He paused. 'What was your next thing? Illness?'

'The people will get sick,' I said, remembering Tom's parents and China, feeling the pain in my face. 'There'll be a virus and it'll spread through the ship.'

'Ah, yes,' he said slowly. 'The pandemics. The warnings were all there too. New strains of bacteria, new viruses, vaccines made from the very sources of the infections and pumped into populations across the globe. People visiting places thousands of miles away and bringing the new strains home, taking antibiotics like sweets. How did they think it was going to end?'

'I suppose they thought they'd make a new antibiotic.'

My father nodded. 'They didn't, though, did they? Science had come to the end of what it could do.' He nodded towards my nose gravely and spoke in a doom-laden voice. 'If we don't get that cleaned up, it'll get infected and you could die.' I cried out – I could not help it – and he laughed at me. 'It's all right. This isn't some poverty-stricken tent city. There's no new strain of disease waiting to unleash havoc upon us here.'

'Your radar will stop working and we'll drift to land.'

'There's the compass and the maps. And the stars haven't gone out yet.'

'You stole that compass,' I said, suddenly certain. 'Just like you stole the people.'

'Better to fulfil your purpose than to rot behind glass.'

'The food will run out, or the freezers will stop working.'

'You've seen the stores. Or some of them. You could eat and eat and eat and not make a dent in what there is. If we all ate like you, we wouldn't need the food at all.' I think I was meant to laugh, but the green line kept up its bleep, bleep, bleep as it swept across the green dot, and in the green light my father's smile looked ghoulish.

'The football will fall to pieces,' I said. 'The knitting needles will break. Alice will run out of thread.'

'There are other footballs. Other needles. More thread.'

'The people will get bored and end up fighting against you.'

He laughed out loud then, and the next bleep showed me green teeth and the green whites of his eyes. 'You don't even believe that yourself.'

'They meet in secret,' I said in spite of myself. 'I've seen them, giving signals to each other after dinner.'

'You have?' he said, faintly amused. 'You don't think they might be – I don't know – discussing something they've read? I trust my people. What else do you have for me? You've threatened pestilence, famine and war. Isn't there another one?'

'Death,' I said.

'Oh, death.' He sounded impatient. 'We are all going to die. We were always all going to die. No one has ever lived who has not died. Death is . . .'

'I know, I know. Death is the only thing all living things share. That doesn't mean we have to go out and invite it in.'

'How else would you suggest we live? Cowering away from death as we did in the time before? Thinking we were immortal because we had seven hundred channels on our televisions and thousands of friends we'd never even met?'

'You wouldn't have found all these people without all that.'

'That's what I keep saying. That's what I'm trying so hard to make you understand. The ship is where human life has been leading, ever since mankind walked upright. It doesn't matter what happens now.'

'It's just a thing,' I said impatiently. 'And things wear out.' I thought about the dresses my mother had cut down for me, my red shoes.

'Perhaps. But this is all new. This is a new way of working, a new way of being. We no longer simply exist, waiting for the next new thing to come and replace the previous thing. We've found rightness. And when something is truly pure, nothing can taint it. It heals where it touches. The ship is healing, Lalla. It has healed the wounds of the people, and the people care for and maintain it. It's perfect, in concept and execution, and nothing will ever need to supersede it.' He paused, and as the green line swept across the dot again, I saw how much he was enjoying himself. There was a spark in his eye and I remembered how he had argued with my mother. Her opposition had helped him, given life and substance to his plans, helped him grow and be purposeful, just as playing football kept Tom's body fit and taut. She had been his discipline and he had loved her for it. But I was not my mother. I lacked her intelligence, her courage, her restraining hand.

Even so, I felt a tiny fluttering of power in my stomach. My secret love, my woman's body. No, my father did not have it all his own way. How could he, when I had Tom?

'I'm not a child,' I said.

'You are. I've lived forty years longer than you have. I remember things you have never even heard of.'

'And I am looking at a future you won't be a part of. You'll be dead and I'll still have forty years to go.'

'Why do you think that I show you all these things? Why do you think I talk to you, allow you to speak to me in this manner? I recognise youth. I recognise idealism. I see myself in you, and I've done everything I can to give you a future.' He stopped and looked around. The screens, the maps. The bleep, bleep, bleep, louder in the silence. The little green dot in the middle of the blank screen. 'You cry about things running out as though it's news. But it's not news. Of course things will run out. But we're stocked for at least twenty years, probably more.

And that's twenty years for you, Lalla. Twenty years for you to learn and create and decide your own future. The future of the next generation.'

The green light on his face. The blood on my hands, the searing pain behind my nose, which struck me anew each time I took a breath.

'I don't know what you'll do,' he said. 'Perhaps there'll be fish again. Or you'll work out how to make cultures in which you can grow proteins. You haven't even started to explore the resources on the fourth deck.' He smiled. 'You could build a rocket ship and fly to the moon to harvest green cheese.'

I drew breath but he cut me off. 'The point is this. You need to think. You need to take responsibility and stop waiting around for everyone else to solve things for you. I've given you at least two decades. I got the ship together in less than half that, with no help at all, in a world that worked against me at every turn. But you are not alone. You've got me. You've got scientists on board, engineers, you name it. Win the people's trust. They want you, Lalla. They want to trust you. You are my heir.'

'Trust, yes. But not blind trust.'

'The people are not blind.'

'They are. Look at Gabriel and the photographs of his father. Helen let them go, because you said she must. Look at eggs. At apples.'

'Apples?'

'Have you ever eaten an apple?'

'Of course.' He looked at me as though we had just met. 'Haven't you?'

'No. I've had apple out of cans, in pies, sauces, things like that. But I've never had a real fresh apple.'

He looked pensive. 'Time goes faster than you think,' he sighed. 'I knew you'd never had an orange. But I thought apples would have been in your time. It was a pity about the bees.'

'Bees?'

'It doesn't matter now,' he said quietly. 'What matters is this room, these displays. The compass. The people. You.'

He looked out of the round window and rested his hands on the desk. It was a beautiful desk, made of wood that glowed warm and red with polish and care. It had drawers with metal handles that looked like gold, just like the desk on the podium in the ballroom. 'It was a lonely thing, getting all this together,' he said slowly, and I felt sorry for him in spite of myself. 'There were times I thought I might die from the loneliness.' I thought of my mother, her feet tucked underneath her as she sat on the sofa saying, *Not yet, Michael, not yet.* 'But I persevered. We have escaped destruction, and disease, and degeneration. We have taken on the guardianship of the things that made humanity beautiful. Friendship. Peace. Love. Trust. Suppose – just suppose – that you're right, and all you threaten comes to pass. We'll seal ourselves in the sports hall and breathe our last together, and all these beautiful things will survive until the end.'

'But there are people out there!'

'Out there? There's nothing beautiful out there.' He gestured out across the waters. 'If there's any life there, it is a life of blame and hunger and misery. Anyone alive out there is dead, even if, at this moment, they still breathe. But the death I suffered has been rewarded a thousand times.'

'What death?' I said. Because even though I was falling into his every word, I still had a ledge I could cling to, a jutting place where I could rest my feet and keep myself from complete surrender. And it was this: Tom and I had found each other. We were young, we were in love, and we had a life of passion and desire that was truly our own. His body, my body. His heart, my heart. Together we had stood on the deck rail and thrown away our cards; together we had balanced on boxes and climbed out of the ship.

'There are many kinds of death,' my father said simply.

And for a moment, my certainty wavered. I saw my father as the others on the ship saw him, as he saw himself. A man for whom humanity was more important than self. A man whose love for others surpassed all else. 'The joy of my life now,' he continued, 'is that I have saved you, my daughter, from all but one of those deaths, and that one is the one we all have a right to, that everyone on the ship may now anticipate, and welcome when it comes. Natural death, good death, a calm goodbye amongst friends to a life truly lived. It may never come. It may come tomorrow. But here, on the ship, we are ready.' I felt tears coming to my eyes. Because what he was offering was so easy. Did it matter that we were all going to die? Everyone has died, always. And if death was the end of everything, what was wrong with living a life in which nothing would attack me in the dark, a life in which I knew what would happen, tomorrow and the next day and the day after? A life of which I was in control?

No one has ever lived who did not die.

My father spoke softly. 'You're stuck in the time before, Lalla, when the sea was the enemy, and ships used tonnes of oil to fight its currents and winds. The sea is our ally now. It bears us up. It shares with us its glorious expanse, gives us space to breathe. It and the ship are as one. There are no destinations, once you have arrived.'

'But Helen's husband?' I said, struggling to hold on to my certainty. 'Why must she forget him?'

'So many people died. Would you have their loss – or even Anna's – define our life on the ship? We move on. We honour our dead by living well.'

It was as though a mist was emanating from my father, a scented, warm mist that covered my skin and entered into my brain, so that his thoughts and mine became one. As I breathed, I tasted the life he had poured into the ship, so that I could be safe. And I realised that the reason he had dedicated his life to creating the ship was because he loved me. Not my mother, who had always argued with him, but me. I was flesh of his flesh. I was made from a part of him; from that part, I had grown under his care and guidance; because of that part, he had planned and created a new world, brought it into being, made it concrete. Because of him, I could weep for the dead in the British Museum, mourn for the drowned in India, feel the luxury of horror at my recollections of the rats chewing on the homeless in Russell Square Gardens. Because of him, the crater in Regent's Park was just a crater in Regent's Park, neither closer nor more relevant to me than a crater on the moon.

'And Tom?' I breathed softly, forgetting the pain for a moment as I readied myself for his anger and gathered myself up to fight. If he denied me Tom, I would be able to hate him. I would find the energy to tell the people what was going on, and to defy him.

But there was no anger in him. He looked younger, and I saw the face my mother had loved before I was born. 'I would not have my children be alone,' he said softly. 'And if a generation yet to come retreats into the sports hall and seals the door – well, it is good to know they will be together, and fulfilled. But that moment won't come. I believe in my people. Their creativity, their ingenuity. I believe in you. I can't tell you what the future looks like, my darling, but I know that it will be beautiful. How can it be anything else, with this as its beginning?' I saw Tom's green eyes looking down on me, and I saw his gentleness with the children, felt his hands upon my skin. Was there really no destination? Were we to glide along for ever, uncomplaining in a field of plenty?

But I wanted more. I wanted to be with Tom, to share everything I was with him. To hold his heart in mine and defend it; to share our stories and determine our own future. That was my hope.

And I understood, suddenly, that it was this hope that had allowed me to leave food on my plate for the walnut-faced man to finish, this hope that had kept me apart as others had wept at my father's speeches. Hope that there were still choices to be made, that my future was not set out in tiny stitches in Alice's tapestry. Hope that whatever miraculous agency had connected Tom and I existed somewhere beyond the ship, and that by being together, we would find it. Hope was the danger. If I threw hope overboard, there would be certainty. Without hope, oranges and eggs would become historic curiosities, like jade axes. Apples would not bother me, and I would never have to worry about where the sun rose. With hope gone, I would have space in my mind to wonder about the glories my father had hidden away in the storerooms, and to dream of the people of the ship all looking at me with love and pride as I fulfilled my father's plans for me.

To give up hope would be to give up Tom, because Tom was my hope, and I could not live without him, no matter what I owed to my father. *I'll go back to London with you,* Tom had said once upon a time, *if it's really what you want.* Tom, not my father, was where my trust resided now. For all his talk of death, my father had not died. It was my mother who had taken a bullet and had her body invaded by poison from the infected wound. My father was alive, adored, standing before me, and he knew nothing of the woman I had become. But Tom did, and together, we would work out what to do with the truth I had discovered.

My father switched the overhead light on again. He stood before me, tall and powerful and smiling, his torso outlined by his rain-soaked shirt, stained with my blood. Only surrender hope, and I would have the universe at my feet. The world beyond the ship would no longer exist, and therefore no longer matter. I could ask my father for deck shoes, throw my old shoes into the sea and consign them to a fantasy world that may never have existed. Hope. The cruellest thing in Pandora's box.

Disease, death, destruction, misery, pain, loss; terrible though they were, hope was the worst. Because it was hope that made humanity bear the rest.

And that was what the ship was. A life without hope.

I looked down at my cracked red shoes, felt them press against my feet. My mother had given them to me. They were a part of the life I had lived before, and if I threw them away, they would still exist, and become shoe-shaped coral beneath the sea. For as long as there were my red shoes, for as long as I could remember the British Museum, for as long as my mother's voice still sounded in my head, for as long as I loved Tom, I would have hope, and my life would be hard. The pain of my broken nose reasserted itself and my father's cabin began to swim.

'Lalla,' he said, coming towards me with his arms outstretched, 'I love you.'

But it was too late for that.

SEVENTEEN

My broken nose ❖ *the doctor's tale* ❖ *stupidity*

I had wanted to know, and now I did. We were going round and round in circles, stimulated, loved, learning, too dizzy on plenty to see. Part of me was aghast that I had not realised what was going on. And yet how could I have realised? My father claimed to have created the ship for me. His chosen people had brought their children on board. They were not cruel, or selfish, or unkind. I could not hate them for their decision; indeed, when I concentrated on today, or tomorrow, or even the day after that, I could understand. Already I was so used to the motion of the ship that I didn't notice it. But we would grow old. We would stumble about, scraping the remains of the preserved foodstuffs into each other's mouths, throwing each other's bodies into the sea with the rubbish as old age or illness claimed us. And when we lost the strength in our arms, the bodies would lie on the deck as they had lain in the streets of London, and those who were just little children now would step over them as they went to the stores, anxiously calculating how long the food might hold out. How different would life on the ship be from life in London then? The passing of time would return us from whence we had come, for as long as we chose to do nothing. How the children would curse us. My father held out the sealed sports hall as some kind of last resort, but slow suffocation seemed a poor sort of future to me, no matter whose hand I might be holding.

My father left me in the infirmary, in the company of the doctor once more. The doctor set about cleaning the blood from my face and injecting my face with something that made it go numb. He pressed white tape over my nose with a grinding crunch that I sensed rather than felt. He stroked cotton wool over my hands and put some cream from a tube onto the cuts. He did not ask how I had come to be injured.

'Michael wants you to stay here until your face has healed a bit.'

'No,' I said. I could not bear to think of the last time I had been in the infirmary. 'Take me back to my cabin.'

'I need to keep an eye on you.'

'I'm fine.' There was a tingling sensation around my nose; it would become painful as the anaesthetic wore off.

'You need to lie still. You can't traipse across the ship every time I need to check up on you. And the infirmary certainly can't come to you.'

'I'm not staying in the infirmary on my own.'

He picked up the clean sheets. I had delivered those sheets only the day before, when I had been a different person. 'All right,' he said. He held out his arm and helped me off the bed. I was aching all over – my hands and nose had been the main casualties of my encounter with the ship, but I had bruises all over me. 'It's time you and I had a talk anyway. My cabin's next door. I'll make tea.'

I had never seen the doctor's cabin before; his clothes and sheets went to the infirmary and he collected them from there. It wasn't like my cabin, or like Tom's, or like any of the cabins I delivered laundry to. The doctor had two big leather armchairs and an infirmary bed instead of a bunk; the floor was covered in red carpet, and there was an intricately patterned rug between the chairs. I leaned on the back of the chair nearest to the door, trying to look as though I belonged.

'You can sit down.'

I sat.

He put teabags into two mugs and poured water onto them from a kettle. They weren't the white mugs from the dining room. One was red and one was blue, and they had gold patterns on them, swirling over and over, like the swell of the sea. These mugs had not come from the fourth floor. Was this man, whom I had avoided for so long, to be my ally? Was this why he had brought me here?

'Have you always been a doctor?' I asked.

He nodded. 'It was all I ever wanted to do.'

'Why?'

He stirred the tea. 'I thought that people were essentially good. I thought I could help us all to stay alive, stay sane, keep it together so that we could get through. Because humanity's been in crisis before. And it's always survived.'

'Even Regent's Park? The British Museum?'

He shrugged. 'It wasn't the first time bodies have been flung into handcarts.'

'So why didn't you stay behind and help?'

'The thing is.' He stopped and stared out of his porthole, as though the thing might be floating in the sea. I willed him to say, *I was waiting for you to come and find me, because I knew I could not turn the ship alone.* But he didn't. What he did say, though, was the next best thing. 'In the past . . .'

'I thought you weren't allowed to talk about the past.'

He gestured dismissively and my heart raced. 'In the past,' he continued, 'no matter how terrible the atrocities, no matter how many lives were lost, there was always a group doing the inflicting, ready to be toppled or challenged or assassinated, or even just to die out and be replaced by someone else. Time goes forward and things change. But that's not true anymore. This wasn't a dictator pounding a people into dust.'

'What was it then?'

'Stupidity, mostly.'

'Stupidity?'

I remembered one of the very few times my mother was angry with me. We'd been to the museum, looking at the mummified cats in the Egyptian galleries. I can only have been eleven or twelve, maybe even younger, because the cases were still quite full. We had just finished eating lunch, and I said, 'Why can't we have a dog? Or a cat?'

My parents both looked at me, eyes wide, a mirror of each other's surprise.

'A pet?' my mother said. Normally her voice was like a soft hand. This time it was a fist and it hit me in the stomach. The pain was sharp and as it faded, I felt the desire for a dog blossom in its place, until I wanted one so badly that I could feel its fur, wiry under my hand, and its breath hot against my skin. I was a lonely child.

'Yes,' I said. 'A dog. It could be my friend. I could take it for walks and look after it. You wouldn't have to do anything. It could sleep on my bed.'

'Lalla,' my father began, but my mother interrupted him.

'A dog,' she said. It wasn't even a question. It was a statement, a flat, bald statement of impossibility.

'Yes.' I could see it. It had big dark eyes, and it was looking at me, wagging its tail against the floor. A shaggy brown and white tail, the length of my handspan.

My father spoke with reason and authority. 'We can't have a dog, kitten. Someone would eat it. It might get sick. And there aren't any dogs around anymore, except the ones that have gone wild.' His voice tailed off as the futility of explaining the obvious overtook him. 'You're being silly, Lalla.'

'She's being stupid.' My mother was shaking.

'OK, she's being stupid.'

'It was a stupid thing to say. What was she thinking about, to ask such a thing? What are we working for, to have a daughter who understands so little? A dog?'

'She didn't mean it.'

'That's even worse. Why ask for what you don't want? We give you everything, everything, and you understand nothing.' Her face was quite white, and I knew that the little brown and white dog with loving eyes I had conjured up in the face of her anger would never return. I had pushed my mother far enough; more than anything, I feared being the reason that she cried.

'She was stupid. That's all. There's no charge. It's all right, Anna.'

'It is not all right. There is a price for stupidity. And it is never the stupid people who pay it. They lumber about like elephants, trampling all over the things other people have planted, then complain when the plants don't grow. But they don't go without. Oh no. They want what they want, no matter what has gone before or what will come after.'

'I know, I know.'

'And that's what stupidity is. Wanting something because you want it. It's not enough, Lalla. It's not enough to want something. You have to need it. To need it with your whole heart and soul, and with every last atom of your being, because everything you get is at a cost somewhere. If people had stuck to that, we'd still be living in beautiful places, surrounded by trees, eating food from the earth.' The image calmed her; her breathing was easier now, and I knew that if she cried, it would not be because of me. The dog retreated across the room and the door closed behind it.

The doctor passed me the red mug, its handle towards me. 'Careful,' he said, 'it's hot.'

'Did you talk to my mother about stupidity? When you were interviewed for the ship?'

He nodded. 'Anna and I agreed that the only thing to do with stupidity is to escape from it. To get away, somewhere where the decisions it makes cannot affect you. She knew it, but she could never make up her mind to go. We were all sorry about that. We talked about Anna in the holding centre, often. But Michael refused to force her. He is a truly great man, your father, and you are a very lucky young woman.' He pulled up his sleeve and looked at his watch. A watch. He had a watch.

'I'll have to go soon,' he said.

'Why?'

'There are some people I said I'd meet.'

'Can I come?'

'No.'

'You're doing something,' I retorted. I thought of all the times I'd watched him in the dining room. 'You and Abigail and Vikram. And that man with the grey hair down to his ears and lots of stubble. Luke. You meet up secretly.' There. I had said it now, and my little piece of hope drew breath and shook out its wings. I watched it fly, sparkling and golden, to the doctor, and willed him to give it a home in which to grow. I plunged on. 'You do know what's happening, don't you? We're sailing round in circles and that's all we're going to do for ever. There's no island waiting for us. But you're trying to take the ship somewhere, aren't you? To land somewhere. I can help you.'

The doctor stared at me and I felt the tape across my nose, the tenderness around my eyes, the scrapes on my palms. The room seemed to turn grey. He closed his eyes and put his forehead in his hands. 'Little girl,' he said into his palms, shaking his head. 'Don't do this to yourself.'

'Do what?'

Hope folded its wings and settled on the desk to wait. The doctor lifted up his head. 'Do you know how I came to be here?' he asked.

'You had a wife called Sarah and a baby who died,' I said. 'That's all I know.'

'Then listen,' he said. 'I knew the baby might die. I knew the moment that I told my Sarah to push, and she said that she was pushing, and I felt the bump and it was hard and frozen and the head was in the wrong place. I had to get our baby out quickly. Really quickly. Don't talk,' he said as I drew breath. 'You need to stay still, so that dressing can set properly.'

I put my grazed hands around my hot tea mug and focused on the pain.

'I needed to cut her open. It was routine once, back in the days when there were proper medicines and all doctors had to do was call for them. But my Sarah was too late for that. Hospitals didn't have anaesthetics and clean blood anymore.'

'What happened?'

'I waited. I don't know what I was waiting for. Some miracle, I suppose. Anaesthetic to fall from the sky. But it didn't. Sarah was screaming, and when I finally got on with it, she passed out with the first cut. The hospital generator was working for once, so I put her on the ventilator. I rummaged in her belly. It was like looking for a working pen in a drawer full of junk. And the baby I pulled from her – a girl, blue and purple, covered in a layer of white wax and her mother's blood – made no sound. I took her, I held her, I breathed for her. I told her I loved her. But I'd waited too long. I couldn't save her. I laid my baby on her mother and left the room, so that they would not hear me howl.'

I sat absolutely still.

'There was a monitor and when I went back in, I could see Sarah's heartbeat growing weaker and weaker. I took our daughter in my arms and sat beside my dying wife, watching. And then Sarah opened her eyes and stared at the baby, and I saw that she was terrified.'

'What did you do?'

'I told her not to worry. I told her that the baby was fine.'

'But that wasn't true.'

'No.'

'And?'

'And then I turned off the ventilator.'

'Why?'

'So that the last thing Sarah knew before she died was love and not despair.'

'Why are you telling me this?'

'Because you're looking for something, Lalla, and you won't find it in me. Or in anyone here. I was truly sorry I could not save your mother. And Lalla – think of this. If I'd acted more decisively, I could have saved my baby, if not my wife. And if I'd had the infirmary and all its resources, I could have saved them both . . .' He let his sentence trail away and I hung onto it with all my might. But he didn't finish it. He took a breath and started again. 'Your father and I . . .' An agonised look crossed his face. 'Try and understand, Lalla. Try and understand what the ship cost, and what it means. I thought I would die with missing Sarah and my baby. But now – now that all time is the same time, the world in which I could have saved them is the same as the world in which they died. So when I look at the ship and all that we have here, I don't see a prison. I don't see a trap. I see love.'

'So do I,' I protested, but he took no notice.

'I see a place where Sarah and my child are with me. Not where they could be with me, or where they might come to me, but where they are. And I love it for that. I love Michael for bringing me here, to live out my days with my family, in comfort, with purpose. And I know what it cost, and that it was a price worth paying.'

'What did it cost?' I asked, but he ignored me.

'Think of the ship as humanity's last song,' he said. 'I've found what I'm looking for, and as far as I know, so has everyone else on this ship. I've told you my story. Everyone else's may be different, but they all come down to this. We are where we want to be. And we thank Michael for that.'

It was a warning. My nose was pulsing and my eyes beginning to droop. But I could not let go. 'What about your secret meetings?' I said.

He pressed down the tape on my nose a shade too firmly; my eyes widened and watered. 'You have secret meetings too, Lalla. You keep yours and I'll keep mine, and we'll respect each other as Michael asks. Now, will it be the infirmary or your cabin?'

The message was clear. I could hide where I liked, but I would not find what I was looking for in the doctor, and I would not be welcome in the community of the ship until I had properly surrendered to it.

We walked to my cabin in the dawn light. The doctor turned his back while I changed into my nightdress, then helped me into my bunk. He held out a couple of pink pills for me, and when I did not take them, he pulled a vial from his pocket, put the pills into it and put it on the shelf above my basin. As he left, he stood in the doorway and said, 'Take some advice. Skip the bit of your life where you have to rebel and go straight to the part where you embrace what your parents have done for you. Skip the part where you throw everything away and cut straight to being happy. I mean it, Lalla. Especially now.'

'Why now?'

'You and Tom need to come and see me. Together. You need to listen to me, and to yourself, and you need to eat. Will you do those things, Lalla? Do you promise?'

I felt my eyes narrow and my face go hard. Who was the doctor, to tell Tom and me what to do? 'Does my father know about your watch?' I sneered. 'And your mugs?'

He turned his back on me and shut the door behind him.

EIGHTEEN

—

*I bite the apple ❀ the fourth deck and what I
found there ❀ Emily's story*

I made a mark beside my bunk; now there were eighty-one.
Eighty-one sunrises. In the time before, that would have been
eleven weeks and four days. More than two months and less
than three. On the ship, it meant nothing, but I would not let
the counting go, no matter how uncomfortable it made Tom or
how much it went against my father. We had been too quick to
throw the mast into the sea; the fact that it lay there, being eaten
by whatever creatures there were, or simply rusting alone in the
junk and poison that had been thrown there over the decades,
did not mean I could forget the bulletins it had once broadcast.

The doctor had forbidden me to work until my face was
healed. I was to lie in my bunk and rest until he gave me permission to get up. All around me, I heard the sounds of the people
waking up and preparing for the day. I heard water running in
the cabin to my left; that was the woman with the long grey hair
cleaning her teeth. The clunk that followed shortly afterwards
was the tap being turned off. Another such clunk came from the
cabin to my right; subconsciously, they had synchronised their
teeth-cleaning. Oh, we were all so safe, so safe, wrapped in our
soft down duvets with our shining white teeth and clean clean
skin, gradually becoming one.

But the toothpaste would run out.

We are better nourished than our forefathers, my father said. *Their bread was only made of wheat; ours is fortified with vitamins and proteins. Their vegetables rotted after a few days; ours will last for ever, their flavour and nourishment locked in until we need it. We are deficient in nothing; if we were, we could take a tablet from one of the millions of little bottles with which we are equipped. We want for nothing. Nothing.*

I gripped my duvet and decided not to clean my teeth. I would never clean them again. If they rotted, the rot would give the ship a marker of time that could not be ignored or banished. My healing bruises would mark time for a while, but when my face healed, I'd smile every single day, so that the people could see my teeth turn yellow, then black, then fall out one by one. The walls might remain white and the crockery unchipped, but they would all remember that Lalage Paul once had teeth.

My mouth was dry. I thought about getting up for water, but my head ached and I lay back on my pillow. The noises were not only those of my neighbours heaving themselves from their bunks, making their beds, slipping their deck shoes on for breakfast. No, the very ship itself seemed to wake up at this time. The rings and clangs were the metal plates of which the ship was constructed expanding as the sun rose, just as we all stretched our bodies to the new day.

I heard Helen's voice shepherding the children to breakfast. Helen's school was now a regular part of the ship; my father had given her a huge touchscreen, and the children sat around it, watching as she showed them how to form letters, read words, navigate the research room and the gallery. I'd seen them going from breakfast to lessons, then tumbling out like so many bread rolls from the basket at dinner, and bouncing to the net to swim, or to the sports hall, where Tom took their football lessons.

My father had created it, and they were happy.

I waited for silence. My duvet was light and warm, the way I always imagined a cloud would feel when I watched them floating across the blue sky, their edges tinged with sunlight. My mother, perhaps, was sitting on such a cloud, looking down on me and wondering whether I was going to be all right. Maybe Tola was with her, laughing at the way some people worried about whether there were going to be any pink cakes left when it was their turn to choose. Maybe there was a cloud big enough for all of us, and we would climb to it slowly as the ship sank underneath us, and we would all sit there, comfortable and warm, eating fruit. *Here, Lalla*, my mother said, *this is for you.* And she put something cold and hard and round into my hands, and I smelled sweetness and sharpness and my teeth stung as I pierced its skin and juice flooded my mouth. An apple, an apple, and the eggs had shells.

I sat up sharply. A sound, not of settling metal but of wood, hard yet forgiving, close to my head. The sound came again, a dull, dense thud, and I realised someone was knocking at my door.

It could only be Tom. *Love Tom, and let it be.*

I was naked under my nightdress. As I raised myself from my bunk, the cotton brushed the backs of my knees and my stomach and my breasts and sent blood rushing to my face. Where the cotton touched, I burned; where it did not, the skin was cold, and the hairs upon it lifted in anticipation.

Tom had come.

Maybe the ship could be my home. We could tell my father, have a cabin together, make a home among the boxes on the fourth deck, install a ladder and make love on the roof of the world. Love, everyone kept saying. Love. Tom had missed me at the breakfast table and run to find me when he heard I had been hurt. Love was the biggest thing after all. If we loved each other, everything else could rot.

Except my teeth. I would clean them after all. There was toothpaste enough for now.

I took a deep breath, steeled myself against the pain in my head, and opened the door. There, on the threshold, was my breakfast on a tray.

I hated them all. I hated Emily and Gerhard and Patience and the doctor and Tom and his green eyes and Helen and the school. I hated my father for living and my mother for dying. I hated myself for being so sure that Tom would come to me, and for giving myself away to the doctor. And most of all, I hated this life, this death, this timeless place of plenty that I had not chosen and over which I had no control.

I kicked the tray, scattering bread and jam and tea over the corridor, and went back into my cabin, slamming the door. I picked up the apple Tom had given me, green and shining, and I thought, what if this is the last apple in the whole world? I clung to Tom; Tom had brought me the apple. This apple is mine, I thought, and I will have it. I brought it up to my mouth; I bared my teeth; I brought them down on the apple as though it was the last thing I would ever do. My teeth cracked; my broken nose jolted under its dressing; I breathed dry dust into my lungs and choked. The apple fell to the floor with a puff of plaster dust, its shining green coat of wax cracked and falling away. For a moment I thought, if that was an apple I'm not missing much. Then pain blossomed through the anaesthetic. I held on to it, and as it receded I refused to let it go. My cabin went dark and I slipped into a place that was something like sleep, where my mother was calling me.

I lay in a haze of pain and followed the sound of her voice, past the infirmary, past the pharmacy. It was dark, but somehow I knew what I was looking at and where I was going, because she was leading me. On the second deck I peered into the games stadium, where a line of footballs waited for breakfast to be over. *No, Lalla, you must keep going.* So I did, onto the third deck, where I opened doors into empty rooms while my mother called, *Come further up, further up.* I climbed up to the fourth deck, where a delicious smell came from behind a closed door. I pushed it open and sunlight poured over me. There was a tree, covered in little pink flowers from which petals fell like rain. I stepped in, and felt grass beneath my feet. *Shut the door behind you, Lalla, and you need never go back.* I could see the grey metal of the ship through the open door behind me.

I opened the next door, where row upon row of floured rounds of dough rose gently in front of an open oven filled with logs of brightly burning wood. Behind the next door, an old woman sat in a rocking chair with a little child on her knee and a storybook in her hands. Behind the next was a garden in which rows of feathery leaves stuck out of the ground; an old man in muddy blue trousers pulled at the leaves and there, dangling from his hand in a spray of earth, was a carrot. The man held out the carrot to me; his eyes were green. 'Are you Tom's grandfather?' I asked, but my mother was still calling.

If you come far enough, you will find me.

The corridor stretched before me lined with doors on either side, hundreds of doors; I could not see their end. I saw a man painting in fat strokes of blue and yellow with a bandage over his ear. A woman in a long lace dress held her hair in a knot on the top of her head and gazed into a mirror; seven or eight girls floated across a wooden floor in pale pink dresses that stuck out; a whole orchestra played something that touched me below my ribcage and made me feel that I could listen for ever. Music. I would love to play music, I thought, and wondered if someone in this orchestra would teach me if I closed the door.

A man wrote with a pen on sheets of paper that he threw over his shoulder as he filled them. Another raised an axe and cut the head off a chicken; the chicken ran around headless for a few seconds, spurting blood from its neck. And behind the next door were thousands, millions of people. At first I thought it was a riot, because so many people were gathered together, but I noticed that they were staring at a patch of green with men running about on it chasing a black and white ball.

The football made me think about Tom. Tom, with his strong hands and green eyes and his desire for me. Tom was not behind any of these doors. Even as I tried to choose between the music and the dancing, the garden and the bread slowly rising, I knew that what I was looking at was as distant and illusory as the idea of my mother coming back. They were images from other people's dreams. That was all I was. A part of other people's dreams. The entire ship was a dream that my father and mother had conjured up for me.

Only Tom was real. He had not come yet, but he would, and if I wasn't there, he would go away. The thought of Tom pulled me back, away from the corridor and the doors, back to my cabin, where the sun was shining full through my porthole and my nose was bleeding and I felt blinded by the pain in my head and my nose and my torn cheek. My hand was being held, and when I opened my eyes, I saw Tom hovering over me, his green eyes wide with concern.

'Lalla,' he said. 'Oh, Lalla, what have you done to yourself?'

'The ship did it,' I said, struggling to sit up. He arranged my pillows and helped me settle back. It was easier to settle when he was with me. 'I went out in the storm. But Tom, listen. I know what's going on. And I know what we should do. I'm sure now.'

Tom sighed, but before he could answer me, there was a knock at the door. He jumped to open it; it felt as though he was avoiding what I had to say. Emily stood there with my breakfast tray at her feet. The tea-soaked bread and broken jam pot had all been gathered neatly together. In her hands she held another tray, this one with two bowls on it – one of soup and another of tinned pears. She gave the tray to Tom.

'The doctor says Lalla needs to eat,' she said as she stepped over the ruined breakfast tray and came in. The little cabin was crowded now.

'I'm not hungry.'

'You're hurt,' Emily said carefully. 'You need to rest and eat and give your body a chance to recover.' She took the soup from the tray and offered it to me but I kept my hands by my sides. 'Lalla,' she said, 'I'm trying to help you. Everyone is.' She put the bowl back on the tray and motioned to Tom to put the tray on the desk. 'What's this?' she said, as a bit of the wax and plaster apple crunched under her deck shoe. 'Honestly, Lalla, you make more mess than everyone else on the ship put together.' I looked at the white and green shard in her hand. She was turning it over, touching the sharp edges.

'That's the apple I gave you, isn't it?' Tom said. 'What happened to it?'

'It wasn't an apple,' I said, my voice wavering.

'You didn't try to eat it, did you, Lalla?' Tom looked as though he was about to laugh, and then he sighed. 'Oh, Lalla, you are an idiot. Why can't you just let things be what they are?' I turned away from him, but the cabin was so small I ended up looking at the wall beside my porthole.

Emily sat beside me with her arm around my shoulders. 'We've got apples, Lalla. I've told you before. Apple pie, apple crumble, apple pancakes, apple strudel, apple cake. Tell me what you want, Lalla, and we'll get it for you. Won't we, Tom?'

Tom stood awkwardly by the door. 'She doesn't mean apples like that. She means, you know – a round apple, off a tree. But what's the difference? Lalla? Really?' I kept staring at my bit of wall, angry that he was speaking for me, angry that he was belittling something I'd cared about. 'I'd better get to lunch,' he said when I wouldn't answer. 'And then I've got work. But I'll come and see you later, all right?' I wouldn't answer, and he was gone.

Emily smiled after him. 'He can't sit still, that one,' she said as the door closed. She stroked the hair away from my face and wiped the tears from my bruises very, very gently. 'Your poor face, Lalla. What were you thinking of?' She took my hands in both of hers.

'We're floating round in circles,' I said, sniffing, tasting blood at the back of my throat. 'No one will listen to me, and I don't know what to do. We're not allowed to talk about the past. We don't know what's going on back on land. And I've broken my apple, and Tom called me an idiot.'

Emily looked around my cabin and saw the pink pills above the sink. 'When I was a teenager,' she said, walking over and picking up the vial, 'I thought the world would end when the law against the manufacture of new clothes was passed.'

'I don't remember that.'

'No, you'd have been a baby then. Maybe not even born. But the point is that the world didn't end. We had to change our ideas of what new meant. And you need to do the same. You've got this idea of what it means to be alive, and you won't even try and accept that this is it. I can't bear it, Lalla. I can't bear to see you turning your back on all this. On Michael. On Tom.' She held out the pills. 'Do you want one of these? Does it hurt?'

'You all knew,' I said, shaking my head. 'You knew we weren't going anywhere, and you didn't tell me.'

'We all told you a thousand times. Alice. Tom. Roger. Even Michael. You just wouldn't hear.' She looked ruefully at me as she put the pills back, and I thought of the doctor and the way he had lost his wife and child.

'What happened to you?' I asked.

'It doesn't matter. I'm happy. I live right here, right now, and Michael is – oh, Michael's wonderful. He's everything. Why would I talk about the past? The ship is just . . . it's like Heaven. Made with love.'

'I missed your testimony.'

'Whose fault was that?' She knelt on the floor, gathering up bits of broken apple in a cupped hand. She put the apple pieces on the breakfast tray and brushed the plaster dust from her hands. 'All right. I'll tell you. But then I'm never going to talk about it again. Do you understand?' I nodded. 'Do you remember Tube trains? Before the stations were all sealed up?'

'I remember the boarded-up stations. I don't remember the trains.'

'Well. This was eight or nine years before the ship, just after the Dove. People risked the Tube if they had work to get to. The gangs down there were at war with each other, after all, not with ordinary people. So when the screen said there was work in Uxbridge – a government distribution centre being built – my husband decided to go.'

'You were married?'

Emily nodded. 'We'd just found a flat,' she said. 'You remember the Possession of Property Act?'

'A bit,' I said, although I didn't.

'It came in just after the Nazareth Act. Any property that had belonged to the banks reverted straight to the emergency government. If you found an empty property and stayed in it for seven days, you could live there. But if you left it, there was always the risk that someone else would take it. And we wanted to have a baby. So Peter went to Uxbridge alone. We'd saved enough food for five days; we didn't think it would be that long.'

'My mother and I went out sometimes,' I said. But even as I spoke, I thought of the locks, the bolts, the keypad whose code we changed as regularly as we checked the government updates on our screens.

'It was a good flat,' Emily said, 'and I had my screen, and

the next biometric re-registration wasn't for a week. I was quite pleased to stay. I never really liked the outside. But Peter was different. Peter liked adventure. He liked challenges. Tom reminds me of him, actually. He took a rucksack and went to the Tube station. Covent Garden, it was. We used to laugh, because we'd never have been able to live in Covent Garden if it hadn't been for the crash. It was Peter's idea. He used to see the best about everything. Even those foul government-issue water-sterilising tablets.'

'My mother used to boil my water.'

Emily nodded. 'Lucky you. Peter just said that at least the taste told us that the water was safe. The second night he was away, the bulletin went live to Covent Garden station. I thought it was a new act, or maybe even a feelgood story about a gang defeat or something. And then the screen showed the lift doors opening.'

'I thought Tube stations had moving staircases.'

'Covent Garden had these great big lifts. And on the bulletin, the lift arrived in the station, and the doors opened, and the floor was covered in dead bodies. One man stood alone in the middle, still alive.'

'Peter?'

'I could see the terror on his face. And blood – oh, the blood. Shining on the floor, filling the gaps between the bodies.' She looked at the floor, where the blood from my nose was congealing. 'The troops arrived and I was glad, because I thought they'd help him.' I held my hand out to her and she gripped it without looking at me. 'I thought they'd bring him home. We had an oil stove for emergencies and I lit it to make him a hot drink, even though I knew he'd tell me off for wasting the oil.'

'What happened?'

'The troops arrested him.'

'Arrested Peter?'

Emily nodded. 'When the bulletin was repeated the next hour, they said he'd been found guilty of exploiting the instability of the transport infrastructure to murder fellow travellers for food. They unpacked his rucksack live on air and put the case to a Peoples' Jury.'

My mother and father had never allowed me to participate in a Peoples' Jury, but it was impossible to use the screen and not see them. If your card was valid, you could vote – the red button for execution, the green for a peoples' pardon.

'The rucksack was full of food. Powdered milk, flour, dried egg, pasta, tinned vegetables. A sponge pudding in a tin. Sugar. And with each item they took out, the red bar kept going up and up. Peter said he'd been given the food as wages, and that the bodies had been thrown into the lift after a gang fought with troops on the platform. But the screen displayed the comments people sent in, and all anyone wrote was that if Peter was telling the truth about the gang, how come the gang hadn't taken the food? I kept pressing the green, over and over, but I only had one vote. Peter was executed, and the next day they announced that the Tube would be closed. Permanently.'

She released my hand and I watched her rocking gently on my bed.

'What happened?'

'I had—' she clutched at her stomach as though she was in pain – 'this burning rage. His face, staring down at those dead bodies, so terrified – it was all I could think of. They used him. They just wanted to close the stations so they wouldn't have to worry about the gangs. He was set up. I had to do something.'

'What did you do?'

'I disabled the Dove and got on the raven routes. I knew I was risking my screen and my registration. I didn't even know what I was looking for. At first it was just obsolete stuff – tonnes of it. Supermarkets, holidays, all that campaign stuff about saving the insects. Insurance. Everything for sale in a place where there was nothing left. But I kept at it, and when I finally accessed the restricted stuff, I was sick. Lalla, it was horrible. People – and animals – and children. And I couldn't even close my eyes in case I missed a pop-up. I had to go through it all until I found the blogs. But I found them, and when I did, I posted and posted. Anywhere I could find. I wrote about Peter, and about the trial, and about the look on his face and the rucksack full of food that had got him executed. I told the Peoples' Jury voters that they were cowards and fools, and that they deserved to lose the Tube. The longer the Dove was disabled, the higher the risk, but I could not stop. And then there was a knock at the door.'

'What did you do?'

'My screen began to burn. Some virus. It was amazing it had held out for as long as it did.'

'Did you have another screen?'

She turned to me and her eyes were huge and shining. Her face was pale; she reminded me of my mother, and I stopped listening for a moment. I was thinking about my mother's face, frowning with impatience, or pale with determination, and finally, purple and strangled with pain.

'Do you think I had a stack of screens behind the door?' Emily demanded. I said nothing. We had had a stack of screens. 'My screen was dead,' she told me, her eyes dry and blazing. 'Peter was dead, killed by the people who were supposed to protect us, and our dream of a family was over. I'd lost everything. Can you understand that? Of course not,' she continued before I could speak. 'You got given everything you wanted, didn't you?'

'I want my mother,' I said.

Emily's face softened again and she put her hand to my cheek. 'I want a child.'

I pushed her hand away from my face. I didn't care about her story anymore. Emily was not my mother and never would be. I wanted my mother. I wanted something of her, something she had touched, worn, owned. I pulled my clothes from the cupboard, tossing them across the room while Emily hopped about, flapping her hands and begging me to stop, but there was nothing of my mother left. My orange dress had never been returned. Even the marks on the broken button had been made by someone else. I called up books we had read together on my screen, but they flashed across the screen exactly as they had the first time, the second time, every other time. There were no pencil marks, no crumbs or stains, none of the million telltale creases and folds we had made in the pages of our paper books. And our paper books were still in London. Was my mother with them, a collection of crumbs and creases? A crumb or a crease was all I wanted.

I ran to the lower deck, ignoring the pain. Emily's voice followed me, calling, 'It was your father at the door. Your father, Lalla, come to save me.' But it might as well have been the troops she'd feared for all I cared.

I stood where I had stood when my mother's body was released into the sea. I watched the part of the sea where she had gone under for a moment, then floated back to the surface, her dress swirling around her in mockery of my father's plans. But as long as I stared, I could not see the swirls and eddies repeated. There were no scars on the water. My mother was dead. The water had covered her over. That was our existence on board ship. It was what my father meant by time no longer. A life of the moment, a life of now, with no yesterdays and no tomorrow. There would be hunger and tears, even death, but the water's surface would never be marked.

What was I to do? Return obediently to my cabin? To accept that this was my life now, and take what sweetness from it I could? To take my place, love Tom, and let Emily love me?

Or to take all the pink pills I could find and hope that my

mother would take me to the fourth deck once more, where I could choose a door, and shut it behind me?

Footsteps came up behind me. 'Lalla?' said a voice, and it was my father's voice, and Emily was tripping along behind him, worry written all over her face. But the hands that were placed on my shoulders were his hands, and the face that looked into mine when I turned around was his face.

'I want my mother,' I said.

'She's dead.'

'But I can't feel her. I can't hear her.' My voice wobbled out of control. 'I can't even remember what she looks like.'

'Darling girl. Darling, darling girl.'

I rested my swollen face on his shoulder. 'I broke my apple,' I sobbed. He kissed my cheek. 'It was made of wax. Wax and plaster.'

'Oh, Lalla. I never imagined you'd think it was real.'

I stopped crying. 'How do you know about it?'

'It came from a museum, before we sailed. I was going to give it to Anna – *have an apple, Michael*, she used to say, do you remember? But she died, and when Tom came to see me, asking if I could suggest a present for you, of course I thought of the apple.'

'You gave it to Tom? To give to me? It was your idea?' He nodded and I felt my stomach drop to the deck.

'Where is Tom now?' I asked.

'He's probably busy. The ship carries on, you know. We can't just stop everything because one person gets hurt. Have a shower. Choose something pretty to wear. Don't just sit and wait for him.'

The pain was creeping back. My eyes were watering and my nose pulsating under the dressing. I could feel blood seeping through the bandages and trickling down my face.

'Why can't I find my mother?' I whispered.

'Because you're looking in the wrong places. You should think of the things you loved most in her, and find them in other people.'

But what I had loved most in my mother was the way she stood up to my father. And that was the one thing I could not find in any other person on the ship.

My father led me back to my cabin and I consoled myself by imagining Tom longing for me, missing goal after goal because he wanted me so much. I dreamed up scenarios in which he got into trouble and had a trial like Helen's, where he stood up and told everyone that the ship could sink for all he cared, because he loved me, and he was going to help me take the ship to land.

Emily brought my supper on a tray. Mashed potato and gravy, carefully selected so that I would not have to chew. I gave the tray back to her untouched, and she rolled her eyes and went away.

Grow up, Patience had said. So had my father. Even Alice had told me to try and be happy, which meant the same thing. But we were speaking different languages. To them, growing up meant acceptance of the world around me. I did not yet know what it meant to me.

What was on the other side of my door that I wanted, anyway? Food made me feel sick. I had no desire for book group, or football, or tennis, or swimming, no urge to learn to knit, or embroider, and no reason to sit quietly and count my blessings as the others did. The ship had taken my mother and my father from me, and although it had given me Tom, the balance would not be even until Tom and I were together, and on our way somewhere. It didn't have to be London. *I would not have my children be alone*, my father had said, and yet here I was, alone. I could not trust him. I had my portal, but there was no facility on it for sending messages now that the mast was gone. We were all flesh and blood friends, my father said; if we wanted to tell someone something, all we had to do was knock on their cabin door.

But Tom clearly thought the football was more important.

I turned my portal on and wandered the galleries of the British Museum, but the photographs were meaningless. I wanted to press my hands against the glass; to be tantalised by the possibility of touch. I tried to read, but my screen wasn't working properly – *Ballet Shoes* had frozen at Petrova longing for a moving staircase and I could neither read on nor load another book.

Emily came back with a mug of warm milk and some biscuits on a tray. It was getting dark, and I wondered if she had left it so late on purpose, so that she would not have to stay with me.

'I want *Ballet Shoes*,' I said.

'Ballet?' she said eagerly. 'I'm sure . . .'

'No, the book. *Ballet Shoes*. I can't get my portal library to scroll.'

'Take it to Christopher,' she said. 'He'll sort it out. Do you want me to do it for you?'

And suddenly, I was gripped by a panic so real that I struggled to breathe. The room swam around me, and I forgot about Tom, about being shut up, about not being allowed to work. I drew breath to scream, but instead found myself sobbing.

'What's the matter, Lalla?' Emily said, putting down the tray on my desk and coming to me. 'Lalla, talk to me. Let me help you.' But I was crying too hard for words, and my breath came in gasps.

'Is it your mother?' she asked, putting her arms around me. I found myself clinging to her. Salt tears set my cut face stinging. What if *Ballet Shoes* was gone for ever? I tried to explain, but fear made me inarticulate, and I found myself sobbing, gulping for breath, until I wore myself out. As my sobs subsided, I became aware of Emily's arms around me and wriggled away.

'Drink your milk,' she said as I hugged my knees. 'If you dip the biscuits in, they'll be soft enough for you to eat.' She went to my desk and fetched the tray. 'Shall I send Tom to visit?' she asked.

'No.' I looked at Emily and wanted to hurt her like I was hurting. 'He'll come if he wants to. You only come because my father makes you.'

'That's not true.'

'It is. None of you care about me. You just want me to be like you. Forgetting what's gone. Forgetting the dead. All of you just want me to be what you want. Not one single person on this ship gives a damn about me or what I want.'

Emily threw the tray. Milk splashed across the wall; biscuits, mug and plate shattered together. The tray fell with a flat crash. The light of my desk lamp caught the fragments of plate as they exploded from the wall. Almost immediately, she knelt and began to gather the pieces together. She held one up for a moment; it was pointed and sharp. If she drives that into me, I thought, I will not flinch. I will bear the pain, and my scars will tell my story.

But she did not stab me. She put the pieces on the tray and spoke slowly and carefully. 'Lalla,' she said, then took a breath. 'Love works both ways. It's not enough to love someone. You have to let them love you, too.' She brushed the biscuit and china crumbs from her hands onto the tray and spoke as though she were reciting a lesson. 'Love is patient,' she said. 'Love is kind. But all you've ever done with our love for you – Tom's, mine, Patience's, even Michael's – is to turn it into some kind of weapon. Tom doesn't know what you want. None of us do. Michael told me to bring you round with love, but my goodness, you don't exactly make it easy.' She nodded towards the milk, its translucent tear tracks marking the wall. 'I'll have this cleaned up. Get some sleep and sort yourself out, Lalla, because I can't take any more of you.' She took the tray in both hands, stood up, and walked away.

The night was black, but I knew Emily would find her way. She would not be left to fall in a storm, to break her face on the ship. She was loved; she let people love her, and neither the ship nor my father had anything to prove to her.

NINETEEN

Oranges ❖ *panna cotta* ❖ *subversives on the ship*

That night, my thoughts circled and clashed and made noises I could not bear. Tom and my father, and Emily, and Roger, all tumbled around in my aching head until I didn't know what to think. Less than three months ago, my biggest challenge had been to remember the code on our keypad. Now my mother was dead, my father had adopted five hundred other people and my lover said he wanted to marry me, then walked away. When the first rays of sunrise came through my porthole, there was a knock on the door. I lifted my head to see, not Tom, but my father, standing in the doorway. He looked at the milk marks on the wall, the blood on the floor, and at me, crumpled and bruised on the bed. I expected sympathy, but he was not sympathetic.

'Emily was in tears most of last night,' he said. 'You can't go round upsetting people just because you're angry.' He sat down. 'You were lucky, compared with other people.'

'I know.'

'I think you forget. Do you know what Diana was doing when I rescued her for the ship, for example?'

'No,' I said, resisting the temptation to say that I didn't care.

'She was standing over her brother's dead body with an iron bar.'

'Why?' I asked, interested in spite of myself.

'She was fighting off poachers. People who came for the freshly dead.' I felt sick. 'There's a lot of meat on a human being. We spared you a lot. Cannibalism. Chlorella.' I shrugged my shoulders. 'It's an algae. You grow it in human urine and eat it to keep yourself alive. Anna never taught you that, did she? It's time for you to stop wallowing and wake up. I've spoken to Gerhard and you're going to the kitchen. You will work there for a while, and as you work, you will look at the food that is provided for you here. You will eat it, and you will stop obsessing about apples. Of course there are things you don't have. But there is so, so much more that you do.'

'You never ate chlorella.'

'How would you know? You have no idea. Literally no idea of what I went through to keep you and your mother safe. Of what the world had become.'

I left him in my cabin and stalked off to the kitchen immediately, so that Tom would not find me if he came. *Accept things for what they are*, he had said. But to do that, you had to know what they were. Otherwise, you would accept something, and then find it was something else, and then you'd have to accept that, and no one would ever know what anything was. How could that be life?

Gerhard nodded as I walked in. He told me to take over making up the orange juice. He and Emily brought up concentrate from the freezers after dinner and put it into plastic buckets to thaw overnight. He showed me the jugs and the proportions and I began. As I did so, I watched the people through the kitchen doors. They drifted in, and I watched the patterns of their groupings. I watched Helen. She had been reabsorbed, forgiven for the photograph album. I saw Diana, and thought about the people who would have eaten her brother. Frozen orange juice didn't seem so bad, when that was the alternative.

Tom came in. I watched him smiling at people who were not me. Was he looking for me? Was my father keeping him away from me, or did he simply not want me anymore? I couldn't tell. Gerhard and Emily hugged him, warm, encouraging touches for which they were rewarded with sighs. This is an orange now, I thought, poking at the ice rock as it turned into slush. This is what an orange means. It is all an orange means.

'This is an orange,' I said, jumping as my words bounced back at me from the walls. Gerhard looked around from the bucket of egg powder. Scrambled eggs for breakfast. Scrambled eggs and orange juice. Those were eggs, these were oranges. Eggs, oranges, eggs, oranges, Eggsoranges.

Tom, I love you. I stared into the bucket. Was it true? If I forgave him for the apple, I would be accepting this world.

'Are there any oranges left?' I asked suddenly, my heart pounding. 'Real ones?'

Gerhard stared at me. *Please,* I begged silently, *please please don't tell me that these are oranges.* I leaned towards him, feeling sick with a struggling maggot of hope inside that, even now, refused to die.

Gerhard looked over his shoulder. We were alone in the kitchen, and he sighed.

'Tom loves you, you know, Lalla. We all do.'

I refused to answer. He looked over his shoulder again, but we were alone, and I stared at him until he said, 'I had oranges once. Long, long ago.'

'Did you have the last orange? The last ever orange?'

'I don't know.'

I hesitated over the enormity of what I was about to say, then pointed at the slush and said it anyway.

'This is not an orange.'

Gerhard looked sharply at me. Then he shrugged. 'Oranges were a nuisance. Most of the orange went into the bin and the rest you had to wash off your hands.' He pointed at the plastic bags of concentrate, the cartoon oranges on its label round and bright. 'This is the way to eat oranges. No skins, no pith.'

'Pith?'

'The white, bitter part under the skin.'

I could no more stop than I could produce a fresh orange from the sea. I remembered the petrolheads on the streets. *I can stop any time I like*, they used to yell at us as we passed. *Any time I like*. 'An orange had white parts? It wasn't just orange all the way through?'

'No. The very outside was the brightest part. It was filled with tiny little sacs of oil.'

'Sacks?'

'Little bubbles under the skin, that burst when you squeezed them. The only way to start peeling an orange was first to pull some of the skin off with your teeth. And the oil would spray out and sting your lips. And then you tore off the skin, and you'd be left with bits of white pith clinging to the orange, and you'd have to tear each bit off, and nine times out of ten you'd go through the membrane into the orange, and the juice would start running out onto your hand and down your sleeve.'

'Through the membrane? But you'd already taken the skin off.'

'No, the individual segments were separated by a membrane. Oranges came in segments. The orange was spherical. But the sphere itself was made of segments – portions – separate parts, each covered in a thin skin of its own. That was what contained the flesh and the juice. You pulled each segment free of the others, one by one, and ate them.'

Any time I like. This was better than a picture. I'd seen lots of pictures. But for the first time, I felt I was learning what an orange was. 'Did you eat the segments whole?'

Gerhard smiled. 'My brother did. One segment, one mouthful. All gone at once, and the juice dribbling down the sides of his mouth. Me, I used to bite the end off each segment and suck out the insides. And my sister used to slide her fingernail under the segment skin and try to pull it away without bursting the little tiny globules of juice underneath, and then she'd lick the surface under the skin until she couldn't wait anymore, and then she'd bite.'

'What globules?'

'The tasty bit of the orange . . .' He suddenly broke off and grabbed a saucepan from the huge metal grid that took up one wall of the galley. All the utensils hung from it, on hooks shaped like the letter S, and when he snatched the saucepan, the handle caught on the edge of the hook. Gerhard yanked it free, and the whole grid started ringing, as though a hundred people in hard-soled shoes were running up the metal staircase.

'What about the tasty bit of the orange?' I insisted.

He slammed the saucepan onto the range. 'It's not important.'

'It is to me.'

He rummaged on the racks, trying to drown me out. But if my father had not managed to drown me out with the vastness of the great seas, Gerhard and his saucepan lids stood no chance. *Any time I like.* But I did not like.

Apples.

Shell eggs.

Oranges.

Life on the ship meant many things. I would never be hungry. I would never be bored. I could make love with Tom for the asking. But I would never be able to decide how I would eat an orange. I would never crack an egg. I would never know how it felt to press my teeth into an apple. How could I feel such a sense of loss for things I had never had?

As though he had heard me, Gerhard said, 'You'll never see

an orange. And okay so that's a shame. But you'd never have had one on land either. If all that mess was so great, why did your ancestors work so hard to get rid of it? What's the point in Michael giving us the essence of oranges if you, his daughter, cannot throw away the rubbish that has gone?'

'My father said the same thing about pineapples.'

Gerhard did not answer. He stared at me across the galley in silence. His eyes were grey; I suddenly saw him floating in the net, with holes for his eyes and the sea showing through. There were five packages upstairs with his name on. This meant that he was forty-five years old. His hair was dark, but there was grey in it too. Then he crashed the pan lid back into the rack, then hooked the pan back onto the wall grid and set all the utensils jangling again.

My father had brought him home. That was the difference. My home had been a flat in London, near the British Museum, with a mother and a father and a plate with rabbits on it. I had lost my home in coming here, and although I had never eaten apples or oranges there, my consciousness of their one-time existence was connected to it. Everyone else on the ship had had their home wrenched away, leaving them floating, rudderless, on an ocean vaster and more terrifying than the one we were floating on now. Gerhard belonged here, feeding five hundred people on frozen concentrated orange juice, making tiny fancy cakes from sugar paste and imagination. I looked into his eyes, and the ship floated there, reflected from his heart.

'Why are you so cross with me?' I asked.

'Because I love Michael.'

'I don't know what he wants from me.'

'He doesn't want anything from you. He doesn't want anything from any of us, except that we should be happy. And if you are lucky enough to have someone in your life whose only thought is of your happiness, then you should be happy.' He paused for a moment and then added, 'I am,' as though that simple statement would change everything for me.

And in a way, it did. I knew that I would never be able to ask questions of Gerhard again. He had gone the way of Finn, of Helen, of Patience, of Alice. Of Tom? Tom had to come to me. If he did not, I would know I had lost him too.

I looked at the rows and rows of identical white mugs, lined up on the shelf. And two mugs came into my mind. Mugs that were not white. A red one and a blue one, that could not be replaced when they broke. The doctor wore a watch. He said he was happy going nowhere, but he was still hiding something. Why else would he meet with others in secret? Suppose he, too, remembered three women who had been swept, broken, into the sea the day we sailed? Suppose the dead in the British Museum were reaching out to him, too? Maybe he sat around with the others, discussing how they used to eat oranges. And if they did, I wanted to be there.

Clover, Tom's grandfather had said. Clover, to clean the soil and make it safe. It could be done.

I crumbled some toast onto a plate in the kitchen and sipped some orange juice. I watched the doctor through the door; I watched the people he spoke to. I observed and deduced. Vikram, Abigail. Luke. They didn't sit together but they spoke to each other, fetching cutlery, taking a second serving, or bringing empty breakfast plates to the hatch. I was not imagining the connection between them. I was more certain of it than I was of Tom's love for me.

I watched the kitchen team bringing in the dirty dishes and processing them through the steel washers, sliding in rack after rack, locking down the great handles and bringing out sparkling white plates and bowls. I wanted to help, but they were so efficient that, although they smiled at me, I knew I'd only get in the way. And then they were gone, and it was as though breakfast had never happened, and I was sitting in the kitchen alone, watching the white frost slowly disappear from the sides of the silver trays that held our thawing dinner.

I tipped the orange juice out of my glass and rinsed it out, and as I filled it with fresh water, I heard someone calling Gerhard's name. The door crashed open. 'Can we have some biscuits?' Tom said, and stopped when he saw me. 'Where's Gerhard?'

'I don't know.'

'What are you doing here?'

'I helped at breakfast. I did the orange juice.' I couldn't help but feel a little pride as I said this, but it soon turned to bitterness. 'I'm to stay here until I've learned that apples aren't important.'

He looked past me to the cupboards. 'I wanted some biscuits. The children need something; they've been running around for ages.'

I got up and we opened doors and rummaged in crates until we found a hoard of bright packets. I pulled one out.

'Not those,' Tom said. 'Emma likes the ones with the smiley faces on them. The others don't mind, so we might as well go with Emma.' I knew Emma; she was one of the younger children, with a row of tiny, white, even teeth and freckles. She worshipped one of the older boys, a boy called Fillipo, who was slightly older than Gabriel. And Fillipo, in his turn, wandered around after Tom, his face tilted up to catch Tom's every smile. I looked through the cupboard again, and sure enough, there was a red cardboard packet with a cartoon picture of a smiley-faced biscuit on it. It had arms and legs; it seemed to be dancing. I handed it over and turned away, but Tom put his hand over mine and wouldn't let go.

'Come with me,' Tom said. 'Come with me now and see their faces. You never saw children smile like this in London.' I hadn't seen many children in London at all. But I remembered the ones on the bulletin, being held up to the windows of the British Museum.

'Where have you been?' I asked.

Tom looked over his shoulder and spoke quietly and very fast. 'Michael said I should give you some space. He said to stop crowding you. He's cross with himself. Angry for making your life so easy that you can't see how lucky you are. I don't like seeing Michael angry with himself. I wish you'd just let yourself be happy. I wish that you could be happy with me. But Lalla, if it's me, if I'm the one making you unhappy, I'll leave you alone, I promise, even if it kills me. You need to decide.'

I pushed aside my glass of water. 'You're the only reason I want to be here,' I said.

He stroked my bruises so gently that it didn't hurt. He kissed my forehead. 'Be with me, then. Let me look after you. It'll be all right, I promise.'

'Is the ship really all there is?' I asked him.

'You've heard the stories,' Tom said. 'You saw what you saw in London. It's not just London either. The ship is our universe, and it's a good one. Let's guard it together, you and I. We can, you know.'

I let his arms surround me. My body began to melt. If I was wrong – if the doctor had no secrets and this was all there was – then there were worse things than being with someone you loved, for ever.

'Can I come to you tonight?' he whispered. 'You won't tell Michael? He told me to leave you alone.' I shook my head. I wouldn't tell my father. He had tried to keep Tom from me, and I was never going to tell him anything, ever again. Tom was mine again, and the day went faster in the excitement of knowing he was waiting for me.

Dessert that night was a thing Gerhard called panna cotta, which I had watched him ease out of tall tins with a long knife

– a thick, fat snake of opaque white jelly that gave a monstrous sucking sound as it slid from the tin. He cut it into slices and I put a frill of red jelly around each one with a giant toothpaste tube as the kitchen team whisked the plates into the dining room. Gerhard had let me empty one of the tins, but the white snake would not ooze out for me. I had to dig it out with a spoon, and when Gerhard saw what I was doing, he rushed to me in consternation.

'No, Lalla, no. You are ruining, ruining dessert.' And he cut the other end of the tin open, and the snake slimed out, whole and perfect except for the concave part where its flat head should have been. 'You see, Lalla,' he said, 'this is why I am the chef and you should go back to the laundry.' But he was smiling when he said it.

When the panna cottas went out to the tables, everyone gave sighs of appreciation, but I could only think of the fat snakes and wonder if being a chef had always meant knowing the most efficient way of getting stuff out of a tin. I couldn't eat it, and while I was busy not eating it, I looked out of the kitchen into the dining room. And I saw Luke raise his eyebrows at Roger, and I saw Roger raise his hand to Abigail, and I saw Abigail turn and look over her shoulder at Vikram, and my breath came faster and my heart beat in my ears, because I knew that if I watched them now, I would find out where they were going.

Vikram left first, going towards the doors that led to the toilets. I could not follow him without being noticed, because the men's toilets were on one side of the dining room and the women's on the other. Abigail left through the main doors into the ballroom. I moved away from the doors as Emily came in. She looked disapprovingly at my untouched plate, and by the time I had shrugged at her and smiled, Abigail was gone.

'Lalla,' Emily said, 'you've got to eat. You know you've got to eat.' I looked back into the dining room but Luke had gone. Only Roger was left.

I walked slowly towards the women's toilets. I could feel Roger watching me. He was waiting for me to go, but I couldn't follow him if I left before he did. Then I saw Vikram, walking past the dining-room doors. Roger's shoulders relaxed as he watched me; I glanced over my shoulder as I opened the doors and saw him pushing back his chair. I almost laughed. Vikram was walking fast and I was behind him. Emily was nowhere in sight. I was safe.

I ducked behind pillars and hid behind cabin doors as Vikram went up the infirmary stairs and doubled back, down a cabin corridor and through to the research room. This was clever, I realised, because anyone watching him leave the dining room would have assumed he was going to his cabin. I saw Abigail approaching the research room from the other direction, and heard voices coming from inside. I waited until she'd gone in, then ran down the corridor and threw open the door, expecting to see them all gathered together. But the research room was empty.

I stood still and listened. I heard footsteps and hid under a table; Roger came in. A door opened and shut and I crawled back out. I scanned the wall with my eyes and saw a door set into it, not steel or shining wood but painted, the same colour as the wall. I had never noticed it before, although I could not say it was exactly hidden. I had simply never looked. I walked over and put my ear to it. Yes, there were voices. I had tracked them down at last.

I pushed open the door. There were no windows, no lights, and all I could see were faces illuminated by the revolving colours of a screensaver. As I edged in, I heard Roger's voice say, 'No, no. Regent Street went all the way down to Piccadilly Circus, and then Leicester Square was just beyond that.'

'That can't be right,' said Luke. 'I used to walk that way all the time. Piccadilly Circus was where the statue of Eros used to be. Right in the middle. And there was a theatre on the opposite side.'

'And Leicester Square was just down from there.'

'You're thinking of Trafalgar Square,' someone else said, and then they all noticed me and fell silent.

'Hello,' I said, because I could not think of anything else. There were six of them. The five I had followed for so long, and one whose presence surprised me so much that I couldn't say anything else. She looked at me through her red snake-hair fringe and paled.

'I just . . .' I began, but the words dried in my mouth and I did not know how to continue. I was there, they were there, and neither party had the slightest idea what the other was doing. But the fear was tangible. Emily was white and Abigail's hand shook as she withdrew it from the table. Roger's eyes were the only ones that met mine, and they seemed to be burning from the inside.

'How much did you hear?' he asked finally, his voice rasping and dry.

'Piccadilly,' I told him, 'and Leicester Square. That's all.'

They looked at each other, and at the lace tablecloth on the desk, which I supposed to be another fourth-deck novelty introduced by my father. I wanted to reassure them that I had heard nothing they did not want me to hear. But that would not be enough. If there was nothing going on, why did they all look so afraid? I wanted to know what they were doing so that I could become a part of it, because I needed to be a part of any activity on the ship that was not being dictated by my father. I wanted them to have something to hide.

'Does my father know you're here?' I asked Emily.

'Does he know you are?' she retorted, staring at me.

'Sit down, Lalla,' Roger said. There was no spare chair and so I moved towards the desk. 'Not there,' he said, but it was too late.

I had already touched the tablecloth, and I recoiled at a strange sensation on my hands – something dry and soft which made my skin crawl with its unfamiliarity. I could see their faces clearly in the light from the screen; they were exchanging desperate looks. I moved away from the desk; the dry softness came away on my fingers, and when I looked at them, I could see by the light of the screen that they were covered in white powder. The entire surface of the desk was covered in it. There was no lace tablecloth, only narrow lines traced painstakingly through a dusting of white, with a great dark emptiness where my hands had been.

'What are you doing?' I asked in a whisper, not daring to raise my voice in case I disturbed more of the pattern. They were all staring at my hands, and as the revolving coloured patterns of the screensaver changed from white to red, they became one great wound, with someone else's lifeblood staining them. I held them out and they all shrank away. My palms were sweating, and little clumps of powder fell to the floor as the red turned to green. No one spoke.

'What have I done?' I asked, scarcely able to hear my own voice.

'That,' Roger said in a voice devoid of any emotion, 'was the National Gallery.'

'And most of Trafalgar Square,' added Emily bitterly. I turned to the desk and looked more closely. And as the colour on the screensaver changed from green to yellow, and from yellow to a bright, turquoise blue, I studied the lace tracery. The delicate patterns resolved themselves slowly into streets, squares, buildings. If I had obliterated the National Gallery, then this was Oxford Street. I remembered it so well, thronged with desperate people trying to secure supplies from people with things to sell, hundreds tightly packed around little folding tables, grasping with outstretched hands, then spreading like an explosion when the sirens came, only to regather as the sirens passed on. Crossing it was Baker Street, which figured in the stories on my screen about a detective called Sherlock Holmes. *From your hands, Lalla, I can see that you have intruded into a place where you have no right to be.* And Baker Street led up to the vast expanse that was Regent's Park, which my mother swore had once been green and open, but which I had only ever seen covered in tents. Blue and purple and green and black and orange, some big enough for families, some so small that only one person could ever have crawled inside.

There was a time when life was an adventure. When the springing up of tents in Regent's Park made walks with my mother more interesting. When eating tinned peaches for tea was exciting, because it was different. When the horrors of other lives falling apart happened somewhere else, on the screens, or in whispered conversations between my parents that I was not supposed to overhear. As I stared at the powder tracings that marked out Regent's Park, what I remembered most was the way the tents had been arranged in streets, the way some people had even put little fences around the front of their tent, like a garden.

I turned back to the six frightened people before me. I realised that I was still standing; I was looking down on them, whereas they had to look up to me. It felt wrong, and yet there was nowhere else for me to go.

'It's London,' I said. 'You're drawing London.' Roger came and stood behind me. I followed Oxford Street up Tottenham Court Road, where a dusting of powder spread to the edge of the desk, untouched. I pointed. 'If you put a road there, it would be Great Russell Street, and then the British Museum would be just there.' I kept my hands well away from the desk surface. 'And there was a theatre there, on that corner. And there, opposite the main entrance of the museum, there was a cafe once.' I was still trembling, but this time I was trembling with life. I could feel blood hammering around my body; I had found people, people who were not confined by the parameters my father had set out, but who were reaching out with their minds and memories, back to the past, back to the way things had once been. To the outlawed, forbidden time before.

'How did you know where to find us?' Roger asked at last.

'I've been watching you all. I've been following you.' I had nothing to lose. 'I wanted to know what you were all doing. Who you were, why you kept meeting up secretly.'

'And what were you planning to do when you found out?'

My heart raced.

'I don't know,' I said weakly. 'I just thought . . . if I wasn't alone. I don't know.'

Emily broke in impatiently. 'Are you going to go to Michael about this?' she demanded.

'I'm not going to say anything,' I said. That, at least, I was sure of.

Luke spoke up. I had not heard him speak since Helen's trial and it seemed to me that his voice had become slower. His hair was longer, too; he wore it in a ponytail now, and his stubble had become a beard that made it hard to guess his age.

'I don't think she will tell Michael,' he said. 'After all, she's part of it now. Those are her fingerprints on the desk. If she went to Michael, she wouldn't be able to prove that the whole thing hadn't been her idea.'

'What whole thing?' I asked.

'Nothing,' Emily said. 'I split a bag of flour and they came and helped me clear it up. What else is there to say?'

'I don't know, Emily.' Roger's voice was harsh, and his face, washed with blue light from the screen, seemed frozen, immobile. 'What else is there to say?'

'Nothing,' she said, and before the others could stop her, she had pushed me out of the way and started brushing the flour to the floor, making great sweeping strokes with her sleeve stretched over her arm, the cuff held so tightly that her knuckles were bright white, green, blue, red in the screen light. 'Nothing,' she repeated, and I could not tell whether her voice was cracked with anger or with tears. 'This was madness. It was stupid, bloody-minded madness. What possessed us? Who cares what London used to look like anyway?'

It was definitely tears. They spilt as she demanded, 'What possessed *me*? I love Michael. I love him.'

'He doesn't know, Emily. Calm down. He'll never know.'

'What if she tells him?'

'I won't tell him,' I said. 'Why would I tell him? I've been looking for you all ever since we boarded. I knew I couldn't be the only one.' Anything seemed possible now. Tom would join us, and we'd find land. Go back to London, even. Five faces stared at me, expressionless in changing colours of the screen-saver. Only Emily was turned away, and a tear shone on her cheek like a leftover sequin from Alice's tapestry. 'What are you all going to do?' I went on. 'Have you got a plan? I thought we could look at the maps, find out where we are. There's a machine in my father's study that shows the position of the ship. I'm sure I saw land on that. We can find it again. That thunderstorm the other night, I think it meant that we're near land. We can check.' I drew breath. 'He turns the ship, you know. At night. With the electricity from the solar panels, or something. The engineers will know. We can chart a course. If he won't let us use the machines, we can steal the compass. There's one in his study, I've seen it. We can find land.'

'You think?'

I nodded. Were they going to exclude me after all? Did they think I was too young for subversion? But I had been up to the fourth deck with Tom. I was not too young.

'Stop it, Lalla,' Roger said. He sighed. 'I wish you hadn't come.'

'But I have. So you have to let me in.'

'Into what?'

'Into whatever you've got planned. Were you making that London map to work out how to distribute our stores?'

Vikram put his arm around Emily, who had started sobbing quietly. 'Tell her, Roger,' he said. 'Go on.'

'She won't believe me. Us. I've told her before, but she won't stop. She just keeps banging on and on. Patience won't have her in the laundry anymore. She's driving Gerhard mad in the kitchen. Breaking Tom's heart. And now she's here.'

'I don't believe my father controls the sun. But I'll believe you. Of course I will.'

Roger looked at me. 'You won't. You'll believe what you want to believe. But I'll tell you the truth.'

I nodded, open-mouthed.

'We meet up because we thought it would be fun to see how much of London we could remember. We didn't want to leave a permanent record, so we got creative. Hence the flour, rather than paper, or the touchscreen in the school, or canvas.' He paused. 'That's all, Lalla. We're just smoking behind the bike sheds.'

'What does that mean?' I asked, as the floor beneath me turned to water.

'Michael's told us not to look back,' Luke said, as though I was stupid. 'And we thought it better to be quiet about this. We can handle it – we're strong enough to know the difference between a game and a dangerous exercise. But not everyone is.'

'I am.'

'No you're not,' Abigail cut in as the screensaver washed her red. 'You're just a silly, pampered little girl. You know nothing, you see nothing, you appreciate nothing. You barely even eat. How ungrateful is that? You make Tom creep around after you, when all he wants to do is stand up and tell us all how much he loves you. He barely eats either, but that's because he's waiting for you. Waiting for you to choose to go to him. You're a spoilt, spoilt, selfish brat. And then you march in here and claim membership of some kind of conspiracy . . .'

'You all know about Tom?'

'Oh, please.'

'Did he tell you? Does he talk to you? Did he tell you that he promised to come back to London with me?'

'Be quiet, Lalla. No one's going back to London.' Roger took a handkerchief from his pocket and wiped Emily's face with it. She took it from him and scrubbed at the reminder of the desk, tears and flour making a sticky paste on the surface. Regent's Park, Oxford Street, the little secret alley and square that was once St Christopher's Place, Baker Street. The space that was waiting to become the British Museum. All blotted out in seconds by misery and shame. The delicate lace, the beauty of memory. Gone, all gone. They were no more plotting to turn the ship around than I was planning to take my father's place.

And that was how I learned that the people who break the rules are the ones who are least interested in changing things.

'Cowards,' I said, my voice thick with disappointment.

Roger turned on me. 'What did you expect? Really, what did you expect? Did you want us all to be making bombs and strapping them to ourselves? To march on your father with guns and force the ship back to where we came from? We've been de-registered, thanks to you. We'd be dead before we got off the ship.'

'Land, then,' I said. 'Just land.'

He shook his head. 'This is what friendship looks like. It's not a life-changing plot. It's just people who like each other sharing something particular to them. We were trying something out. It didn't work.'

Emily sank onto a chair, the floury handkerchief hanging

stiffly from her hand. 'Michael's right,' she said. 'We shouldn't look back. He's always right.'

'I think so.' Roger took the handkerchief from her.

They stood up, straightening their clothes, and filed away together. Abigail and Vikram were holding hands. They left me alone with the doctor and the handkerchief.

'Thank you, Lalla.'

'What for?'

'Bringing us to our senses. It was a silly, pointless thing to do really. I don't suppose we'd have realised how pointless if you'd stayed away.' He looked at me curiously. 'Did Michael know? Did he send you?'

'No. I followed you. By myself.'

He looked at the handkerchief, the sole reminder of the map in flour. 'There is nowhere for us to go,' he said. 'There's nothing left.'

'But . . .'

He put on a high-pitched whining voice and screwed up his face. '*I want to go back, I want to go back*. If you want to be heard, say something worth listening to.' He sighed. 'Beautiful things are happening here. Right here, right now.'

'To you?'

'Yes. But to you too. You have the potential to bring us all happiness beyond anything we've dreamed of.'

'Me? How?'

'Because you've never suffered. Because you're young and healthy. Because you're Michael's daughter. Because of Tom.'

Tom. I was meant to be meeting him in my cabin and I'd completely forgotten. I hoped he had, too.

'I broke my nose the other night,' I protested. 'I know about pain. I do know about being hungry and all that.'

He shook his head. He seemed about to say more, then he changed his mind. 'You'll see, Lalla. I hope so, anyway, for your sake as well as ours.' He held out the handkerchief. 'Would you slip this through the wash?'

'I don't work in the laundry . . .' I began, but then I nodded. Perhaps this was a gesture of faith; an invitation to friendship. Patience would be glad to see me, surely, if I stopped asking her about eggs? I could wrap the handkerchief in a shirt, or a sheet, and bundle it into the machine so that no one else could see. I'd have to whip it away at drying time, and sneak it into Patience's ironing pile, or do it myself. And then, and only then, would I be able to return it to Roger's cabin, white and fresh and folded, so that no one would ever be able to tell that it had been used to wipe out London as we once knew it.

TWENTY

Tom is angry ❧ *the museum of the ship*
❧ *how do you know you exist?*

When I got back to my cabin, there was a note on my pillow, written on the back of a biscuit box. *Where the hell were you?* The dancing, smiling biscuit on the reverse mocked me. Tom had not forgotten; he had come to me. He had disobeyed my father's injunction and I had not been there. How long had he waited? I told myself it was too late to go and find him now; I would talk to him at breakfast. I knew I ought to feel guilty, but I had other things to think about, and very early the next morning I went back to the little research room. It was completely empty. Just the desk and the screen and the gently shifting colours of the screensaver. I passed my hands over the surface of the desk, where I had wiped out Trafalgar Square and the National Gallery, and I understood why they had come and traced the roads and the monuments with their fingers instead of just looking up a map on the screens. Great Russell Street, I thought, tracing a path with my fingertip. Bedford Street. Russell Square Gardens. Bloomsbury Street.

All my father had done on the ship was to reinvent the Dove inside our heads. Our admiration and gratitude was a filter that made the creation of a map in flour into a crime. And yet, only my presence had turned their activity into something forbidden.

I wondered if they would ever forgive me. *What harm*, someone once asked me, and I had grown less and less sure of the answer.

As I reached the end of Goodge Street, my fingers met something hard and irregular, like a small stone stuck to the edge of the desk. I pushed at it with my thumb and it snapped off. I placed it carefully on my open palm and looked at it in the changing colours of the screensaver. It was a lump of flour paste. There was London in it, and Emily's tears. It was smaller than the button but it held a story just the same. I wrapped it in Roger's stiffened handkerchief and put it in my pocket.

I found an empty room on the third deck, above the infirmary, and carried the little lump of flour and tear paste there. I took Helen's photograph album, too, and Tom's letter, and the skylight screws and what was left of the broken apple. And I took my button in its velvet jewellery box. It wasn't a real museum, with an atrium and glass cases and more galleries than could be visited in a lifetime. But it was a museum of our lives, and I didn't want Emily to throw it away. Six objects. The British Museum had held thousands, millions, and when I thought of the significance of my six and multiplied it by those millions, the world began to spin around me with the sense of what had been lost, and with what I had saved.

I was late to breakfast; Tom had already gone. I thought about going and finding him in the sports hall, but I had a handkerchief to wash. I bustled about the laundry work, and as I was careful to keep my questions about anything other than sewing or knitting to myself, Patience began to look kindly on me again. She didn't ask whether I had my father's permission to be there, and I didn't tell her. Tom was not speaking to me at lunchtime. I understood what it had cost him to go against my father, and I owed him an apology I did not know how to give. Every smile he shared with someone else made it harder and harder for me to find words. At dinner I took my old place at my father's table, and stared at the pink, pale slices of gammon ham. There were rings of pineapple on the top; they reminded me of my first meal on the ship. Eighty-three marks ago. Eighty-three marks.

'I saw you'd tidied your cabin,' Emily said as she sat beside me, glowing, and my father looked happy: I felt as though I had come home after a long absence and that everyone apart from Roger and Tom was pleased to see me. Was it really this easy? I thought. Were they really so ready to see what they wanted to see? And yet I liked it, too.

I never saw the people who'd made the London map in flour together again. Emily took her place at my father's side, a penitent shadow, looking up at him with wide eyes and an open face. Roger avoided me; at first I thought it was coincidence, or my paranoia, but as the marks grew in number it became clear that he did not want to be alone with me any more than Tom did. He was never in the pharmacy when I delivered the clean towels, nor in the infirmary when I went in with the laundry. I left the handkerchief in his pile of clean clothes, and looked and looked for an answering nod or smile over the dinner table that evening, but he looked away whenever he saw me, and I am sure I saw him frown with frustration as he did so.

Luke started helping Tom with the football, and Patience told me that the two of them were teaching each other tennis now too, and that soon we would all be able to learn. I feigned delight to make her happy, then found that I was actually looking forward to the first lessons. Helen spent less and less time with Gabriel; she had given him up to the ship, and when she saw him she smiled briefly and let him go back to whatever he was doing. I took him swimming, half expecting him to comment on the change in his mother, but he talked only about the next thing he intended to do. He sang a song that Helen had taught all the children in the school. Helen had written it herself, he told me proudly, and it went *The ship has saved us all, grown-ups and children small, and life is new. Happy and future-proof, borne on by trust and truth, safe under Father's roof, Father we love you.*

The tune was familiar, although I couldn't place it, and although I found the words ridiculous, they wormed their way into my mind, so that I would find myself singing, 'The ship has saved us all,' as I folded laundry and took it to the cabins. The tune was a dull one – there were thousands, millions of better ones that we could listen to just by summoning them on the screen. But it was hypnotic. It floated just below the surface of my conscious mind, and whenever I thought, I must stop singing that song, I'd find I was already doing so. *Happy and future-proof.* I wasn't alone. Before long snatches of the children's song could be heard all over the ship.

Future-proof. It was printed on the Dove-governed screens, although I didn't mention that to anyone. Mentally, I consigned the Dove to my third-floor museum; like the other artefacts, it had no place in ship conversations. It was in my museum that I let my memories roam; I went there most days, and because I was smiling and eating and had stopped asking questions, no one seemed to mind, or want to know what I was doing. Like Roger and his friends, I'd learned that obeying the rules means you can break them. Eight days after I'd found them out, I sat on the floor of my museum, staring at the dried-up ball of paste that was all that was left of their London map. I remembered watching the bulletin after the bombing of Regent's Park, and the announcer's sorrowful voice announcing fifty-four deaths.

'Fifty-four?' I'd said to my father. 'Did all the others escape?'

'Yes,' my mother said at exactly the same moment as my father said, 'No.' My mother had a way of arranging her face with her eyebrows slightly raised and her eyes wide, with the corners of her lips turned up but no warmth in her eyes. It meant, *There are things Lalla does not need to know. There are things I will not discuss here, in front of her.*

'But there were thousands of people living there,' I said.

'Only those fifty-four existed,' my father said; as he spoke my mother turned away from him and bit her lips together so hard that it looked as though she had new, thin, white ones.

'But I saw them,' I said, puzzled. 'They existed.'

'How do you know anyone exists?' my father asked me. 'How do you know you exist?'

I was fourteen years old when Regent's Park was bombed. I had never thought about how I knew that I existed. How could I know such a thing? It wasn't something to know or not to know. It just was. I remember looking at the challenge in my father's face and thinking of all the other things that just were, like water, and air, and food when I was hungry and the fact that I could walk and run, and that there were clothes for me to put on to keep my body warm, and that my mother and father and I lived together in a flat in a place called Bloomsbury.

And I remember how I thought, even then, about the number of things that had always just been, and which were no longer. Books. Shops. Restaurants. The fact that I had once been able to walk around the display cases without tripping over foul-smelling people in sleeping bags, and that the cases themselves had once been full. I thought about the objects, and realised that they, too, had once just been. The iron spoons had once carried food into the mouth of a living, breathing person who lived and loved just as I lived and loved now. The necklaces had been worn; the pots had held valued possessions; Lindow man had walked and talked and held someone close. Once upon a time, they all *just were*, and somehow they came to be shut behind glass, hundreds, thousands of years later, until their only existence was as part of someone else's *just am*.

'I breathe,' I'd said at last, and when neither of them stopped me I continued. 'I feel pain when I fall over, or when I burn myself on the fire. I get cold. I get hungry.'

268

'And when the tent city you live in is bombed to oblivion?' my father asked. 'What happens then?'

'But I don't live in a tent city,' I said.

My mother turned to me and the blood rushed back into her lips so quickly it looked like she was returning from the dead. 'That's right,' she said quickly, and as my ship-self relived the conversation I winced, because I realised now how important the conversation had been. 'She doesn't live in a tent city. So that's fine.' She clapped her hands, as though celebrating the departure of an unwelcome guest. 'What shall we have for dinner?'

'A roast chicken, I think,' my father had said dryly.

'There isn't any chicken,' I said.

My father shrugged.

And my ship-self watched my long-ago self take the final step inwards as my thoughts pulled in once more, to the central circle, the smallest one, which was also the biggest because it encompassed absolutely everything else.

'But doesn't the fact that I remember roast chicken mean that I exist?'

My father kept his eyes fixed on mine. 'Try that the next time we go to re-register. Leave your card here, and tell the official that you remember roast chicken.'

My mother laid her hand on my father's sleeve. 'She's right, Michael,' she said softly. 'If she remembers roast chicken, she exists. That's all right. Once upon a time, we thought we existed just because we thought. Let's leave it now. There's corned beef.'

My father's laugh was harsh and short, more like the coughs that came from the sleeping bags in the museum than a laugh. He had invented the Dove to bring fairness, equality, hope into a desperate situation, and it had not worked. 'The tent people remembered roast chicken, Anna.'

'Corned beef,' my mother repeated, emphasising the words in an attempt to puncture my father's thoughts. 'Good protein.

And fat. For energy. Lucky we got to the food drop quickly.'

'Only because we knew where to go.' Now, on the ship, as I remembered the conversation, I could see that my mother was playing into my father's hands. By trying to get away from the subject, she was bringing him back to it. From the safety of the ship, I could look back and see that my father was right. I was there now. Ninety marks into our voyage, I had arrived.

'How did we know where to go for the food drop?' my father had asked.

'The screen told us.'

'Now think of yourself with no card,' he said to me. 'How do you get your food?'

Two days before, the screen bulletin had given the address of the food drop. An hour before it was due, the drop address changed. And as we went to the new address, we passed the old one, and the queue there wound around the building, down the street and around the corner, so long that we could not see its end.

'Shouldn't we tell them?' I had asked. But not even my mother said yes. That queue, hundreds, thousands of people we did not know, became the left behinds. In the hour since the change in the food drop location, they had fallen from the government list. They had re-registered late, or searched for something outlawed on the screen, or not renewed their identity cards. Perhaps the internet hot spot they relied on had gone cold. They would starve. Or be bombed. And no one would count them.

We killed those people, Father, I thought, straightening my stiffening legs. My ankles were beginning to swell. I looked around at my exhibits. What was the difference between the Nazareth Act and the manifest?

My mother had never been able to commit to the ship. *The ship will be the last thing we do*, she had said. Every additional day we stayed in London had been a chance she was giving me to find a way of my own. But she had never had the courage to turn me loose, and I had never learned enough to leave. She had loved me too much, and she had failed. I knew now. I had begun to understand.

I had been kneeling on the floor of my museum for too long; my legs had gone dead. I forced myself to stand up and it hurt to do so. The light was fading; I had missed dinner, but I found that I wanted to go to the goodnight meeting. I wanted to see my father, to look at him, to study his face and see if there was any trace there that he, too, remembered where we had come from. I pictured myself apologising to Tom, too, and the prospect of reconciliation was soothing. Being in trouble all the time was exhausting, and I was very tired.

I slipped into the ballroom and stared around me. Pleased, confident, shining faces, all turned towards him. Michael Paul, father not only to me, but to all the children. No longer challenging his own child about her existence, but bestowing existence generously, lovingly, openly on everyone. The only things that mattered now were the ones which were in front of us every day. Rivets were metal and round; bolts were metal and hexagonal, but the stars were made of diamonds, or kitchen foil, or light bulbs, or holes punched in a vast swathe of black velvet. And the sun bounced over the ship, controlled by a rope in my father's hands, and the ship was the centre of the sky and the entire world was nothing more than a plate of water.

Father, we thank you.

. What, after all, was I fighting for? The world was gone. There were no apples, no oranges, no eggs. I saw Tom, sitting with an empty place beside him. There was a place for me here. Gerhard put a hand on my shoulder in greeting. Would I, like Helen, be forgiven for my childish questioning, my doubts?

But my father was speaking, and I sat still to listen.

'The glitches with our portals may be irritating,' he was saying, 'especially if you were halfway through a good book. But glitches remind us of what we have gained. I know, Chris,' he said, as a man in a dull green jacket put his head into his hands, 'you've tried to sort them out, and I know you'll keep trying. I also know you'll succeed.' So it wasn't just *Ballet Shoes*, I thought, then put the thought away. 'What I'm saying is that it doesn't matter. We're not defined by screens and cards anymore. Now we exist because we learn.' He looked at Helen, who smiled and pulled Gabriel a little closer to her. 'We exist because we play together, eat together.' He held one hand towards Tom, the other towards Gerhard, palms upwards, as though he were offering them something. 'We exist because we create.' Here he bowed towards Alice, who blushed and looked at the floor. 'We exist,' he said, lowering his voice so that we all had to lean towards him, 'because we love.' I wanted him to look at me so badly that I turned my head away, but when I looked up it was Emily who was pink-cheeked, Emily who attracted tender, approving smiles, Emily whose head was inclined to the side in prettiness and pride.

And then, before I could feel jealous, he looked at me. 'We exist, my darling, because we remember roast chicken.'

My father had won. This, then, was the end, the triumph of humanity, the final destination of mankind. No mast, no screens. Learning, playing, eating and loving. It was sweet of him to remember the roast chicken, but it really didn't seem to be important anymore. I looked at Tom, and my heart contracted. Tomorrow, I promised myself silently. Unless the ship sinks tonight, I'll join it tomorrow. I'll apologise to Tom, and I will never go looking for anything beyond what I am given, ever again. I slipped away to my cabin and lay in the dark, my body aching for my lover. Sorry, Mother. I was not strong enough, and I am in love.

I lay awake and I thought about the water. All around us,

bearing us up, supporting us. But threatening us, too. My mind raced. Water will not be stopped, I thought. Hold it in your hands and it will seep through your fingers. Hold it back with chains and it will trickle through the links. Hold it back with a walled dam and it will burst through, all the more powerful for having been contained. My father dictated, and my mother broke away from him, went to the window and threw open the curtain. If she had not broken away. If she had not . . .

I remembered the shot, and a figure in faded black running away. I lay in the dark and I suddenly realised there was one place I still had to look. There was one final question to be answered. One place where, even now, I might find what I was looking for.

TWENTY-ONE

I search for the truth and find a stranger
❈ *an engagement*

Four or five hundred years ago, people walked the streets with oranges stuck with cloves held to their noses, or little posies of sweet rosebuds. They believed that terrible diseases were carried by terrible smells, and if they could not smell the smells, then the ghastly rashes that marked the dying would never blossom on their own skin. They were wrong, my mother said. But we had no oranges, no cloves, no scented flowers, so I don't know how she could have known. It wasn't as though we could do what she always told me to do, and find out for ourselves. Do things really change? Four hundred years. What did it mean? Four hundred years on, we were no further on than we had been. They had oranges stuck with cloves; we didn't even have oranges. And in four hundred years more, the ship would be at the bottom of the ocean with the mast; my museum would be gone; everyone would be dead.

I felt my marks with my fingertips. Ninety of them. I thought of going on my quest in the dark, but it was another moonless night, although there was no storm in the air now. I tried to sleep, hoping that my mother would lead me to the fourth deck again. But the things she had shown me there had been her dreams, not mine. The things Tom and I had found, the cots and the clothes and the crockery and the paint and tools, were my father's dream. And wrapped in my father's dream were the dreams of everyone else on board. Roger dreamed of healing the sick; here he was, healing the sick. Helen taught the children. Gerhard provided food. That was why my father had interviewed so carefully, searched out the people he would save. That was why no one argued with him, why the little secrets I had uncovered had, as Helen said, hardly been subversion. What would you subvert, if everything was as you wanted it? Tom's grandfather had wanted something that my father could not provide; he had not been allowed to come on board. Those who were here had all been chosen, not just for their good deeds, but because they, too, had surrendered hope.

We are every human being that has ever lived, has ever thought, has ever created. We are the ultimate expression of humanity, and it is humanity that we celebrate here. Every kindness that has ever been done in the name of humankind, from the first man who reached out his hand to a crying child, to the last person back on land who broke his sole piece of bread in order to share it, is here, in us. In our floating home, we contain all that has ever been. Let us savour, and enjoy.

Let us savour, my father said, and enjoy. The difference between his chosen people and me was simple. They could rush forward, immediately, and throw themselves headlong into the riot of learning and experience my father had put before them. The only prospect before them was of better things, wonderful things, a richer, more beautiful, more profound life than they had had any hope of before. There was no risk.

But my inclusion had been automatic. No one had made sure I was starving before they set a feast before me.

Savour, and enjoy. Perhaps I could have done. If my mother had lived, I thought, we would have walked together, to the library, the gallery, the music room, and embarked upon a sweet, clean journey of discovery. We would have walked without looking over our shoulders, looked at paintings and artefacts without the weight of my father's warnings pressing us down, experienced the wonder of learning without the fierce oppression of guilt. I saw us walking down Great Russell Street together, she in her floating dress, me doing double skips to keep up with her, only this time the street was safe and bright, and the bodies were gone, and the sun shone on green trees and white buildings, and the blue plaques on their walls were the colour of the sky. We would have had the past to live again, and live differently, for however long we were granted.

But what was I, now that my mother was gone? Who was my father? The man who had once loved my mother? Or the man who had created this world for me, and in so doing, had made sure I would never be able to find out who I was?

At first light, then, I left my cabin. My hard red shoes set the gangways ringing; I stepped as softly as I could, but I could not help the noise. Eventually I took my shoes off and dangled them from my hand. The cold metal impressed itself on the soles of my feet. Was this man, sailing his people in circles with no thought for the future, also the man who had rushed back from his trips just to be able to kiss me goodnight, who had scoured London for my red shoes and said nothing of their origin? Just how great had been his desperation to sail? Around me, behind the cabin doors, the people began to stir. When I got to my father's cabin, I hid behind the stairwell. I watched the sun rising; when he left for his breakfast, I slipped inside.

There was nothing in the instruments, or in the map I found in the top drawer of the great wooden chest. There was nothing in the green dot that still went bleep, bleep, bleep as the circling green line swept over it, although I studied these things carefully. Nothing in the telescope I found in a corner cupboard, or in the compass that lay beside it. I looked quickly and thoroughly, because I wanted to be at breakfast if I could. I searched the surface of the desk, the floor, and the padded cushions of the chairs. And it was while I was searching the chairs that I finally found something important, sitting on top of the little table beside the leather armchair. It had not even been hidden.

The manifest.

I opened it. I was struck once more by its texture, dry and yet solid, the smooth surface on which we had inscribed our names. I turned page after page, trying not to tear them in my anxiety to find what I was looking for.

Harry Oz. Round, fat letters, carefully formed.

Lalage Paul. My own signature, a little shaky in the middle.

And between them, my mother's page. There was no signature. She was gone. No more present in the manifest than she was in the clothes store upstairs. I sat on my father's chair, breathing hard. It was not enough. She had been too ill to sign the manifest. The fact that her name wasn't there proved nothing.

I kept searching. I didn't know what I was looking for, only that I would know what it was when I found it. In one drawer, there was a notebook. It fell open at the ragged remnants of a ripped out page. I did not need to go back upstairs to know that Tom's grandfather's letter was written on the missing page; I recognised the paper, the pattern of the torn edge; I could see the words indented on the page beneath. And I wondered how my father could have borne to watch the old man writing those words. *I love you, and I let you go.* What more had my father been prepared to do, to ensure our departure? The notebook gave no further clues; my mother was not there. *I was terrified that one of you would be hurt before she would agree to come away. I am only grateful that it was not you.* But we had both been hurt. She by a bullet, me by her death. Where had that bullet come from? I pulled out every drawer, searched in every cupboard, but could find nothing more.

I went back to the manifest. In my head I heard my father's voice. *Anna's gone.* Fine. I would look beyond her. I turned the pages of the manifest one by one. I read the summaries my father had written at the top of each page. I looked at the names; I studied the signatures. And there, just seventeen pages in, I found it. Neil Bailey. Engineer, twenty-seven years old. Used scavenged items to create rainwater savers; distributed them without charge to those without access to water. There was no Neil Bailey on the ship. But here he was in the manifest. A man, a history, and no signature. What had happened to him? Where was he now?

I marched out of the cabin and into the dining room.

'I need to talk to you,' I said to my father. 'Right now.'

'We're just about to eat, Lalla,' Emily said, walking behind me with the toast basket. 'Surely it can wait.'

'Sit down,' my father said patiently. 'You're so hungry you're forgetting your manners. Eat something. And then afterwards, if you still want to, we'll go to my cabin together and talk for as long as you like.'

I looked around at the people, all so familiar now. At Emily, eyes wide with love for my father. At Patience, head inclined in pity or despair. At Roger, whose frown still held a secret. At Tom. Roger, Patience, Finn, Luke, Helen, Gabriel, Mercy with the embroidered patch on the left knee of her trousers. Alice. Emily. My father. Tom. All here to die. Tom was going to die. And something in me broke, and the nausea I had been feeling for weeks became a vast, all-consuming hunger. I burst into tears, and as my tears emptied out, the void inside me grew, and I wanted to eat and eat until there was nothing left in the stores.

Tom got up from his table, and the people around us began to clap and to cheer, a sound that started small but that spread over the whole dining room like spilt water. Was this what it all came to in the end? Floating aimlessly, waiting for certain death, saved by love?

I had thought he was my rebellion.

He smiled at me, and I tried to smile back, and after all it was quite easy to whisper, 'I'm sorry.'

He held my hands in his, and went down on one knee in front of me. 'Lalla,' he said, 'you know I love you. Will you marry me?'

And the room went silent, and every person in it held their breath in a joyful pause. My tears stopped. I looked around and saw the floodtide of happiness that my next word would bring forth. All the people who had cared about me, who had been angry or frustrated with me, who had argued over and over again that they were happy and that I could be too, were gazing at me with approval. I felt loved. I felt enfolded and included. We were all going to die. Where was the harm in enjoying ourselves first? What harm? I felt utterly drained.

'A wedding!' Gerhard shouted, his deep voice booming in triumph over the general delight. 'A feast.' And the people shouted and laughed, and I stood in the middle, a little tiny dot, sheltered by Tom as I stood inside the circle of his arms without saying a word.

And as I stood being shaken to bits by all the people who came rushing towards us, hugging and kissing our cheeks and kissing each other and waltzing around in each other's arms, I saw my father look at Roger, and Roger look at my father, and something hit me from the inside, and I knew that my happy ending had been as carefully orchestrated as the existence of the ship itself.

TWENTY-TWO

Preparations for the wedding ❀ Ballet Shoes
and the Art Trials ❀ *my mother's last chance*

I meant to ask more questions before the wedding. I meant to stop everything, and ask how they dared to dictate the course of my life in this way. I meant to demand the full history of Neil Bailey, whoever he was. But for the first time since my mother's death, I felt loved. And it was not just Tom who loved me. Everywhere I went, people smiled at me. I started going to book group again, just to feel the warmth of people celebrating the engagement. My father offered to release me from laundry duty while we planned the wedding, but I refused. I liked going into people's cabins and have them say lovely things about Tom, and about me, and offer their congratulations. And I liked it when Patience, having smothered me with kisses, held me at arm's length and said, 'Child, you are so beautiful when you smile.' Just as the first time we went up through the skylight on the fourth deck, time had condensed into a single moment, so being with Tom, thinking with Tom, spending time with Tom, stopped other thoughts from growing and developing. The sun rose and set unencumbered by my concerns; if I didn't accept Alice's tapestry, I was at least happy to watch with everyone else and admire the way the universe had shifted to accommodate us.

In any case, the tapestry was no longer an issue. Alice put it aside to embroider a wedding veil. Gerhard disappeared into the stores for hours on end and came back with menus which he pored over with my father. I went with my father to the fourth deck, and I tried on the dress he had chosen for me. 'You saved us at the start, Lalla,' he said to me, 'and now you are saving us again.' Saviour. It had quite a ring to it, and I stopped wondering why everyone seemed to love me so much. He offered to take me to his cabin and answer my questions, but every day, I decided that tomorrow would do, until at last it seemed too late to bother. Maybe Neil Bailey had just missed the boat. And the dress was so beautiful.

I learned to be happy. I thought of my early days on the ship as a troubled night that had given way to dawn, and the dawn was so bright that I could not see the darkness beyond. I had Tom and I had the ship. I had my father and I had myself. I was a new person, a happy person, and to be that person I had to let go of anger and doubt and enjoy each moment as it came. I stopped feeling that the weight of the world was on my shoulders and my shoulders alone. The children were a creative lot, and would surely think of something if the time ever came that they'd need to. I did the laundry and joined the knitting circle and danced about the ship as the others did. I put my red shoes in my museum and asked for deck shoes. I ate and ate, and got fatter every day, and if I could not quite give up making the marks, at least I made them on a different part of the wall, for I was in a different place now, and it was better.

And then one day, thirty or so marks later (although I could not be sure; I did not always remember to make them), I came back from swimming too tired to walk up to the sports hall and find Tom. We shared a cabin now, and I went to it, and as I sat on our bunk, I thought that I might like to read again. I picked up my portal and found that my library was still frozen on *Ballet*

Shoes. Petrova, the only one who hated ballet, stuck at a station, forever longing to travel on a moving staircase.

I had always loved *Ballet Shoes*. My mother read it to me, from a paper copy that had been hers. Later I read it myself, from the screen. The world of the Fossil girls had always been impossibly exotic. They descended into the depths of the city as though it was the most normal thing in the world. The Tube, where tunnels and corners could hide anything, where a power cut would plunge you into pitch dark, where a cry for help would echo for so long that there was no way of telling where it came from. Once the gangs had been smoked out, the petrol dealers moved in, and the sealed entrances swarmed with muttering people who carried the petrol smell with them. I loved the way that smell sent my mind circling above me and set me slightly dizzy where I stood, and I would pretend to have forgotten something, or seen something, so that I could go back and smell it again. The filthy, incoherent people did not frighten me then. They seemed to belong to a different world, and held no more threat than if they were already dead.

'How can they still be selling petrol if it's all gone?' I asked my mother.

'This is the end of it,' she told me. 'The bits left. The last drops in the bottom of tankers, of storage tanks. They scoop it up and sell it to kids.'

We had a Tube map at home, and I followed the familiar names – Russell Square, Regent's Park, Oxford Circus – to the outmost edges. Amersham. Uxbridge, where Emily's husband had gone to work. *Here be dragons*, my father said when I asked him what was there, which made my mother laugh, although I never understood why. And, safely on the ship, sitting in my cabin with my frozen portal in my hand, I finally realised that I had read *Ballet Shoes* for the last time.

The British Museum was all about last times. Every object in there had been used for the last time. Did the person who used the iron plough know that it was the last time he would prepare his fields with it? Did the person who wore the silver buckle know, when they took it off, that they would never put it on again?

You change. You move on, and life where you are becomes the only life that is, until it changes, and the next new reality becomes the only one. For the Fossil sisters, going to dancing school was so normal that they could complain about it. For me, school had been as impossible as eggs, as tantalising as oranges. And travelling daily by Tube – three girls and an old lady, un-armed, with no guard – was an idea from another world. The frozen page contained the illustration of the girls asleep on the Tube. No matter how many times I stared at it, they were never attacked. Not once. No petrol dealers approached them, and in the picture they all wore shoes and socks and coats. They looked so clean.

And the illustration itself had been drawn by hand, not digi-tally generated. Painting and drawing had still been legal when *Ballet Shoes* was first written, but I could not remember it. It was just another thing that belonged to another time. The Optimum Resourcing Act as I knew it simply stated that what resources there were, were needed for important things, like eating. I didn't remember the act coming in – like the Seasonal Food Act, it predated the collapse – but I did remember The Art Trials that started just before we sailed.

'If this man was working today,' the screen bulletin said, 'his working methods would have destroyed acres of rainforest. If this man were alive today, the oil in the paints he wasted could have been used for fuel. The canvas he ruined would have made blankets, clothes, tents. It is criminal waste, and has been a factor in the shortages we experience today.' They were talking about an artist called Van Gogh, who had been dead for hundreds of years. I was fifteen; even I could see that this was a way of placing responsibility for the shortages in the past, where no one could do anything about it.

'Why now?' my father asked, staring at the screen, where bright yellow flowers were overlaid with the words recounting Van Gogh's crimes. 'Why outlaw dead artists now?'

'Because the Optimum Resourcing Act got rid of all the living ones.' My mother shrugged. 'We're the dinosaurs, thinking that it matters.'

'But of course it matters!'

'Why?' My mother threw down the word like a challenge, and I remembered that there had been bread on the table at lunch, actual bread, soft, with a crust that crunched as I bit into it, not dried biscuits. Had my father been trying to persuade my mother onto the ship with luxuries? At the time, I'd just been pleased to see the bread. 'Why does it matter?'

'Anna,' my father said, looking at my mother as though she was a stranger, 'why are you asking that?'

'Because I want to know the answer.' My mother's cheeks were pink, and her eyes were brighter than usual. 'It matters, you say. It matters to have paints in many different colours and brushes, and canvas, for the sole purpose of putting down a picture that could easily be created on the screen?'

'But it couldn't,' my father said, his tone at once hesitant and exasperated. 'You know that. No screen can match the image I might create with my hands if I had the chance. Anna, what is this about?'

'I'm just saying. You have – what – fifty metres of canvas at the dock?'

'Five hundred and three.'

'Whatever. And outside our window are at least that many people with nowhere to live. You could distribute that canvas, Michael. They'd have something to sleep under.'

'But our people will need it. There'll be another Van Gogh on the ship. Another Titian, another Michaelangelo. Another Leonardo da Vinci. You should be grateful to these Art Trials, not picking fights with me.'

'Grateful to them?'

'The hoarders will lose their nerve now they know that the Optimum Resourcing Act will never be rescinded. We'll be able to get clay, oils, pigments, remember?'

'I remember,' my mother said, but my father was riding the wave of his enthusiasm and didn't react to the dryness in her voice.

'They'll give me the stuff for nothing if I time it right.' He paused and looked at her. 'It means I'll be away for a while,' he said gently, and stepped towards her. She moved away, towards the window, and shrugged his hand off when he placed it on her shoulder. 'I'll be back for Lalla's birthday,' he said. 'Don't be like that.'

'Like what?'

'So cold. At least say that you'll miss me.'

'But I won't,' my mother said, staring out of the window with her back to him. 'Not in the slightest. Why don't you leave Lalla some paper and pens, so that she can draw a picture for you while you're away? You've got a lovely fat blank book there. Leather bound. That would do.'

I started up, ready to protest that I could not draw a picture, hardly ever got to hold a pen, but neither of them was looking at me. They threw me into the debate as a way of challenging each other's ideas. If they were the knives cutting through the difficulties of the world in which we were living, then I was the whetstone upon which they sharpened themselves. No wonder I had remained a child so long.

My father opened the door to leave. 'I need that book for the manifest.'

'But Lalla needs it to express herself creatively. That's just as important, isn't it, Michael? After all, a human being deprived of the means of self-expression is nothing better than a slave to the undignified mechanics of physical survival. That's right, isn't it? That's what we said.'

'I'm thinking of the ship.'

'And I'm thinking of the people we're leaving behind.'

'Anna, please.'

'Please what? Please just accept what you say without question? Please stop expecting you to live what you preach? Please just let you take a vision we used to share and change it until I don't recognise it anymore? Please what, Michael?' And there she stopped, as though she had been walking a tightrope and had just looked down.

My father's face clouded over. His eyebrows drew together, and I saw a glimpse of something dark in his eyes as he drew a deep breath.

'You'll never let us leave, will you?' he said. He stood over her as she sat on the sofa, her legs curled beneath her, her dress pooling over the balding velvet. Her face was tilted upwards; she was looking directly at him. Their eyes were locked together. The waters were pressing relentlessly at the dam. Her eyes fell, and the dam held. Right up until the day she died.

TWENTY-THREE

The thing about museums ❀ *I am married*
❀ *Van Gogh and Lalla Paul*

I shouldn't have tried to read *Ballet Shoes* again. It sent me up to the fourth deck, to my neglected museum, to fetch my red shoes on the morning of my wedding. If I hadn't thought about Posy's ballet shoes, the ones her mother left her, such sentimentality would never have occurred to me. But my mother had given me those shoes and no one would see them under the long white dress my father had chosen for me.

And the thing about museums is that they set you to thinking.

There was a button, scratched and worn. There was a wax and plaster apple, broken by my desperate teeth. The screws from a skylight, from back in the days when I had thought freedom was important. Now, nothing was forbidden. Tom and I did whatever we liked, and it wasn't the same. A photograph album and a letter, whose stories I had almost forgotten. A lump of pastry, turning greyer and greyer. And my shoes. My red shoes.

I shut the door on my museum and walked slowly down the infirmary stairs. I let myself into my old cabin, which stood empty now, to add the final scratch to my tally of the days and to change my shoes. There were ninety marks in the original section, sixty in the new, but I was getting married now and it was time to stop. Tom was right.

I went on to the ballroom where my father was waiting with his people. The dress was made of heavy, smooth satin. The shoes my father had given me had high heels, but my red shoes were low, and the skirt puddled around my feet. I gathered it up so that I wouldn't trip, but the fabric simply slipped through my arms like so much water and I gave up. I moved more slowly these days anyway; there seemed to be more of me. Had my body expanded as my brain surrendered? Once I'd have asked. Now I simply accepted that the dress only just met around my waist.

Tom was there, waiting for me outside the ballroom door. He took my arm and we walked through the ballroom together. There was music, and the people smiled on either side of us. My father stood on the podium, behind his desk. The manifest sat open and the trumpets finished as we came before him.

'We have won,' he said, and even then it seemed a strange opening for a wedding speech. 'Every battle that humanity has ever fought, every cause that any man or woman ever felt was worth fighting for, or dying for, we have won. There is not a man or woman in history who struggled for a cause that has not triumphed here, on the ship. There is not a dream that has not been realised here, on the ship. Tom and Lalla stand before us as the expression of what we have achieved.'

I looked at Tom. But he was looking at my father, and they were as radiant and proud as each other.

'We know what wealth means now. We know that wealth is living for and in each other. That every stroke of paint on a canvas, stitch of a tapestry, kick of a football, is an investment in our lives. We know that every meal shared, every activity enjoyed, is an investment in humanity itself. We are everything man was ever intended to be. We are creatures of love, of togetherness, of creativity.

'So, Tom and Lalla, take the legacy of the millennia that have brought us here, and live. Live! Love each other. Till the end of all our days.'

I barely heard the people cheering. At that moment, as though my father had called it into being with his words, I felt a movement inside me, a bubble in my stomach that could have been hunger. I looked at my father, who was preparing his pen to write in the manifest. I looked at Tom, who was grinning around the room, nodding at the people as they shouted our names. I saw Patience holding out her arms in blessing; I saw Finn wiping away tears and Gabriel calling my name while Helen made a pretence of wanting him to quieten down. And then I saw Roger. He was looking at me, and I felt another bubble burst inside me and a soft fluttering, as though I had swallowed a butterfly. And suddenly I knew.

Where had my father been standing, the moment that he made the decision to buy the ship and offer five hundred good people the chance of a perfect death? In my imagination, he was on the top of a mountain, looking down on a mighty city, or sitting on a golden throne in a room filled with oil paintings and marble statues. But he was probably doing nothing more than walking down a road. Certainly, when I realised what was happening to me, my body just carried on, while my mind wrapped itself around the revelation and stared at it. My father put the pen in my hand and I signed the manifest for the second time. I passed the pen to Tom, and then my father joined our hands and we were married.

The people bore us off to the dining room, where Gerhard had prepared a feast. Emily stood smiling and crying beside a vast arrangement of artificial flowers. They were everywhere, and when my father told me that I should throw the bouquet I was holding, it was Emily who caught it. She looked so young. So full of hope. And I realised that this would be neither the last wedding, nor the last birth.

The dining room was decked in bright colours, not only the flowers but the clothes people wore, the little cakes, the decorations that were everywhere. I thought about Jamila's tales of Bangladesh before it had been drowned, of the spices and the heat and the way that rain turned everything a bright, vivid green and of a pink and gold sari she had once worn. I thought of Patience, tending to ripening watermelons, deep green on the red earth of her homestead, and the pale bleating of her goats. I thought of the tulips of Holland leaving their scarlet kisses on the ocean floor when the dykes gave way. And my mother, her green silk dress floating about her, at one with the sea.

Yellow sunflowers in the paintings of Van Gogh.

I'm having a baby, Mother, I whispered silently, and I saw her, sitting on the balding velvet sofa in London, picking at its arm. My father had just set off his expedition to secure now-outlawed art materials for the ship; the sound of the locks being set behind him was still reverberating in the air.

'Van Gogh killed himself,' she said quietly, dropping her hands. 'He created a thousand paintings, but still he died, mad with his inability to show what was inside him. Your father hasn't got enough canvas for even one Van Gogh. Not one. Vincent would clean him out in a week if he came on board.'

'But Vincent's dead.'

'We're all dead,' my mother said, looking out of the window onto the square. 'All of us.'

We're all dead, she said into my wedding celebrations, breaking her silence at last. *All of us.* And I knew what I had to do. It was not a decision I made over time. It was sudden and absolute and irrevocable, like the moment the overhanging cliff falls into the sea, or the moment my child was conceived.

I think my father knew too, because he watched me leave the dining room without a word, my long white satin skirts trailing behind me. I don't know what Tom thought; he was a dream from a place I should never have visited, and he wasn't even looking at me. I left them celebrating with their people, and I thought, maybe this is what has happened to me. I am going mad with the inability to express what is inside me, and my father has run out of canvas.

TWENTY-FOUR

Tom and Roger ❁ *the speeches at my wedding*
❁ *Tom and my father*

I went to my cabin and picked up a bag, and then I went down
to the stores and filled it so full I could barely drag it to the little
boat, from which I had learned to swim. The people were busy
singing and dancing in the dining room; the rest of the ship was
deserted, and no one saw me heave the bag into the boat. The
solar panel showed that the engine was fully charged. I went
back for some clothes, although I did not stop to change, and the
gown swept after me, rippling over the diamond pattern on the
walkways. It was but the work of moments to release the pulley
and lower the boat into the sea, where it bobbed cheerfully at the
end of its rope, like an image from a holiday picture in another
world.

The ladder was fixed to the hull; it would not take long to
climb down to the little boat, even if I went slowly.

I saw my mother's body floating away from the ship. The sea
had borne her up; it would do the same for me. The canvas was
still on the fourth deck, waiting for my father's Van Gogh. I
had never tried to paint a picture. If I stayed, he would give
me canvas. He would give me paint, and brushes, and I would
paint my pain onto the canvas, even though I did not know
how. People would look at my painting like they looked at Alice's

embroidery, and there would be a point to existing. There was no canvas on the little boat, which looked pathetically flimsy now. I imagined the next great rainstorm, my slowly swelling stomach and I hunched in the cabin as the sea and sky became one. And I knew that my mother had been afraid of the ship, just as I was now afraid of the world beyond it.

I heard the door behind me swing open.

'Lalla. Where have you been?'

He had come. Tom had come. And when I saw his face pink and his green eyes alive with concern, I wanted to stay. If his heart beat like mine, if his hopes were wrapped in me as mine were in him, then we could live and love and die on the ship, and the future would be for our baby to sort out. He had come for me. I could do it. I could brave the degeneration of the ship. I could eat from tins and packets of powder until they were exhausted, and then I could starve with him and say nothing of my hunger. I could stand between him and my father, and take one of their hands in each of mine and press them to my growing belly, and see them look at each other with pride, and their love for me would make our inevitable descent to the ocean bed as nothing.

I could do this, if Tom loved me.

'What are you doing, Lalla?'

'I'm leaving,' I said, and as soon as the words were in the air, I knew that they were true, and that I could no more stay on the ship than I could change my father. Tom followed my eyes to the little boat.

'You're what?' he said, his voice constricted. 'Just – please, Lalla. Don't even joke about it.' My hands were shaking in his. I held his hands more tightly.

'I love you,' I said, and my voice was steady. He tried to take me in his arms, but I could not lose him now.

'Lalla,' he said.

I looked at him, and I saw how we had changed. This was not the face of the boy who had jumped eagerly at the gift of a football. The sun had coarsened his boy-skin; there were tiny red veins in his eyes and lines on his forehead. And I – I was no longer the grieving child who had come on board, so needy, so lonely, so desperate to be liked. We had grown together on the ship, and now it was time to leave. 'We're married,' he said, this man who held my hands. 'You don't mean this. You're ill, Lalla. I'm going to fetch Michael, and Roger, and we'll help you. All the excitement – it's sent you a bit mad. That's all. I'll get Michael.'

'Don't,' I said. My husband. My lover, who was going to be a father.

But of course, he didn't know. Did he know? I took his hand and pressed it flat against my belly. 'This is why,' I whispered. 'There's a tomorrow now. We can't be right here, right now any-more, and the ship won't let us be anywhere else.'

'I know.'

'You know?' I said, and the colour drained slowly out of my world.

'Roger said it was possible. He said to keep an eye on you. How long have you known? Why didn't you say anything?'

'I've only just realised,' I faltered. 'You sound angry.'

'I'm not angry. But you've got to stop saying stupid things now. You just ruin things. This ought to be the happiest day of our whole lives.' He pulled me towards the ballroom door, just as he had once pulled me onto the top deck. 'Let's go and tell Michael. He ought to be the first to know.'

'Stop it,' I said, and I held myself hard and would not be pulled. 'It's our baby. Yours and mine. Not his.'

He stopped pulling. 'Of course,' he said. 'But he'll look after you. I'll look after you. I said I'd always be with you, and I will.' He put his hand back on my stomach, but the baby was still.

'Roger said to take you to the infirmary as soon as you said anything. Just to be certain.'

But I was certain. I didn't need Roger, and I didn't trust him.

'Have you said anything to my father?'

'Of course not,' Tom said indignantly. He paused as though he expected thanks.

'Let me go, Tom,' I said.

'Go where, darling? Tell me, where?' He came and stood beside me at the deck rail, and the warmth of his hands on mine made me waver as his words had not.

'Just away. Away over there,' and I gestured at the horizon, beyond which was land or death. Or land and death.

'No,' he said. 'I won't let you. How can you even ask me? There's nothing out there. I saw it. I know. Trust me.' And I could not hold myself apart from him anymore. 'Come back,' he said. 'Eat. Cut the cake. Dance with me.' He smiled and wiped his eyes with the back of his hand. 'Would that be so painful?'

I shook my head. No, it would not be painful. If dancing with Tom had been painful, leaving would have been easy. 'You said you'd come with me,' I burst out.

'We'd starve.'

'So will the ship.'

'We'd die on the sea.'

'So will the ship.'

Tom let me go then, and stepped backwards. 'What if you die, like Roger's Sarah?'

'Then you'd have our baby.'

'What if the baby dies?'

'You'd have me.'

'And if you both die?'

'You'd have yourself. Free. And maybe none of those things will happen. We might find land. You have to choose, Tom.'

'There is no choice,' he said. I felt a terrible tearing in my own breast, as though a part of me was being clawed apart. 'I'm going to be a father. Do you know what that means? It means not breaking your promises. It means putting your children first.'

'Did my father tell you that?' I asked.

'He's done better. He's shown me. All the plans he made, the provisions he stored. For you. Do you know what frightened me most when I came on board, Lalla? Do you know?'

'What?'

'That I wouldn't be worthy. That I could never be what he wanted me to be for you. He loves you so much, and he trusts me. He chose me for you. It wasn't the China pictures I posted on my blog. It was his plan for you. That was why he told me to give you space. He needed to know that you'd chosen me for yourself. And you did. You love me, and I love you. He was right.'

'He chose you?'

He nodded eagerly, and the last fibre holding me to the ship strained, and snapped.

'You say you love me,' I said quietly. 'But you don't. You love the girl my father sold you. And I've tried to be that girl. But I'm not.'

'And the girl you are can't love me?'

'Not on the ship.' The baby moved. 'Tom,' I said, 'if there was ever a moment when you loved me for myself, then you have to come with me.'

He put his hand in his pocket and there, held between his thumb and index finger, was one of the skylight screws. 'I wanted to give you this instead of a wedding ring,' he said. 'But Father had the ring ready, and . . .' He put it into my palm and folded my fingers over it. He pulled me to him and kissed me, and I clung, not to my father's creature but to the boy who had followed me out through the skylight and into the world.

The ballroom door opened and the people spilled out onto the deck. They were laughing, and when they saw Tom and me, kissing on the deck, they began to cheer. Tom put his arm around me.

'The cake.' I heard my father's voice through the open door. 'Where's the happy couple? We should cut the cake.'

I put my lips to Tom's ear and whispered, 'Let me go. Now.'

Tom hesitated for a moment, and in that moment, my father appeared in the doorway, all smiles and pride. 'Tom,' he said. 'Lalla. Come back inside. Cut the cake. You'll be together all your lives. Today you have to share each other with the rest of us.'

Tom put his arm around my shoulders and pushed me forwards, back through the doors into the ballroom, smiling to left and to right. My red shoes had no grip and I slipped along, propelled by his strength. 'I'm sorry,' he said quietly, guiding me up onto the podium. The clapping and the stamping that greeted us drowned out the music and made it impossible for me to reply. He bent down and kissed me again, and the ballroom exploded in cheers. And I liked it. Oh how I liked it, even though I was furious. There was nothing simple here.

Patience and Mercy bustled over with the cake knife, its handle tied with ribbons and flowers. Tom took it and offered it to me, and I ran my finger down the flat of the blade. The cutting edge caught the light; it looked wickedly sharp. Patience and Mercy looked at each other, delighted, as though they'd overheard me saying something lovely. I held the knife, and Tom put his hands over mine, and together we pushed it through the smooth white icing and into the cake below.

'Speech,' someone called out, and the word was taken up. 'Speech, speech.' Tom grinned and held up his hand as though he was reluctant to comply. But I could see his eyes, and I could see his pride in standing where my father had stood, speaking to the people as my father spoke to them. My father was there, standing with his people and gazing at me. He took in my dress, my veil, the tiara in my hair. But he could not see his compass, tucked inside the bodice of my dress, warm against my skin.

'Speech,' the people called, but not until my father held up his hands and joined in the cry did Tom lean over to the microphone.

'Is this on?' he asked, and it clicked into life. 'I just wanted to say one thing. Only one. And it's this – that I really, really wish Lalla's mother were here.' Silence fell, broken only by murmured agreement. People looked at Tom, and at each other, and at the floor. Only my father continued to look directly at me. 'Lalla loved her mother, and I know we all lost people, but Lalla actually lost her mother here on the ship, and I think that's why it's taken her a bit longer than the rest of us to be happy here. But Lalla's happy now, aren't you, Lalla, and I'm going to make sure she stays that way.'

People began to clap, but I leaned across to the microphone and said, 'Wait.' I spoke louder than I had meant to, and the word echoed slightly. Hundreds of pairs of eyes followed my father's and fixed on me.

'What are you doing?' Tom asked, frowning.

'I've got some things to say.' I tried to say this to him quietly, but the microphone was on and Tom was leaning over me, so our words were picked up and broadcast across the ballroom.

'We're going to tell Michael first,' Tom said quietly. I shook my head. My father raised his eyebrows. The unconditional joy that had reigned only a few moments before dissipated, and in its place was an air of unease.

'Let Lalla speak,' my father said, and Tom stepped aside. I could see the satin of my bodice pulsing with my heartbeat and wondered whether I was going to be able to say a word. The bride did not normally make a speech, my father had said casually as he brought the flowers down from the stores. But I had not planned the wedding. I had not chosen to be standing where I was. They had no choice but to listen.

'I've got some things to say,' I repeated, my voice unsteady. 'It can be my testimony, if you like. I never got to say what brought me here, like the rest of you did.' Tom shifted nervously beside me. 'I wish my mother was here too. But she isn't. And there's someone I wish was here even more than my mother.' My father was looking grave, and Emily's hand tightened on his arm. 'Tom had a grandfather. Tom's grandfather was the only family he had left. The only family. And he took Tom into the country, to find a plot of land to grow things on.'

Tom hissed in my ear. 'This is an old story, Lalla. Everyone knows it already. We've left the past behind, remember? The testimonies are over.'

'Mine isn't,' I said. 'The point is that Tom's grandfather wasn't allowed to come on the ship. It's not that he was dead. It was because he wanted a garden. And what I wanted to say is that I wish he had been allowed to come, because he had a right to be saved too. You can't just pick and choose. Not people. Because people aren't things. You can't just store the ones you like, as if they were tinned tomatoes or cooking chocolate.'

My father removed Emily's hand from his arm and strode up to the podium. 'Let's talk later, Lalla,' he said. 'Stop this now. Say thank you to your guests, and go and dance.'

'I won't be dancing,' I said, and I could feel my smile tight and false. 'I'm going to leave now. I'm going to find apples. Real ones.' I gathered my skirts. 'Thank you,' I said as I got to my feet. 'Thank you for looking after me, and putting up with me for so long.' There was an uncertain smatter of applause as I stepped down from the podium and began to walk towards the doors.

'What are you doing?' Tom called.

'I told you,' I said, and the room was so quiet that I didn't need the microphone. 'I'm leaving. You won't let me go, but it's not your decision to make.' The wedding was crumbling; people looked around at the flowers, the cake, the clothes they were wearing, as though they expected these things to melt. I kept walking, and the people stepped aside. When I reached the door, I heard my name echoing around the room, and I knew that my father had taken the microphone.

I spoke to him without turning round.

'Tom doesn't love me enough,' I said. 'Do you?'

Patience began to cry, and her sobs cut through the set air. Mercy held her. I looked at Mercy, her wide soft eyes turned pleadingly towards me. But I could not stay just because Patience wanted me to.

'Close the doors,' my father called, but no one moved. I kept walking.

'Close the doors,' came another voice, higher, more desperate, but still the people hesitated, scared to do at Tom's command what they had failed to do for my father.

'Look at me, Lalla,' my father ordered. 'Look at me.' His voice was cracking and I knew I had to get out of the ballroom before he began to cry. I remembered my mother, how she had stalled and stalled and stalled the sailing of the ship. If she had not been shot, we would still be in London. I knew this now, and I had a suspicion of the lengths my father had gone to, to create the world he wanted.

I heard the desk drawer open and shut.

There was a scream, and another, and I knew what I would see when I turned around as clearly as though it was happening in front of me.

'I can't let you,' my father was calling, his voice choked. 'I won't let you. Where do you think you'll go?'

I was trembling so hard that I wasn't sure I could turn without falling. *Let me be wrong,* I begged to nothing. *Let me be wrong.* But I remembered a figure in faded black running through the crowd and my mother collapsing to the floor. I was not wrong.

I turned around. My father was holding a gun, and he was pointing it at me. The room was so still people did not seem to be breathing. He held the gun steadily and said, 'I would rather kill you myself than have you suffer what you will suffer before your death in the world beyond the ship.'

'And I would rather die out there, looking for a future, than die here, knowing there is none.'

'Michael.' Emily stepped forwards, her hands held out. She kept her eyes on my father and walked towards him. 'Lalla is your daughter. You love her. We all love her. This is not the way. We convince her with love, remember?' But my father was not deterred. His gun was trained on me and he did not flinch, even when Emily joined him on the podium and touched his arm.

'What will you do?' I said, turning to the ballroom in general. 'Will you leave your children to sink with the ship? Will you live this glorious life of plenty, knowing that your children will starve because of it? Or will you help me take the ship to land?'

'The ship is for the children,' my father said, and for the first time I saw a tremor in his hands.

'And their children?'

'A beautiful life makes a present of death,' my father said. 'I gave my daughter a beautiful life. I have given you all a beautiful life.'

I looked around at the people, frozen in dismay, in shock, in fear. 'Tell him,' I said to them. 'Tell my father to take the ship back to London. Or anywhere. I've seen the radar and the charts. There is land. Let's find it, and go there, and start again. We can use the stores to give us a good start. We'll grow clover.' I looked at Tom and willed him to join his voice to mine. But no one said a word.

Then Helen spoke. 'No,' she said. 'I'm not going back. If you make me go back, I'll throw myself into the sea and take Gabriel with me.'

'Me too.' Patience pushed Mercy from her and got heavily to her feet. 'Lalla, child. Africa's burned. India's drowned. China's dead. You saw London. There's nowhere. Nowhere but here.'

'And even if there was somewhere else, why would you go there?' Mercy joined her voice with Patience's. 'We've got everything here.' She looked around shyly, the guardian of a secret. 'Michael told me there's pianos. We're going to learn to play music.'

'Things may have got better,' I said. 'How will we know unless we go and see? You threw away the mast.'

Tom looked at me, and for a wild, glorious moment I thought that he was going to tell the engineers to storm my father's cabin and set a course for the nearest land. I would not have to leave. We would be together, and find a future for our child.

'But it's safe here!' my father cried, the gun now trembling in his hands. 'That's all I ever wanted. To keep you safe, to keep you nurtured. Why are you doing this to me, Lalla?'

I looked at him. 'Who was Neil Bailey?' I asked.

My father's self-command was gone. Emily cradled his head in her arms and he cried, gripping the gun as though it was the only thing stopping him from falling. 'No,' he cried. 'No.' I looked at Emily, waiting for her to shout at me. But she did not.

'It was an accident,' Emily said. 'You need to understand that we were in the holding centre for a long time. Years, some of us. We wanted to sail, but your mother would never quite agree. We had food and shelter and the guards – we were all right as far as your mother was concerned. She was more interested in the street people. I wanted her to bring you to meet us, but she never did. Michael said she was scared we'd hold you hostage until she agreed to sail. We were so insulted by that. We said too much to each other, got ourselves too wound up. And one day, Neil disappeared. That same night, Roger got the message from Michael that we were to sail at last.

'When Neil came back, we were singing and dancing. Only Roger wasn't joining in. When I asked Roger why not, he showed me the rest of Michael's message. Anna had been shot in the stomach. She was barely breathing. Roger didn't think she could possibly survive. And Neil – when he realised what he'd done – he went outside and shot himself.'

'Where did he get the gun from?'

Emily didn't answer.

'Did you give it to him?' I asked my father. 'Did you tell Neil Bailey to shoot my mother?'

'No,' my father sobbed, his face contorted. 'Not to shoot her. A broken window, that was all. She was sleepwalking into hell and she was holding your hand. A warning. To wake her up. To save your life.'

'Is this the same gun?' I felt myself drawn to it; I imagined taking it in my hands. My father was cradling it like a child. *No, Lalla, never a gun. Just my toothbrush and my wit.* I had been so naive.

'We didn't know what to do with it,' Helen said. 'It all happened so quickly. Neil died, then you arrived, and we sailed. We couldn't just throw the gun into the sea, not with all the government troops, and the mob on the quay.'

Gabriel clung to Helen and began to cry, 'I don't like the gun, Mummy. I don't like it.'

Helen held his hand. 'No one likes it,' she said, keeping her eyes on me as though the gun was my fault.

'But thank goodness we've got it,' Roger said grimly.

He took the gun from my weeping father and aimed it at my skirts, and the tilt of his chin and the light through the ballroom windows told me the truth. Roger, who had red and blue mugs and made maps in flour. Roger, who broke the rules and changed nothing. A broken window wouldn't have been enough to persuade my mother to board. It had been Roger's idea to shoot her. An arm, he would have said to poor Neil Bailey. A foot. I imagined Neil Bailey's trembling hands, his fear. I could forgive him. But I couldn't forgive Roger. I couldn't forgive my father.

I walked backwards towards the deck doors, facing Roger and the gun. Any moment, I would hear a shot and feel the searing pain of a bullet in my foot, or my leg. The train of my dress caught under my shoes. I tripped, and as I struggled to my feet, I saw that Finn and some of the engineers were blocking my path to the deck door. The internal door – the door into the ship, through which the doctor had carried my mother one hundred and fifty days ago – stood wide open. I could escape into the ship, I thought. I could live in my museum and sneak down to the stores at night, the hidden, ghostly conscience of the ship. And I knew, as clearly as though I had seen it happen, that one day, someone on the ship would do this.

But I had a life of my own to find, and another to protect.

'Please,' I said to Finn. 'Move aside and let me through.'

'We can't do that,' he said. 'You're not well. You've never really been well, not since we sailed. Isn't there something you can give her, Roger? To help her a bit. She doesn't know what she's doing.'

I looked at Tom. Did he think I should be winged, like a captive bird, or tranquillised, like the zoo animals in screen documentaries? Is that what I was to him now – a sick elephant, incubating his heir?

But Tom did not speak. Instead, he reached over to Roger and put his hands gently over the hands that held the gun. 'This isn't the way, Roger,' he said gently. 'It's not what Michael's taught us, or what he wants.' Tom took the gun, and spoke softly and calmly, using a monotone that made me think of lullabies. Emily looked at Tom gratefully; Tom looked at my father. 'We are your people, Michael,' Tom said. 'We will be with you, and be grateful to you, for all of our lives, and our children's lives.' For one wild, ridiculous moment I thought Tom was going to shoot my father. But he didn't. He called to the engineers, 'Let Lalla go.' My father was shaking now. Tom carried the gun towards me. My father shrank into his chair, like a speeded-up film of a man growing old.

Emily knelt in front of him, holding his hands. 'Are there any more guns?' she asked him. He shook his head, and a great cry rose from him, involuntary and animal. Tom stood next to me, holding the gun, facing into the ballroom.

'Stay there,' he said. 'All of you. Stay where you are.' He stepped backwards through the ballroom doors, motioning to me to go through first. I went through to the deck, and he came with me, bringing the gun. The doors shut behind us, and we were alone.

'Lalla,' he said. 'Don't do this.'

'I don't have a choice.'

He took the gun in both hands; he looked at it; he looked at me. Then he raised his hands high over his head and, with all his strength, he threw the gun over the deck rail. It flew in an arc and plummeted into the water near the little boat, and the splash it made caused the little boat to rock.

'You do now,' he said.

I wanted to kiss him. I wanted to hold and hold him, and never, never, never let him go, but I knew that if I felt his lips against mine, I would decide that tomorrow would be soon enough, or the day after, or the day after that. I had to live, even if I died as a result.

I could neither live in a grave, nor birth my child into one.

Tom looked at me. He waited. He waited a little longer. And then he went to the ballroom doors, opened them and looked back at me. I stayed still. He stepped into the ballroom and pulled the doors shut behind him.

TWENTY-FIVE

What happens in the end

And so I climbed, and my red shoes made the deck rail ring. I pulled myself up and swung my legs over, so that I balanced like a child on a swing, gripping the rail until my palms were numb. My satin train hung heavy below me.

If I let go and threw myself forward, I would hit the water. I could push off from the deck rail with my feet, and launch myself away from the ship, beyond the little boat, to the true unknown that awaited all of us. It would be quicker that way, and my mother would be waiting for me.

But no. The end was not going to be so easy. I gathered up my dress and felt the little boat rocking beneath my feet, even though the deck rail was still pressing cold into my thighs. It would be firm and solid decades after the little boat had fallen apart and rotted away. On the ship, I lived and worked with hundreds; the little boat was barely big enough for just me. The ship stored food for years to come; the little boat held only what I'd been able to carry, and a map from my father's study. If time on the ship was running out, on the little boat it had practically gone. And yet I was going to take myself – take us – from big to small, from plenty to dearth, from the known to a place I had no power to predict.

I felt with my foot until I found the first rung of the ladder. I wondered whether Tom would betray me at the last. I looked

307

back at the ballroom door, half-hoping for a tall shadow, a foot-fall. But there was nothing. Tom had chosen, and he had not chosen me.

For you, Lalla, my father always said about the ship. I did this for you, for your future, so that you could be safe.

For me, Father? I thought, remembering his arm slipping softly around Emily's waist. For me? I remembered the cots waiting on the fourth deck. The looks of adoration on Alice's face as he presented her with more silk, more beads, embroidery threads in ever brighter colours. The bewilderment in Tom's green eyes as I reached for his hand in the sunlit air, and the sudden clearing of his face as my father showed him the way forward. *I think this is what Michael would want, Lalla. I think this is what would make him happy.*

When you are born, little one, I will never say that I did this for you. I will never place that burden upon you. These are my feet climbing down the ladder. Mine is the heart that longs for another way, mine the eyes that have seen the emptiness in the way we are living. You, as yet, are nothing. But even now, even before I am certain that you will ever draw breath outside my body, I know that I cannot, I must not, feed you for ever. You will be mine for a time, and then you will feed yourself.

On what?

Mother, you are out here somewhere. Mother, look after me. After us.

There is land. I have seen it on my father's maps. And on that land are people. I will find them, or drown. My child will not be born into the safe, dying world of the ship, but into the desperate, shifting world of the living. My child will be born in a place I do not yet know, among people I have never met. They will welcome me, because I have given everything I have, everything I am, to find them. I will steer my little boat on the high seas, and one day, if I am lucky, I will see the vast trunks of the wind turbines towering above me, their giant arms reaching for stardust in the air, and I will know I am almost there. Maybe my hands will be the ones that reconnect the wires. Maybe, little one, those hands will be yours.

I had my father's compass. I was leaving my museum to the ship; it was a fair exchange. They could read my story there if they wanted to.

I climbed down the ladder, my train weighing on my arm, each foot secure for a matter of seconds before taking its turn to bear my body down.

The ship was not the beginning, but the end. In a day, or a year, or a decade, or a century, the food would run out. The ship itself would rust and sink. And the people upon it – these people whom I knew, or their children, or their children's children – would die. Burnt out, like night's candles.

I was seized by the desire to know where the thought of night's candles had come from. Maybe it was not too late. I would find out in a moment if I went back. I felt the cold of the metal rungs pressing into my palms, their solidity beneath my feet. Now that I was leaving, the certainty of the ship seemed very precious. I longed for it, for the knowledge that there would be food, that there would be shelter, that there would be meaningful work for me, a life in which I could flourish, love, grow. And yet, it was this very certainty that made it essential to leave. Because there is no such thing as certainty, and in creating it, we lose the very thing that keeps us alive.

I stepped into the boat and released the pulley ropes. The boat shivered on the surface of the vast sea.

I blinked away the tears that were clouding my vision, and I saw a halo of bright rust surrounding the rivet that held the ladder to the hull. Like a sunrise trying to burst through, or the creeping orange embers on a paper's edge before the paper bursts into flame. Or a sunset, or a dying fire.

ACKNOWLEDGEMENTS

My agent, Jonny Geller, who understood the apple, and my editor, Arzu Tahsin, who bit into it.

Anna Davis, Kirsten Foster, Alice Lutyens, Jennifer Kerslake, Sophie Hutton-Squire and everyone at Curtis Brown and Weidenfeld and Nicolson.

My supportive and talented writing friends Emily de Peyer, Emma Sweeney and Rachel Connor, my long-suffering non-writing friends, in particular Ali Jezard, Rebecca Singerman-Knight and Julie Walther, and my sister Carissa Honeywell.

Everyone I've been taught by or alongside, with particular thanks to Maggie Gee, Katharine McMahon, Louise Doughty, Andrew Miller, Helen Dunmore and Erica Wagner.

All who read and gave feedback on the manuscript, including Jessie Burton, Geoff Curwen, Laxmi Curwen, Lucy Eyre, Emma Haigh, Daniela Haller, Sue Harris, Sarah Hooker, Tim Jordan, Rosie Pearson, David Salmon, Rose Mary Salmon, Ruth Shabi and Gillian Stern.

Helen Lappert and the wonderful women of Amersham A Cappella, who know why.

Kate Honeywell, Maureen Hancocks, Howard Hancocks, Jane Diduca, Charlotte Yeoman and Jane Davies, who have given me time.

My children. OK, so I could do it quicker without you, but the thought of doing so takes away all meaning.

And James. I thank you from the bottom of whatever it is that drives me to write. My heart belongs to you already.

THE
SHIP

READING GROUP NOTES

IN CONVERSATION WITH ANTONIA HONEYWELL

Q Where did the idea for *The Ship* come from and how did the
   plot begin to take shape in your mind?

A The idea for *The Ship* began to form when I married but in
   many ways the novel has its genesis in my childhood. I was
   an odd child – I didn't make friends easily and used to spend
   school playtimes wandering round the playground writing
   notes to the ladybirds in chalk. Then came an apocalyptic divorce when I was thirteen. The legacy of that divorce and the
   bitterness that led up to and away from it meant that I walked
   through life on eggshells. Relationships were a snare and a de-
   lusion; arguments were like the molten lava beneath the earth's
   crust, showing the seething dangers beneath. I became a skilled
   mediator and peacekeeper, but those skills came from a genuine doubt about my right to inhabit the space I took up. I also
   became a constant observer of other people – the way they
   talked to each other, influenced each other. I began to understand that lack of self-confidence – constant reliance on other
   people – can be a form of tyranny. I couldn't just wait around
   to be rescued by some insightful teacher, or doctor, or hand-
   some prince – I had to become an island in order to join the

mainland. And when I married, I wanted to keep my hard-won happiness safe – but how could that be done without shutting out the flawed and damaged aspects of the world? And that got me thinking about the ways in which the hugely privileged defend their privileges, and the ultimate consequences of that. The financial crash in 2008 sharpened my nebulous ideas, and then I saw Lalla, a bored and angry teenager, through a display case at the British Museum and began to write.

Q *The Ship* is set in the near future in a world which is unfamiliar to us. How did you create an alternative history for Lalla? Did you plan a timeline from the present day to the time of the book, and if so, do you think the world into which Lalla is born could become a reality for us?

A I think we're living in it already. What are the people found dead in lorries, or drowning in fishing vessels, or relying on food banks, or dying of exposure on the streets, but an expendable underclass? How fully are you able to participate in modern society if you have no access to the internet?

Q Lalage is an unusual name. How did you come across it and does it hold particular significance for you?

A I first came across the name Lalage in John Fowles' novel *The French Lieutenant's Woman*. I was thirteen when I read it, and it had a powerful effect on me. Sarah Woodruff is a woman whom society has defined in a particular way. She is powerless to reject the definition, but maintains her sense of self in spite of it, and becomes a pariah. I don't want to spoil the novel for people who haven't read it – suffice to say that a small child named Lalage appears in its final pages, and that the outcome, not just for the individuals concerned but for the progress of society as a whole, depends entirely on the über-Victorian Charles' reaction to her. My Lalage is John Fowles' Lalage, a fair few decades on.

Q There are a number of religious references in the novel, for example the Nazareth Act, the symbolism of the apple and the ship, and the way those on board start to call Michael Paul, 'Father'. What value does religion have in *The Ship*?

A There is no religion on board the ship – not overtly, anyway. But by choosing the people he will save, Michael creates a bond between them, and nurtures their very human desire to believe that their good fortune is due to more than mere luck. Their elevation of him is necessary to them – without it, they would have to challenge his decisions, and their own. They'd have to answer Lalla's questions. And it's necessary to Michael, too, because without the people's unwavering, uncritical faith in him, the ship would be torn apart. They create a pseudo-religion that suits them. Religion can be a deliberate anaesthetic for your conscience, or a means of finding it. Look at the Church of England's struggle to embrace equal marriage, for example, or the strength with which huge swathes of avowedly religious people clung to slavery. It's Lalla, at the end, who faces the true conundrum of faith.

Q Have you considered writing a sequel to *The Ship*? How do you respond when readers ask what happens to Lalla?

A I love questions from readers – one of the main joys of being published is meeting readers and grappling with their questions, particularly in a book group context where we don't have to worry about spoilers. Lalla belongs to anyone who reads her story and every reader brings something new to her decision. I've had readers draw parallels with their own lives – one spoke of Lalla's story resonating with his own struggle to come out to parents, for example, and another talked of the pressure to take on the family business her parents and grandparents wanted to pass down to her. Readers have talked about divorce, about facing infertility, about end-of-life treatment and assisted dying. Every life contains a Ship moment – a time when a particular course of action becomes the only possibility, regardless of what happens next. Some people commit everything to an idea and succeed beyond their wildest dreams – which is wonderful – but I feel that we're living in a world where success is seen as an inevitable consequence of total commitment, when in fact it's no such thing. I'm interested in the no-man's land between commitment and success. Suppose *The Ship* had never achieved publication? What about the young people who give their lives to developing their tennis or swimming, yet never win Wimbledon or an Olympic gold? What about the couple who've sunk all they have into IVF but never become pregnant? It's an underexplored area, and *The Ship* is about the decision Lalla comes to, rather than its consequences. Any sequel would have to respect those stories – the ones that look like failure, but which contain sacrifice and devotion equal to any success.

Q You have four young children. Do you find it difficult to find the time to write? Have you developed any strategies for balancing the demands of parenthood with your writing life?

A It's impossible. It could be made possible by a full-time nanny, or boarding schools for the children, I suppose, but . . . but . . . It's not just money. We wanted the children. And for reasons too complicated to explore here, it's a complete miracle that they came and were all healthy. They'll grow up and leave us soon enough, so for now I juggle and contrive and cry for help, and maybe when they fly away, the time and space to write will soothe the pain. It might help aspiring writers in the same situation to know that these replies have been written a) in the kitchen while the porridge bubbles b) in the café at a local activity centre and c) hiding in the bathroom. I have to look hard at how I spend my time, and ruthlessly cull the non-essential. Some activities are easy to let go – like dusting, ironing and clothes shopping. Others are harder, particularly where the children are involved. It takes a good deal of discipline. But it's right that the children should see that I work. And that writing is my work is a privilege in itself.

Q Who are your favourite writers and how have they influenced your work?

A I love to read. I always have. Benson Village Library featured largely in my childhood and I read indiscriminately. I had no idea whether a book was well-written or improving or *suitable* for a child; I absorbed the lot. The insidious erosion of our libraries is a terrible thing. When I was eleven, my English teacher suggested I try some classics. I started with *Jane Eyre* and just kept going. At sixteen I discovered Thomas Hardy and fell heavily in love; by eighteen I was boasting that I didn't read living authors. I wore long full skirts and lacy blouses with high collars and wondered why I didn't get invited to parties. But literature was so much easier than real life. Now I read living authors constantly and despair at the impossibility of reading even the novels that were published yesterday. But those classics are part of me – Lucy Snowe, Dorothea Brooke – women who reject the narrative they've been brought up with and reach for a creed of their own. (But not Maggie Tulliver or Tess Durbeyfield; pre-death self-actualisation is preferable. I'm working on it.)

DISCUSSION POINTS

'I think he was a little bewildered that his great triumph, the Dove, had not saved the world, and so he set about saving his own world – my mother and I – another way.' Is Michael Paul a bad man? Do you feel any sympathy for him? How difficult are moral judgements in a world in which civilisation has collapsed?

How fine is the line between caring for children and controlling them?

The Ship has been described as a coming-of-age novel. What does Lalla learn during the course of novel, and can you see any differences in the choices she makes at the beginning of the story and at the end?

'Eat. Smile at me. Be happy.' Why do you think Lalla struggles to follow her father's instructions?

If you found yourself on board the ship, what would you miss most about the world you inhabit now? Do you think you would be more or less content than Lalla?

How many religious images or references can you find in the novel and why are they significant to the narrative?

'*Have an apple*, she used to say when I asked for the impossible.' What does the symbol of the apple represent in *The Ship*?

Lalla and her mother are walking home from the British Museum when they see a button fall from a man's coat as he wraps it around a woman. While Lalla's mother thinks the button is a token of love that should be in a museum, Lalla's father sees it as a 'broken button . . . not worth anything.' Discuss the differences in their ideology, and who you think is right.

What contemporary political, social or environmental parallels can you find within this novel?

'And that was what the ship was. A life without hope.' Do you agree? Is the overall tone of *The Ship* hopeful or pessimistic?

Discuss the tension between love and freedom in the novel. Consider Lalla's relationships with Tom and her father. How well do they know Lalla really?

Why does Antonia Honeywell include phrases at the beginning of each chapter? Do these affect the way you approach the story?

'We honour our dead by living well.' Do you agree? How does Lalla experience grief?

Do you think that the five hundred people on board the ship are worthy of salvation? How do you feel about their willingness to forget those left behind?

'*I don't have answers, Lalla. Only questions. That's how you learn.*' How are these words brought out in the novel?

**If you enjoyed *The Ship*, you might
also like to try these novels**

The Handmaid's Tale by Margaret Atwood
The World According to Anna by Jostein Gaarder
Ballet Shoes by Noel Streatfeild
The Bees by Laline Paull
The Hunger Games by Suzanne Collins
Never Let Me Go by Kazuo Ishiguro
The Girl With All the Gifts by M. R. Carey
The Machine Stops by E. M. Forster
The Burning Book by Maggie Gee
The Siege by Helen Dunmore
Children of Men by P. D. James
Our Endless Numbered Days by Claire Fuller
After Me Comes the Flood by Sarah Perry
The Carhullan Army by Sarah Hall
Z for Zachariah by Robert C. O'Brien
The Testament of Jessie Lamb by Jane Rogers
The Bone Clocks by David Mitchell
Nineteen Eighty-Four by George Orwell
The Little Mermaid by Hans Christian Andersen
The Ones Who Walk Away from Omelas by Ursula K Le Guin

THE TIME BEING

A short story prequel to *The Ship*
by Antonia Honeywell

Sometimes, I sit in my front room and wonder what life must have been like before I was born. My mother tells me about history, but she also reads me stories, and it's often impossible to tell one from the other. For example, she tells me that people once ate food that grew in the ground. I believe that, because there are pictures on our tins and packets that show fields, and there are lots of books which describe the land before the soil became poisoned and exhausted. But she's also told me that people once used whole aeroplanes to bring green beans and roses from Africa to England. And I can't see why anyone would have done that when the soil was still good. Not that it matters much; there are no longer any aeroplanes, no beans and not that much of Africa either. So much for history.

And then there are the stories. The ones my mother reads to me are mostly about young girls who have to do difficult things. 'Once upon a time,' my mother says every time she opens a book, even if that's not how the story starts. Three girls grow up learning ballet when only one of them really likes it. One girl has an aunt who hates her, who shuts her into the terrible room where her uncle died. Another one is forced into a vast arena, to kill people in a kind of game. My mother is trying to show me that things have always been difficult, everywhere, across every time, and that I'm nothing special. 'Once upon a time,' she says, and I think, *any time but this one*. And that's the difference between story and history. The once-upon-a-time girls may not have much fun, but they can do something about their lives. They become ballet dancers, film stars, governesses, heroes of rebellion . . . it doesn't matter what. They have tomorrows. But my life is made up of glimpses of the past; my tomorrows are made only of yesterdays, and the only food that's left now is the preserved stuff that yesterday left behind.

Our flat is very close to the British Museum and my mother has been teaching me there for as long as I can remember. My father would not let me go to school. He said that schools were bound to become a target and he was right; the last schools closed years ago. We eat in the flat with the doors locked and bolted, and walk to the museum with nothing but our identity cards. I used to like it, but even in the stasis of now, things change. The homeless are settling into the museum, quietly, hiding their sleeping bags in corners. They smell bad and I don't like being near them. My mother talks to them, but I won't. I keep my distance and open my eyes. Things are going missing from the display cases – not the rusty ploughs and the iron spoons but the gold, the silver, the jewels, even the ivory statue of St Margaret of Antioch escaping from the dragon. There are little cards instead, saying that the objects have been taken away for cleaning. But I see the curators watching the homeless, and the homeless watching the curators. My mother tells me that the things are being put somewhere safe, but blind eyes turn both ways and everyone is hungry. I prefer to stay in the flat, where my mind can wander and I don't have to think about other people.

Other people belong to another time, when I was not afraid of the troops. When the streets were not as empty as they are now. When my father was home more often than he was away, and there was always something to look at. A market stall for example, constructed as soon as the troop patrol had passed and then dismantled before there was any chance of them returning. Or a screen party, when the street people would find an ancient television, or a computer from the time before the collapse, and rig it up to a power source, and then tweak and connect and twist cables together until a moving image appeared, captured from the random bits of the past that still floated outside the government firewall. Once it was women in huge dresses and men in black and white suits, all dancing together. And another time, it was an excited man chopping up fresh carrots – real, true-life, fresh carrots – so fast you could barely see the knife move, while a room full of people sitting in rows watched and laughed. My mother said that it must have been recorded as a live broadcast, and that that was ironic because everyone in it was probably dead now. Even when there were no markets or screen parties, there were the street prophets, making poetry of the barren world. '*The fig tree shall not blossom, neither shall fruit be in the vines; the labour of the olive shall fail, and the fields shall yield no meat; the flock shall be cut off from the fold, and there shall be no herd in the stalls...*' I used to stand and listen to that one for ages, letting the words thunder around my head until my mother pulled me away. But everything changed after Regent's Park. Regent's Park is why I don't like thinking about people any more.

My father was away at the time. My mother and I were at home, and through the window of the flat I saw troops in Bedford Square. They were setting something up. At first I thought it was a registration station or a food drop, but then I saw cables and a generator, and a large screen, and amplifiers. People began to creep out of the alleys towards the screen, and the troops stood around with their guns trained on the growing crowd. Then the whole screen was filled with the face of a smiling woman. Her skin was impossibly clean, her lips bright red and her hair dark and smooth. Her lips moved, showing white teeth, but the only sound was a high-pitched screeching from one of the amplifiers. The soldiers argued, shaking bits of cable at each other. One started shouting into a communicator; I could hear his voice through the closed window and opened it to try and catch his exact words. A woman in a long blue skirt, dingy with grey, stepped from the crowd with her hands held up so that the soldiers could see she had no weapons. I couldn't hear what she was saying, but the soldiers moved things about when she pointed, and then there was a buzzing thud from the amplifiers. The screeching sound stopped and the red-lipped woman's voice, smooth and shiny as water, spread over the crowd, quietly at first, then louder as the soldiers worked out the controls. I leaned out of the window to listen.

'So let's work together,' the woman on the screen said, smiling and shaking her beautiful hair. 'Whether you fell behind on your rent, or lost your mortgage in the collapse, there's a place you can go while our emergency government sorts things out.' She held out a hand as though she was inviting us into her home. 'Regent's Park,' she said, and music started – bright, cheerful music, like the song on that little snatch of old film. As the music played, the screen showed children sitting at desks, grinning and holding up their hands. Grownups talking seriously, walking together with bulging bags of government rations. A close-up of a tap issuing clean water into a clean bucket. A child lying back on a big chair while someone in a white coat looked at their teeth. Best of all was a red and blue roundabout. The children sat on it in warm brightly coloured jackets, laughing like pictures from the time before as it went round and round and round. And there were swings, and the grownups pushed the children and the children stretched out their legs. 'More,' the children shouted, their voices rising over the music. 'More, more.'

'Regent's Park,' the woman said over the images. 'A place to be, for the time being.'

For the time being. It looked like fun. It was something different. I was fed up with being dragged to the British Museum and back every day. And the people on the film were clean and brave, and the shiny haired woman cared about them, walking among them and asking them questions. They all walked proud, not shuffling in corners. I was almost twelve, and the children in the playground went round and round in my head. I wanted to meet them, to play with them, to know them.

'Can we go and live there?' I asked.

'Live where?'

'Regent's Park. There was a film about it. Just now. Look, you can see the troops taking down the screen.'

My mother had not come to the window; she was tapping and tapping at our screen, frowning with frustration. I went over to her and saw that she was in the middle of updating; a hollow line appeared and starting filling with blue. We stood in silence, watching, waiting for the blue to reach the end of the bar. If the update was successful, then the Dove – the government firewall that protected our screens from legacy viruses – would sweep across the screen and we'd find out when and where the next food drop was due. The blue crept up, millimetre by painful millimetre. If it froze, we'd have to start again. If the connection went down, we'd have to start again. There was no choice. If we didn't update, our cards would be invalidated, and we would lose our flat and be turned away at the next food drop. But at that moment, even the threat of homelessness and starvation didn't seem important.

'If we lived in Regent's Park we might not need to do this,' I said. 'There weren't any screens on the film. Or registrations, or food drops. The people had food in bags. I think they just fetched it from a food tent.' The blue was edging to the end of the bar; I could see my mother beginning to relax.

'We have a flat,' my mother said. 'A solid flat, with walls and food stores of our own. We have a secure entrance. Why would we swap that for a tent?'

'There are children there,' I said. 'Ones I could play with.'

'There aren't any children,' my mother said. 'Not any more. There's only survival.'

'There were children. I saw them, on the film. How could they have shown children if there aren't any?'

'Lalage, you can only be a child because you've got all this. The food, the screen, a safe place to live. You think it's ordinary. But it isn't. The children you see on the streets, in the museum, they're not *like* you. They don't have what you have. They're just clinging on. And this Regent's Park thing – it's just a way for the government to push them off.'

'Off the roundabout?' I asked. She didn't answer. She was looking at the screen, holding her hands together and muttering.

Suddenly, the update bar went blank. The blue disappeared, and the solid bricks of our home suddenly felt as fragile as paper. My mother got our identity cards out and scanned them again, her hands shaking. She breathed on them and rubbed them with her sleeve. 'They're not scratched are they?' she said anxiously. 'They can't be scratched. Is it the card or the connection?' I rattled at the cables while my mother pressed our cards onto the screen again and again, and before the fear had truly taken hold, the bar went blue. Completely blue. The white feathered wing swept across the screen. *Update successful*, the screen informed us. *Please click for the latest bulletin*. I felt dizzy, and realized that I had been holding my breath.

My mother closed her eyes and massaged her temples. The Regent's Park film began to play on our screen. *So let's work together*, the woman said, her voice as musical and comforting as it had been the first time. My mother watched in silence.

'Can we at least go and look?' I asked as soon as the film was over.

'No,' she said. 'No, we can't.'

And that was that.

But I couldn't forget the roundabout. I couldn't forget those children. The film was shown automatically whenever we used the screen and I watched it every time. I'd have recognised those children on the street. I gave them names from my mother's stories. Posy. Jane. Peeta. I imagined talking to them, finding out about their lives before they moved to Regent's Park, sharing out the food my mother had stored. Taking turns on the roundabout. And through the window, I saw small groups of people walking towards the park, bags in hand and bundles on back. I wanted to join them. I wanted to be part of something bigger than my family. 'What about the cold?' my mother said when I asked again. 'What about the rain, and the storms? And security. Suppose someone has a knife? What good would a layer of canvas be then?' I stopped asking, but I didn't stop thinking.

Then there was a second film, showing great rolls of razor wire being stretched around the perimeter of the park. The same red-lipped woman spoke over the film, saying, 'In Regent's Park, your security is your government's priority. Let our emergency government keep you safe until the crisis is past. Regent's Park. A place to be, for the time being.' And with that film, my desire to go there rekindled and grew. My mother was wrong; I wouldn't be knifed in my bed.

'Why can't we go?' I cried. 'We could help.' I began to prepare, reading the government blogs on my screen when my mother thought I was playing games. I read about how to maintain your tent, about keeping in good health under canvas, about using your rations to feed a child under three. When I'd read so much that I felt I could manage in Regent's Park on my own, I spoke to her again, hoping she'd be impressed with my research, my independence. I was almost twelve, I told her. Couldn't I go on my own, just for a night or two? Just to see? No, she said again, just no, until I almost hated her.

But it didn't stop me reading. *Community and friendship in Regent's Park. My first week in Regent's Park.* And the streets got emptier and my mother spent more and more time messaging my father. When he came back, I said how much I wanted to go.

'No you don't, kitten,' was all he said. 'You really don't.'

'I do,' I said. 'I really do.' But my father just shook his head, smiling, and went back to his screen and his computer as though I wasn't even in the room.

And so, the very next day, I ran. My mother and I were leaving for the British Museum. My mother was busy locking the front door behind us. There was no one in sight and I took off down the empty street, in the direction I'd seen the people walking with their bundles. I ran and ran, alone for the first time in my life, feeling the wind blowing into my eyes and the grain of the pavement through my thin-soled shoes. When I turned the corner into Gower Street, there was a patrol coming the other way and I waved, grinning, thinking how happy they'd be to show me the way.

'Hello,' I called.

They stopped dead and pointed their guns at me, and before I could scream, I heard footsteps and a woman's voice shouting, 'She's with me, she's with me!' My mother was running. She had my card in her hand and was waving it like a tiny white flag, and just as she reached me, she tripped and fell, skidding on her hands and knees. The nearest soldier took the card from her without helping her up. As she struggled to her feet, the soldier grabbed my hand, pressing my finger hard against the pad on his card reader. When it registered, he dropped my hand like so much rubbish and took my mother's. She winced, and when he let go, I saw the white circles where his gloved fingers had gripped her slowly turning red. Her precious thick tights were shredded at the knees and there was blood running slowly into the unravelling wool.

'You're Michael Paul's family,' he said. He stood between my mother and me, so close I could smell sweat and leather on him.

He moved away from me, towards her. She backed away; there was a wall behind her and she felt for it with her hands. The other soldiers were watching.

'I'm teaching my daughter,' she said. I could barely hear her; the soldier was right up against her now, pushing her against the wall.

'Teaching her what?' he said softly. She'd turned her head aside and he was talking into her hair. 'I hope you'd teach me better than that.'

'It was my fault,' I called. 'I wanted to go to Regent's Park.' But he didn't turn around, or even look at me.

'You're under government protection,' he said. He ran a black leather finger slowly across her cheek, down her neck, to the collar of her coat. He slipped his finger inside the collar and pulled my mother to him. 'Don't push it,' he said as she tried to move, 'or it might start costing more than your husband is prepared to pay.'

'Michael's paying *you?*' my mother whispered. A communicator crackled, and the soldier pulled his hand away and stepped back into formation. The squad moved on and my mother pulled me out of their way, holding my wrist so tightly that I couldn't move my fingers. She held me like that until they had gone, and it wasn't until the noise of their boots had faded away that she began to move, walking back towards the flat. She didn't let go of me, and I was forced to follow her, skipping and stumbling. I tried to wrench free, but her hand had become iron. Everything about her had gone hard; the set of her head, the set of her shoulders. When we got to our front door, she threw my hand away from her, her face white, her lips drawn together, as though she was daring me to run away again. She tapped in the entry code and put the key in the lock, but her hands were shaking so badly that it took her three tries to fit it in. I wanted to help her but fury fizzed from her as though, if I were to touch her, she would spark and burn. I didn't run away. I walked before her into the hall and when she shut the door, it felt like leaving the sunshine for the dark.

'They shoot people, you know,' was all she said. 'People get shot.'

She finished locking the outside door and bristled ahead of me up the stairs to the door of our flat. She gave our coded pattern of knocks and my father let us in. Then she walked past us without saying a word and shut herself in the bathroom.

'What's up?' my father said, securing the door behind us. 'Is she all right?'

But I couldn't answer, because I didn't know.

My father closed his screen. He never did that. He laid the fire carefully. I trailed after him, not sure what to say. I couldn't stop thinking about the soldier's finger, the black leather against my mother's skin, inside her collar. What had I done?

'I ran away,' I said. 'I wanted to go to Regent's Park. But the troops...'

'Did they hurt her?' he demanded. I shook my head, hovering in the kitchen doorway while my father reached into one of the high cupboards. I heard a packet crackling under his hands and knew that it meant some kind of treat. But I didn't deserve a treat.

'These were meant for your birthday,' he said, handing the packet to me. 'I'll let you choose what to do with them.'

Biscuits. It had been months since I had seen biscuits, and the packet showed that these ones had little nibs of chocolate in them, and nuts. I felt my mouth watering. I wanted to take them to my room and eat them, one by one, all to myself until they were all gone. That was what birthdays were for. And these were for my birthday. I could go to my room, shut the door ... but oh. That soldier. And the guns. The guns, all pointing at me.

When my mother came out of the bathroom, her skin scrubbed raw and her eyes dangerously red, she found the fire lit, and a plate of biscuits on the little table in front of it. My father had made coffee, too, and the smell of it spread all through the flat.

'What's this for?' she said. 'It's not Lalage's birthday yet.'

'They're for you,' I said quietly. 'All of them.'

'All of them? I don't want them all.'

'That is Lalla's choice,' my father said evenly.

'I'm sorry,' I told my mother. 'I'm sorry I ran away.' Something else was bubbling up inside me, something hard and angry that would hurt them both. *I'm sorry I even exist*, I wanted to say. But I bit my lips together. Hard. The flat was too small for words like those now.

'Oh, Lalage,' she said, 'my Lalage. I know it's hard. I know you're lonely. But your father and I . . . we need you to just put up with the way things are for a bit longer. We're working on things, aren't we, Michael? We've got ideas. There will be a change, and you'll have friends and pianos and songs and biscuits every day, if that's what you want. But you need to be quiet for the time being. You need to stay still, and listen, and do what your father and I tell you. Because if you run away like that again . . .' She stopped, and when I looked at her, I could see that the reason she had stopped was because she was no longer capable of speaking. Her face was wet and her mouth open, as though she was screaming. And I looked at her and touched the edge of the fear I had put her through, and I knew that I would never run away again.

'Is that what happened to the fig man?' I asked eventually.

'To whom?'

'The fig man. *The fig tree shall not blossom, neither shall there be fruit on the vines; the labour of the olive shall fail, and the fields shall yield no meat; the flock shall be cut off from the fold, and there shall be no herd in the stalls* . . . Him. Did they shoot him?'

My father knelt on the floor before me and clasped my hands in his. He looked up at me as though I was the grown up, and he said, 'That man was just repeating something he'd read. But he didn't learn the whole thing. Do you know what comes next?'

'No.'

335

He looked at me, hard. 'Listen, Lalla. Listen to what comes next. *Yet I will rejoice in the Lord, I will joy in the God of my salvation.*'

'Whatever that's supposed to mean,' my mother whispered under her breath, lifting the strips of material she'd tied around her knees to see if they were still bleeding. But my father's eyes were holding mine so completely that I didn't even look at her. 'That man – the one who's disappeared – he chose to end his story with fruitless vines, with figs withering. He never bothered to look further than that. But you – you must look further. Rejoice in the Lord. Joy in the God of your salvation.'

'You mean I need to pray? But why? And to which God?'

'There aren't any gods. There's only man. But salvation and joy – they are real. You have to believe it. If you run, that means you don't trust me. Do you trust me, Lalla? Do you?'

And that was the last time I asked questions. It was the last time I tried to be a once-upon-a-time girl, with choices and tomorrows. It was the only time I ever ran away.

And so I spend my time being sitting in my front room and imagining what it must have been like before I was born. What it must have been like to have fresh fruit, and flowers, and things growing in the ground. I don't believe that people used whole aeroplanes to bring green beans and roses out of Africa to England. But I do believe that apples grew on trees, and when my mother reads me a story that begins, 'Once upon a time,' I don't think about the girls in the stories any more, or about choices, or about tomorrows. I think about apples and wonder what they might have been like. I think about a tree covered in bright apples, ready to be picked.

'The Time Being' by Antonia Honeywell was first published in audio format in 2015 by W.F. Howes Ltd